W9-BXX-893

THIS'LL BE
THE DAY
THAT I DIE

JOHN MICHAEL GRIFFIN

DENVER, COLORADO

Outskirts Press, Inc.
http://www.outskirtspress.com

ISBN: 978-1-4787-2423-0

Outskirts Press and the "OP" logo are trademarks belonging to Outskirts Press, Inc.

PRINTED IN THE UNITED STATES OF AMERICA

Because I could not stop for Death
He kindly stopped for me;
The carriage held but just ourselves
And Immortality.
— Emily Dickinson

Prologue

December 26, 2012, 6 p.m.
Vatican City, Italy
The Associated Press

The Vatican released a statement today from Pope Benedict XVI strongly denouncing claims made yesterday by the Cold Spring Harbor Laboratory in Cold Spring Harbor, N.Y., that scientists have discovered a gene that can accurately identify the exact date of a person's death.

In a press release issued by the Cold Spring Harbor Laboratory on December 25 at 6 p.m. Eastern Standard Time, Todman Russo, President of the laboratory, said, *"After four years of testing on four hundred human subjects selected at random, the findings of the study show that we can identify final life expectancy date, without reason or cause of death."*

The release states that some one hundred and sixty five study participants out of four hundred test subjects, all volunteers, had succumbed to their deaths at exactly the dates that their genetic test results had predicted, and that the remaining subjects have expiration dates in the future.

The laboratory's statement added, *"There is no link between the genetic predictability factor and the reasons for the deceased subjects' deaths. They have succumbed to natural causes and accidents, as well as suicide and a homicide. Cold Spring Harbor Laboratory tests claim accurate identification of each deceased subject's expiration date and not their specific and varied causes of death. However, each person has lived until his or her known and identified genetic calculations."*

The news release added that there is zero probability that the results to date could be in error.

"The numbers are the facts," said Russo. *"Each subject was tested against the genome formulas, starting with their exact moment of birth. At this point, there are no errors in the predictability factors. All one hundred and sixty five subjects to date have died on their identified date. In short, we have now found the gene inside all of us that is our life clock. If we know the exact moment of a human's birth, we can now know, within a single day, when he will die."*

In the statement tonight from the Vatican, Pope Benedict said: *"For as long as man has existed, there have always been those who would question and challenge the authority of He who brings life and He who holds domain over all peoples. Science has, throughout the centuries, tried to refute God's existence by putting together what it claims is evidence that the elements of our earth, God's universe, and even man's own inventiveness and ingenuity, control life. But this is false and unsubstantiated. As followers of Christ, we invite all the sacred brotherhoods of believers in the almighty God to turn away from this most recent attack on the core of our faith: that God is the father of us all and that it is by His will alone that we live and we die so that we may join him in his eternal kingdom, where all that we seek to know of the mysteries of our world will be ours."*

Part I

Chapter One

Dr. Todman Russo dropped the transmission into low gear as he headed east down the steep, winding hill toward the Victorian gate house and past the gold-lettered sign indicating the Cold Spring Harbor Laboratory. The promised morning sun had not yet appeared. A white, low sky hung dreary over Long Island this Christmas morning. There had been snow flurries the night before and an overnight drop in temperature left icy spots along Route 25A. He'd already skidded on a patch of black ice as he made his way toward his life's work, as well as his first, probably last, and perhaps only true love.

It could be said of Russo that he had never in his adult life deceived anyone, including his two divorced wives, about the things that mattered to him most. His work as a genetic scientist had gripped him from his first school biology class through sixteen years of study and a long career in medical research. His dedication to his work was his true lifelong companion. Now, at seventy-one, alone and without a family, he was about to spend his Christmas Day engaged not in the traditions of the holiday, but rather in a position of responsibility that would take him to places and emotions he had never expected to encounter.

Russo had one other passion; tellingly, one he could indulge alone. Since his childhood spent in Corona, Queens, he had succumbed each year to the summer charm of baseball and the New York Mets. The Mets played at Shea Stadium in Queens, a mere twenty-minute walk from the small bungalow where he lived with his naturalized Italian parents, grandparents, and other assorted members of an extended immigrant family. That family was all gone now, dead or distant. Tod lived with his science and his Mets. And not much else.

He punched the signal to indicate a left turn across 25A and gently touched the brakes to ease past the gate house entrance toward the Nolan Pavilion parking lot. His office was there, as was the laboratory's board room.

He spotted a shiny black Escalade with Jersey plates in the lot, and a large chauffeur seated behind the wheel. That meant Dr. Ritu Mhatra had already arrived. She was married to a wildly successful real estate developer and they lived in a magnificent condo in northern New Jersey, right on the Hudson River. Ritu only consented to the luxury when her husband agreed she'd be driven to and from work each day.

No sign yet of Dr. Zach Weitzman, but a glance in his rearview mirror revealed what he expected, the familiar grillwork of Dr. Ellen Guitton's BMW. She'd been right behind him, coming down the hill to the harbor where the laboratory had stood since 1889, when the Brooklyn Institute of Arts and Sciences established a biological lab to train high school and college teachers in Cold Spring Harbor on the north shore of New York's Long Island.

The genetic research in which Russo and his colleagues were engaged had been spawned by two events: the appointment in 1898 of Charles Davenport as director of the laboratory, and the discovery, in 1900, of Gregor Mendel's work on osmosis and cellular mutation.

Now, more than a century later, Cold Spring Harbor Laboratory, a private, not-for-profit research and education institution at the forefront of molecular biology and genetics, stood on a hundred and sixty acres, its mission to generate knowledge that would yield better diagnostics and treatments for cancer, neurological diseases, and other causes of human suffering.

Home to seven Nobel Prize winners, the lab played a pivotal role in the emergence of molecular genetics, the scientific foundation of a contemporary revolution in biology and biotechnology. It was at Cold Spring Harbor in 1953 that James D. Watson gave the first public lecture on the double helix, the structure of DNA, for which he and Francis Crick each won Nobel Prizes. Later, Watson helped develop the lab into one of the world's most influential cancer research centers.

There were a great many good vibrations in this place, but on this snowy Christmas morning, Todman Russo, Ph.D. was faced with the fact that science had a way of leading researchers down paths unsought and to conclusions unexpected. While conducting a research into neurons, the lab had developed a mathematical "wiring economy" within the brain that minimized the length, and hence the volume, of that wiring. Researchers were thus able to shorten the cycle of tracking neurons, and as a result, developed the first system for viewing how the central dogma of biology unfolds in its entirety, from DNA to RNA and eventually to protein within living cells.

That in turn had led to the 2005 discovery by Russo and the small group working with him. The loss of a certain gene called p63A accelerated aging in lab mice. Since p63A was also in human DNA, they concluded that it was likely to play a role in human aging and they began to break the gene down. What they found was that, at least in mice, p63A didn't just affect aging, but that manipulated in certain ways it was also predictive of death. Regardless of a given mouse's reason for expiration, the DNA formula was invariably correct. Not one mouse survived past its expected final date. So if this p63A gene was also consistent in humans, might it be possible to track and calculate a person's genetic date of expiration? In other words, to know when someone was going to die?

There was no way to resist the impulse to test the thesis.

Russo and his team assembled a group of human subjects, none of whom were informed of the purpose of the study. One hundred volunteers per year for the last four years had been recruited from different age groups. All were given complete physical examinations and any with identifiable diseases or chronic ailments were excluded. Those that remained were guaranteed anonymity if they would participate in the study. Their results would not be revealed publicly by Cold Spring Harbor Lab and, they were told, would also not be revealed to them. The lab would take a sample of saliva and a clip of fingernail in return for which the participants would receive one thousand dollars.

Subject number one hundred and sixty-five, a white male aged thirty-nine with an expiration date of December 22, 2012, had passed away in Naples, Florida, as a result of an automobile accident. He had been tested in 2010 and his death confirmed the accuracy of the study. There had been no failures. The remaining two hundred and thirty-five volunteers still had dates in the future, some as far as sixty or more years.

Russo had looked at the results and called this Christmas Day meeting. He had no choice; he and his team had crossed the Rubicon.

The scientists and the laboratory's board had agreed before testing began that the entire project would be kept secret only until the results offered forty percent certitude. If it was established, with zero tolerance for error, that forty percent of the tested subjects had expired on the day the scientists predicted, it would be concluded this gene did, in fact, predict the length of a person's life.

That marker had now been reached.

Russo stepped out of his car and took a deep breath of the salty air. Whaling had once been the main occupation in these parts. Often, Russo knew, a life threatening occupation. But perhaps each man who set foot in a whaler may have known whether or not he would return to shore.

He waited for Ellen Guitton to pull in beside him, glancing meanwhile over the harbor and down to the icy waters. They were as calm as glass this morning.

"Good morning, Tod, and merry Christmas." Ellen pulled herself out of the front seat of her sleek 750iL BMW. "I see Ritu has beaten us both." She nodded to the Escalade.

"Maybe because she's a Hindu. Didn't have to go to Mass this morning." The walk was icy. Russo offered Ellen his arm.

"Oh, that's right, I forgot," Ellen chuckled. "It's actually a holiday for us Christians today. Silly me. I thought it was just another workday."

"How sentimental. Anyway, I wonder what George has to pay a driver to work on Christmas Day?"

"I hope he's not as cheap as you. Poor guy leaves his family Christmas morning to drive from Jersey to Long Island. He should get some kind of bonus."

Tod slid his key card through the security receptacle. The glass door opened, admitting them into the vestibule of the three-story building. Ellen glanced into the retinal scanner, waited for it to click green, indicating identification and clearance for Dr. Ellen Guitton, then followed Tod through the steel door.

It was she, once they were on the elevator, who raised the question on both their minds. "Tod, what do you think are the mathematical chances that four persons in the same test batch can have the exact same death date?"

"Extraordinary," Russo said, "but not impossible. A hundred and fifty-one people, on average, die each day on Long Island. The chances of four of them coming together in a single hundred-person pool, based on random selection criteria, is probably mathematically akin to winning a lottery." He smiled. "Every lottery has a winning ticket, right?"

"But that it will be your ticket?" Ellen said. "Not such good odds. We didn't see confluent death dates in any of the previous test batches. Not even a matched set of two. Now we've gone from zero to four. That I think is very strange."

Russo thought so as well. It was perhaps the most compelling reason he'd called this emergency meeting for Christmas Day. There were, nonetheless, two other concerns: After four years of testing this hypothesis, they had reached the point of mathematical certainty which would trigger a release of the study's findings. Inevitably that would mean dealing with the remaining test subjects who might press the lab to reveal their own data. Never mind that every one of them had signed an agreement that the results of the testing would not be revealed to them.

But Ellen's question was the key. It was the odds that really troubled him. He'd had four years to accustom himself to the notion that science could predict an individual's date of death. But there had been no such preparation for what now confronted them. The last test group of one hundred random volunteers had revealed four subjects with the same death date. One year from today, Christmas Day, 2013, four complete strangers, all in the same test batch, were marked for their final day of life. Four individuals had beaten millions to one odds in a lottery none would probably choose to win.

Russo was mildly surprised at his reaction to the project's findings. His devotion to the science of genetics had always been about cellular study, finding answers that would extend life, not threaten it. He had always enjoyed the impersonal, almost anonymous nature of his work. Now that was gone. He felt the cold chill of being closely involved with human mortality, and for the first time ever, he felt conflicted..

The elevator door opened and they stepped into the hallway outside the board room, to the welcoming smell of fresh-made coffee. The brightly lit room meant that Dr. Mhatra was already inside. Ritu, easily the most brilliant member of their team, was exceedingly punctual and exacting. It was no surprise she was here first, and halfway through the debriefing report Russo had sent out the night before.

Ellen breathed in the rich smell of coffee and began peeling off her red Burberry duffel coat. "Let's get some coffee and one of the good doughnuts before Zach gets here and gloms all the chocolate-covered ones."

Tod followed Ellen into the board room, marveling at how a woman so distinguished in the scientific and intellectual field remained so down-to-earth, and with such a young and playful spirit.

He flipped his Mets cap around backward so he would feel some-what equal as he began searching the mahogany server for a choco-late-covered doughnut.

Once he'd filled a coffee mug and settled into his seat at the round table in the board room, his thoughts turned to the four test subjects and what they might be doing this Christmas Day. Somewhere out there, he mused, a billionaire member of his board, a housewife with two children, a Roman Catholic priest and a young black woman were celebrating the last Christmas of their lives.

The thought chilled him.

Chapter Two

December 25, 2012, 9:57a.m.
St. Patrick's Roman Catholic Church
Huntington, New York

Dan Brannigan stepped through the brass doors at the side of St. Patrick's Church and held them open for his three daughters and his wife, Kate, who was carrying their crying grandson, Matt. Then came his sons-in-law David and Adam, husbands to daughters Debbie and Allie, holding the hands of the other Brannigan grandchildren.

Dan, Kate and the family were hurrying away this morning because Matt, the youngest, had chosen the holy sacrifice of the Mass this Christmas morning to release the contents of his stomach down the front of his holiday outfit and his grandmother Kate's sable coat.

Dan hadn't assessed the damage to Kate's fur. He was busy with his usher's duties in the church where he had been baptized, married Kate Kelly, and where all their daughters had later made their marriage vows. Dan had grown up at this church and the adjoining elementary school, and had remained throughout his life, one of its most ardent supporters, eager volunteer workers and prominent donors.

As for Kate, she adored her grandson. And perhaps today even more so, since she secretly hated the coat little Matt had just ruined. She had always felt it was a symbol of being married to a rich man.

And although she was, Kate's style was strictly cloth from a catalog, not fur from Bergdorf's.

Matt's indigestion had generated an unwelcome odor about the Brannigans, so they left the Mass before the final blessings and headed to the supersized Suburbans that had carried them to the nine o'clock service.

They had all risen just after seven and gathered in the main entry hall of the Brannigan home, dubbed Colcroft House, which dated back to 1908. The house had been expanded twice since then and renovated several times. It stood three stories above ground, and boasted eleven bedrooms, all with private baths and working fireplaces. It covered thirty two thousand square feet and sat atop a gated ten acre garden with unobstructed views looking west across Oyster Bay, toward the magnificent magenta sunsets of Long Island, and then beyond the Centre Island peninsula to the Connecticut shoreline. Dan, Kate and the children had moved to the house in 1989 when it had become available after the passing of Madame Chiang Kai-shek, who had occupied the former Taiwanese Embassy to the United States for some fifty years. The Brannigans spent fourteen months and several million dollars restoring and modernizing the house, and had renamed it after a castle in Ireland where they had spent a night on their honeymoon.

A second residence on the property was home to a family who cared for the house and grounds. As they did every holiday season, the husband and wife team entered the house before dawn on Christmas Day to lay out the family's meal and stoke the fireplace that was nestled under the dual circular staircases leading to the second floor.

A thirty foot Christmas tree surrounded by four royal red sofas filled the center of the gargantuan main reception hall at the center of the house and stretched the full three stories above the entrance. With the lighted garland and green velvet ribbons and bows trimmed with baby's breath and white poinsettias circling up the staircases, their home looked like a Christmas card.

Against the wall, toward the north wing of the house, a huge serving buffet had been set with breakfast. Hot food was served in silver chafing dishes and accompanied by chilled fruits, pastries and juices.

As the family gathered, the caretakers discreetly disappeared and the Brannigans, all clad in the special Christmas pajamas Kate had distributed the night before, delighted as the children tore into their toys and presents.

Kate distributed the packages, each of which she had personally selected and wrapped. If you could ignore the regal surroundings, the Brannigans seemed as normal as any typical family.

But they were not.

Dan and Kate knew they had realized more of their dreams than most people ever would, and they shared a common guilt over it. Dan had always had a burning in his soul to make piles of money. Kate grew to be embarrassed while Dan was bored by being rich.

The couple had learned to share their wealth in many ways. While their family enjoyed their opulent Christmas, hundreds of thousands of dollars anonymously donated by Dan and Kate to charities and local churches had provided a better holiday for multitudes more.

Dan had felt Kate's eyes on him and glanced across the room to where she sat with the children on the floor, a distant look on her face. He'd nodded and blown her a kiss. Then he realized she wasn't staring at him. She was staring beyond him.

Dan had turned to see what she was looking at, but no one was behind him. When he turned back, she was engaged again in their grandchildren.

Later, after they dressed for church and she'd put on the sable coat, he had asked her, "What were you staring at before? You looked like you were staring at me, but when I threw you a smooch, you just kept staring. I actually thought there was someone behind me."

Again, Kate just stared at Dan, her eyes glazed over. "I don't know. I was just thinking. Why are we so lucky? Sometimes I still feel like the bottom may drop out on all the good fortune we've had."

"Not a very happy thought on Christmas morn, Kate. You OK?"

"Mmm," said Kate, and they had both moved on.

Chapter Three

December 25, 2012, 9:57 a.m.
35 Sunnybrook Lane
Hicksville, New York

Janet Bates glanced up to her left, where she could get a glimpse of the digital clock on her microwave. The phone was ringing in her kitchen. Maybe it was the call she had been expecting. Her Christmas wish.

A call from her youngest child. Her baby, Michael.

Of course, Michael wasn't a baby any longer. He was nineteen, six feet tall and a lean one hundred and seventy pounds. He was also a specialist second class with the 37th Special Field Communications Platoon of the 2nd U.S. Army Reserves occupational forces in Afghanistan.

Janet believed she had never truly cut the umbilical cords of either of her two children. She knew she felt a physical connection down deep in her body whenever she heard their voices or whenever the thought of them entered her mind. When they were babies and their first cries of the day would come from their cribs, Janet would feel something physical stir inside. She always believed it was an everlasting maternal connection to their bodies and souls that began when they were first conceived.

Janet knew the exact moment of their conception. She never said anything to her husband, Rod, the evening in Bermuda when she first felt "the connection" to their firstborn, Michaela. Mickey. She and Rod had gone back to the room in the middle of the afternoon and "the mood" had struck them as they changed from their swim clothes. That night, as they sat over dinner, she knew somehow that she was carrying a child. Six weeks later, when her doctor confirmed her pregnancy, she quickly calculated back to that date in Bermuda and confirmed her suspicions.

She also knew the night when, Michael, her second child was conceived. She went to the bathroom after she and Rod had had an above-average love-making session, and when she returned to bed, she folded herself into Rod's arms and whispered, "I think we made a baby tonight." Rod was already snoring. And again, six weeks later, the doctor confirmed Janet was to give birth. This time she reminded her husband of her prediction, which he hadn't heard when she uttered it, and his response was, "Yeah? Can you make it a boy this time?"

She reached out for the phone on the wall and closed her eyes so she wouldn't see the caller ID. Behind her she could sense that Mickey had bounded into the room, hoping as well that it was the call they'd been waiting for. Mickey and Michael shared an extremely close bond as brother and sister. Besides having nearly the same name, they both were fair-skinned and freckled-faced, with the same light hazel eyes and strawberry blond hair their mother had.

"Did he call yet?" The voice of Janet's best friend and soul mate, Kathy Jonas, anxiously whispered on the phone line.

"Not yet. Merry Christmas," Janet replied as she waved her disappointment at Mickey, who was standing directly in front of her now with her hands clasped prayerfully and her eyes nearly popping out in anticipation.

"Merry Christmas to you, too," Kathy responded with little enthusiasm. Besides being Janet's oldest friend from childhood, her next-door neighbor, confidante and pseudo older sister, she was also Michael's godmother.

"I won't keep you in case he calls, but we'll be over in a few minutes and I was wondering if you need anything. Billy just got back from the 7-Eleven with the OJ and I laid the cinnamon rolls out on a pan already, so I just need to put them in the oven," Kathy said.

As Kathy spoke her last word, a call-waiting alert beeped, and Janet felt a stirring inside that was unmistakably familiar. Michael was calling from Afghanistan. She knew before she answered that it was him.

"Gotta go, the other line is beeping," she blurted, cutting Kathy off as she pushed the talk button on the phone.

Knowing who was on the line, Mickey bolted from the tiny kitchen and bounced up the short flight of stairs back to her bedroom in their split-level ranch, eager to hear the voice of her brother, whom she missed as if "she'd had her skin peeled off."

"Michael?" Janet croaked as her throat tightened and her eyes began to fill.

"Yeah, Mom, it's me. HO, HO, HO and M-e-e-errry Christmas," he bellowed in a terrible faux Santa voice, made worse by the noise from the satellite hookup linking them across seven thousand miles.

Mickey cut in before Janet could answer. "Hey, dork face, keeping the towel heads in line?" Janet could hear the familiar thickness in her daughter's voice and had a vision of Mickey's quivering lips as she tried to hide her true emotions.

"Ha! They stay away from me, Mick. They know I'm from the 'ville," Michael shouted into their ears, referring to their hometown of Hicksville.

"Michaela, don't call those people towel heads. That isn't nice," Janet scolded her daughter.

And for the next ten minutes, the threesome traded banalities about winter weather in their parts of the world, the latest local gossip, whether Michael had received his Christmas packages, the "Clark Griswold" Christmas lights on some of the houses in Hicksville, the state of the current NFL season.

They spoke about anything that would help them avoid the reality of the distance between them. As close as they all felt to each other, it was painful for mother and sister to deal with Michael being in a hostile place. It wasn't much better for Michael.

Michael had brought his plan to the family as an evening dinner discussion when he was beginning his senior year at Hicksville High School. The plan was to join the Army under its college fund guarantee program and get experience that would later help him reach his goal of becoming a New York City policeman.

Janet was adamantly opposed. So was Mickey. "Mom, Mickey: It's my choice. It's my life," he told them.

Janet disagreed. She believed that Michael's life was attached to hers. That it was a physical part of her.

Michael's father, Rod, was ambivalent, but not opposed entirely. He privately thought a few years in Uncle Sam's employment might do Michael some good. Rod thought his son was a bit lazy and he was certain that Michael would rather tap Mom and Dad's wallets then come up with his own capital.

Rod had been constantly employed in some way or another since he was fourteen. Even now, secure in his longtime union job as a track switch operator for the Long Island Rail Road, he sometimes worked weekends with a moving company to make extra cash off the books.

So, in some ways, this plan Michael had presented to the family had merit, Rod thought. Though he feared the risks, they weren't enough to make him dismiss the plan outright.

In July, after Michael's graduation, Janet cried for three days when her son reported to basic training. In November, he was assigned to his present unit and shipped to Afghanistan. The Army had been in Afghanistan as occupational peacekeepers since the war in 2006.

When Michael shipped over and went into harm's way, Janet struggled not to blame Rod for agreeing to their son's plan. For months, she was cool toward her husband. Rod didn't really seem to notice. That hurt Janet as much as it angered her. Rod had always been aloof to most of the world around him. He was a man of schedules and routines. Like his job, he saw life as being regulated by the clock. There was barely any spontaneity in Rod's world and showing emotion for him was as rare as snow in August.

It was Kathy who had brought Janet back from that cold place.

"Rod is who he is, Janet," she counseled. "He hasn't changed since the day you met him. That's who you married. Remember that what you fell in love with was someone dependable and loyal. Someone who was on this earth and committed to his oath and his promises. That's how he sees his life, Janet. You married him because he was dependable."

That had struck home with Janet. Her own father had been a barfly and had flitted from job to job most of his life.

By now, Kathy had arrived from next door and was on the bedroom extension, having pushed Mickey aside. "So, are all the women in the outfit lining up outside your door, gorgeous?" Kathy sent an e-mail to Michael every day without fail.

"Well, not exactly, Aunt K," Michael replied. "There is one kind of special one that keeps coming around. She *may* have a chance. Slightly." he said

As she listened to Michael and Kathy talk, Janet's mind went completely blank. Her defense mechanisms went to full alert. Like a mother wolf, she felt instinctively that her cub was being stalked. Somewhere, thousands of miles away, he needed her to protect him. Her insides flipped over, and her knees actually buckled slightly. She sensed danger.

"Hey, can I get a word with my son?" she heard Rod ask.

Janet absentmindedly handed him the phone, forgetting to say goodbye to Michael. There was something very different about what she'd just heard Michael say. Something that brought a sensation of fear. It was almost as if the earth had stopped spinning. She needed to sit down. This gift, her connection, was suddenly and unexpectedly turning on her.

Why?

Chapter Four

December 25, 2012, 9:57 a.m.
St. David's Roman Catholic Church
Oceanside, New York

"The Mass is ended, go in peace to love and serve the Lord, and may God bless you, in the name of the Father, and of the Son, and of the Holy Spirit. Amen"

Father Edward Hayslip brought his right hand down completing the final blessing, then left the altar, and followed the pastor who'd concelebrated the Mass and the deacon and altar servers in their crisp white cassocks down St. David's center aisle. The parishioners stood. Some were waiting to follow them to the rear of the church and into the gray Christmas morning. Others moved to the side aisles and exits, busily wrapping scarves, buttoning coats, bundling children.

Ted had gone about a third of the way toward the main door, walking with the very slight limp engendered by the prosthetic device that was the legacy of his military service, when he remembered he'd forgotten a closing Christmas greeting. He raised his voice over the din of movement and awkwardly called out, "Oh, and merry Christmas to you all." Few smiled back. In fact, few heard him. Without the aid of the loud speaker system his voice lacked the power to carry much beyond the altar.

The success of parish ministry was always about sentiment. People loved their priests to display warmth and friendliness. Ted had a hard time remembering to make that effort. He continued to the rear of the church, half-heartedly joining in the final hymn, 'Hark, the Herald Angels Sing.'

The highlight of every service for him was standing in the vestibule and greeting people as they left the church. During the few minutes it took the flock to file by and nod or speak with him, he would have some kind of connection. That was what had kept him going as a priest for twenty-eight years. Even if the contact seemed shallow and insincere, it was human interaction. Ted Hayslip had a hole in his soul that could only be filled by human contact.

He took his place by the carved wood doors, opened to the cold and gloom outside. As it was Christmas day, the pastor, Father Schmidt, stood opposite him, as did the deacon. Usually, as the celebrant, Ted would be the only one on exit duty. Seeing the other two men present, he knew he'd be shaking fewer hands. The pastor and the deacon were both extremely well-liked.

Ted was hopeful that two uniformed soldiers he had spotted at Mass would pass by on his side so he could speak with them. He'd been a much younger priest when he had been given his first assignment in Kuwait during Desert Storm, and his experiences there had taken hold of his life. They had damaged his heart and soul, a disfigurement more profound than the explosion that had torn off his left leg from the knee down. But his affection for those in uniform never chilled, and he never had a problem connecting with those in the military.

The two soldiers never appeared and eventually the church emptied. Ted released the hardware holding the doors ajar and moved back down the main aisle. Modern science was remarkable. His prosthetic device was so advanced that one had to look closely to see his limp. You could easily miss it completely. He could make pretty fair time as well.. He wanted to see the other two men before they took off their vestments and left, so he could pass along a couple of small Christmas gifts.

Ted wasn't going to bother taking off his vestments as he was also scheduled to celebrate the noon Mass. He'd simply slip back into the rectory and call his two sisters in Baltimore. Colleen was likely to be easy to reach. Patty on the other hand was never available when he called. Patty lived a fast life. "Good for her," Ted muttered to himself.

Chapter Five

December 25, 2012, 9:57 a.m.
The Reese Public Housing Projects, Building Four, Unit 102
Middle Island, New York

"Oh, Deke, honey," she exclaimed. "This is so pretty. I love it. Is this a real diamond? I ain't never had no diamond, so you could be fooling me for sure." Sharona Watts beamed as she moved from the tiny living room to the bathroom so she could look at the necklace in the only mirror in their small apartment.

"Yeah, it better be real, baby, or the salesman at that store gonna wish he was never born." Deke smiled as he followed her to the mirror. "It's real, baby. It's real and I'm real," he whispered as he stood behind her, fastening the necklace clasp and softly kissed her neck.

Sharona admired the quarter carat of freshly purchased diamond. It came from one of the commercial jewelry mills that populate the malls of Long Island, and run endless streams of TV ads during the holidays promising eternal devotion and gratitude to any man who buys his woman a diamond from their "collection of fine jewelry." Instant credit to qualified buyers and easy payment terms on any purchase over a hundred dollars were also assured.

Deke hadn't even tried to make the case that he was a qualified buyer. He knew that any computer check would identify him as a convicted felon and bring yet another rejection. Life for an ex-con was an extension of the state of suspension he lived in starting the day he was convicted.

"Baby, you can't afford this. It's beautiful, Deke, but where you get the money for this?" Sharona asked. She turned and put her arms around his neck and kissed him hard on the lips before he could answer.

Deke's expression darkened as he felt that pang of doubt. Was his generosity being questioned for its honesty? But just as quickly, the feeling passed. Sharona Watts, standing in his embrace, was the only person on the planet who had complete and unqualified trust in him. He wasn't at all certain why or how she had come to that point in her life, but she had, and that was all he needed to know. If he told Sharona to sit down, he knew she wouldn't even look to see if a chair was behind her.

"Deke, you about the best man this girl is ever going to find," she whispered as she snuggled her head against his chest.

"Now, ain't I been telling you that all this time, girl? About time you realize it, baby," he merrily and loudly exclaimed, as he squeezed her tighter in his massive, rock-hard arms. "Now, how about some more of that sugar you been passing out this morning?" His voice dropped lower as he referred to the love-making they had awakened to and were both breathless from until just before Deke had handed her his gift.

"Mmmmm, now diamonds are a girl's best friend, baby, but we got a date with Gran to take her to church, and services start at eleven, so we got to be moving, Deke." Sharona smiled as she unwrapped his arms and walked to the tattered consignment-shop couch that sat next to a white Christmas tree placed on an equally drab end table in the cramped living room. "Besides, I got something for you that I been busting to give you." She leaned down, reached behind the tree and grabbed a small, white envelope with a red ribbon tied in a tiny bow.

He held his gaze as she leaned behind the tree and her loose-fitting nightshirt rode up, exposing her backside. "Ain't nothing on this earth better than your sugar, baby girl." Pure fire was sparking up in Deke's loins again.

"Be that as it may, we still going to church with my grandma and we can't be late. So merry Christmas, Deke. I love you." And she handed him her gift.

He shook the feather-light envelope in his hand and pretended to be listening for movement inside. "Feels awful light for a man been handing out diamonds," he teased.

"You saying I ain't worth diamonds, boy?' she pouted as she put her two hands on the center of his chest and shoved him backward into a hard landing on the couch. Had they listened closely they would have heard the frame of the couch crack slightly beneath the sudden weight of Deke's massively muscled two hundred and forty pounds. "And you better open your present, fool, before I decide you ain't worthy and give it to one of the many flirting, useless men who come by my register every day, looking for me to pay their rent the rest of their no-good lives."

"Them useless men best not let me hear them or the only rent they gonna be paying will be at the cemetery," Deke replied.

Sharona felt a light chill at the resolve in Deke's voice. "Yeah, yeah," she said as she flopped next to him. "Don't you worry about what that present weighs. You just open it up, Deke. Come on, I been waiting to see your expression."

Deke quickly slipped the bow off and flipped it at the tiny, sorry-looking tree. The ribbon hung limply, caught about halfway up the little tree, which Sharona had bought at Target, where she worked as a cashier, and toted home on the bus.

He tore open the envelope and slid out a Christmas card with the greeting "To the man I love" across the top. He quickly flipped the card open. Falling into his lap, wrapped separately in tissue paper that he stripped away, were two tickets for the New York Mets' opening game in April.

Sharona knew Deke was a rabid Mets fan, but that he hadn't yet been to the team's new ballpark at Citi Field. The Mets had moved into the new stadium in 2009, when Deke had been a guest of New York State. Since his parole about a year ago, he hadn't been able to get to any games because of his work schedule and lack of a car. Traveling the fifty miles to Flushing from Middle Island by public transportation was far too time-consuming and expensive.

Deke had told Sharona that while he was inside, where inmates could sometimes watch games on TV, he would pretend he was sitting in the stands. He said he could imagine the smell of hot dogs and cold beer, and the sight of fresh-cut, green grass. "Grass so green only the Lord could've made it that way," was what he had said.

Deke sat stunned as he realized what he held in his hands. He picked up the card from the floor where it had slipped and looked at Sharona's careful printing inside: *This is keeping it real, Deke, no more dreams about green grass. I luv u. S.*

Deke looked up from the card and peered at Sharona. She saw his eyes filling; that made her throat tighten and her own eyes moist.

"Baby, nobody cares about me the way you care about me," Deke said. "Man, you listen to all my dreams and then you make them come true. Where was you when I was coming up? If I'd have met you before I started gangbangin', maybe I'd be something now. This is the only present I ever got in my whole life because it was a dream of mine. Thank you, Watts. Thank you so much, baby." His lower lip began to quiver as he spoke, so he turned his head and glanced up at the Christmas tree next to them, half its lights no longer working.

Sharona leaned in closer and put her arms around his bull neck. She whispered in his ear. "I know the man you been, and I know the man you are, Deke, and we're going to have a long, good life. You're a good man, Deke. You just had to find that out."

Deke Williams, his emotions back under control now, turned to her, smiled, and brushed a tear from the corner of his eye. "Look at the time, baby. We got things we got to do today. People's waiting on us."

Chapter Six

December 25, 2012, 10:30 a.m.
Cold Spring Harbor Laboratory, board room
Cold Spring Harbor, New York

Zach Weitzman entered the board room, shedding his black ski jacket. Tod and Ellen were working on their second cups of coffee; Ritu's tea had gone cold. Three doughnuts were missing from the box, two devoured by Russo. The third, only half eaten, sat in front of Dr. Guitton.

"I'm sorry, I should have called. They took forever bringing the car over from the garage this morning," Zack apologized. "I should have anticipated the holiday would leave them shorthanded. Sorry."

"What time did you start out?" Ritu chirped.

"About nine-fifteen and it's usually just a forty-five minute trip, but the roads from the expressway were icy," he replied as he filled a mug with coffee and grabbed two chocolate-covered treats.

"No big deal," Russo said. "Ellen was just filling us in on some of the more glamorous people who have graced her apartment over the years: Princess Grace, Bogart, Harrison Ford."

"What I wouldn't give for that apartment," Zach sighed.

"Excuse me, but that place of yours overlooking Gramercy Park isn't a hut," Ellen shot back.

"I'm with you, Zach. Her place is an *Architectural Digest* cover, every issue." Ritu chimed in.

Ellen grinned at Ritu because it was true. Her apartment was one of the most celebrated locations in New York City and had been used forty times that she knew of as a location for movie or television shoots. It had been willed to her, and its expenses were paid for in full every year out of a fund left by two aunts whom she'd barely ever seen.

"Ritu," Ellen retorted, "George has built you the Taj Mahal on the Hudson over there. Not bad."

"Too new. None of the character and craftsmanship your place has. It's too nouveau. Trashy, actually. At least I think so. But don't ever tell Gitesh. He adores black marble everywhere. Bathtubs, countertops, the pool!" she added with a note of disdain.

"Who's Gitesh?" Ellen asked.

"George is Gitesh. His real name is Gitesh, but he changed it. Said it helps him in his business," Ritu chuckled.

"Right," Zach jumped in, "like the last name Mhatra doesn't tip people off that he didn't come over on the Mayflower? My grandfather was Yaakov, which he later changed to Jack, thinking that would make him more acceptable to Jew haters. He never really caught on that his yarmulke was a dead giveaway. Oy!"

Ritu and Ellen giggled.

"Folks, we have a reason to be here today that takes priority over our real estate holdings and ethnic origins," Russo said as he tried to focus his team.

"I have nothing. Mitzi owns our place," Zach continued, "and she's forbidden by her trust agreement to even put me on the deed."

"Probably for the best," Russo said, allowing his colleagues to draw him into the banter. "Less fuss with the lawyers if she ever throws you out. I know. Believe me."

"She can have it. Give me the beach house," Zach said as he reached for another doughnut.

"OK," Ritu sat forward in her chair as she opened her file. "Mister Dominic Pagano has left this earth. On time. Or at least on our scheduled time." She stopped suddenly. "That sounds harsh. I didn't mean it that way."

"Poor guy," Ellen said. "A car accident in Florida? How many does that make who have had accidents?"

Weitzman responded through a mouthful of doughnut: "Of the one hundred and sixty five subjects with identified genetic death dates up to and including today, all have died on schedule. Sixty percent male, forty percent female; ten percent between twenty one and twentynine, thirty percent age thirty nine to fifty five and the rest above fifty five. One hundred and twenty eight were of natural causes, with the rest accidents, suicide or homicide. Not one person has missed his or her date. Mister Pagano was our thirteenth accident, and we had four suicides and a single murder."

Zach was both a brilliant oncologist and geneticist. Born into a Hasidic family from the Lubavitch sect in Williamsburg, Brooklyn, he had eschewed the family's diamond business and gone into medicine. Although that sorely disappointed his grandparents - Zach was the only son of their only son - his career was still a source of pride. His parents didn't stand in his way and his mother was secretly happy he wouldn't be in the family business, as she had no taste for the murky, ugly side of the diamond trade.

A star athlete at Yeshiva, Cornell, and NYU Medical School, he lettered in swimming, basketball and baseball, and although he had been considered a pro prospect in baseball, he had no second interest beyond medicine.

He had no second interest, that is, until he met Mitzi Rosen, an education major, in his sophomore year at Cornell. She was a freshman, a knockout, with raven black hair and heavy, dark eyebrows that formed a spectacular frame around her Mediterranean features. She had a self-deprecating sense of humor and a world-class figure. Even better, Mitzi was an orthodox Jew, from a wealthy upstate New York family. She easily became one of the most sought-after girls in school.

They married after graduation while Zach interned at NYU Medical Center, where he specialized in the treatment of latent cancer cells believed to be traceable to genetic medical histories.

His reputation flourished and he became widely regarded as a top man in the field. He published several papers that caught the eye of Dr. Todman Russo, who had invited him to lecture at Cold Spring Harbor, and then brought him on at the lab.

Life had always treated Zach well. His family had not fought his ambitions. He had more than lucked out with Mitzi. "Thank God she's not a princess," as his father often said. Their marriage was vibrant, and they enjoyed each other as friends who shared a cosmopolitan lifestyle.

But now, the results of the four year study were going to have an impact on his life. His family's ultraorthodox Jewish community had a high regard for medical science, but condemned anything that they felt contradicted the Torah. Zach knew that once his connection to the research was identified, he and his family would be under pressure from the world which he had left behind, but which his parents were still very much a part of. It darkened his mood whenever he thought about what was coming. This was so unfair to them. But he also knew as a scientist that he could not deny the findings.

"It's the accidentals and the suicides that keep me up at night," Russo said. "Not that the poor murder victim doesn't, too."

"That's also what everyone is going to point at to challenge us," Ellen said.

Dr. Ellen Guitton could have posed for a cover of *Vogue* under the headline *"Beautiful People,"* in any way you measure that phrase. At sixty, she still swam thirty laps every day in the basement swimming pool in her building. She was rewarded with a sculpted body that had not changed much since her days at the Sorbonne, where she studied human anatomy. These days she had only about twenty percent body fat and no trace of cellulite. Her body had made few concessions to the laws of gravity. Her curves were still pretty much where they had been thirty years ago when she married John Guitton, who had died within the last two years. Ellen had a few streaks of gray in her dark, shoulder-length hair now, but rather than detracting from her looks, they gave her an air of grace and nobility.

Ellen was born into a Tulsa oil family and had been raised to take over their business. She was fifteen when her parents visited Mexico on a second honeymoon and disappeared. They left their hotel one evening to take a walk and never returned.

Ellen and her brother, a year younger, became wards of her missing father's twin sisters, Esther and Myrtle. The twins had left Tulsa years earlier - "The whole place smelled like oil," they said - and moved to Manhattan, where they bought a fourteen-room apartment with a wraparound balcony overlooking Central Park. They joined New York society, the art crowd, and the boards of the Guggenheim and the Metropolitan Opera.

When Ellen and her brother became their "caretaker problem," the twin aunts quickly shipped them to boarding schools in eastern Connecticut; they kept their distance from the young orphans. Ellen was later sent to study in Switzerland and finally to the Sorbonne in Paris. There she began the medical research that eventually brought her to Harvard and the University of Pennsylvania. At U Penn she met and married John Guitton, who was studying engineering. During the sixteen years it took her to become a doctor, Ellen traveled the world and absorbed the culture and grace that were her signature today.

Her brother was enamored with British theater, but had never become more than a bit player in London's West End. Ellen, an oncologist and cum laude graduate of University of Pennsylvania's Medical School, became chief of surgery at Columbia University Medical Center in Manhattan. When the aunts, whom Ellen referred to as "Cinderella's stepsisters" died within weeks of each other, they left their apartment, lock, stock, and art collection, to Ellen, along with a trust that paid the annual taxes, housekeeping and maintenance. Their only request was that she maintain the "glory of our beloved household, or, eschewing such privileged surroundings, sell it to a worthy new proprietor." Ellen's aunts understood what being a snob meant.

But whatever their other shortcomings, Esther and Myrtle didn't turn their backs on her or her brother, Bobby. He inherited an estate in southern England, a favorite haunt of the sisters, and a numbered

Swiss Bank account, which assured he'd never be a starving actor.

John Guitton quietly worked on the Grumman Aerospace team responsible for designing the lunar module that delivered Neil Armstrong to the moon. The team was awarded a Nobel Prize. John retired from Grumman as senior vice president of aerospace design and, a year later, died in his sleep.

At John's funeral, Ellen's roommate at Harvard, Ritu Mhatra, asked if she might want to tackle something new. John's death had led Ellen to re-evaluate her life. Ritu had been working with genetic scientists at Cold Spring Harbor on some fascinating research. They needed someone with Ellen's experience. Ellen said yes on the spot. It's so strange, she once thought, our lives don't depend as much on ourselves as we think. Mostly, it's the people and events around us that shape our destiny.

"You're right, Ellen," Russo agreed. "I thought we should comb through the details of each case once more. We know we'll have to have to defend these findings and every shred of evidence has to line up perfectly."

"People are going to go on the greatest witch hunt since the Salem trials," Zach said. "We're telling the entire world that we knew when a hundred and sixty-five people were going to die, we did nothing to prevent it, and we will not release the names or case files that prove our claim."

"Whoa, we didn't know when they were going to die," Ritu said. "That was speculative. And the reason behind the study. We now assume they were programmed to die by virtue of the DNA evidence, and the evidence supports that the subjects died on the days we expected, with a small, inexplicable number meeting their date through unnatural events. By the way, that murder gives me the chills," she whispered as she wrapped her arms around herself and shivered.

Dr. Ritu Mhatra had always been the smartest person in the room. Early on, school officials advised her parents to never let their daughter know her IQ; they felt Ritu might not work as hard in school. They were wrong. Ritu soaked up knowledge. She excelled at every type of learning she ever attempted and was a freshman at the Sorbonne when she was barely seventeen. After Paris, there was medical school at Harvard, and a double doctorate from MIT.

Ritu loved solving puzzles, from the mystery of the foundations of the universe to how to set Vegas odds on college football games. And, more often than not, in her thirst for learning, she would uncover questions unanswered, knowledge unknown. As she sought solutions in medicine, she was drawn to stem-cell research and deeper study of DNA. Now, she was the leading geneticist at the lab and its most tireless and avid researcher. It was not uncommon for her to work twenty-hour days for weeks at a time as she hunted down a single shred of information. Her focus was unbendable, her work flawless. That she was able to maintain any kind of a life away from genetic research was a tribute to her husband, George.

George Mhatra, like Ritu, was a naturalized citizen. He had been introduced to Ritu by mutual friends while he was starting a construction business along the Jersey waterfront, which would eventually make him extremely rich. He was one of the few developers who sensed the real estate boom ending in 2006. As the markets crumbled, he prospered. Ritu wasn't sure what they were worth, but she also didn't care.

"We're not involved with interfering with our subjects' destiny," Russo said.

"Exactly. This whole thing has been about trying to understand if what we've found is indeed the genetic clock that sets your death date. Fortunately - or unfortunately - we have," Weitzman said.

"OK. Let's just break up the files in the database in case number sequences and when you've checked each one, resave the file and add today's date so it'll tell us it's been checked. Anyone want more coffee?" Russo got up from his chair and turned to the buffet.

"Thanks, Tod, I'll take some," Ellen said.

"Any chocolate doughnuts left?" Weitzman asked.

Chapter Seven

December 25, 2012, 2:35 p.m.
Cold Spring Harbor Laboratory
Board room
Cold Spring Harbor, New York

"OK," Russo said. "We've checked every file and we're signing off on all of them. We need a consensus on how to proceed. I say we need to study the genetics of the four with the same date with a fine-tooth comb."

"I agree," Dr. Mhatra said. "This anomaly is an opportunity in my mind. The identification of their dates being the same suggests that there may have been some common factor, something they share genetically."

Weitzman leaned forward. "Forgive me, that's not really the point. I'm convinced that what we see here in the test result is probably a result of some level of genetic mixing in their background. What's remarkable to me is that it comes out of such a small random sample. Having said that, we have some serious digging to do, and quickly, to see if there is something about this that, if found and identified, can help them escape their fates."

"By all means," Dr Mhatra agreed.

Ellen had been writing notes to herself as her colleagues spoke. She put down her pen and the others instinctively turned toward her. " OK, what I really want to know is not whether these four break the rules of probability. Mathematical anomalies happen in science all the time. What I need to know is why they are all going to die; and does that have anything to do with something common to the four. Let's look at the possibilities that could possibly lead to all four having their DNA render a common date.

"There certainly could be a mechanical explanation. By that I mean the four could all somehow be linked to a destructive event of some sort. A traffic accident, a fire, some kind of traumatic event that claims the four of them. If that is a possibility, we could attempt to pre-empt such an outcome by keeping the four of them under guard next Christmas Day."

Ritu stood and moved towards the window considering what her colleague had said.

"The laws of probability that could bring about such an over-whelming occurrence as you describe, Ellen, are enormous."

"I agree wholeheartedly, Ritu. That's why I think it should be the first theory we eliminate." Ellen flatly stated.

Russo held his hand up and joined in, " I agree that mutual de-struction of the four of them by some perilous event is probably ten million to one but until we think we have something more defining and reliable to go on let's not just brush it aside."

Zach, sitting with his arms folded over his chest now re-entered the discussion. "I need to go back to their possible common DNA mixing. What we know from our findings to this point is that this human clock we have identified is accurate on the date it renders without exception. The fact that we have yet to catch even two iden-tical dates may or may not be unusual, we haven't got a large enough sample yet to assume that will never happen. My guess is that as we widen the scope we will see a great deal more evidence of similar patterns emerging. But the anomaly of four coming up in a single testing says to me that they are bound together in some probable way through their DNA. "

"I am persuaded to agree with you,' Ritu said from the window, ' the fact that they share no common links to each other today doesn't necessarily eliminate the possibility that they have crossed paths at some point in their family ancestry. If we can find that to be a fact, and I have my doubts, that will still present us with the conundrum of their mutual common death date. Regardless of where they came from genetically, why are they all headed to the same unfortunate interruption of what appears to be four healthy, ordinary lives?."

Ellen was nodding in agreement. "And' she paused, 'that could be something that is medical as much as anything. For all we know they may be victims of a pending disease that hasn't shown up yet. Which says we need to try and get them in here quickly and take a toes to nose look at each of them"

"You really think it's possible that they could; A, be linked genetically and B- that they can all fall prey to some malady on the exact same day. None of them are even the same age!" Russo said, seemingly expressing doubt in where his colleagues were taking this discussion.

"But on the other hand' he added, 'why not? The fact is that we have in front of us a mysterious happenstance that defies the laws of probability. He shrugged his shoulders. "But more than likely we have been given a chance to look inside the two possible trails behind the single clue we have. One would be by medical elimination: that the four are going to come to their demise by medical circumstance, not necessarily a common disease. Or, alternatively, there are multiple factors that could bring them down. One dies by accident, another from disease etc. There is no reason in front of us to assume a single cause theory here."

Ritu began to slowly walk back to her chair. "Tod, instinctively I know that your assessement is correct, I doubt any of us would argue the logic. But, I think we have got to study the genealogy of these four in parallel with a constant study of their DNA patterning if the work we've begun is to become valued. There may be some link in their past that tells us something about them that is bringing this sentence upon them. The fact that we know who they are and what they have in common is an invitation to possibly unlock something we can't see right now. The study of DNA has so much more power to be found that we can't let this interesting circumstance pass without a very deep dive that at least attempts to find a hint to the reason for it. Maybe there's nothing. But even knowing that is an answer in and of itself."

"The time factor involved here in DNA analytics is daunting," Ellen said. "Finding the common denominator linked somehow to their death date is incalculable, isn't it? I mean we need to search three billion codes in each subject and then cross-match those! And oh, by the way, so much of what we are looking for is not standing still. We know that their codes may be shifting continuously in reaction to human protein changes. I want to be reasonable, but aren't we wishing on a star here?"

Russo was ready with an answer to her reasoned objection. "You're correct, Ellen. But Ritu is right, and there may well be some evidence somewhere inside the search that reveals the cause for their scheduled deaths. If we discover that, we may find a way to save them. Don't we owe them that much?"

Ritu held up her hand. "I think the clues will lie in their genealogy. If, as Ellen says, we can't break the genetic codes in time, and she may be right, we can certainly go after their genealogical history and see if there is something that is common to the four that is driving this mutual death sentence on them."

"OK then' Russo concluded, "we put the four under full DNA scope looking for any trace of possible demise arising from their ongoing biological or psychological mediations from now until next Christmas Day; we begin to drill into their family trees to see if we can find common crosschecks in their ancestry; and let's hope that we aren't forced to consider destruction of the four by common trauma next Christmas day."

Russo glanced thoughtfully at his colleagues as he stood and walked to the glass wall that looked out on the gray, gloomy Christmas Day. "Let's take a break and think a bit longer about the issue of anonymity here. There is a responsibility that comes along with this that chills me," he said.

The other scientists glanced at each other. Finally Dr. Mhatra broke the silence by reaching for her cell phone and leaving the room. Taking his cue from her, Zach stood and stretched his arms full length above his head and groaned as if drawing his final breath.

Ellen slipped quietly from her chair and whispered, "Who knew becoming God could be so tough?"

Tod stared at the bleak, icy landscape, drawn back to the day he was called from his office to this room and confronted with the early results of a project whose purpose was to explore the human genome and identify a genetic link to dementia. He thought back to the moment his team presented their suspicions to him. He was raised a Catholic, and although his practice had long since lapsed, his first response was, "God decides when we will be born and when we die."

That was four years ago. He believed very deeply in his science and he knew the findings were verified and that he would become the voice and face of the man who refuted centuries of religious dogma that gave domain over life and death to God. Now here it is, Russo thought. But this isn't about lab tests any longer and this key to existence isn't about lab mice. The work the lab was about to bring to the world could alter humanity and the way people function for all time.

The implications and the burden of discovery were overwhelming. He was thinking now of what this information could mean to people's lives and dreams. He was conflicted and troubled by the reality of knowing one's final moment, and what that information could do to people. This was not an anniversary or birthday. This discovery offered people the knowledge of when he or she would be leaving their life behind. Is there anything in our existence more valued than our own right to life? How would parents react if their newborn's death date revealed a short lifespan for their baby? What about people planning to wed if long life for both was not assured? We all know when we were born; but how would each of us live if we knew when we would die? What kind of lives would we choose for ourselves? How many of us could bear the fear as that date loomed? Could we stand knowing when the time was almost up for those we love? Russo was heartsick at the implications of their discovery. His work was supposed to provide humanity with solutions. Not create problems.

"But that leaves us open to a lot of crap," Zach Weitzman's voice broke Russo out of his tormented reverie.

"Like what?" Ellen asked.

Russo had been so lost in thought he hadn't heard his colleagues re-enter the room. He turned to join them and, keeping his dark thoughts to himself, pulled out his chair and slid into it.

Zach was heading to his chair. "Well, for one thing, they could drastically alter their lives when we tell them what's coming. These results were to be kept anonymous. We tell these four guys their dates, and the rest may want theirs too. And maybe the dead people's families come after us for not having told them."

"Good points, Zach. It does open a can of worms," Ellen said.

"Let's break it down one at a time in terms of the potential is-sues," Ritu said, "and I agree with Zach as well. We need to be cau-tious. But we also need to be fair. To both sides."

Russo cut in, finally surfacing from his mental morass. "OK. Up to now, all the results were anonymous. We did that to protect the subjects from unnecessary fear and anxiety. It's great for those who have fifty years left, but not for people with nearby dates. Those hundred-plus unfortunates certainly would not have appreciated hearing they were on a short rope. What we call their death date, they could have argued was an execution date." He glanced around the table seeking agreement. "But until we knew for certain that the data were correct and irrefutable, what could we have told them? You may die on a particular date? That wouldn't work. We can only deal in absolutes. And until two days ago, we had no reason to hand out any absolutes. Now we do." Russo removed his Mets cap and ran his fingers through his lush salt-and-pepper hair.

"And now?" Ellen asked.

"The results remain silent within the study," Ritu piped up.

"I agree, except in the case of the Christmas Day group," Russo said.

"Me too," Ellen said.

"Make it unanimous," Zach agreed.

"Absolutely" Ritu confirmed.

Russo quickly added, "In my view, if we hand out the dates to everyone who was tested, we could destroy their lives. And their families' lives."

"OK, so what about the families of the deceased?" Zack asked. "What about their coming after us for not divulging their loved ones were ... what? Mortally identified?"

Ellen glanced at Russo, who seemed to be shrinking in his seat. Ellen had a sharp sense of empathy and knew he was aware that he was about to enter a whirlwind of controversy. She decided to offer to take some of the burden on her own shoulders. "Do you want me to call the PR people and do the release, Tod?" she said.

Russo glanced at her and took a few seconds to respond. "Thanks, but I think I'd better do that, Ellen. I'll get it started and then we can look more deeply at the cases of the four. I'm not looking forward to the discussions with them. Maybe you guys have some ideas about how we approach this?" Tod shook his head. "I know Brannigan is going to flip out. He went along with this but I know he didn't think much of it to start with. Do any of you know any of the others?" They shook their heads silently. Tod rose and as he headed to his office to call the public relations director to discuss the press release, his colleagues sat with glazed looks on their faces. No one felt any exhilaration about the research. They each knew they were about to become a page in history. Their astonishing discovery was about to alter mankind and change their own lives forever.

Chapter Eight

December 25, 2012, 8:47 p.m.
St. David's Roman Catholic Church Rectory
Oceanside, New York

Father Ted was bone weary as he quietly put his key in the rectory door. He knew he would be the only person in the building that was both his home and office. Marge Gomes, the residence secretary, had been kind to him today. He had joined her and her husband for Christmas dinner. Ted was surprised how little enjoyment the visit gave him. Having dinner with Marge and Ralph Gomes didn't do much to lift his spirits. They lived a kind of penitential life, much like his.

Ralph was a retired auto muffler mechanic, who, for most of the day, kept his hearing aids turned off. But it didn't seem to matter much anyway, as he rarely took his eyes off his big-screen TV, which was always tuned to sporting events. The couple's only daughter had gone off to college years earlier, became a computer scientist and moved to Seattle.

After early Mass, he had tried to call his sisters. He felt an acute loneliness on holidays when he couldn't be with them. Even though he wouldn't describe their relationship as close, he still felt a need to hold on to family ties.

Colleen, his older sister, lived alone, except for a tenant who rented a room in her modest Baltimore row house. Never married, Colleen taught sixth-grade history in the public schools, and usually spent holidays at home, the sole keeper of the Hayslip family traditions. He knew she would have a tree in the front window, lights on the porch rails and a wreath on the front door. She would roast a small turkey with all the trimmings, and invite coworkers and neighbors for some Christmas cheer. He was always invited, but his duties usually meant he couldn't make the trip.

Ted was disappointed and surprised when he got her answering machine. He called back later, after his sick call rounds at the hospital, just in case she hadn't heard his message. Still no answer. That troubled him. He had counted on Colleen to shake him out of his funk. In his second message, he asked if she was OK, and to be sure and call back.

He hadn't fared any better calling his younger sister, although that was no surprise. Patty could almost never be found and rarely on a holiday. At forty-seven, she was the youngest and had been a free spirit from birth. Like her older sister, she had never married. Unlike Colleen, she lived to spend her time with the opposite sex. Patty was tall, athletic, outgoing, funny and sexy. Often described as "a hot number." She was a senior marketing executive for the Baltimore Orioles, owned a condo on the Inner Harbor, drove a red Porsche, and nearly always had a new guy in her life. She always said she would make a terrible wife and mother because she enjoyed men too much. And she obviously didn't care who knew it. She kept a sign on her desk that said "Go slutty or stay home." She had long ago abandoned her strict Catholic upbringing, but Ted never tried to play the priest with her. He felt guilty about that, but he knew a confrontation would likely alienate her.

He admitted he was a coward about not challenging her lifestyle, but he'd decided to live with that. He loved both his sisters deeply and needed their love in return.

Patty preferred staying in touch by text rather than phone, so Ted tapped a message into his cell phone and sent it off. Wherever she was or whatever she was doing, when she came up for air, he'd get a response. He entered the rectory's office. It was cold, so he kept his cashmere topcoat buttoned. One of his few indulgences, he rarely wore that coat except for holidays and special occasions. Father Ted liked to dress up for Christmas; wearing this coat was a way to make the holiday feel special.

The answering machine's blinking indicated that seven messages had come in while he had been at the hospital and during the dreary dinner with Marge and Ed Gomes. The first few were from parish members. He listened absentmindedly until the fourth message. "Hi, Teddy, it's Colleen. Merry Christmas, little brother." This part of the message was kind of warbled in the nervous, sing-song way used by people who feel embarrassed to be talking to a machine.

Then her tone changed. Ted sat up and leaned on the desk as he listened with a deepening frown on his face. "Sorry I missed your calls today. Well, actually, I just didn't answer the phone today at all. Wasn't feeling up to it, Ted. I just couldn't get into the holidays this year. Guess I missed you all too much. You know, with Mom and Dad gone, it's just us three. I miss the old days and seeing you. Patty is … Oh, who knows where she is? She's never around. I don't know. I didn't put out any lights or even a tree this year. Just couldn't get into it. I did buy you something nice, but I haven't gotten to the post office yet to send it. Anyway, hope your day was good, sweetie. I miss you. Love you. See you soon, I hope. Bye-bye."

The last few words were gulped through tears. Something was wrong with her and Ted was alarmed. He immediately pulled out his cell and speed-dialed her, but the phone rang and Colleen's answer message, delivered in her usual cheery voice, announced she was "not available and would you leave your name and number, and I'll be sure to get ya back real soon!"

He didn't try to hide the concern in his voice. "Colleen, it's Ted. Pick up the phone if you're there, honey. I need to talk with you. You sounded so down when you called. Call me back as soon as you get this. I don't care what time it is. Just call me, all right? Merry Christmas, Col. Call me." He hung up. He sat for a minute, trying to think what could be troubling his sister. While he pondered her life and loneliness, he punched the answering machine for the next message and heard, to his surprise, the voice of Dr. Russo at Cold Spring Harbor Lab. Ted sat, half-listening as he recalled vaguely hearing a report on the all-news radio station in his car on the way home after dinner. There was something about a denial by the Vatican, if he heard it right, and some new thing the lab had announced. He hadn't really been paying attention as the roads were treacherous and he was trying to keep focused. He briefly wondered if it had anything to do with the DNA tests he had submitted to last spring. He'd never heard anything more and had forgotten about it until now.

His interest sharpened as he listened to Russo's message. "Good evening, Father Hayslip, this is Dr. Russo at Cold Spring Harbor Lab. I would appreciate it if you could return this call at your earliest convenience. You participated in one of our DNA tests and we would like to have a short discussion with you about the findings. I'll be in my office all day tomorrow and the rest of this week. We'll set up an appointment with you at whatever time works best. But as I said, it would be helpful if you could see us at your earliest convenience. Call my direct line," and Russo left his number. "If the call goes to my assistant, she'll be able to make the appointment with you. We shouldn't need more than an hour of your time. OK? Thanks. Oh, and merry Christmas, Father."

Ted replayed the message again, listening for anything that would offer a hint, but Russo's voice gave away nothing. Ted thought back to how he had come to participate in the study. He had seen an ad in *The New York Times'* science section seeking DNA donors for blind tests at Cold Spring Harbor Lab. The ad promised a short, noninvasive test and a thousand dollar payment. He had been saving for a new car and decided to apply.

Suddenly his cell phone vibrated, the signal for a text. The room had warmed up a bit, so he stood and shed his coat while he flipped the phone open. "PATTY" was spelled out on the screen. *"In belize. hevenly! hvng blast. how was xmas? talk to col? back in 2 days. Luv P merry2u"*

Oh Patty, he thought. Maybe you have the right idea. Here I am on Christmas night in the ice age, alone in this empty house, and getting ominous messages from my sister and some weird science lab. There has to be a better way.

With that, he picked up his coat and closed the door to the office. He shuffled down the hall and entered the kitchen, where he opened the refrigerator and grabbed a bottle of chardonnay. He poured a generous amount into a tall, stemmed glass then walked to the living room and flipped on CNN, where he hoped maybe he'd get some information about whatever was going on between the lab and the Vatican. Had he even heard that right on the radio?

As he sat, his thoughts took him through his day. So many contacts. So few connections. Except for those two soldiers, none, in fact. He must have been in front of seven hundred parishioners today. He saw perhaps forty people in the hospital. Nothing. Spent Christmas dinner with two "friends." Nothing. Both sisters, no contact. The biggest holiday in the Christian calendar in terms of connecting with family and friends, and he had spent time today with hundreds of people. And here he was, at the end of that day, having had barely any intimacy on a human level. Most people could relate to others at some level that allowed for human connection. Why not him?

Warmed by the wine, he fell asleep in front of the television. While he dozed, an interview moderated by a CNN talking head discussed the announcement by Cold Spring Harbor Laboratory that its researchers had discovered a gene capable of predicting the date of a person's death. The announcement had come out at about six in the evening, New York time, and CNN's Rome correspondent was predicting that an almost certain rebuttal would be forthcoming from the Vatican.

The guests on CNN - a rabbi, a Buddhist monk, and an author - were asked to comment. Not surprisingly, the rabbi and the monk said that science could never assume death was determined by anyone other than God. That was fundamental to all religions sacred teachings, that only God ruled our domains. The author, who specialized in writing about science, disagreed, saying the lab's announcement was a major breakthrough and that genetics, while complex and highly difficult to understand, was never wrong. He contended that the scientists had probably uncovered one of the mysteries of life.

Father Ted woke at three-thirty in the morning, turned off the TV, and stumbled to his room, where he went to bed. The next morning, he called Dr. Russo and made an appointment to visit the lab at four o'clock. The phone conversation lasted less than a minute.

Chapter Nine

December 26, 2012, 9:48 a.m.
Colcroft House
Cold Spring Harbor, New York

"Honey, leave the shower running so the water stays hot, OK?" he heard Kate say as he stepped out of the marble double shower in the master bedroom suite.

He stuck his hand back in and reset the single water control valve. Steaming hot water, perfectly heated to a temperature of one hundred and fifteen degrees, gushed out of the three stainless steel shower heads. As he turned and reached for the towel on the heated bar, Kate burst out of the walk-in closet that adjoined the massive bath, a closet Dan always said could house the wardrobe of the Queen of England. Kate was wrapped in a well-worn terrycloth robe, which she'd had for probably a dozen years. Even with several newer robes hanging in that oversized closet, she stuck to what she liked best. That was Kate. "What time is the car coming?" she asked Dan, who was already across the room at the counter housing dual marble sinks that ran the full length of the bathroom.

Dan turned to face Kate as he began drying his privates, hoping, as he always did, that his actions would get Kate's attention, which they never did. That wasn't what Kate was about. "Ten-thirty, ten-thirty sharp," he responded as he rubbed the towel over his head and began to move farther down the counter toward the double hair dryers cradled in stainless steel mountings. "And that's the fourth time you've asked. It's not going to change, Kate. Ten-thirty. Get moving."

"I am moving. When have we ever missed a plane because of me?" she shot back.

Dan ignored her question and began using one of the dryers on his thinning white hair. Glancing in the mirror, he didn't miss the opportunity to watch Kate drop her robe before she stepped naked into the cascade of hot water. Dan still lusted after Kate as if she was his first sexual awakening, which she had been, a long time ago. To this day, he appreciated what a natural beauty she was and how just a glimpse of her body stirred him. She had grown older, of course, and perhaps was softly sagging in a few places, but she still pushed his buttons. "You know," he said, as he put the dryer back into its holder and kept his eyes glued to the mirror, "we put a separate tank behind that shower so you wouldn't have to run it for ten minutes to get hot water. You do remember that, don't you?"

"Yeah, I know, but it never feels hot to me until it's been running a while. You know me; if I don't turn red, it wasn't hot enough."

He watched as she placed a pink bath puff between her legs, getting aroused. He quickly snapped back, "How about I come in there and we'll see how hot you like it?"

"Oh shut up, you old fool, and stop staring at me. Go get dressed."

Dan glanced down at the Rolex Daytona on his left wrist and seeing that it was nearly ten a.m.; he knew he had come to a couple of realities. One: In nearly thirty-six years of married life, an exotic, impulsive interlude with Kate in the shower had happened maybe twice. Two: They were, in fact, being picked up in a little over thirty minutes for the ride to Republic Airport, where they had a G6 Gulfstream waiting for an eleven o'clock departure. They were flying to Eagle County Airport for their annual family ski trip at a rented seven bedroom house in Bachelor Gulch, high above Vail, Colorado. "Yeah, yeah," he surrendered, and opened the twelve-foot cherrywood door leading to his changing room, across from Kate's closet. His salon was equally as large but contained far less wardrobe.

"You'll miss these opportunities someday."

"What?" she gurgled and said something back, but he couldn't understand her as she held her head under the water to rinse her freshly shampooed hair.

"Nothing," he muttered. As Dan stepped into a pair of plaid boxers, the phone on the built-in credenza in his dressing room purred softly. Reaching for the handset, he glanced at the caller identification, but since he didn't have his glasses on, he couldn't read the text.

His first thought was that it was one of their girls looking for something she had left behind at the house. Even though they had officially moved out and were married with children, there always seemed to be something still back home that they needed Mom to find for them. And the frantic calls always came, like this one, at the last minute.

But the caller ID this morning read "Cold Spring Harbor Laboratory," with the private number of Dr. Tod Russo. Dan was not only a member of the lab's board of directors, but also a serious seven figure annual donor and a recent study participant. Had Dan seen who was calling, it's likely he wouldn't have taken the call. He would have returned it from the plane. "Hello, what did you forget?" he said as he pressed the talk button, certain it was Allie or Debbie, who both lived nearby. He knew it couldn't be Diane. She was at the other end of the house with her toddler, packing.

"I haven't forgotten anything," responded a baritone voice that startled Dan. "Have I reached the home of Dan Brannigan?"

"Oh, I'm sorry. I expected one of my daughters to call," Dan replied. From the bathroom, he heard the hair dryer and he moved across the room to peek again at Kate, but she had closed the door. Her modesty always denied him his lust. "Yes, this is Dan."

"Hi, Dan. I'm sorry to bother you on a holiday. This is Tod Russo."

"No bother, Tod. Merry Christmas. We saw a shot of you on the late news last night. You looked great. Is it true? Do we have a discovery?"

"Yes, Dan, it is true," Russo said, skipping the holiday salutation.

Dan walked from the dressing room to the bedroom, which had floor-to-ceiling glass walls running for thirty feet along a western exposure, offering captivating views and breathtaking sunsets. He cradled the phone between his chin and shoulder while he fumbled with a pair of copper-colored corduroy trousers and an Irish knit turtleneck.

"We went public last night and issued a release from the press room on the website indicating that we can confirm we've located and identified the gene p63A. And that our study will prove that this gene accurately identifies the day an individual will die. Pretty heavy stuff, Dan, but we've done it," Russo said with a slight hint of pride in his voice.

"So," Brannigan responded with just a trace of skepticism in his voice, "you can safely say that it is now possible to know someone's actual day to die … from his genes?" Dan was far from convinced, even as a financial donor and a board member, that this project was worthy or plausible. He had gone along and supported it, even participated as a subject, out of curiosity.

Ever since Dan had amassed a fortune, he had deliberately tried to give something back, as he liked to call it. So, when they sat through a Mets game at Shea Stadium four years ago and Russo had broached the subject of Dan coming on board, he had accepted.

"Right, Dan. Earlier this week, we had another subject, our hundred and sixty-fifth, to be exact, die on the calculated date. So, out of the four hundred test subjects, we now see that each has died as the test results predicted. This now sets the mathematical probability as a certainty. We are at more than forty percent of the tested sample. And as the board had agreed, we are at the point of irrefutable mathematical evidence. So the release was sent out last night."

"Why break the news on Christmas Day?" Dan was irritated that the lab would send out information like this on the holiday.

Russo sighed. "We were kind of hoping to fly under the news radar a bit and not hit the wires. It turns out we may have been wrong about that. If you come by the lab right now, you'll see we've had to post security cars out on Route 25A to direct traffic and prevent people from getting onto the grounds. The media have descended like locusts."

"Get out of here," Dan exclaimed as he stepped into his pants and stood up from the bed.

Kate came into the room in her underwear and mouthed "Is that the girls?" Dan waved her off, but fixed his gaze on her rear as she turned and went into her closet.

"Yeah, we may have underestimated how quickly the press would respond. The website has crashed because the traffic is exceeding our bandwidth."

"Well, that's awesome. I think," Dan replied. "Thanks for telling me. We're heading out to the airport this morning and I'll avoid going that way."

"Then I'm glad I caught you. Is there any chance you could stop by, Dan? There's something that came out of the tests that I'd like to put in front of you."

Dan's heart accelerated. He would later look back at that instant as the moment he knew his life was coming to an end. And sooner than he had thought. He would know later that his survival instincts and his uncanny perception of events around him, which helped him build a fortune, were now telling him that danger was near and loss was coming. Dan had spent his entire life knowing what to do, when to act, how to win, when to get in, when to get out, and, most importantly and more than everything else, when he was in danger.

Russo's statement told Dan that loss was coming.

Chapter Ten

December 26, 2012, 6:27 a.m.
Reese Public Housing Projects, Building Four, Unit 102
Middle Island, New York

Sharona frowned deeply as she glared into the dim light of their bedroom at Deke's still, sheet-entangled form. "Don't be giving me no bullshit, Deke. I want to see you standing on your feet right now. You know if I leave here now for my bus, you're gonna go back to sleep and then you're gonna wind up losing the only job you may ever get. Now get your black ass out of that bed before I throw some cold water on your sorry ass."

Deke groaned quietly. "Girl, you cold."

"I'll be cold if I got to pay this rent next month by my own self like I always did before you got this job. I'll be cold then. And ya'll ain't gonna like that. You know what I'm sayin'."

"How come every time you start hollering at me, you go sounding like some old mammy from Mississippi?" Deke teased, knowing he had to get his day on the move.

"Never you mind what I sound like. You get your ass up and get to work so your boss don't have to come here and find you got drunk again, on Christmas night, no less. And it's because you was out hooting around with that no-good Nicky Storms. He ain't never had a job, and he probably never even been up to see the morning sunlight since he's born. Now, come on, Deke. Get out of bed," she pleaded.

"OK, OK. I'm getting up. Lord, you unmerciful," Deke said. He swung his heavily muscled legs out of the bed and flipped the pillow in his hand back toward the ruffled sheets. He stood in black briefs as he moved toward the window to peek through the blinds to see what the day after Christmas might look like. But the bedroom window looked over the back of another building and even if it hadn't been pitch dark at six-thirty on a late December morning, light seldom shone down that alleyway and into their bedroom window.

Deke's briefs could barely hide the erection he always woke up with. Attempting to be discreet about it was useless, as Deke was well-proportioned. He usually wore a T-shirt, which he'd pull down to hide his embarrassment, but for some reason he did not have one on this morning. Deke had always been modest about his body and was never comfortable with nudity.

Sharona came back into the bedroom, bundled up from the top of her head to her toes against the cold. A stocking cap, puffy coat, and boots hid her sculpted, compact figure and shaded her large brown eyes and dazzling pixie smile. "That's right. I see what you're trying to hide. If you'd have come home at a decent hour without that nasty wine breath, I'd have been taking care of that thing. But you got your boy, Nicky Storms, so I'll be saying bye-bye now and ya'll can do whatever ya'll does with one of them when ain't no sugar around." She laughed at her own teasing.

"Come over here, you nasty witch," Deke said as he reached out to grab the woman he surprisingly felt so much love and gratitude for. Surprising, because Deke was as cold as they come.

Giggling and satisfied that she had gotten Deke awake enough for him to catch his bus to work, Sharona scampered to the door of the tiny, one-bedroom apartment. As she left, the cell phone in her pocket jangled. Letting the door close behind her, she stepped into the dreary December morning and began her trek through the parking lot of their public assistance housing development. The bus she needed was still a good walk from their door and missing it meant she'd be late for work.

She expected the call to be from Chita, her coworker and neighbor, so she didn't bother to check the LED readout. Chita missed more time than anyone at the store and Sharona anticipated hearing from her today, the day after Christmas, the worst and busiest day of the year. Chita would want to stay at home and enjoy Christmastime with her two boys. "So," Sharona said into the phone. "What kind of excuse you want me to give Bernadine when she sees me come in the door alone?"

"I'm sorry, this is Doctor Russo calling for Sharona Watts. Do I have a wrong number?"

"This is Sharona. Who did you say this was?"

"Sharona, it's Doctor Russo at Cold Spring Harbor Lab. You were one of the volunteer subjects for a study we have been conducting. Is this a bad time to call?"

"No, I'm just going to my bus and thought you were my girlfriend. Yeah, I was in your test, but I never got my check."

"I apologize for that, Miss Watts. I'll look into that and find out what the glitch was."

"The glitch was that it was mailed to me, according to the woman at your place, but I never got it. Somebody stole it out of my mailbox, 'cause the woman said the check cleared, but whatever name is signed on the back isn't mine. I never saw that check."

"Well, have we sent you another check?" Russo asked.

"No. Nobody said nothing about that. I asked, but the woman said she'd have to look further and then no one called me back."

"Well, I apologize for that and I promise you we'll get to the bottom of this. If your check wasn't delivered, we should get you another check. I'll look into it, Miss Watts. But I have another reason to be calling you today."

"OK, well, is this going to take long? Because my bus will be here in about four minutes and my phone don't work so good when I'm on it."

"That will depend on how quickly you can answer a simple question for me, Miss Watts. Is there any way that I could meet with you at our lab at some point tomorrow? We have concluded the tests on your DNA samples and there are certain aspects of the results we feel we must share with you directly."

"What kind of aspects are you talking about, doctor? Am I OK?"

"Yes, Miss Watts. You are perfectly fine and what I need to discuss with you isn't about any immediate concerns, but it is highly personal information that you should hear in person."

"Doctor, you're scaring me. Am I going to be OK?"

"Miss Watts, I would not want to mislead you. The news that I must share with you is not the best news you will ever hear. But you are not sick or in any immediate danger. You may want to make some plans, but as far as what we know from your results, you are perfectly normal."

"Well, I got work tomorrow from seven to three, plus I don't have no car, so I can't say how I would get to you."

"I think I can solve the transportation issue, Miss Watts. I can have one of our people come by and pick you up, and then bring you back home after. I'll even have your new check waiting for you when you get here. How's that?"

"This must be pretty important for you to go to all that trouble."

"Miss Watts, do you have someone you'd like to bring with you? Someone who you rely on? A parent, a boyfriend, or someone close to you?"

"Doctor, I'm liking the sound of this less and less."

"Miss Watts, there is nothing in your present health to be afraid of, we just need to share some information we found with you and possibly get your permission for further testing."

"My bus is here. I suppose it's OK, but I want my grandma to come with me. She lives where I live. I get off my shift by three."

"OK, I have your work address here. Is it still the same?"

"Yes, the Target store in Coram."

"OK, any particular spot where we can meet you?"

"I'll come out the front door on the left. I may be with my friend, Chita."

"OK, look for a white van with the lab ID on the doors and a half-bald driver by the name of Lou. He'll be there and he'll take you home to change if you like, and he'll also take you to get your grandmother."

"Can he take Chita home with us? She lives in the projects, too."

"Sure, that won't be a problem. So we'll see you here tomorrow, Miss Watts."

"I guess so. You'll have my check like you said?"

"I promise. Have a good day and I look forward to meeting you."

A cold gust of wind blew on Sharona's back as she climbed the steps onto her bus.

Her friend Chita, as she had guessed, was not at the stop, which meant that Chita wasn't going to work. Sharona shivered as she paid her fare and moved past the driver to an empty seat.

Sharona had developed an acute sense of self-preservation growing up in a hardscrabble world.

She knew instinctively the things in life to be frightened of, and what not to worry about.

Something about this appointment tomorrow frightened her.

Chapter Eleven

December 26, 2012, 11:22 a.m.
Aboard Gulfstream R4TW8
Over New York City

Kate fell asleep just as the Gulfstream rose above the Manhattan skyline, heading west. The holidays had taken a huge chunk of energy out of her. The traditions of a Brannigan Christmas, along with her charity work, were draining.

She knew the overload was her own fault. Their wealth could easily allow her to pay others to take care of the preparations. That just wasn't her way. This was her family and there were parts of the season that Kate treasured. Nothing could change her.

So with the family in their seats, the kids busy with their treat bags full of puzzles and coloring books, the big boys tuned to football games on the Comsat hookup and their daughters settled into their wine and cheese chat, Kate quietly grabbed a *Redbook* and a hot tea, and plopped into one of the last captain's chairs available on board, as close to the rear as she could get.

She wrapped herself in a comforter. It wasn't long before her eyes drooped and the *Redbook* fell back on her lap, still open to the page she'd been reading. She usually slept well on planes, but today she was in one of those semi-trances, where it felt as if she were asleep but she could still hear what was said around her.

It was in this twilight state that she heard Dan's annoyance with the children; several times he asked them to keep the noise down. After a soda spilled into one of their laps, he rose from the front of the plane, grabbed a set of sound-blocking headphones and walked back to the captain's chair across from Kate, where Dave, Debbie's husband, was working a crossword puzzle. "David," he mumbled, "can I grab that seat from you? I should be doing what Kate is doing instead of mopping up soda."

"Sure, Pop. Help yourself. I'll tell the kids to leave you and Mom alone for a while." Dave tucked his crossword book under his arm and moved up the plane's aisle.

Kate kept her eyes closed and wondered what had brought on Dan's bad mood. It wasn't like him. Usually, when they were on the plane with the kids, he was in the middle of their activities. Dan soaked up his time with his grandkids. He even enjoyed their spills and drops. It seemed like he was always laughing at their energy and focused on the fun they brought into his life.

Kate opened her eyes a few moments later and saw Dan staring at her. His headphones were off, and he simply sat, his gazed fixed on her. She could see strain on his face. She and Dan had been through a lifetime together and each read the other's emotions as easily as if the feelings were their own. She knew something was wrong. "Hi there," Kate said. " Needed a break from the noisemakers?"

Dan avoided her eyes. "Yeah, they're really cranked up today. Guess as they get older, they get louder."

"Hmm, didn't wake me up. They seem to be all settled in now," Kate said.

Dan glanced at the front of the plane, where the rest of the clan was in various stages of sleep and quiet activity. "Yeah, for the moment, until the next soda can gets knocked over."

"Well, they're kids, Dan. You usually find that so amusing."

Dan ignored the comment. He reached into the magazine rack, put on his reading glasses, and began to thumb through a copy of *Vanity Fair*.

Kate watched him for a few minutes and then leaned across the aisle. As quietly as she could, she asked, "What's wrong?"

Dan peered above his eyeglasses, stared at her for a few seconds, then leaned over and kissed her cheek. "Nothing, just a bit tired."

Kate's eyes widened. "Just tired? I don't believe you. You never read *Vanity Fair*. And even if you did, you can't read it upside down."

Dan looked at the magazine in his hands and realized Kate was right.

"Who called this morning just before we left, and what did they say that has you reading magazines upside down and being short with your favorite little buddies in the world?" Her tone was more serious than curious.

Dan's defenses went on alert. "That was Russo. I'm more than a bit annoyed about how the lab handled the results of this research they just finished, the gene study they've been at for the last four years. They kind of botched the press release and let it get out yesterday. It wasn't exactly the best timing for what they had to say and I personally think they made a mistake. That's all."

Kate sensed hesitation in his voice. "Since when did an announcement from the lab matter so much? What was it all about?"

"I'll tell you what it was about, Mom," piped up Diane. "I heard about it last night on CNN, and it was all over the news this morning."

Dan wished he had kept his mouth shut. Kate's eyes opened wide as their other daughters gathered in a semicircle in the aisle near them.

"Oh my God, I couldn't believe it," chimed in Debbie. "Dad, did you know about this? It's kind of scary."

Before Dan could say anything, Allie spoke. "Yeah, I saw it on the news this morning. Some priest at the Vatican was calling it the greatest heresy in centuries. Are you going to stay on the board, Dad?"

Before Dan could respond, Debbie added, "I think the whole thing is sick. Predicting when you're going to die from your genes? Yikes!"

"What?" exclaimed Kate. "Predicting what from your genes?"

"Stop it, everyone. Just stop. The lab has uncovered some really interesting stuff and it isn't life-threatening at all to anyone," Dan said as he tried to restore order.

"And what is all over TV?" Kate asked, looking up at the girls.

Diane spoke first and outlined the lab's discovery.

"What's this?" Now Dave and his brother-in-law had joined the discussion.

"Makes sense if you think about it. Why not?" Allie shrugged.

"Because God decides those things," Debbie quickly retorted.

Before anyone else could speak, Dan, as calmly as possible, described the study from its inception to the announcement yesterday. It was a roller-coaster ride of a discussion, as the family interrupted endlessly, debating the merits of the study, it's conclusion, and its impact.

"So how does this affect you, Dad?' Adam asked finally.

Kate, quiet the entire time, now looked right into Dan's eyes.

Feeling her gaze and knowing she would be measuring his response, he carefully kept his voice casual and calm. "Not at all. Why should it? I'm a member of the board, not a scientist. This isn't my claim, although you could say I am a part of it. But I make no decisions about what the lab puts out. Hell, if that were true, I'd be a seven-time Nobel laureate."

Diane looked at him closely, "But how do you feel about it? This is against your religion."

Dan shrugged. "Yeah, I hear you. I'm not sure how I feel yet. I respect that science gets better each year at predictability. But I also have my doubts, confidentially speaking. I don't believe that life or death is outside God's power. I think God chooses for us. So I'm at odds with this. I don't know what to say about it yet, because I only heard the results myself this morning."

Dan had never told his children that he was part of the study and that somewhere there was a test result with his DNA and his death date listed. Now he regretted that he had ever joined the study.

"Dad, a few weeks ago I was having lunch at your office with Laureen," said Allie. "And she mentioned something about you and the lab, and said, 'Who knows, maybe someday the lab will use your father's DNA to clone a new line of Brannigans.' Why would the lab have your DNA?"

"Who said they have my DNA?" Dan said, trying to cover up, although Laureen had been his assistant for more than twenty years.

"Laureen was talking about how wonderful you are, as always, and she made that remark. I didn't pay much attention to it then, but now that this has come up …"

"Well, she talks too much." Dan said.

"Dan, tell the kids. They have a right to know," Kate said quietly.

"OK. I participated in the test last year," Dan confessed.

Bedlam broke out. The three girls became apoplectic, talking over each other. The grandkids, hearing the fuss, raised their heads to listen. "What's wrong? Why is everyone hollering?"

Diane walked to the front of the plane, distracted the kids and got them back to their activities. Then she retrieved the wine bottle and her sisters' glasses, and returned.

"What's the big deal?' Dan whispered. "I gave some spit and a nail clipping, and that's it."

"The big deal is that there is a file on you now that supposedly says when you could die," Debbie moaned.

"Will die," added Allie.

"Let's not go into that. God forbid." Diane said.

"Dad, this is horrible. Why did you do this?" said Debbie.

"Keep your voices down. The kids will get upset," Kate whispered.

"Hold on," Dan tried to settle everyone down. "We are all going to die. Nobody gets out of here alive, remember? I was curious about the project and offered myself as a test subject. What do I care if I'm in a book somewhere with a date on it? I would have assumed that was true in heaven or on earth. God's got a book he keeps, believe me."

"Don't you want to know what the date is?" Adam asked.

"Not interested in the least. Folks, listen to me. This test is only the beginning. The entire structure of our humanity may well be locked in our DNA. That's what genetics research is about, to unlock the codes that make us all who and what we are. This test seems to confirm that a clock is ticking on all of us. But we all know that anyway, don't we?"

Dan looked at his daughters and sons-in-law for confirmation but none was forthcoming. "If Cold Spring Harbor has now found the clock, as they claim, that's all there is to it. They can't tell you if you are leaving by accident or disease or whatever. So forget about this stuff. It's just another discovery. It isn't making anything happen that wasn't already bound to happen anyway."

"True, but it's also the last page in everyone's book and if you read that, you can spoil the story," said Diane.

"I don't like it," said David.

"Me neither," Allie and Diane said in unison.

"Well, it's here now, so what can you do?" Dan replied and finally they calmed down.

Kate looked at her husband as their family returned to their seats. She picked up her magazine as Dan stared out the window.

When everyone was outside of earshot, she turned quietly to him. "What did Russo want the day after Christmas? Don't tell me he called just to let you know that the lab had gone public with its research."

Dan had vowed he would never lie to Kate again, a vow made years ago and for a very good reason. He hated himself now for that promise, but not as much as he hated the need to keep his vow. His voice barely audible, he leaned toward Kate. "He wants me to come in and see him. With you. He said my test has some kind of finding that he needs to discuss with us."

A look of concern crossed her face. "Us? That sounds ominous."

"Yeah, I'm hoping he wants to tell us that I am a descendant of King Kong and that my wiener is going to grow bigger in my old age."

Kate chuckled in spite of herself. She knew Dan was trying to push back against what was on his mind. There was more to this, Kate knew. Dan's instincts were acute. Whatever his suspicions about this lab business, it was probably real, she thought. And she also knew it wasn't about a King Kong-sized wiener. But Dan could always make Kate laugh and that was how they both shielded each other when they needed protection.

"You're already in your old age and believe me, it's not growing. So when are we going in? What's your guess as to what he wants?"

"The day after we get back. As to what exactly it's about, I haven't the faintest idea," Dan said dismissively.

Kate knew Dan was in fear. She knew he would never lie to her. But that didn't mean he wouldn't lie to himself. And what she had just heard, she knew from a lifetime of listening to her husband, was a lie.

Dan was lying to himself so he wouldn't have to lie to her.

Chapter Twelve

December 26, 2012, 9:28 a.m.
37 Sunnyfield Lane
Hicksville, New York

The phone rang in Kathy Jonas's bedroom, and when she picked it up she heard the voice of her best friend.

"Kathy? I just got off the phone with Doctor Russo," Janet Bates said, all in a rush, forgetting her usual "good morning."

Kathy had worked full time in Cold Spring Harbor Lab's accounting department for more than seven years; she knew who Russo was. "Why is he calling you? And you're not canceling for later, are you?"

For years Kathy and Janet had spent the day after the holiday together, taking care of the inevitable exchanges and returns. It was a grueling, exhausting task, but they always made it fun. They would start early then treat themselves to a nice lunch and a manicure to recharge their batteries. In the evening, they would meet several girlfriends for dinner. Tonight, they would be heading to Captain Bill's, a toney restaurant overlooking Long Island's Great South Bay. They loved this tradition. The notion that Dr. Russo of all people might interfere with it was bizarre.

"I'm not sure." Janet said flatly. In fact, her nerves had gone on alert after the brief call from Russo. She had been on edge already, and his call left her even more anxious. "He asked if I would be free to come in to meet him today. Something about an unusual test result from the stuff we did with them, and he wanted to discuss it personally with me."

Kathy sat on her bed, moving the phone under her chin as she slid into a new pair of jeans she had received for Christmas. Once both feet were inside the pants legs, she stood and tugged them up, realizing that they would slide over her hips just fine, but, as usual, were too big in the waist. "Oh, the DNA test we did? Hmm? What the heck?" Kathy checked her rear end in the full-length mirror on her closet door. "Well, don't panic, kiddo. This could be good stuff. Maybe your results included some winning lottery numbers," she teased.

"Yeah, sure," Janet replied. "My luck doesn't run that way. You know that. Anyway, I told him we were supposed to go to the mall and return some Christmas stuff this morning, but I could pop by after that. What kind of a guy is he? He seemed nice."

Kathy began to take the jeans off. "Oh, he is. But he's not really my boss. He's kind of like the absent-minded professor. But, then, most of the scientists over there are. I hardly have anything to do with him except once in a while I may have to get him to sign off on a check. He seems OK. I never hear anything bad about him. Did he ask about me?"

"As a matter of fact, he did, when I mentioned we were going to the mall together, he said your name sounds familiar." Janet hadn't told Russo that both she and Kathy had volunteered for the p63A DNA test. Actually it had been Janet who saw the ad seeking test volunteers. Kathy hadn't heard about the research even though she worked at the lab.

"A thousand bucks to get a swab of saliva and some nail clippings? Duh! Count me in," Kathy had said at the time. "I'll go by the recruitment office tomorrow and get us some applications." Ten days later, they showed up, signed some legal papers and submitted their samples. The entire process took less than fifteen minutes. When their checks arrived Janet used hers to save for a protective

Kevlar vest for her son, who was going to Afghanistan. Kathy put the money toward repaving her driveway.

"Nice. I work there seven years and he's the president and he says my name sounds familiar. That's all I get after seven years?" Kathy tried to sound insulted even though she wasn't.

Janet sensed her friend's hurt feelings. "No. As soon as I described you, he laughed and said, 'Oh yeah, Kathy in accounting. Sheesh, what was I thinking? I didn't know you guys knew each other.' So I told him we grew up together and lived next door and that we were godparents for each other's children. Anyway, he asked if Rod could join me and I told him Rod was already at work. Then he asked if maybe you could come. He said he wanted someone to be with me."

"What? That sounds weird. Wonder what the heck it could be?" Kathy said.

"That's what I said when he asked if you could be with me. I said 'Why, am I in some kind of danger?' And he kind of danced around the answer."

"Really? What did he say?" Kathy was getting a little worried now, too.

"He said that the latest test results had produced some peculiarities, and that I was one of only four persons tested who they were calling in for more information. That I was in no immediate danger, but that he'd rather we had the discussion in person."

Kathy decided to make light of it to tamp Janet's fears down. "Mmm. Sounds technical. Probably some new gene pattern or stuff like that. Not for nothing, honey, but they are always finding something new over there. He didn't ask you to come with Rod? Why me?"

"Kathy? Hello? Are you listening to me? I just said that I told him Rod was at work today, and that when it came to details you would probably remember more than my husband anyway. Maybe I shouldn't have said that, you know? That kind of threw Rod under the bus a bit." Janet said.

Kathy thought she heard some fear in her friend's voice now.

"Are you OK? You seemed a little off your game yesterday."

"I don't know. That call with Michael kind of bothered me and then this. Something's not right. I have a bad feeling."

Kathy knew Janet was overly anxious about the potential peril her son faced. She felt some of the same anxiety, but she knew that her friend bordered on paranoia about Michael being somehow taken from her. Janet had been one of those mothers who followed her children's school buses until they were safely inside their classrooms.

Kathy knew there was little she could do to help Janet with the fear that clutched her. So when she could, she tried to make light of her best friend's dread. "Oh, come on now. Michael sounded great, and don't be making a bogeyman out of Russo. The guy is harmless. He wears a Mets hat to work, for Christ's sake. These people are after Alzheimer's, not a couple of mopes like us."

"I know," Janet said, unconvinced. "But you know me with the kids. I have this umbilical cord that stretches across the world and I got a weird feeling when Michael called."

"Weird like what?" Kathy asked.

Janet sighed heavily. "I don't know. Just weird. Like maybe he is in some kind of danger or something."

"Janet, he's fine. He runs the telephones back in the rear command post. He's not out shooting bad guys."

"No. It wasn't that. I don't know what it was, but I got spooked."

Recalling the conversation, Kathy asked, "You think he's got a girl, don't you?"

"Maybe. He did hint at something, right?" But Janet tried to shake off her dread and instead focus on their exchanges-and-returns trip. "Anyway, let's get going. I'll honk when I'm ready. Should be about a half hour. Want to grab a bagel before we go?"

"Sure. See you in a bit. Oh, and Billy tried the sweater on last night and it's too tight," Kathy said, referring to her husband. Then added, "Yeah, right, it's not that he's too fat."

"OK. See you in a few. Just need to dry my hair and put some paint on this sagging face," Janet said.

"Me, too. Or maybe a bag over my head would be better. Ciao."

Kathy hung up the phone.

Both women had their TVs tuned to the Weather Channel to check the day's forecast. Had they turned to CNN at that moment, they would have seen a live report of a demonstration outside the lab's front gate by a group of ultraorthodox rabbis from Brooklyn, protesting "the abomination of the attempted destruction of the teachings of the Torah."

Neither woman had watched a news program or seen a newspaper in days. Neither knew anything of the maelstrom that was swirling around the announcement made thirty-nine-and-a-half hours ago by Cold Spring Harbor Laboratory.

Chapter Thirteen

December 27, 2012, 4:20 p.m.
Cold Spring Harbor Laboratory, Office of the President
Cold Spring Harbor, New York

S harona sat in a wingback chair placed so that she could look out onto Cold Spring Harbor. Gran perched sideways on a matching loveseat so she could take in the view, too. The comfortable, patrician furniture was set up before a large picture window in Dr. Russo's office. Neither of them had ever seen Cold Spring Harbor before, other than the time Sharona visited to have her DNA collected last year. But that was at night and the view from the lab along the water's edge could not be appreciated.

The sun at this time of the year, just about a week after the winter solstice, dropped early and quickly below the horizon, and the two women marveled at the changes in the sky's color, which they saw reflected on the water. "The Lord gives us wonders each day," Gran murmured as she took in the changing palette of color before them.

They had been ushered into Russo's office while his assistant explained that he was doing a radio interview and would be with them shortly. She apologized profusely, explaining that the staff hadn't expected them to arrive until closer to five, but understood from Lou, the driver, that they made "exceptionally good time coming in from out east." "Well, I could sure use some wonders that include my check that this doctor says he's giving me." Sharona was still thinking that this was going to be a payday for her. Money was, as always, scarce.

"Shoney, honey, the Lord doesn't do money," Gran admonished her beloved granddaughter, using her pet name. "How many times you have to hear that before you listen? Lord, you a stubborn one."

Sharona's grandmother, Valerie Stalls, was the rock in her life. A solid, hard-core working woman, she'd raised three children, raised her grandchild Sharona and supported other family members while employed as a nurse's aide at a hospital. She had never taken her husband's last name, expecting that he would turn out to be no good. Her instincts were right; he ran off after her last child was born. One of her sons had died after a car accident, and the other was missing.

Gran had a special spot in her heart for Sharona and believed that the girl would someday do something great. She didn't allow her own daughter, Sharona's mother, Vanessa, to be in the house when she wasn't home to watch over her. And for good reason. Vanessa had always been trouble. She bore Sharona at age sixteen with no father recorded on the birth certificate. She never married, but changed her last name to Watts, thinking that a local thug might be the child's father. Sonny Watts didn't agree and never saw Vanessa again after she announced she was pregnant.

Vanessa gave birth to four more children after Sharona and had at least five more pregnancies, as well as an arrest record for drug abuse, robberies, shoplifting and prostitution. She also had a badly disfigured face, courtesy of a drugged-out sex partner. Vanessa, a welfare recipient most of her adult life, was now off drugs and working part-time in the kitchen at the county jail. Gran suspected she had stolen Sharona's check from the lab. Vanessa manipulated nearly everyone she had ever come in contact with, but she was afraid of Gran. And she ran if she saw Deke Williams.

Russo's assistant gently tapped on the closed door and without waiting to be invited, came bustling in. She walked directly to Sharona and handed her an envelope with a clear front window.

There, Sharona could see her name, preceded by the words "Pay to the Order of." "Dr. Russo left me explicit instructions to hand this to you the minute you came through the door, Miss Watts. I apologize for having nearly forgotten it. Dr. Russo said the original was stolen and forged. How terrible," Jenny said sympathetically. "What kind of people would be that desperate?"

"Oh, there's all kinds, miss," Gran said. "I can tell you that."

"Yes, I suppose. But Dr. Russo also asked me to apologize for not following up with you on this. You shouldn't have had to chase us for it. Probably come in handy now that the Christmas bills will be showing up. I know it would in my house."

With that, she left and when they heard the click of the door, Sharona giggled, looked at her Gran, and slipped the envelope open. "I thought you said the Lord don't do money, Gran? Well, here I just about got the words out my mouth and there's a check in my hand for, yep, a thousand dollars. How you like me now?"

"That's blasphemous, Sharona. You should say a prayer to thank the Lord for looking out for you and getting you your check back. Never mind making a fool's joke from your good luck," Gran said, with the emphasis on the word "fool."

"I'll be thanking the Lord if this doctor don't have me here to tell me bad news, Gran. That's all I got on my mind right now. Although, I will say this check does make my holiday spirits bright."

Russo swung into the room wearing a Mets cap and a moss-green roll-neck sweater over gray corduroy jeans and Puma running shoes. Neither Gran nor Sharona got what they were expecting. They had been anticipating a white-coated, silver-haired, soap opera archetype, and Russo was none of that. He was tall, lean, and athletic, and his wardrobe gave no hint that he was one of the most prolific scientific minds of his time.

"Ladies, please stay seated. My apologies. We thought you'd be here much later, but this is great that you got to see the sunset. Pretty, isn't it? I sometimes think I should work here for free just for the view. Miss Watts?" he turned to Sharona. "Did you get your check?"

"Yes she did. And a happy new year, too," said Gran, evoking a mild chuckle from Russo and a look of rebuke from Sharona.

"Well, let's hope so. A little cash around this time of year is never a bad thing, hey?"

"Nooo, doctor. This time or any other time of year," Sharona responded and they all smiled.

"Now, what can my grandchild do for you, doctor?"

And then Sharona Watts, twenty-seven, grandchild of Valerie Stalls, sixty-five, began the worst hour and eleven minutes of their lives. By the time the meeting ended, the two were devastated, their souls split down the middle.

"You said I wasn't in any danger, doctor," Sharona pleaded.

"I said you weren't in any danger at this time, Sharona, and I don't believe you are. These results do not provide evidence of any illnesses or conditions. As I explained, there is no prediction here about what may cause your eventual demise. We simply know when it will happen."

"And you think that maybe because I have the same day as these other folks that there could be some connection? But they're all white folks, you said."

Tod sat forward in his chair. "The fact that the others are all Caucasian doesn't mean that you aren't linked genetically. We have traced many thousands of cases back through their genealogy and found racial mixing in evidence. Your ancestors were probably mixed races just as mine could have been.' Tod paused for a breath, "There can be coincidences in your four medical makeups that are going to become revealed at some point in this year ahead. That's one big reason that we want to stay close to the four of you and keep a constant watch on your health. If something develops in one of you; it could develop in all. And it could be something we can treat. Possibly even prevent."

He leaned back and continued. "We hope to find out within the study group we're forming what, if any, common link you may share and how it happens that all four of you, born on different days and at different times, can somehow end up with the same date of death. Believe me, without revealing anything about the others, because we don't have their consent yet, the four of you are from completely different backgrounds."

"But we all going to die next Christmas Day?" Sharona started sobbing.

Gran put her arms around her, saying nothing. She, too, was overcome. "Please God, don't take this child," she said, as she reached for her purse and a packet of tissues.

Tod was being drawn into their emotional storm but didn't know what he could do to stop their fall into that abyss. "I know this must be devastating for you both, and I have no wish to try to sell you on opting into this study. And I understand if you choose not to, but what we might discover through further study could help perhaps hundreds of thousands of others. Our genetic structures are the roadmaps of our living and dying. They are the deciding factors in who and what all of us are and what we become. Any evidence that we can unlock can be meaningful."

He was grasping at anything to convince them to join the study. "Your participation will have some monetary reward as well. I know that seems meaningless right now. The lab will compensate you for your participation on the basis of your time spent with us as if you had a consulting contract with us. That would be a thousand dollars a day for each day, or part of a day, in which you would be actively engaged with us. In addition, we will give you complete medical coverage and your costs for transportation."

"And what do I do for a thousand dollars a day? Be one of your lab mice?" Sharona sounded completely uninterested in the financial details.

"Not at all, Miss Watts." Tod was trying not to sound defensive. "Mostly we expect we will be taking simple DNA samples, much like the ones you gave when you first entered the program. We'll also monitor your physical condition in detail throughout the year to see if perhaps there are any clues leading you toward your date, and if those coincide with the results we get from the others. So, if nothing else, while you are a participant, your health will be completely scanned twice a month and you'll know the minute anything doesn't look right. I know that may not sound like a great deal, but if something were to show up that was threatening, we would be on top of it through early detection. And who knows? Maybe we could head something off."

Russo paused briefly and shifted in his chair. He sensed that they had moved away from the pragmatic points he was presenting. "We really have no idea what to expect because this has never happened before. We estimate you'd need to be here a minimum of about four days a month. The process should be entirely painless and completely at your convenience." Russo's voice began to trail off. He didn't know what else to say.

"Did I hear you say that if she got sick you would find out what she had and at least be able to get a head start on whatever treatment she needs?" Used to dealing with medical crisis at the hospital, Gran was able to listen - and hear - despite the emotions she was feeling.

Tod nodded. "I'm sure the continuing monitoring of her physical condition would yield anything that came up, and we'd react accordingly."

"But you ain't saying that you could stop me from dying?" Sharona said.

Tod crossed his legs as he squirmed in his chair, hearing the pleading in her voice. "No. I would never say that until, and unless I knew what your particular symptoms could or would be. We don't know now what we are going to find. The body doesn't work that way medically. What medicine finds in patients isn't always curable. We can't offer you any promises. We aren't even sure we will see anything in this study. I assume that you are perfectly healthy today, and I would expect you to stay that way. We have no doubt about what your DNA tells us. But we have no idea about what is going to happen to make that truth a reality."

Sharona looked directly into Russo's eyes. He could see her fear. He detested himself at this instant for having to be the grim reaper to this energetic young woman who thought she had her whole life in front of her. Russo had a good nose for people and he sensed that Sharona, and her grandmother, had experienced their share of bumps in the road. He wished that he could remove the pain for them.

Sharona began to tremble. Then her eyes began to fill and she leaned her head over until it fell on her grandmother's shoulder. Gran was keening as quietly as she could now, trying to hold back the pain, but losing the battle with her emotions. Sharona's nose began to run and she put a tissue up to her face while sobs came from deep inside her. Her pain was beyond anything she had ever felt. " Gran ... I don't want to leave you. ... I'll miss you so much."

Russo got up from his chair and slipped quietly out of his office. They didn't see the tears rolling down his cheeks.

Chapter Fourteen

December 27, 2012, 7:10 p.m.
Captain Bill's parking lot
Massapequa, New York

When they left the lab Kathy thought Janet was holding herself together amazingly well. She even insisted they continue with their dinner plans. Kathy was the one unsure about what to do next, and not in the mood for holiday chit-chat. And she was sure, whatever brave front Janet had mustered, her friend must be far worse off. The doom predicted by Dr. Russo was beyond imagination.

Kathy knew Janet had been in an emotional hole since Michael left for basic training, the toll his departure had taken. So Janet was already living on the razor's edge. Now this.

At first Janet had seemed not to comprehend what Russo was saying, while Kathy had grasped at once that Janet had less than a year to live. Kathy could see from Janet's questions that her friend had not yet digested that sinister information. She had continued the discussion as if she were somehow outside the results, finally asking Russo, "So what does this actually mean for us, doctor? You mentioned something about December 25, 2013. Does that have some meaning?"

When she heard that, Kathy's heart felt like it had jumped into her mouth. Russo had taken a deep breath, exhaled audibly, then glanced down before looking straight at Janet. Later, Kathy would swear she had seen him age in the instant before he spoke. "Mrs. Bates, December 25, 2013 is the date that your DNA indicates you will die. I'm sorry."

Janet blinked several times. Now she understood. She went stone cold silent, staring down at the table. Kathy kept her eyes focused on Janet. Russo sat back.

A minute of intense silence passed before Janet glanced out the window and muttered, "Is it possible you've made a mistake here, doctor?"

Russo seemed to be struggling to hide his sorrow and maintain a professional detachment. "Mrs. Bates, I wish it was. But these test results have been run over and over to be certain that the origins of the samples, the known timing factors and calibrated numeric, is perfected. We have one hundred-percent certainty."

Janet had shifted her gaze to Kathy and exhaled loudly, "I never was the lucky one, was I, Kath? I finally get picked for something and it's got to be a dirt nap."

Kathy always had whatever answers Janet needed; this time, she had nothing to say. She slid across the couch toward Janet and grasped her hand.

The rest of the meeting was a blur. Like sleepwalkers, the two women had awoken to find themselves back at Janet's pale blue minivan in the lab parking lot. Kathy offered to drive. When they got in, Kathy said she would call the girls and cancel dinner.

At first, Janet didn't say anything. She just stared out of the window at the dark blue waters of Cold Spring Harbor, white caps rising as a strong breeze blew over the waters. Then she began to sob. "I always thought I would be the grandmother who had all the kids at my house all the time. I saw myself in my old age with teenaged grandkids sneaking around the kitchen stealing cookies. Me chasing them away. I dreamed about being the person they would tell their secrets to because they knew I'd understand and have good advice for them. And that their secret would stay safe with me. Now none of that will ever happen. I won't even see my kids walk down the aisle." Janet's words were barely audible.

Kathy couldn't stop her own tears; words were not even possible.

After a few minutes, Janet took a deep breath ."I'm not ready for this, Kath. I can't leave Michael or Mickey. I can't leave them. What will happen to Rod? And what about us, Kath? How can I not have you?"

With that, Janet's emotional restraint collapsed. She put her face in her hands and shook uncontrollably. Long, deep sobs rose from deep within her.

Kathy joined her best friend in the depths of grief. "I know, Jan. I can't be without you, either. How could this happen? What are we going to do, Janey?"

The winter winds, turning the harbor into a cauldron, dropped a shroud around them. In much the same way, Janet's hopes and dreams were also swirling in a tempest.

When they emerged from their grief, Janet insisted they should still have dinner with their friends. Kathy drove to the restaurant and they parked. They even began applying makeup to cover their swollen eyes. Then Janet stopped, a mascara wand still in her shaking hand, and whispered, "Can we go home, Kath? I need to talk to Rod and Mickey, and then write to Michael."

"Good call," Kathy said as she restarted the minivan's engine.

Chapter Fifteen

January 3, 2013, 10:30 a.m.
125 Main Street
Cold Spring Harbor, New York

Dan Brannigan's large cherrywood office, like his home, was richly appointed and exquisitely designed. Each piece was impressive, from the Bokhara rugs to the Chippendale furniture to the Baldwin sconces above the fireplace.

Behind Dan's desk, which was large enough for a grown man to lie across, was a broad picture window. To the right of that window hung a framed check made out to Brannigan, payable at Chase Bank and dated January 19, 1984. The check was drawn for a sum exceeding a million dollars, and was countersigned by the treasurer of Morgan Stanley. The check was real and it had remained in the frame since the day he got it.

Others would have long since spent that check. Brannigan considered it a motivational tool. To him, it would always be secure and if he ever had to, he could break the glass and take it to the bank. The check was backed by a promissory note guaranteed by Morgan Stanley and had no expiration date. So, as he had for twenty-eight years, he kept it as a symbol, even as he joined Gates, Buffett, Bloomberg and Soros on the annual Forbes list of richest men in America.

Dan told Kate the night he brought it home, "This check is going to be a daily reminder of possibilities. It's the biggest score I ever made and I want to see it every day to remind myself there's more where this came from."

Kate, as usual, kept it real, joking, "Is that glass breakable in case I need milk for the kids someday and you aren't around?" Then she handed Dan his daughter Diane and asked him to keep the baby busy while she put the wash in the dryer. She ended the discussion as she kissed him and simply said, "Thanks." Dan knew she meant the check, not the child care.

Currently, he kept a million dollars on hand in both their checking accounts. Other assets and cash were spread around the world, amounting to billions of dollars. No one, including *Forbes* magazine, had an accurate count. He never missed that uncashed check. Instead, he touched the frame each time he went to his office chair and took from it a sense of possibility and ambition that he carried with him in all his business affairs.

One of those was the subject of a boring conference call he'd been on for the past twenty minutes. Dan hadn't uttered a single sentence in the mix of voices trying to decide his interests in a global communications company supplying bandwidth to the aviation industry for in-flight Internet service.

Dan already owned a decent-sized stake in the company, which had lined up a contract with the rapidly expanding China World Airways. But they now required an infusion of a hundred and forty million dollars to supply equipment to the Chinese fleet. Dan was considering a fourteen million dollar cash outlay. The rest was to be supplied by two investment banks. His potential return on investment within a year could be tenfold. The longer term plan was to flip the company to a worldwide telecom firm seeking acquisitions. The shorter story was that Dan's cash would give him a thirty-percent stake in the company and a return of somewhere close to two hundred million dollars when the company was acquired. He liked the deal and had decided to clinch it weeks ago. Today was simply a formality.

The door to his office swung open and Kate entered, wearing a classic double-breasted, cream colored coat that just barely touched the tops of her cordovan boots. Underneath the unbuttoned coat was a black turtleneck sweater with a single string of pearls draped across her chest. Her skirt was gray wool, knee length, and atop her head a white wool knitted beret was worn to one side. A matching white wool muffler hung casually around her neck and shoulders. Covering her hands were matching gloves; on one shoulder was slung a large leather purse.

Dan looked at her and hit the mute button. "Hey, cutie! Don't you look like a million today!" Hitting the mute button again, Dan re-entered the discussion. "Listen, guys, my apologies, but I have to move along. My wife and I have an appointment this morning that won't keep. But to put this in a nutshell, let me just say I love this deal and I think we'll go forward with it. Jack" - he was Dan's CFO - "will get the transfers done with you and we'll get it closed as soon as possible. I think that's all you need from me, so I'll buzz off now and leave it to you guys to settle it up. Just let my assistant, Laureen know when you need me for signatures. Good?" And before anyone could reply, Dan hung up and faced Kate.

"You didn't need to get off the phone. I was a few minutes ahead of schedule this morning and thought I'd stop by to see if you're OK with all this. What was the call about?"

"Nothing, just some investment crap. How's Diane? Did she get away on time this morning?" Dan came over to where Kate sat on the arm of one of the sofas in front of the wood-burning fireplace.

"Yes, she and Matt are on their way to your nation's capital as we speak. The baby was crying this morning when he couldn't find Grampy."

Dan kissed Kate's cheek as he passed in front of her and flopped down on the couch. "Oh, your cheek's cold. Still freezing outside?" he asked, reaching for a cup and saucer from the silver service on the coffee table. He poured, handed her the coffee, and filled another cup for himself, skipping the saucer.

"Yeah, it's freezing still. Diane had Matt all wrapped in a scarf around his face up to his eyes and his hat pulled down so all you could see of him were these two little slits." Diane had returned from Colorado with the rest of the family to Cold Spring Harbor to retrieve her au pair, and was headed back to Washington.

"So. How you doing with all this?" Kate asked, wanting to know what Dan was thinking about the meeting with Russo.

Dan knew where she was going and decided to try playing dumb. "With Diane being a single parent? Matthew living away from us? Lousy. How do you think I'm doing with it? That's why I snuck out before everyone was up this morning. I didn't want to see them off. Too painful."

Kate knew Dan was trying to redirect the discussion. She wouldn't allow it. "No. Not that. I know why you left way ahead of everyone this morning. I'm talking about the Russo meeting. I know it's on your mind, but you haven't said much about it."

Dan put the coffee cup down. "What's to say? We'll find out what he wants when we get there. Like I said, it's probably some quirky thing that has to do with my gene pattern or something. Why would I be troubled by that? Nothing anyone can do about their genes."

"Dan," Kate's voice lowered. "I know you don't like this whole business. Don't try and fool me. Are you troubled that your results may be something you don't want to hear?"

"No. Of course not," Dan shot back. "I'm not going down that road with this. That's a fool's chase. I don't care what the tests show, although I won't say that publicly. I'm sure when God is ready for me, he'll let me know, but they say the good die young, so I expect another hundred years."

Kate wasn't buying this bravado. His instincts were so sharp he would know an hour before lightning would strike—and also where. It had also been said of Dan Brannigan that he could "talk his way out of a sunburn."

And she knew that meant especially if he was talking only to himself.

Chapter Sixteen

January 3, 2013, 11:25 a.m.
Cold Spring Harbor Laboratory, Office of the President
Cold Spring Harbor, New York

"Learned doctor," Dan smiled as he entered Russo's office with Kate, extending his hand as Tod rose from his desk. "Great to see you again. How's the world press treating you these days? I see the Fox News truck outside the gate."

"Dan, the press is only annoying and invasive; the religious conservatives are warriors," Russo replied as he shook Dan's hand and leaned down to kiss Kate's cheek. "Hi, Kate. You look like a million, as always," he chirped.

Kate's eyes rolled toward her husband, who smiled broadly. "See? I told you!" he said.

Russo's expression changed, thinking he had perhaps inserted himself somehow into a private discussion. "What? Did I say something wrong?" he asked.

"Not at all, Tod. Don't pay any attention to my husband," Kate smiled.

"I make it a policy to listen to everything my board members say, Kate. How about some coffee? Tea?" He led them to the seating area in front of the picture window looking out over the harbor. The day was astonishingly cold, the temperature at eleven degrees. But it was crystal clear and the sun was shining off the snow, set against the dark blue water of the harbor. A few small oyster boats were still on their moorings, even though the ice was creeping toward them. Over the years, artists had painted hundreds of canvases of this picturesque setting. Today's view could have provided yet more inspiration.

They made small talk about the weather and Dan pointed out that if you stretched to see, there was a chimney above the ridge on the far shore that belonged to the Brannigan house.

Finally, Russo rose from his chair, went to his desk, picked up a thick file, and returned to his seat, facing Dan. Kate sat on the loveseat in front of the picture window.

"How do we want to proceed with this discussion, Dan? I can talk with you about the climate our announcement has produced in the press, or we can go first to your case and my reason for meeting with you and Kate."

"Let's do that first," Dan said, direct as always. "I'm curious why we couldn't have this discussion over the phone and why my bride has to be involved." Dan often referred to Kate as his bride, casually and not for the effect. He meant it. He still thought of her as his bride.

"OK. Dan, as you know, you were part of the last batch of one hundred tests. What I need to discuss with you is something we came across in your tests. You are not sick or abnormal in any way, so let me say that first. Then, I want to know how well you understand the findings of the study and what its implications are for participants."

"Well, I know that you have come to the conclusion that these tests are proof positive that you can identify when any of us is going to die. And I have, as you know, great respect for the science and the methodology followed here. I have my own reservations about the findings. I believe in God and that He decides these things, but, having said that, I know you don't become an old dog without learning new tricks. So I am open to the suggestion that the findings of the study may well be irrefutable. Hopefully, the lab may win yet another Nobel. What I'd like to understand is how foolproof your tests are and what possible relationship I could have to any of this beyond having been one of four hundred subjects."

For the next forty minutes, Russo broke down, line by line, the genesis of the study and the protocols behind each step, building to the unshakable conclusion the lab had publicized on Christmas Day. Tod drew Kate and Dan deep into a discussion of the genomic patterns, and how the research team mathematically tested and confirmed data to align with the physical realities of the subjects tested, from the lab mice to the most recently deceased volunteer. The Brannigans were appalled that suicides and a homicide were among the causes of death. They had difficulty accepting that there were no links between the causes and the actual death dates, especially with the unnatural causes, where dates had been known only by CSHL researchers.

Deep in both Dan and Kate's minds, the idea germinated that this phenomenal discovery could be divine inspiration, but neither of them said so. Dan thought, and suspected Kate probably agreed, that it didn't seem possible a fatal accident could be predicted in someone's genes or that a suicide was predictable through DNA to a date on the calendar. A murder predicted by DNA? Unbelievable. Yet it had occurred. With each twist in the evidence and every shred of explanation that Russo carefully and patiently provided, Dan and Kate understood that regardless of how they felt, Russo presented a scientifically solid case. Indeed, the evidence led to a single conclusion. Science would now be able to predict the end of life for each person on earth. But science didn't have any answers for how that person would die. That seemed ominous to the Brannigans.

As the discussion moved forward and the study's validity took root, Dan became increasingly uncomfortable. He had hoped Russo had only asked them to come in together to sell them the lab's findings. Now, his stomach began to tighten and he could feel sweat beginning to form in his armpits. His intuition was taking him somewhere he didn't want to go.

Finally, Kate asked, "So, Tod, all of this being said, why are we here?"

Russo reached out and brushed some lint from an exposed sock. Then he looked into Dan's eyes as he sat back in his chair and crossed his legs. "Dan, what I need to share with you is not good news."

Kate gasped. Dan's brain began to scream as if he had just jumped from a tall building.

Russo kept speaking. "As you'll recall, you signed a waiver just like all tested subjects, that guaranteed full anonymity of your test results, assuring that whatever the tests would show would be kept from you entirely. But the last batch of a hundred subjects revealed four people with no apparent links to each other, who all carry the exact same death dates. The four are different ages, genders, and races. In fact, there is absolutely nothing we can see that would indicate any links among them, either through DNA or anything else."

"Why is that so surprising?" Dan asked.

"In four hundred tests we have seen not even two duplications of death dates. This four-way matchup, of which you are one, is the only such anomaly we have uncovered. Even more coincidentally, all four of you were in the final test batch, and, have a date exactly one year to the day of our announcement."

Dan went cold. Kate fumbled in her bag, looking for a tissue. Russo looked first at Kate, then at Dan. Haltingly, he said, "I'm sorry, Dan."

Dan sat staring back at his friend. He well knew that Tod Russo was not a man of errors in his scientific pronouncements. In fact he was, as far as Dan knew, fully reliable. But the coincidence of Dan being somehow connected to four others so randomly selected and yet so mortally linked had a mystery about it that chilled Dan's senses of survival. He wanted to deny what he intuitively knew to be the truth. He naturally knew nothing about his three mortally marked colleagues but in that instant he felt a flash of connection deep within his soul. And, for a flash of a moment, he fought back a dark presence coming over him. Then truth crept inexorably into his soul and mind. Fear clutched him as it had never done before.

Dan took a deep breath and glanced over at Kate, who was looking down at her boots, avoiding eye contact. Tears were beginning to roll down her cheeks. He looked beyond her, out of the window, and saw a seagull gliding against the sky above the harbor. His jaw tightening, his voice catching in his throat, he whispered, "So. ... What I just heard ... a year from now? On Christmas Day? Christmas? ... This'll be the day that I die?"

Chapter Seventeen

January 4, 2013, 7:46 a.m.
Colcroft Hall
Cold Spring Harbor, New York

Dan Brannigan hadn't had more than three glasses of wine at a single sitting in over thirty years. Once he'd been pretty well acquainted with booze. Now, his drug of choice was wealth. But the alcoholic stupor he'd deliberately put himself into last night was only one of the mistakes he would need to atone for today. Slowly, his brain came back into focus, as he tried to recall the last twenty hours. The meeting with Russo had ended badly. Very badly.

Gripped with denial and fear, he had lashed out. "This is bullshit, Russo. You think you're God? You think you can deliver this black magic, and we're just supposed to accept it and drop dead? Well, I have news for you. You're not God. You think that because there are three other fools who are all supposed to be tapping out next Christmas that I'm supposed to put my life on hold and get a headstone ordered? This is nuts, Tod. Completely off the charts."

Russo remained stoic as Brannigan vented. He had guessed Dan would react this way. Denial of one's own mortality was common, and Dan was no exception to that emotion. Russo was committed to taking anything Dan threw at him, knowing that he would eventually accept this reality. How Dan would go about his last days was anyone's guess, but Russo was fairly certain it would not be in a state of denial or anger. Dan was too good a man for that.

"And another thing. First, you have the balls to call me the day after Christmas while I'm with my family. Then you drag Kate into this. Why, Tod? Look at what you've done to her. You thought that as God almighty, it was necessary to make my wife cry? Who the fuck are you?"

"Dan, keep your voice down," Kate whispered.

"No. I'm not keeping my voice down. This is bullshit. All of it. Don't tell me you're buying any of this, Kate." With that, Dan stood up.

Kate rose also, realizing that Dan was going to bolt from the office. She wasn't going to let him get behind the wheel in this state.

"I should work with you on further testing? Fuck you. I won't have another second of my life involved with you or this operation I don't care how many Nobel laureates you have here. I'm done. You have my resignation and you will never see another penny of my money."

Kate glanced up, expressionless, at Russo. As Dan reached the door, his voice turned threatening. "I know how to get ink, Russo. I know the press is after this story. I'm going to talk to them. I'm going to tell them what bullshit this is."

And in an instant he was gone. If Dan had still been in the room, he would have seen Kate stop and turn back to Russo, who said, "Kate, I'm sorry for this. I really am."

"Thank you, Tod," she said. Then she turned and left.

Now Dan lay, staring at the ceiling. The only sound in the room was the ticking of the clock on the wall. The mansion's library could challenge the literary collections of many universities. The main level rose to a balcony that wrapped around the room, which contained a numbered collection covering just about every possible interest and at least nine languages. The room's contents, except for the carpets and furniture, had come with the house when they bought it.

Dan heard water running and caught the scent of coffee brewing. Kate was stirring. First, he needed to apologize to her. He had stormed out of Russo's office and insisted on driving, and he'd nearly crashed as he peeled on two wheels through the gates of their property.

"Dan stop it, you're scaring me. You're going to kill us both!" Kate had screamed.

In a second they were at the entrance and Dan kicked the car door open with enough force to crack the window. He slammed the keys onto the lawn and stormed into the house without a word to Kate. He kicked an umbrella stand in the entry foyer and then threw the library door shut, making a thunderous clap.

The library contained a fully stocked bar; Dan went straight to it. Before he was finished, he'd gone through nine Heinekens and a bottle of Cristal. There was also a highball glass with the remains of what looked like Scotch, but he couldn't be certain. God, what a shameful performance, he thought. He slowly rose from the couch and walked to the window.

The sky was overcast and the landscape covered in snow that had turned icy and was beginning to gray. He could see their cars in the circular driveway but not the housekeepers' car. That meant the help was not in the house, which was fine, since he had some major patching up to do with Kate.

His thoughts turned to the news he had tried to deny: I'm going to be gone this time next year. His heart rate began to accelerate. He felt it and realized it was what terror does. He began breathing deeply, trying to calm the pounding in his chest. Get your game face on. he thought. Settle down. But the fear was mounting.

The door to the library opened and Kate entered with a large, steaming mug of coffee. She was bundled in her frayed terry robe. Her flannel pajamas, a bit long, almost hid a sorry-looking pair of fuzzy slippers that had been ready for the trash long ago. Her hair was pulled back in a cute ponytail, and her face was expressionless until she glanced at the bar and saw the empties.

She was laughing as she approached Dan to give him his morning caffeine. "Are you serious? You don't know how to get drunk. Look at what you drank. No self-respecting bartender would even serve you. What's that?" she asked as she pointed to the glass that looked like it held whiskey

"I don't know," Dan whispered, his heart rate slowing.

Kate laughed again. "You never stop surprising me," she said. "At a time like this, you would choose to get drunk? I'd have never guessed it."

Dan watched her over the top of his coffee mug as she picked up the glass, sniffed it, and said "Eeew!" as she put the glass down.

"All right, Brannigan, you've had your tantrum; now let's talk about this." She plopped onto the couch next to him.

"Kate, I'm sorry. I made a complete jerk of myself."

"Given the news you got, who could blame you?" she cut him off. "How do you feel now that you've had a chance to digest it, along with some of the finest booze that money should never buy?" She was trying to lighten the mood and hoped Dan's sense of playfulness would kick in. She knew he didn't think well when gloomy, but if his attitude brightened, he would make good decisions.

Dan chuckled at her, and sipped some coffee. "Is this where I do the Jackie Gleason imitation and go 'Hammana, hammana, hammana, baby you're the greatest'?"

"The second part of that statement wouldn't be bad."

"I guess I have to face this, eh? What choice is there? You were there. I know you came to the same conclusion I did.. Russo's study is too precisely correct to be wrong. He's found the clock that regulates our lifetime, and my death date is coming. Not that everyone's date isn't coming, but I went into this experiment and now I get to live until next Christmas. Christ, what a mess."

"The coincidence with the other three is really curious. The odds of us all being here on Long Island and involved in this study is mysterious. I wonder if there could be something about us that connects a dot one from the other. Not that I want to share their fate believe me. But I know Russo well enough to know he is certain of his facts. So somehow it's going to turn out we share a mortal connection."

Kate leaned over and put her head on his shoulder. "I know. It sucks. I feel bad for you. You don't deserve this. And the kids. The kids are going to be devastated. Do you think there is any chance he could be wrong? What about a second opinion?"

Dan shook his head. "The Church has pretty much told you what the second opinion is. As far as the scientific community goes, they're applauding. No one else is doing any research like this. I wouldn't know who to ask who could offer anything other than a personal opinion. They wouldn't have any scientific findings to refute this. Cold Spring Harbor has got this thing cold, Kate." Dan leaned back. "You're right that it sucks. But I'm not sure I don't deserve it."

"Don't say that. You're a good man, Brannigan. What are you going to say to the girls?" Kate asked.

"I need to think. I'm not sure I'm ready to admit this to myself, much less anyone else. Least of all the girls," he shook his head.

Kate nodded," I know. That's how I feel, too."

Dan put his hand on top of hers, "What do you think about all this? Where is your head? You were probably up all night analyzing."

Kate glanced down. "I don't know yet. On the one hand, I believe what Russo told us yesterday is the truth. But I also think science doesn't always get it right at first. Sometimes they think they have it right and then they find something different. They're always telling us what's bad for us, and then you hear a year later that now it's OK."

She looked directly into Dan's eyes. "So I'm hopefully ambivalent, to tell you the truth. I think Russo means well and the lab should be respected. But I feel like this isn't the end of it. That maybe something is going to come along to show that the information isn't right. Or isn't right every time."

"Hmm," Dan grunted. "I hadn't thought of that. You've got a point. They don't always get it right." Dan began to move just slightly, from fatalistic to mildly optimistic. "So what should I do? Make plans for my funeral or just wait and see what happens? I'm not sure I like either game plan. Are we trying to talk ourselves out of the inevitable? Kind of whistling past the graveyard?"

Kate bolted upright and slid to the edge of the couch as she glared into Dan's eyes.

"Bad choice of words. No talk of graveyards. Not yet. Hopefully never," Kate said with a tinge of anger. "I won't be naïve. It's a threat. But anything can happen." Kate's throat began to tighten and her eyes started to fill, as did Dan's as he saw her emotions climb. "I can't think of our world without you. I can't think of our children and grandchildren not having you around. I can't think of our bed with just me in it. And I can't think of this world without your kindness and laughter. You're the best man I have ever known and if you have to leave us, I won't accept it until I can't look into your eyes anymore and see life, or I can't listen to your heart beating next to mine. Not a second sooner. Oh, Dan ..." Her emotions choked her; she was unable to speak.

Dan wrapped her in his arms, as her sobs drenched his shirt.

He had never imagined sadness like this.

Chapter Eighteen

January 4, 2013, 3:16 p.m.
The Boardwalk at New York Avenue
Long Beach, New York

The winter sky appeared cloudless all the way to Europe. Azure blue, with bright sun, and an occasional vapor trail streaking white from the giant airliners from Kennedy Airport, a few miles away. The air was crystal clear, the temperature at a single digit. The northeast had been locked in a record cold snap. There had been above average snowfall since before Christmas, and temperatures hadn't risen above twenty in weeks. Most of the snow had turned to ice.

Long Island's South Shore was blessed with some of the world's most extraordinary sandy beaches. The Atlantic shoreline, from Breezy Point in Queens east to Montauk, boasted more than a hundred miles of white sand that rivaled beaches anywhere. Most Long Islanders had easy access to this beautiful waterfront. In Long Beach, for instance, a two-and-a-quarter-mile stretch of public boardwalk bordered sand and sea.

Father Ted, like so many others, was drawn to the cool surf and the hot sands on a summer's day. But he had discovered the soul-restoring wonder of occupying a bench and watching the surf roll in any weather. He came here to jog, and found he wasn't the only runner on a prosthetic leg. Two people even exercised in wheelchairs.

Over the years, his best times on the boardwalk were when he needed to be alone with his thoughts. More often, his search was for a human connection. But today he needed the elixir of the salty ocean breeze and to be alone. As he sat in the unforgiving cold and ceaseless winds from the Atlantic and stared out at the beauty of the snow-covered beach against the clear sky and the roiling deep-green water, he tried to grab hold of the emotions swirling around his death watch.

He'd met with Russo the day after Christmas. At some point during the doctor's discourse, Ted's mind had disconnected. It was as if he had been elsewhere, not consciously grasping the discussion. He understood this was what psychiatrists would call a defense mechanism, a denial of reality. He'd been in this state before, when he'd learned what had happened after he'd lost consciousness in Kuwait. That news had taken away his true heart and cloaked his existence all these years.

"And so, Father," Russo had said, "do you have any questions?" Russo had been astonished by the lack of response from the priest. For the entire hour that Russo had gone through all the facts, Ted had asked only a couple of questions. Russo suspected he wasn't absorbing any of it.

"Not at this time, Doctor. Thank you for being so thorough."

"Father, if you don't mind me asking, are you OK? You seem to be taking this news awfully well." I know from your records that you were decorated for your actions in combat during Desert Storm. And being a priest, perhaps you have a bit more grace then most of us. But for a man faced with what I've just shared with you, your reaction, as far as I can see, is as tranquil as if you had just found your missing umbrella."

"Let me ask you something, Doctor," Ted replied in a level voice that betrayed no trace of anger. "What possible response should I have? Is there a correct way to receive this news?"

Russo felt foolish and embarrassed.

Ted continued, his hands clasped before him. "There is also the question of dealing with what my superiors will have to say when they find I'm involved in what's sure to become a very public debate between theology and science. I may well be in serious trouble. That was not expected, and I may add, is not welcome. I need to step back and think this through, Doctor."

Ted leaned forward in his chair and waved his hands in a dismissing gesture. "My Marine Corps experience in Kuwait gave me this artificial limb and a medal. Trust me, I was in the wrong place at the wrong time. It was friendly fire that took me down. So I am no hero, sir. Perhaps my vocation does have something to do with my calmness. But I doubt it." Ted's voice cracked as he glanced out of the window beyond Russo's chair. "Doctor, I have to cool down and get my bearings before I can really absorb this. You asked if I would agree to meet with the others. Fine. I'll sign anything you need right now. I just need to go somewhere and think. And call my sisters."

Russo placed two documents in front of him, which Ted signed without reading. He shook Russo's hand, walked out of the lab, and into a nightmare of anxiety, fear and introspection. He felt abandoned.

Now, Ted sat on the boardwalk, huddled against the winds. Glancing to his left, he saw someone on a bench farther down the boardwalk and a lone jogger who appeared to be a woman. He'd phoned his sisters and reached Colleen. Her call to him on Christmas night had been troubling him. She had remained evasive about her holiday message, saying only, "It just didn't feel like Christmas."

He had given up trying to find out what had been bothering her. He let her know why he was calling. Predictably, she fell apart. There was hysterics and panic. "None of this makes any sense, Ted. These doctors are always wrong on this stuff," she sobbed.

Rather than debate, he told her what she wanted to hear. "You're right. This will probably be nothing." He knew she was grasping at straws to convince herself that he would survive, but he also knew that Russo's discovery was reliable and factual. He would be gone by this day next year, but for now he wanted to soften the blow for his troubled, emotionally fragile sister. The conversation wandered until she promised to come to see him in a couple of weeks. He agreed that would be great and they ended it there.

Colleen, he knew, would be in denial all the way to the end. He'd seen that during the long, drawn-out illness, the cancer, that claimed both their parents. Colleen was one of those "If anything happens to Mom, God forbid" people, even after Mom had been diagnosed with stage 4 brain cancer.

Ted had also told Father Schmidt what was going on, as he was bound to do, and the discussion had been sympathetic.

He'd sent his sister, Patty, now back from vacation, a text: *Have news. Dont speak w collen b4 u speak w me. Call me luvu t*

She'd called him back quickly. "So, good Father." Patty, typically bawdy, enjoyed toying with her brother. "You finally met some filly up there who floats your boat, and you want to ask your wayward sister how to get around the chastity vow thing?"

He'd laughed in spite of himself. She always teased him about being a priest. She was proud of him and defended his vocation with zeal when others joked about the scandals concerning Catholic clergy. "First of all, I don't take a vow of chastity. I'm a diocesan priest, not a member of an order. And if I wanted to know how to get around it, I would probably ask someone who at least knew how to spell the word," he zinged her back.

She had laughed boisterously. "It starts with a 'c' right? Or is it a 'k'? I always get confused. How are you, big brother? What's the news that I can't call Colleen about?"

"First off, where have you been?" For ten minutes he'd listened as she regaled him with tales of her vacation, which had run through New Year's Day. She'd rented a beach condo with a friend and the two had come back tanned, poorer, but "satisfied," as she put it . He didn't ask for details, afraid she might have given them.

When he had told her his troubling news, she had gone stone silent. He could hear sniffling, accompanied by nose blowing. He imagined her curled up on the couch in the fetal position. He knew his sister was a lot deeper than she pretended to be and she would be absorbing the information. As soon as they hung up, she would be on her computer, looking up every fact she could uncover about genetic research, DNA, and especially the Cold Spring Harbor Laboratory.

She was a serial researcher with a sign in her office declaring "Nothing beats knowing." That was a creed to her. She'd disciplined herself to always be certain of all relevant facts.. Her first response - "Ted, what the fuck?" - was immediately followed by "Can I meet with Russo?"

He knew she was crushed. "OK," he had said, but the line was already dead.

Now, a couple of days later, she still hadn't called him. He was still struggling, pissed. Angry mostly at God. "Why me?" kept running through his mind. "Why do I need to get the beating all the time?" He felt he had tried all his life to do good. His understanding of the teachings of Christ pushed him to act toward mankind as He would have. That was his calling and he was comfortable in his decision. The self-denial and sacrifice was daunting at times, but his faith was deep. He truly was a believer, even though he often had trouble understanding God's purpose.

Desert Storm had changed him forever. As he recovered from his wounds and tried to piece his shattered life together, he had prayed, "Why God? Why do you not step in and stop this? Why do these young people have to die? Why this injustice among the innocents?"

He was shivering now and the sun was beginning to set. His mood was getting darker as well. Asking in his whispered prayer "God almighty," he felt his temper and voice beginning to rise, "you led me here. What for? I'm a priest. All I want is to serve you. I know if this gets out, I'll be an embarrassment to your Church. But you know I never understood that it could turn out like this. Why me? Why?"

He stood and took a step toward the ice-covered railing. His emotions were still turbulent. He needed to come to terms with his fate without resentment. He had to leave blame behind. That had robbed him of the peace in his heart and soul ever since the war. He knew it was a thief of energy and emotion. And he feared another dose of it darkening him further. "What is this for? What message are you sending? Help me, please God, help me. I'll gladly die in your name. But please don't let me die thinking my life was wasted. What did I ever do to deserve that?"

His cell phone buzzed. He put his hand to his mouth and bit down on his glove to take it off so he could answer. He wasn't startled by the message: *i'm here where r u? at rectory pats.*

He closed the phone and walked briskly from the boardwalk to where his car was parked. The south wind blew hard at his back as he went to see his sister. With Patty's love for him in evidence, he felt like a weight was starting to lift.

When he entered his room, his sister rose from the overstuffed leather chair where she'd been napping. She walked over to him, put her arms around his neck, her head to his chest and began to sob. "Why you, Teddy? You were always so good. You never did anything to anyone. What is God thinking?"

She looked as though she'd been up all night. Her strawberry blond bangs peeked out from under an Orioles baseball cap, a ponytail pulled out of the back. Without makeup, but tanned, she had black shadows under her eyes and her face looked drawn. She smelled faintly of wine and as Ted looked beyond her, he noticed the half empty glass next to a thick manila file on an end table. He assumed the file held the research she'd been doing since their call. "Ha! Those are the exact questions I've been asking myself. Actually been asking the Boss as well," he said as he pointed upward.

Patty pushed back and muttered, "Yeah, well what did he tell you?" She turned and went back to the chair, flopped down and folded her feet underneath herself.

"Not sure yet. He may have started throwing me some hints. But I'm not in the clear yet."

Patty had done her homework. She picked up the file while Ted poured himself a glass of wine. "Man, these are some serious scientists," she said. "Seven Nobels? Are you kidding me? I'd never even heard of this place until yesterday. I'll say this for you, brother, you don't fool around. Only the best."

Ted grinned. "So what have you found, Sherlock? Any happy news?" he asked as he settled onto the couch, hoping Patty could punch some holes in what Russo had told him.

She had done a masterful job in running down the background of the lab as well as the scientists on the team, Russo especially. They were impressive, she told him. "This Doctor Guitton and the other one, Doctor Mhatra, attended the Universite Pierre et Marie Curie at the Sorbonne, as well as the Centre National de la Recherge Scientifique. That's like the Holy Grail of scientific research in Europe. And that's before U Penn, Harvard, MIT between them. One married a guy who helped build the lunar space module that put Armstrong on the moon. I mean, these people are top shelf. Not the kind who make big, messy mistakes."

She had to agree that Cold Spring Harbor Laboratory stood among the foremost research centers in the world in genetics and its record was impeccable. As far as she could see, there wasn't any scandal to be found. She was looking for something she could be critical of. No luck.

She wondered aloud about four persons in a single batch of tests with the same mortality date then dismissed that as a probable mathematical anomaly, adding "But it does sound kind of creepy."

"So what's your bottom line, Pats?" Ted asked, although he already had a good idea what she was about to say.

"It's the real deal, Teddy. It sounds to me like these guys really did stumble onto our human clock. Who knows? Mine could run out before yours. So could anyone's. The shitty deal here is that you know about it. If you don't know when you're going, then it's a surprise, right?"

She took a deep breath, trying to keep her anger and fear under control. "This sucks. It really sucks. I talked to Colleen about it. She's Colleen. You know. Always a Pollyanna."

Ted sipped his wine. Patty looked better now than she had a few minutes before, the color returning to her face.

"Let's go to dinner," he said.

"Sure, but I need a shower first."

"You can use mine."

"Nah. I'm in the guest room down the hall. Schmidt hooked me up. He's cute." She walked quietly out of the room.

Chapter Nineteen

January 4, 2013, 9:10 p.m.
The Bay Towers, Apartment 1810
Bayside, New York

Russo heard his cell phone buzzing as he prepared to step from the elevator. He tried to maneuver around one of his larger neighbors and her shih tzu, who partially blocked his exit.. The woman failed to notice - or chose to ignore - that Russo was carrying several plastic bags of groceries in one hand, and enough dry cleaning in the other to constitute a year's worth of ready-to-wear.

As he squeezed himself around her and the dog, Russo was also trying to retrieve his cell phone from inside his parka coat, with a bag of groceries wrapped around his right wrist. The bag, over-packed with a two-liter bottle of Diet Coke and other groceries, ripped as the elevator door closed behind him.

He cursed and walked the forty yards to the end of the hallway, where his three bedroom apartment faced west toward Manhattan, offering a panoramic skyline view. But before the skyline was Citi Field and the Mets, the reason he had chosen this unit which exceeded his needs by two bedrooms and a bathroom.

The phone had gone silent. He didn't check to see who had called. He dropped the dry cleaning onto the sofa, where it promptly slid to the floor, and went back into the hallway to retrieve the spilled groceries, hoping that none of his neighbors had witnessed this slapstick episode.

Back inside the apartment, he shed the parka and opened the phone while he hung the dry cleaning in a closet. He scrolled to the call log and stared at a number he didn't recognize, as the phone again indicated an incoming call. It was the same number. He punched the green receive button at the first vibration and put the phone to his ear. This was his private number, so he simply said, "Hello?"

"Russo, have you ever known a bigger asshole than me?" The unmistakable voice of Dan Brannigan was on the other end.

Smiling softly he replied, "You're not an asshole, Dan."

"Peace pipes, Tod?"

"Peace pipes, Dan."

"Thank you. Although you shouldn't let me off so easy. I was really out of line." Dan sounded relieved by Tod's quick acceptance of his apology.

Tod walked across his living room to the glass doors. "Forget it, Dan. That was a hard blow. How's Kate doing?"

There was a pause before Dan replied and when he did, Russo suspected that Dan's throat may have tightened before he spoke. "We're both struggling some, Tod. Right now, we're trying to figure out how to tell the kids. Or even if we do tell them. They've all called here today, but for the moment, we've decided to say that our meeting was postponed until next week. We're trying to buy some time while we sort through this. Kate's a rock, but I'm not exactly at the top of my game at the moment."

"No," Tod murmured. "How could you be?"

"I tied one on last night and locked myself in the library. Woke up this morning with no recollection of how or when the night ended, but I was passed out on my couch with a pounding headache I still have. Listen, Tod, did the others agree to the continuing research?"

Russo turned away from the view. "Actually, yes, they did. That surprised me. We'll begin that process probably sometime next week."

"Well, include me in that, Tod," Dan said. "I didn't mean any of the things I said yesterday. I'll go along with whatever needs to be done to help. How did the others take it? I assume since you haven't been hospitalized, they were better at it than me."

Russo was putting groceries away now. "It was difficult for all of them, Dan. One poor girl is only twenty-seven and she was with her grandmother, who raised her. The grandmother is devastated, as you can imagine. Then there's a really nice woman who has a son in Afghanistan. She seemed to go into a cocoon when I told her. Finally she asked, 'so how does this affect me?'"

"Oh God!" Dan groaned.

"Yeah, exactly. The priest - he's the fourth - reacted the same way. Kind of distant while I was breaking it down, but when it was over, I knew he had connected the dots. He seemed more pissed off than anything else. But he has signed on to keep going with the research."

"A priest?" Dan seemed surprised. "That's interesting. Wonder what made him do this? You must be exhausted, Tod. It can't be easy being the grim reaper."

Russo grinned at his friend's intuition. "The hardest part is keeping my feelings to myself. I'm a researcher, not a neurosurgeon. Those guys train themselves to remain impersonal. But guys like me get emotional about petri dishes and math equations. People and their emotions are on the other side of what we usually do."

"How are you doing with the press? Are they still up your butt?" Dan asked.

"Yeah, pretty much. The PR guys are taking most of the flak, but the networks are all asking for time. CNN has contacted them for a special report on the findings. Some assistant director from the Department of Health in Washington is asking for a full report. Matt Lauer has been in touch. Katie Couric's representative has asked for an exclusive, wants to come out to the lab, and on and on. We haven't responded yet to any of them. I gave one radio interview to CBS here in New York because they swore they would keep it to four minutes and I could get the questions in advance. *Newsday*, of course, is on the phone all day long. Surprisingly, we haven't heard yet from the *Times*. We've had to shut the front gates and screen everyone entering the grounds. It makes the place appear to be a crime scene with a police cruiser out there. You saw what it looks like. Then there was a group of rabbis protesting, but they were harmless." Tod waved his free hand as if to dismiss the incident..

Earlier this afternoon Russo had spoken about the protesting rabbis with Weitzman, who had been raised in the same Hasidic community they were from. Zach told Tod he had been expecting this reaction, and that they would not be brushed off easily. Zach's only fear was for his parents.

"My people make no compromises," Zach had said. "There is never a negotiation on the Scriptures. None. No exceptions. If it gets out among the Hasidim that I have anything to do with this, then my parents would become outcasts."

"Will we be kept out of the press, Tod?" Dan asked, concerned. He also wanted to maintain his privacy. He had billions of reasons for it.

Russo assured him. "Yes. As much as possible. I have no way of knowing whether the others will reveal themselves to the press but if your identity gets out, it won't be from us. That confidentiality agreement is one of the documents you didn't sign yesterday. That binds both parties, but there is little we can actually do to control other people in the study."

Dan probed further. "Have you been hearing from other people - beyond the four - who were in the study?"

Tod answered as though he were speaking with one of his board members, which he was. "Not as many as we thought. My three colleagues have agreed to handle those cases as they come forward. In each instance, if these individuals request their personal test results, they will need to sign a waiver freeing the lab from all liability, as well as a confidentiality agreement to not reveal any persons from the lab staff. We may decide to conduct this part of it through our legal guys. I'm already exposed and I'm OK with that, but the others have lives to lead and this could possibly place them at risk."

"What kind of risk?" Dan asked.

"Someone doesn't like his DNA test, blames the messenger for it. Goes after the messenger. One of the team - you know him, Zach Weitzman - is a Hasidic Jew, and his parents would be ostracized from their community in Brooklyn if his identity is revealed. He doesn't care about himself, because he doesn't abide by the strict customs any longer, but his parents do."

Dan saw the dilemma. "Ouch. I hadn't thought of that. Although what you say makes perfect sense in light of the hissy fit I threw. I suppose people could lose it and decide to take it out on whomever they think is responsible. And I hadn't realized Zach's background. How do you protect our guys, then?"

"By trying to keep them out of the spotlight, which is all we can do. Like I said, they'll handle the requests from the test subjects, but they'll probably wind up doing it through our lawyers so that they remain anonymous."

Dan sounded satisfied. "Maybe you won't get many requests. If you hadn't told me, I wouldn't have asked in a hundred years."

"I agree." Tod answered.

"Yeah, morbid curiosity is fruitless. Anyway, if you need me to sign off on the papers, I will. Is there anything else I can do?" Dan was tired and wanted to wind up the discussion.

"No, just try and relax, Dan." Russo knew that sounded trite. "In a couple of weeks, we'll pull the four of you together. I'd appreciate you being available for that. We hope to find what you four may have in common, and perhaps vacate the predicted results. At worst, we find what you have in common and can do nothing about it. Or, as is often the case in this business, what happens may take us down another trail. Honestly, anything is possible. But finding the link could be essential to your well-being. So while there is time, we hunt for the answer. Otherwise, I think all is OK for the moment."

"OK. You've got it. You've been a gentleman as always, Tod. Thanks."

But Russo didn't want to let Dan off the phone until he was certain there were no lingering doubts. "Dan, do you have any questions for me about anything?"

"As a matter of fact I do, but you may not want to answer it."

Tod grew slightly apprehensive. "Try me."

"Where the hell did a nice Italian boy like you, from Queens no less, get a first name like Todman?"

Tod's apprehension evaporated. "Ha! That's easy. My mother was pregnant with me when she and my dad were sworn in as American citizens. The judge who presided over the ceremony was Eileen Todman. My father was so grateful, he vowed he was going to name his first child after that 'nice judge who welcomed me to America.' Of course, he couldn't call me Eileen, so my folks named me Todman. But they gave me an authentic Italian middle name."

Dan was chuckling now. "I'll be a son of a gun. That's a great story. What's your middle name?"

"'Lorenzo' he answered laughingly, 'but you can call me Larry." As he rang off, he heard Dan's raucous laughter. It was good to hear.

Russo felt divided. On the one side was the proud scientist who had uncovered a world-changing discovery. There had been talk of a Nobel for his work at the lab. He knew how proud he would be to win such a venerated and exalted award. But on the other side was straining at his emotional soul. Death is the inevitable outcome of birth and most medical professionals weave Teflon around themselves to avoid that aspect of their work. Russo had done that. He excelled at doing that. He had kept his heart and soul to himself all his life, living in an emotionally barren landscape. Fair enough, he had always thought. He was born to be a research scientist and just about all of his being was centered there.

Until now. Now he was inextricably intertwined with human subjects who had real lives. Now he was going to chaperone them to their graves. All their love, all their emotions, all their humanity would slowly fade away. He was going to be intimate with another person's soul. It was the very thing he'd avoided all his life.

How do I stay outside of this? he wondered.

Part II

Chapter Twenty

"Janet, wake up. You're having a nightmare. Janet? Janet?"

She opened her eyes; there was Rod. She was still on the sofa in their TV room, where she'd fallen asleep. Sweat beaded around her neck, but the pounding in her chest was settling down.

"Are you OK, Jan? I came in last night and you looked so comfortable, I left you alone."

She stared at Rod, in his saggy boxer shorts, now walking over to turn off the TV. The remote was missing. She felt a chill and clutched a pillow close, pulled her feet up underneath her and shivered. Sitting back from the edge of the couch, she closed her eyes when Rod asked if she needed anything. "No, I'll be fine," she whispered listlessly without opening her eyes.

"You sure? You were calling out and I could hear you from upstairs. It woke me up."

She opened her eyes and glared. "So sorry to wake you up." Rod didn't respond; he sensed that Janet wanted to provoke him. She had been trying to draw him into a confrontation ever since that night back in December when their world had changed forever.

Janet was held captive by demons. She couldn't accept that her life was slipping away, that her dreams would never be. But Rod was trying his best not to argue with her until she straightened out her emotions. It was tough enough for her that Michael was in Afghanistan. This news from the lab was beyond comprehension. It was for him, and he shivered whenever he thought about it.

They had yet to discuss it. Janet had clammed up on him and everyone else around her. Rod was having a hard time imagining life without Janet. He felt guilty that he was already mourning her, but he managed a show of apparent calm.

Janet had arrived home with Kathy that night, and the arguing had begun immediately. Rod said he didn't remember her ever telling him she was volunteering for the study. That annoyed her because she knew she had. She could see in his eyes that he had no idea what she was talking about and hadn't been listening when she mentioned the DNA tests.

She blew up and began to scream and cry at him. "This is so typical of you, Rod. Typical. Anything I've ever told you that you don't care about goes right by you, like one of those trains you play with all goddamn day long. I'm going to die, Rod. One year from now, I will be dead and gone. Do you think you can remember that? Do you think you can possibly not work overtime that day? Do you think you could give a shit for once in your life about anything that involves me? Once? Maybe?"

She had screamed the words at the top of her lungs and stomped out of the room. The rest of that day had been a nightmare. He remembered saying she was being unfair to him, that she always demeaned his job, saying he was like a kid with a model railroad. But that was what he did for a living. H e moved trains along their routes and maintained the central switching signals, providing safe passage every day to hundreds of thousands of commuters traveling between Manhattan and Montauk.

Looking back now, he realized that trying to debate his career after she'd received such traumatic news was a mistake. Janet had lost all reason and lashed out like a cornered snake. Her most dangerous bite was aimed at Michaela, who had arrived home from work just as the argument was building.

"This is just great, isn't it?" Rod recalled her saying, desperately. "Everybody gets what they want out of life but me."

And before anyone could comfort her, she lashed out, scarring the people she loved more than herself. "Thanks to you, father of the year, my son is in the Army on the other side of the fucking world, where he could be dead at this moment for all anyone knows. But at least he's earning money, right, Rod? That's what really counts. And Kathy, perfect Kathy. Your life, as always, turns out perfect. Your kids are at home where they belong. Your husband waits on you hand and foot, your job is great, Bill's pension pays the bills, and oh, by the way, your test probably shows that you have another forty fucking years left, which means weddings, grandchildren, retirement in Florida, maybe a cruise around the world and who know what else. But it's all heading toward a finish line way down the road just the way you expected it always would. Roses and violets for you, babe—as always."

Then, as if the attacks on her husband and her best friend weren't enough, she turned her venom on her daughter. Michaela was bewildered by the maelstrom she'd walked into, unaware she was about to be kicked in the teeth, too.

Rod had always doted on Michaela; Janet worked hard not to be jealous. Her own father, a drunk all his life, had rarely ever acknowledged Janet's presence. Her most fervent hope for her own family was that she would have a husband who would treat her like a queen. She needed to be Rod's beloved. Rod had been many things in their life together. Most of them were good, but romantic or attentive? That had never happened.

But unlike the distant relationship Janet had had with her father, from the day Michaela was born, she had been her dad's shining star. He obviously favored her.

Janet teased them both about "Daddy's little girl," but her joke was a disguise, a mask that she ripped off with her next words. "And Daddy's little girl. Now Daddy won't have any more distractions he can pay all his attention to you. Won't that be nice, Mick? All he's ever cared about was you and his goddamn trains. If you were in the mess I'm in, or you were sitting in Afghanistan like your brother, he'd be all over that."

As soon as the last syllable left her mouth, Janet recoiled, horrified at the hatred she had just spewed. She began crying hysterically, her nose running and stomach churning. She ran to their bedroom, slamming the door, and headed to the master bathroom, where she vomited violently. Her sobs were uncontrollable. She had nothing left inside.

Janet imagined herself as a carved gargoyle leering from the façade of a Gothic cathedral. A hideous limestone monster with no heart, set in stone forever, snarling, spitting venom at the world while masking its fear and self-loathing. At that moment, she wished that she didn't have to wait a year for her life to end. Better if she was gone right now.

Later, she had fallen into a troubled, restless half-sleep, still in her clothes and lying on top of the covers on their bed. She heard Rod quietly tiptoe into the bedroom. He reached out for her hand. Janet knew that her fears and need for denial would make any discussion treacherous and painful. She wasn't ready for intimacy or sharing. Wordlessly, she rose and left the bedroom. She quietly tiptoed past Michaela's room, where the door was cracked open. Janet could hear her first-born gently breathing in her sleep. The light on Michaela's desk was on, and she could see used tissues scattered around the room. "Some mother you got," she whispered. She crept down to the kitchen and peered out of the window, where she could see Kathy's house next door. There was a light on in the second-floor bathroom, and she wondered if her friend was still awake. Then the light went out and Janet apologized to the darkness. "I'm so sorry, Kathy."

In the living room, she picked up a framed picture of Michael in his middle school basketball uniform. She sat on the couch and stared out at the still, cold, moonless night.

While the world around her slept, Janet looked inside her soul for some comfort, some redemption for what she had said and done.

She found nothing.

As morning dawned, one day after she'd learned the fatal news, she awoke on the couch. Rod had left for work and Michaela for class. She was alone.

Chapter Twenty One

April 4, 2013, 8:40 a.m.
35 Sunnyfield Lane
Hicksville, New York

"Michaela, I'm going now," she called up to her daughter's room. "I'm supposed to be done by four, but just in case I'm late, could you please just turn the oven on at five? The chicken is already in the refrigerator. All you need to do is stick it in at three hundred and fifty degrees. See you later."

"OK," Michaela called back in a flat, listless tone. She was still reeling from the verbal assault Janet had delivered back in December. Aunt K and her father had tried to console her then, to make her understand that her mom was suffering, in shock.

Janet had apologized and left a card with a hand-written message written on her pillow the next day. *Hi, Mick, I didn't mean any of the things I said last night. I'm sorry if I upset you. You've always been a wonderful, cherished daughter to us both and I would never want you to think that I really think that your father is unfair in how he treats us all. He worships you, but not more than I do. I'm just in a bad place right now. I hope you can understand that and forgive me. Please. Love you. Mom.*

Michaela felt like she was trapped in quicksand. Her brother was on the other side of the world, her mom, on death watch, had grown distant and edgy. Her father was quiet.

Not that he didn't have an opinion on the lab's findings. "That's fine if you want to buy into these things, but I don't," he had told Janet and Mickey as they all sat down the next night for dinner and Janet's contrite apology. . "I don't think it's that simple. There has to be more to it."

Janet had brought it up, saying she wanted to "clear the air". "I owe you both an apology for the way I spoke last night. It isn't anyone's fault what's happening to me. It can't be helped. I'm upset, obviously, but all I really care about is getting Michael home safe. Then I'll worry about what they say is happening to me. Doesn't make sense, any of it."

As she finished, Michaela had begun to cry. "Mom, I spent the day reading up on all this stuff in the library and from what I can tell, the genes are supposed to hold all the secrets of our bodies, like who and what we are. But I didn't read a single thing about predicting death for someone. Why are they doing this to you?"

The conversation soon dissolved. Rod didn't add much. "Let's just see how things go," he said finally. "You never know, anything can change."

Michaela knew from the glare in her mother's eyes when Rod spoke that she was hurt and angry over his lack of thoughtfulness and visible emotion. Michaela, unlike her mother, realized that the thoughtfulness and feelings were there; he just hadn't found a way to express them.

This was nothing new. Getting an opinion on which ketchup to buy was a challenge. "What's the difference?" was his usual reply to nearly any choice he confronted. Even if he made a decision, it never felt quite final, and was always followed with a phrase like, "I suppose." Michaela sympathized with her mother. Janet had a right to expect more from him.

Meanwhile, Janet was also holding Kathy, her alter ego, at arm's length. Later, Janet came to realize that she was pushing her friend away rather than admit to herself that death would be what parted them.

While Janet was in denial, she also completely accepted this fearsome reality. If she had any thoughts about how she wanted to spend her last months, she wasn't sharing them And if she had any fears or doubts, no one heard them. She ordered Rod, Michaela and Kathy to keep her fate secret. She didn't want to risk Michael getting wind of it; he had to focus on staying safe and not be distracted by worry.

That meant Michael couldn't provide any emotional support to Michaela, who fell into isolation and loneliness, terrified at the thought of losing her mother. She couldn't share her feelings, except with her dad, who wasn't much help. "Don't be so worried, baby," he told her. "Everything will be OK."

Michaela didn't feel worried. She felt fear. For her mother's life; and for life without her mother. The phone on her desk lit up and started to peal its distinctive electronic shriek. Michaela glanced at the display and saw it was a Skype call. That meant Michael, and she instantly grabbed the receiver from its cradle and thumbed the green receive button. There was a rush of noise, like wind passing through the receiver. "Hey, dork face," she said, her dark mood lifting a little.

"Hey, fat ass," he answered back with a giggle.

The siblings' pet names for each other were laden with sarcasm to mask their deep affection. Except their affection was so strong it couldn't be masked.

"What are you doing home when you should be in school?" Michael asked.

"This is my early day. I was there at eight and just got home a little while ago. I work tonight at seven. What's up, dork?"

"Nothing. I just came off duty and thought I'd see how things are back in the 'ville," Maybe it was her brother's voice. Maybe it was his silly reference to their hometown, a sprawling mix of middle-income, working-class suburbia and strip malls, as the 'ville. Maybe it was simply that she couldn't bear the isolation she felt for one more second. Her emotions welled up; she emptied her heart and soul to her brother. She told him everything. She heard him sniffling. She knew he would be emotional. He asked all the same questions she and Rod had asked; he uttered the same kinds of denials. But, as they had, he knew deep inside that this was not an error and that these research findings wouldn't be announced without solid facts underlying them. Endgame facts.

He told Michaela that he had heard about the study on CNN. There had been a pretty fair amount of discussion and debate among his buddies about it, but he had never imagined that his own mother was at the epicenter of the research.

"I'm sorry, Michael," Mickey said, crying. "Swear you won't tell Mom. She's so bad right now. If she knew I told you, it might send her over the edge. Really, Mike. Swear to me that you won't tell her you know."

"Mick, what do you expect me to do with this? I'm supposed to rotate out of here in September, but I can't wait until then to see her now that I know."

"What? You're coming home? Why didn't you say so?" she said, her heart pounding.

"Well I was about to, sis, but this kind of got in the way." He thought for a moment, and started putting together a plan. "OK, here's the deal. I won't say anything to Mom about her news if you don't say anything about mine. In the meantime, I'll try to get home for a quick leave as soon as I can. My platoon leader will fix me up. We're pretty tight. As soon as I know when I can get a few days, I'll let you know, and come home and surprise Mom. Maybe when she sees me, she'll tell me herself."

"That's great. She'll flip when she finds out you're coming home. Maybe that's what she needs to bring her out of her funk . Oh, Mike, that is such great news. I can't wait."

"Well it's still a ways off, but, yeah, I am getting out of this shit-hole, finally. But this news about Mom is unbelievable, Mick. How's Dad?"

"He's putting up his usual front. But he's kind of whistling in the dark, Mike," Michaela replied.

"That's Dad. Fuck! I can't believe this, Mick! What are we going to do? I'm going to have to call you back. Can I reach you tonight at work? Give me a number there. I need to see how soon I can get home. I have some other news, too, but I'll wait till I get home and tell you all at the same time."

"What other news? Tell me now."

"No chance, sis. Give me the number for later."

"Come on, Mike." She recited her work number, but continued to wheedle him. "No fair."

"Yup. No more from me. Later, fat ass." And the phone went silent.

"Bye, dork face" she whispered. A tear slowly rolled down her cheek as she held the phone to her lips and kissed it.

Chapter Twenty Two

April 4, 2013, 9:28 a.m.
St. David's Roman Catholic Church Rectory
Oceanside, New York

The letter had sat unopened on Father Ted's dresser for two days since he had picked it up from the hallway table. He had hoped this business with the lab and his role in the research wouldn't get out. He especially did not want the Church's hierarchy involved. The Vatican and just about every other religion in the world had attacked the findings, and the world press had an insatiable lust for details. So far, the lab had stood by its word and kept the four test subjects with identical death dates anonymous and out of the press. The foursome had all given the lab permission to try to connect the dots among them.

They were now getting twice-monthly physicals, and he'd met the others on those occasions. Like him, they were frightened and suspicious. The exception was the rich guy, who was also on the lab's board. He acted as if he were running for office; he had fallen over himself being nice to the rest of them.

Ted looked at the letter. The envelope wasn't the gray recycled stock the diocese customarily used. It was heavy, brilliantly white linen paper, and the lettering in the upper left hand corner almost looked like it was engraved. The return address was the office of the bishop of the Diocese of Rockville Centre.

Bad news, all his instincts said, even though Father Schmidt had told him that he'd gotten almost no reaction to the news from the chancery administrator at the diocesan office, .

The letter was propped against a framed photograph, half-covering the image of a young Ted Hayslip in vestments, holding the Eucharist above the hood of a jeep. He was saying Mass in a field in Kuwait surrounded by young Marines in camouflage and flak jackets. They kneeled or stood, heads bowed. *Mass before Patrol, February 25, 1991.* The snapshot had run in *Time*, part of its coverage of Desert Storm. He was twenty-six then, a year out of the seminary. It was the last day he ever spent on his own two feet. He had woken up in a military hospital in Germany and found out that his left leg below the knee had been blasted off in that field in Kuwait.

The photo was a reminder of a much darker wound. Lance Corporal Jason Bonnie was in the image, too, standing to Ted's left, wearing Marine field dress and flak jacket. He looked like the rest of the troops: solemn, hopeful, anxious, fearful. Dreading the unknown.

Bonnie had asked for a word with the chaplain after Mass that day. Being available to discuss personal problems was part of the sacred covenant between military servicemen and their chaplains. The troops knew Ted as a ready and trusted listener. Often he was aware of issues that could affect a combat Marine's ability to do his job. And, if he thought it wise, Ted discreetly and promptly reported these problems to the superior officers who ran the Marine's outfit.

His advice and counsel were rarely challenged because his assessments were usually accurate. Both officers and troops knew he wasn't a pushover for a good story intended to secure light duty or extra leave. But if your problems were real, Father Ted Hayslip was a good man in whom to confide. So when Lance Corporal Jason Bonnie asked for some time, Ted agreed to chat, though his next Mass was scheduled some distance away and he was running late.

Bonnie was around twenty, blue-eyed and fair. He was trying to grow a mustache, but so far it was only a few light blond tufts. All pretty ordinary, Ted thought, but the kid's story was something else.

Turned out he'd decided he could not fire his rifle at another human being. "I'm not fit to be here, Father," he told Ted

"You aren't the first person I've heard that from. Why not, Jason?" Ted dropped the formality of military titles and read the Marine's name tag so he could address him by his first name.

"Father, I have been in at least four situations since I've been here and I can't do this. I can't fire my rifle at another person."

"Have you told anyone else about this?"

"No, Father. I think my squad leader has his eye on me, though. He said I have the slowest reaction time in the world. Says I either think I'm Superman or Chicken Little."

"Why did he say that, Jason? Did you freeze up?"

"Sort of, Father. We were on patrol and came under fire from some insurgents staked out in a couple of houses. They'd dropped a few mortars at the column ahead and took out the lead Humvee, which blocked the road. Once we stalled, they opened up some pretty heavy fire. Sergeant Lee, that's my squad leader, he ordered us out of our Hummers. I followed him into a drainage ditch. We were supposed to return fire. The goat eaters were in some houses maybe two hundred yards from us."

"Goat eaters" was among the gentler names the Marines called their enemies. Ted had no problem with the term, but the kid's issue didn't sound as if it could be dealt with quickly. He needed to let Bonnie know they'd have to connect another time.

Bonnie went on with his story. "I took a position alongside my buddy, Macklin and everyone just started pounding these two houses. They weren't much more than mud huts. I took aim and just kind of froze, Father. With all the noise and firing that was going on, I just kind of stood down and took my weapon off automatic and fired single rounds. Macklin went through three magazines before I was halfway through one."

The young Marine took a breath before continuing. "All of a sudden, Sergeant Lee is kneeling next to me, screaming, 'What the fuck are you doing, Bonnie, trying out for the rifle team? This ain't no goddamn shooting contest. I want to see some smoke coming out of your ass. Get that weapon on auto and send these fucking fleas to the vestal virgins.'"

Bonnie blushed. "Sorry for the language, Father. But that's what he said. And I did what he told me to do, but truth is, I was firing above the houses. I knew I just couldn't fire straight at the targets. I had this vision of some Kuwaiti family being held hostage in there by some goat eaters and us finding out after we'd shot the place up that we'd killed them. Sure enough, the return fire from the house finally stopped and when we broke in, we found six gunmen and two families nearly wiped out. There were a couple of kids and a woman left, but eight civilians were greased. I couldn't even go in and look at them."

"I remember hearing about that," Ted said, shaking his head. "Nasty stuff. As I recall, we lost four Marines that day as well."

"Yeah. When it was over, Macklin pulled me aside and asked why I was holding fire until Lee jumped me. I told him I didn't see the sense of just dumping fire into targets I couldn't see. He just kind of looked at me like he knew I was covering my butt and said that if I was gonna be on his flank, he'd prefer I not make it target practice. I think he was pissed, but he let it go. We've been buds a while, so I got a pass for now."

There was pleading in Bonnie's voice now. "What am I gonna do, Father? I can't tell him or anyone in the platoon that I can't do this. And I'm afraid if we get into the shit again sometime, I'm gonna let my buddies down."

"Jason, sometimes when we actually get out here," Ted waved his arms to indicate the desert battlefields that surrounded them, a vast, endless and pitiless stretch of colorless sand, "we find the reality of war too much for us. I understand that. But you can't hide your fear of taking the lives of the enemy from the Marines in your platoon. You can't let them down. I'm sure you understand that."

Bonnie shook his head. "I just can't fire my weapon at another living thing." His voice dropped several octaves and he gritted his teeth.

"Why did you enlist, then? Surely in your training you knew you were committing to being a rifleman and that you'd be in combat at some point. What did you think was going to happen?" Ted realized he sounded a bit annoyed, but he couldn't seem to help it.

"I know I made a mistake, Father. But a lot of us from my town were going into the Marines and I thought it could be cool. I know that sounds stupid, but I never thought it could be this bad, Father."

"OK. I need to speak with you again, Jason. Can we do that? I have to get to B'har Al'bein for another service for Alpha Company and I should be back mid-afternoon. Will you be around?"

"I'm not sure, we have patrol mounting out at eleven hundred, but we should be back before chow call if we don't run into any shit. One thing though, I don't want to let the others see us meeting."

For Ted, this was a familiar request. "Yeah, I know that." They arranged to meet at the camp PX. Bonnie said he would hang around there and they could pretend to bump into each other and continue the conversation.

Ted offered Bonnie a few consoling words to boost the young man's confidence. Then he said, "I think you did the right thing coming to me and I promise you I'll do whatever I can to help, OK?"

Bonnie nodded.

"I'll see you later, Jason. *Semper Fi.*" He clapped the youth on the shoulder as he uttered the Marine motto, *Always Faithful.* It was a covenant of trust which meant all Marines were brothers, on guard for each other's well-being. *Semper Fi* was intended to let the boy know that a promise was being made to support him. But for the novice priest it was a promise he would regret the rest of his life, because it was a vow he never kept.

Now, in his room, Ted picked up the letter. There are, he reminded himself, worse things in this life than anything that could arrive by mail. He opened the envelope and began reading to the last chilling paragraph: *If you are deemed to be in violation of your religious Agreement of Subordination, you could be subject to possible prohibition of the exercise of your ministry and a loss of ecclesiastical rights.*

The letter was signed by Monsignor Gregory Petraglia, General Counsel, Diocese of Rockville Centre. It was copied to the Bishop of the Diocese, Terence Thomas Molloy and the Reverend Raymond Schmidt, Pastor of St. David's Parish. So Father Schmidt knew about this letter, too, Ted realized.

Sitting on his bed, he felt the same feeling of dread as he had back in the hospital in Germany. Part of him might be amputated. Only this time he wouldn't lose a limb. It was his vocation that might be cut away.

Ted had spent six weeks at the seminary when he returned from Germany. He'd been offered a position in the Diocese of Rockville Centre on Long Island, where he'd been ordained. His orientation had included a course on how to serve the parish; mostly situational instruction in family management and interpersonal skills training, as well as public speaking and developing what the Church called community and communication assets. In the end, he was assigned to one of the diocese's hundred and forty parishes.

St. David's was his eighth parish. Not a record he felt happy about. Part of the orientation had involved signing documents pledging fidelity to the Church and agreeing to accept Church policy and administration. It all seemed like nothing more than formalities. Obviously, he had already pledged his fidelity to the Church and its canonical leadership when he took his vows as a priest.

One of the documents was referred to as the "Berrigan sanction" after two priests, brothers, who had been active in the anti-Vietnam War movement. Actually called the Agreement of Subordination, the Berrigan sanction was not insignificant.

Any priest subject to the rules of the Diocese of Rockville Centre would "*commit to no public events or public disputes, politically affiliated organizations or associations, including any medical affiliations that support or in any way lend meaning to policies or practices outside of the accepted and known teachings of the Church, any research projects or public denouncements against the teachings of the Church.*"

The list of forbidden activities went on for half a page.

Monsignor Petraglia had been good enough to attach Father Hayslip's signed agreement just in case he had misplaced it. The document stipulated that should any priest feel he needed to attend or in any way become attached to functions that were listed, he could do so only with a superior's prior written permission. Failure to obtain such permission would subject the priest to a disciplinary process and an appearance before a diocese review board. *"If you are deemed to be in violation of your religious Agreement of Subordination,"* the letter read, *"you could be subject to prohibition of the exercise of your ministry and a loss of ecclesiastical rights."*

All he'd done was answer an ad in the Sunday *Science Times* that sought tissue samples to be tested for gene composition. The volunteers would be paid a thousand dollars and guaranteed complete anonymity regarding their test results. Ted took up the offer because he was saving to buy a new car. It occurred to him now that he was paying a pretty heavy tax on this money. Not only was he going to lose his life, he might also lose his calling.

As he sat and contemplated the letter, the cell phone rang in his pocket. The caller ID began with 917, a New York City code, but he didn't recognize the number. He punched the ignore button and let the call go to voice mail.

So he did not speak with Dr. Zach Weitzman, and it was much later that day when he listened to his message

"Hi Father, this is Doctor Weitzman at Cold Spring Harbor Laboratory. We met two weeks ago, when you had the CAT scan series during your scheduled check-up. Father, I'd like to get you back in the lab as soon as possible. There's an abnormality in your scan and I want to run the series again, as well as get some blood. It's very early in the diagnosis and I don't wish to alarm you, but I must convey how important it is that you come back in as soon as possible. I'm leaving my private number. Please call me immediately."

Then, after a few seconds of silence, Weitzman said. *"I'm sorry, Father."*

Chapter Twenty Three

April 4, 2013, 9:45 a.m.
Colcroft House
Cold Spring Harbor, New York

Dan stood in the pantry that adjoined the kitchen, watching Kate sitting at the breakfast island at the center of their over-sized kitchen. When the mansion had been an embassy, this area had been expanded into an entire wing built onto the back of the house. Now it could stand in as a hotel kitchen, with duplicate appliances and every culinary device imaginable. Beyond the solarium, a sprawling glass dining area, was a spacious concrete and slate veranda skirting the entire rear of the house, all of which was a level above the swimming pool and cabana.

Kate, seated below a fully stocked pot rack stretching the length of the center island, was absentmindedly thumbing through some catalogues as she dug into a grapefruit.

Earlier, he'd heard her get quietly out of bed and slip into the shower. Dan pretended to sleep. He knew she was on her way out to Mass at St. Pat's, her daily regimen during Lent. Easter was a week away. Although Dan was a practicing Catholic, he wasn't diligent enough to make that daily sacrifice. And if asked what he was sacrificing for Lent, his response for years had always been, "I gave up meatloaf." Which he had - at eleven years old.

They hadn't been communicating much lately and Dan wasn't in the mood for talking this morning. He had slipped quietly out of bed again last night and wandered through the corridors of the second floor, stopping at each of his three daughters' bedrooms. He poked about at some of the mementos they'd left behind, warmed by pictures of them in younger days. He found himself reaching back to his memories and the photo album in his mind, the life they had lived together. The truth was, he couldn't get enough of that now. It was more restful and restorative than sleep.

In Diane's room, he had sat in an armchair and wondered where the years had gone. His little girls were women now. Mothers and wives, with important careers; stable, beautiful, smart, strong. Wondrous.

Everything he had ever hoped for them had come to pass. They had had their rough spots growing up, like most kids, but they had all turned into the great people he and Kate had dreamed they'd be. Reflecting on a photo from Diane's high school days, he mused at how life is lived full speed ahead. Only when things are complete do we look back and assess the risk we took when we plunged in, breathlessly unaware of what the job might demand. Who knows how to be a parent except those who have already done it? There's no qualifying test before they hand you a helpless, dependent child.

Kate had handled all the planning and strategies that went into their parenting. Instinctively, she raised the girls with total confidence and understanding. He saw, almost from their first day as parents, that Kate was completely, intuitively competent. Since she was so assured, he was relieved, knowing she would be the boss in all matters related to the children. To the girls, it appeared that they were a united team because they had agreed to never disagree in front of their daughters.

After yet another fitful, sleep-deprived night, he pondered his mortality. He'd fought against the truth for just a short time. As a pragmatic man, he had finally accepted that, like everyone else, he had no reason to expect life everlasting. His time was just coming sooner, rather than later, and, unlike most people, he knew when that was coming.

Maybe the knowledge that death was imminent would present an opportunity. He could confess his various sins and leave with a clear conscience. Or maybe that was the salesman in him, trying to sell the reality of his fate to himself.

He knew he'd had more than his share of good fortune and life's pleasures. He also knew he'd been exceptionally lucky. He was rich and respected; his children successful, healthy, stable; his grandchildren adorable and smart. And his marriage? It was in the best shape it had ever been. He and Kate were still deeply in love, still passionate about one another.

Two problems weighed on him. He was devastated that he would have to soon leave Kate, the girls, the grandkids. "How?" he murmured to himself, "can I just not be here anymore?" It seemed impossible; the concept made his heart weep.

But a darker problem was at the root of the sleepless nights. It was guilt. There was a hidden side to Dan. There were black spots on his soul, indelible, that rose up to haunt him as he pondered his date with the grave. Dan knew that the opportunity to redeem his life and cleanse his spirit was ticking away. He headed to the kitchen. He headed to Kate.

"Hey," he said as he stood before the fresh pot of coffee. Kate had left a large mug standing next to a sugar bowl and creamer. A spoon and napkin lay atop the empty mug.

"Hey, no kiss for me? What am I, on the pay-no-mind list?" Kate pouted playfully.

"No, of course not. I'm just on the sleepy list; kind of a zombie this morning," he mumbled, as he bypassed the coffee and planted a kiss on Kate's lips.

Kate didn't need to ask why he was sleepy. She'd felt him get up last night and knew he hadn't come back to bed until sunrise. She understood that some things in life were so personal that you had to go through them alone. He was in that place now and she prayed he'd find peace.

She held his kiss for a moment and then purred as she released him. "Mmmm. A girl can't do better than that, Brannigan," she said as she stood up.

"Indeed. So what's up for you today?" he said as he poured his coffee.

"Well, I'm going to the eight thirty and then Debbie is bringing Tommy over later this morning while she runs some errands. They're looking for a swing set and she's going over to someplace in Glen Cove that she saw an ad for in the paper."

"So why not take Tommy?"

"Because he's wild about swing sets and she went to another place with him and he cried when they left. You know Tommy. He's full speed ahead all the time and it's easier for her if he stays here."

"Does she want one like ours? I can just call the guy we used."

"No. It's too big and besides, she and Dave are working with a budget in mind and this place is supposed to be the cheapest around."

Dan realized this was yet another discussion about their girls where Kate had better information and instincts than he did, but he plunged ahead anyway. "We can give them one any size they like," he said, stubbornly trying to turn the issue his way.

"Debbie and Dave don't like to do that, Dan. You know that. They want to do things on their own."

"Yeah, but he's our grandson, too. Why can't they just let us help once in a while?"

"You mean like when you sent a new Jaguar to their house after Debbie cracked up her Jeep?"

"It was almost her birthday. Besides, it's the same car as yours, and she loves your car. They didn't need to make such a fuss."

"Dan, a Jaguar station wagon worth a hundred thousand dollars isn't what most young housewives get as birthday presents. We never give the kids gifts that large. Besides, Dave is embarrassed that he can't provide those things for Debbie and they're uncomfortable with it. Why do they have to take our money? Let them alone, Dan. It's their lives."

This door was closing on his foot. He knew he should just drop it, so he changed the subject. "Well, that's about to change isn't it?

They're about to come into their own money whether Dave likes it or not. I'm not about to leave without the joy of seeing our girls receive their fortunes. We agreed on that, Kate, and the paperwork is just about done. The paperwork will be here for signature very shortly."

Dan and Kate had decided not to tell the girls that their father was going to die soon. There was nothing that could be gained by it, so they planned for Dan's last year to be full of the usual family closeness and homey warmth, and none of the negative emotions that knowledge of the truth would arouse. They reasoned that the girls would have time enough to mourn if the lab's predictions came true. Knowing it a year ahead of time wouldn't change anything. Dan and Kate were having enough difficulty accepting it. What possible benefit would come from the girls knowing?

Kate had remained insistent. "Not until I can't feel your heart beating next to mine will I accept it," she had said more than once.

"That's different," Kate said, as she picked up her bag and car keys.

"OK. Just as long as you're not changing your mind," he said as he sipped from his steaming coffee mug.

"I'm not changing my mind. I want the girls to have their inheritance while we're both still able to see it work for them. But they still need to feel that buying their child a swing set is their own responsibility. OK?"

"OK, OK. I get it," Dan surrendered, holding his hands up in capitulation.

"What's up for you today?" she asked as she got ready to leave the kitchen.

"Nothing really. Just another day. I'll be around here mostly. May go over to the office for a bit. Is Debbie staying for dinner?"

"No. She has to bring Tommy to the dentist, so she can't stay. I'll be back right after Mass. If you're still here when Debbie gets here, don't try and talk her into a jungle gym big enough to cover Vermont. Promise?" Kate knew Dan well enough to suspect he would still try to butt into their daughter's business.

"Promise. See you." Dan chuckled knowing Kate had anticipated that he would take a shot at convincing Debbie to let him help with the swing set. He heard one of the garage doors rumble open as he turned to the solarium and looked about for his morning paper. It was as much a ritual as his first cup of coffee. "Ah," he said aloud to himself when he couldn't find it. "Who cares about the paper?"

He reversed his steps and decided to shower and get dressed before Debbie and Tommy arrived. He was having trouble sitting still. His anxiety and restlessness was mounting. He knew he had to clear his conscience soon.

He entered the bedroom and walked to the windows looking out over the harbor. His stomach was churning. He was gripped by fear. It wasn't the dying. He was afraid of confessing. He knew he had to come clean with Kate. He hadn't kept faith with her in more ways than one and he no longer could bear his guilt. More than anything, he needed Kate's love. In their marriage, he'd found a life of grace. But that couldn't change him or what he'd done. He couldn't live with the truth, but was afraid to die with the lie.

He stared out at the budding spring morning, sun shining on the sparkling water, and he thought about Kate's brother, Joe Kelly. After graduating from Villanova, Dan worked on a Wall Street trading desk. Two years later, Joe had graduated from Northwestern, *summa cum laude* in finance, and Dan had recruited him as his trading partner.

From the start, Dan had shown exceptional ability and quickly rose to become one of his firm's top traders. He was a natural, everyone had agreed. He not only seemed to be able to ferret out the best unseen values, but he also had a knack with potential customers and was winning new accounts at a record rate. It hadn't taken long before Dan's reputation was carrying him toward the possibilities of his dreams. The wealth that was available to Dan appeared bottomless. He had selected a career that worked towards his strength and intuition.

But the luxury of high reward, brought with it the great loss of time in his other career, that of husband. To buy himself time, and to offload the work of research and detail, required to maintain his stunning success in picking growth stocks, he turned to Joe Kelly.

Joe and his wife, Loretta, had both been at Dan and Kate's wedding party. Dan knew that his brother-in-law looked up to him and convincing him to join his team at Morgan Stanley was relatively easy. Joe had jumped at the chance.

Joe was a wizard with computers as well as business processes but was introverted, the polar opposite of Dan. While Dan came on mighty, Joe remained almost meek.

In the years that followed, Dan and Kate had their family of three girls while Joe and Loretta struggled to get pregnant. Meanwhile the business the Brannigan team brought in set records at Morgan Stanley, making them among the highest compensated traders on the street.

Joe was the desk man and handled the financial details and research. He was never wrong in his assessments of companies he viewed for investment. His acumen was always perfect. Dan would say it was organic. His part in their ability to create wealth was enormous.

With every new financial plateau Dan surmounted, his ego grew. Along with his increasing appetite for greater gold, he developed an almost mystical belief in his entitlement to the rewards and pleasures of the world. Self absorption led to self delusion and paved the way to degrade his moral compass.

In the mid '90s, AT&T split its corporate operations into multiple business units. One of those units was Networking and Communications Operations, which provided the backbone support and switching equipment to large networked computing enterprises. The personal computer had moved to a dominant role on the office desktop and the need to connect millions of global workers into cohesive operating networks across vast global enterprises and commercial operations was about to usher in the Information Age.

To accommodate the market, AT&T decided to split their equipment manufacturing operations into a separated company from the core business, then take that company public. The man behind this strategy was a rising star in the AT&T executive suite by the name of John Barnes. John saw the opportunity of a lifetime as the newly formed company, Lucent Technologies, would come out of AT&T with a twenty billion revenue base in place. The IPO was going to be a blockbuster. John Barnes was named by AT&T as the CEO of Lucent.

John Barnes and Dan Brannigan had been fraternity brothers and roommates together at Villanova and remained connected. Over a dinner of steaks in January of 1996, John told Dan of his impending assignment to lead Lucent. Soon after, Dan Brannigan submitted his resignation to Morgan Stanley, leaving behind his team, including his brother-in-law. On September 30, 1996 Lucent was spun off from AT&T. The next day, a press release in the *Wall Street Journal* announced that Dan was forming his own investment firm and soon thereafter, it had acquired the exclusive trading rights to the newly formed Lucent Technologies.

John knew the Lucent IPO was going to create a market capitalization that would become a nearly endless fountain of cash for Lucent investment and expansion. He also knew that the telecommunications business was going to change the way all commercial enterprise was executed, and that the trail of development would be far longer than the 'experts' were predicting,. The benchmarks for his new company were going to be far greater than what was reasonably possible. The revenue returns would never match the predictions the market was following.

Dan knew it as well. Because back at that dinner in January that changed so much,, John had said, "So, as you can see, I'm taking the wheel of a ship that's going to be overloaded with investment cash in the next few years. But I'm going to get thrown overboard by the passengers for not serving up their favorite meals at dinner."

Dan knew his old friend well. He knew that John would never put his head into a hangman's noose. He used to call him 'the edge man' back in college knowing that he always maintained an edge in any endeavor he took to himself. Dan instinctively knew there was more to come in the tale he was hearing.

"So?" Dan asked, "how do you take the short reward, when long reality can be sudden death once it gets revealed? You need to be safely off of that course before the scorecard gets totaled. I assume you're still the edge man and you have another plan?"

John was ready with a response and true to Dan's instinct, he held an edge in the game he was playing. One that needed Dan.

John Barnes planned on giving the investment community exactly what they wanted from Lucent. He would spend their dollars in as many ways as possible, to merge, acquire and expand Lucent exponentially in the next two to three years. The stock would become fashionable to own and few, if any, would see that a house of cards was building. The future was much farther away than investors expectations and in the meantime there would be a fortune to be made in trading the stock. This fortune was delivered in two ways; one in owning the stock and the other in trading and handling it.

"But what happens when the music stops, John?' Dan asked. "Eventually there won't be revenues to support the investment and you'll need to make good on the promise of invested dollars."

The next thing John Barnes said changed Dan forever.

"By that time, you as the exclusive trading licensee, and myself as the ultimate silent partner, will have banked several hundred million dollars around the world in transaction fees from the sale of the stock. I need to spend the capital to keep the stock climbing. Who cares on what? The fashionable expectation is that we need to expand. So I'll give them what they want.

When the music starts to fade I'll know it and we'll ease our way out before the drop. It's like being in the casino business, Danny. I run the gaming, you handle the counting room and the skimming. Only the suckers at the tables get poor. Fuck 'em."

The plan was executed flawlessly between 1996 and 1999 as Barnes drove Lucent to the top of the market and then back down to the bottom. The story became textbook fodder on how to bankrupt an enterprise.

Lucent became a market darling in the late 1990s as the eight dollar a share spinoff price climbed to eighty-four dollars. In 1997,

Lucent began an overly aggressive acquisition strategy intended to keep pushing the stock upwards. By 1999 its acquisition spending totaled twenty four billion dollars.

By the end of that year the stock had increased its original value by 1,100 percent. It had become the most widely held stock in the United States, claiming 4.6 million shareholders. Each of those shareholder's transactions ran through Dan Brannigan's exclusive rights to the sale and distribution of Lucent stock.

During those three years, Dan Brannigan earned one hundred and sixty seven million dollars in commissions, which he diversified outside of technology stocks, building himself an impenetrable firewall of personal financial security.

At the same time, through a sophisticated process of money laundering and computer accounting maneuvers, John Barnes, pocketed approximately half of that amount in cash, paid outside of the United States and deposited in numbered bank accounts and investments in shell corporations on five continents rendering it twice the taxable value.

By the end of 1999, Brannigan's exclusive trading agreement expired and was not renewed and Dan began quietly selling off his considerable stake in Lucent. Later, to Securities and Exchange Commission investigators, he characterized that move as "portfolio correction and asset balancing."

In January 2000, the death knoll rang on Lucent as the company made the first of a long line of announcements that it had missed its quarterly estimates. The company's first quarter results for the year fell short of analysts' expectations and its stock lost twenty-eight percent of its value in a single day, reducing the company's market capitalization by approximately sixty five billion dollars. The crash had begun.

Later that year, Lucent revealed that it had used dubious accounting and sales practices to generate some of its earlier quarterly numbers. By October 2002, the stock bottomed at fifty five cents per share. The company now had less than thirty-one thousand employees, reduced from a hundred and sixty-five thousand at its peak.

John Barnes, ousted as CEO, had been thoroughly investigated by the SEC, the Treasury Department and the attorneys general of at least four states. He never faced criminal charges. Dan Brannigan established a Wall Street reputation of legendary proportions, for his cunning and sense of timing.

And somehow, in all of the investigations into the rise and fall of Lucent, the dots between Brannigan and Barnes were never connected.

Dan always knew he had risked jail to partner with John. What he had not thought about was the corruption of his morals, his betrayal of his brother-in-law and worse, what his self absorbed years without conscience would mean at the end game.

Everything comes back to Kate, he thought. Except one thing. His emotions began to swell and a dark cloud entered his brain drawing him toward what felt like the gates of Hell. His sins of betrayal went beyond leaving Joe Kelly behind as he entered the criminal alliance with Barnes. At least that was only about stealing money.

His affair with Loretta, Joe's wife, was different. Nothing he could tell himself about it would justify that stain on his soul. Ever.

"Pa-Pa!" The voice of his two year old grandson snatched him from the abyss he was facing. He heard Debbie calling too.

He could put his mask back on. It was time again to be Grampa and Daddy.

How much longer could he hide behind it?

Chapter Twenty Four

April 4, 2013 4:10 pm
Colcroft Hall
Cold Spring Harbor, New York

Kate's trust in Dan had collapsed. He had finally cleared his con-science and confessed everything about his business dealings. She was more saddened then angry as he explained how he had set up her brother Joe to dissolve their partnership. He described the truth of the unholy alliance with his former frat brother, which had sent a company from obscurity to global dominance and—deliber-ately and maliciously—into ruin to manipulate their wealth, hurting millions of shareholders and thousands of company employees. It left her heartsick.

But she sank beyond Dan's reach when he finished talking about his business dealings and confessed that he had been attracted to Joe's wife, Loretta, and the two had had an affair. Kate sat at the end of the bed, listening in disbelief as he clumsily tried to explain how it was that he could turn away from her and find himself in her sister-in-law's bed.

Kate asked only one question. "What did you need from her that I wasn't willing to give you?"

Dan answered Kate as honestly as he could. "It wasn't planned," he told her, as if that somehow mattered. "It just happened. And the only answer I have is that she fed my ego, Kate. I needed to feel like a king to you and honestly, I didn't. Loretta was going through a really tough time emotionally with Joe. You know how Joe can be, Kate. Not good in terms of showing his feelings. And according to Loretta, apparently not much in terms of being a lover. Loretta wasn't too happy with him."

Dan felt Kate's eyes boring into him as he continued. "She was taking every possible opportunity to have a baby. You remember that, don't you? They went through years of trying and had every test imaginable. But Loretta told me at some point Joe lost interest in doing his share of the required essentials, and he'd shut down where the bedroom was concerned."

Kate's cold, blank stare remained steady. She had made no response to anything Dan had said so far. He continued uncomfortably. "But that wasn't what happened between us. Truth is, it was more me then her. I was full of myself then and, well, she put me up on a pedestal, frankly. It kind of started with her asking for any advice I might have on how she could keep Joe interested in her. She said he kind of considered me his idol and so she thought maybe I knew if there were some buttons she could push. It became apparent she thought I was a pretty hot ticket. And I liked that. I have to say it kind of attracted me to her, and she, in subtle ways, let me know that if her husband wasn't, you know, taking care of business, it set her free to take care of herself."

There was no break in Kate's gaze and Dan was becoming even more uneasy. "I knew what she was hinting at and at first I steered clear. But then, before I knew it, we were seeing each other more and more, and spending time on the phone and all that. And, then, somehow, there we were. It was right after Allie was born and you were completely under water with the three girls, and to be honest, we weren't exactly tearing the sheets up. But really it came down to her thinking I was the answer to every question, every need she ever had. And it seemed real for both of us. For a time, we actually thought we had fallen in love. Not that either of us wanted it, but it just seemed so real. We knew we weren't in it just for the sex. It was our emotions that needed what the other could supply and so it happened."

Dan wanted to get away from Kate's laser glare, but he knew he needed to finish what he'd started. "In the end, as they moved toward adoption, the affair began to tail off. We both realized this was wrong. And I knew that I didn't love Loretta, that I loved you. And it didn't really matter that you didn't treat me like I was the master of the universe. Somehow that didn't seem to be so important after I met someone who did treat me that way. It just sort of vanished in me nearly as quickly as it happened. And I think she realized that Joe was a man worth loving and he loved her back, and she could always count on him. And so we both decided to end what we had started."

Contempt brimmed in Kate's eyes. "Why are you telling me this now?"

"I can't leave this earth and not tell you the truth, Kate. I've been carrying this around for years and now that I know I am going to die, I have to clear the books. The guilt is too much for me, Kate. I love you. I just needed to get this out so you'd always know that I put you in front of everything else in my world."

Kate got up, walked to her closet and pulled out a small bag, threw a few items into it and turned to Dan. "At this moment, Dan, I don't love you anymore. You have betrayed me and you have humiliated me. I didn't deserve this. I'm going out to the beach house and I don't want to speak with you or see you. Leave me alone. I am going to contact our lawyer. I need to sort out what I own on my own. I don't want anything that was yours, especially anything that was stolen from my brother, from his job, or from his bedroom."

Her reference to her brother's bedroom was accompanied by a wave of her hand towards Dan's midsection making Dan feel more humiliated than he had ever been in his entire life.

She lowered her voice, but the words came out just as forcefully. "I am going to tell the girls that we are reviewing some things and for the time being they are to butt out. I expect you to do the same and under no circumstance will you discuss this with them. If you do, and I find out about it, you will never see or hear from me again. Do you understand me, Dan?"

Dan nodded. He began to move to her.

"Stay away from me, Dan. I'm leaving the house now and I can't tell you when I'll be back, or if I'll be back. I thought our life was real. I can't believe it wasn't."

Chapter Twenty Five

April 4, 2013, 9:45 a.m.
Reese Public Housing Project, Building Four, Unit 102
Middle Island, New York

Beyond her front door, Sharona heard the thump of music, then silence, and the thud of a car door closing. She lifted her head from the sofa where she had been resting; through the window she saw Nicky Storms walking up the path to their front door.

Deke was still in the shower, so she wearily rose as the chimes rang twice.

"Word, Sharona. How you feeling? Man says you got the flu. That ain't fun," Nicky said as he came in. She nodded but there was no kiss on the cheek or hug between them. Nicky and Sharona had always been suspicious of each other. Only recently had Sharona come around to seeing something of value in Deke's friend; he had recognized her positive influence on his friend, too, but they still kept their distance.

"That's what he says, Nicky, but I don't know. I just been feeling low for a while now. This been coming on for couple of weeks now and started for real the other day. Then I thought it might've gone away because yesterday I was OK. But this morning was terrible. I ain't sure it's anything except my mind, Nicky. You know what I'm talking about? I'm scared for what's coming."

"Yeah I imagine you got cause to have things on your mind these days. Ain't never heard bad news like yours, God knows. But it's going be all right, Watts . Everything always works out for the best, you know," Nicky didn't sound convincing.

"I don't know about that, but while Deke's still in the shower, I just wanted to tell you thanks for the nice things you said about me and my Gran to Deke. You about his only friend and hearing from you made a big difference. Least that's what he said."

"It's cool. He's a lucky man to have a good woman wants to make him into a father. That's the best chance he's ever going have to become something. I hope he never forgets it. And he gonna make a good pops, you'll see."

"Well thank you. He's late because of me. I had the bathroom tied up with this ugly stuff. I believe the water was cold when he got in there, besides. I ain't got no coffee to offer you but I can get you some tea."

"No, that's cool, Sharona. I got to step outside to make a call for a minute. If I ain't back when he gets out the shower, let him know I'm here. Man ain't never on time for nothing anyways. And thanks for the ticket today. You sure you don't want to go? I'll loan you two my car still."

"Thanks, Nicky, but I can't see myself anywhere today except on that couch. Besides, I ain't never cared about baseball, and you and him was always about them Mets. He'd rather be with you anyways."

"That's where you're wrong, Watts. That man is crazy in love with you and there ain't nothing in this whole world he rather have then time with you. That's money." Nicky closed the door behind him as he punched the speed dial.

Sharona felt her heart skip a beat and her throat tighten. She knew that Deke loved her, but she had never been sure he would let anyone else see it. But Nicky wasn't one to blow smoke. Sharona knew Nicky was playing back to her what he had heard from Deke because the words he used were the same.

Today was opening day at Citi Field and Sharona's Christmas gift was about to become Deke's reality. They'd planned the day together until a few hours earlier, when she started feeling sick and couldn't hold anything in her stomach. She suggested he ask Nicky to attend in her place. Deke had balked at going without her, but she convinced him. He was surprised when she mentioned Nicky, but Sharona now saw Nicky as a worthwhile mentor and adviser. It was Nicky who had set Deke straight a couple of months back, when Sharona had first suggested they have a child together.

After meeting with Dr. Russo at Cold Spring Harbor Laboratory, Sharona had felt almost completely numb. The news that at twenty seven years old she had less than a year to live was beyond her comprehension. She simply could not envision her life being taken away from her.

Her grandmother tried to comfort her, but Sharona was deaf to any reason or logic; she was especially hostile to Gran's talk of faith in the Lord. Nor did she find much comfort from Deke. He was dumbstruck by the news. To his way of thinking, there was a simple solution: If you know what the problem is - in this case, some kind of rogue gene - then remove the gene, and the problem. "Why can't they operate and take it out before it does what they say it's going to do?" he asked.

As Sharona sunk into despair, Deke spent more time with Nicky. At one point he disappeared for several days after Sharona accused him of sounding like a fool because he didn't comprehend how DNA worked. He had turned to Nicky, and even though he was sworn to keep Sharona's secret, he had confided in his only friend.

When Deke told him what was happening, Nicky went to his computer and spent hours researching the human genome and the news of the research findings from Cold Spring Harbor Laboratory.

After hours of browsing the web, he returned to the living room where Deke was brooding in front of the TV, picked up the remote, and shut it off. "We got to talk, brother. This shit is real," he told Deke as he sat down in an overstuffed chair.

"What you find out?" Deke asked. Nicky was more than a former gang member; he lived well because he was smart. He hadn't gone very far in his formal education, but Nicky spent most of his free time reading and learning. He kept up with politics, social issues, economics, science, finance, entertainment. To the world he was a gangster but beneath that exterior, he was a self-educated, erudite and sophisticated man. He read *The Times* from cover to cover each day, believing what could be learned in those pages could be as useful as four years of a college education

"There ain't nothing about the four people with the same date. But they said they'd keep all of that secret for now, right? I did all this other stuff about it. I can't believe how much shit is out there on all this gene stuff. It's everywhere. And here it is: If what they told her is true then it could be that she is gonna die."

Deke's eyes widened, but he stayed silent. He realized Nicky had more to say. "Word. The genes control everything. They decide how big you gonna be, how smart you gonna be, how long your hair can be, how much you weigh, color of your skin, eyes, if your teeth are gonna rot, everything. All that is kind of coded inside when we born. Thing is, ain't nothing you can do to change all this stuff."

Deke was confused by Nicky's explanation. "You telling me that my genes made me a gangster?"

"No, it don't work that way. But it did make you as strong as you are. It made those biceps like iron and probably gave you that mean streak down your back. You used what your genes put inside of you to be one of the baddest dudes I ever seen. That's all you, brother. But if you had been raised right and been from the right place, as you grew up maybe none of that would have happened and you'd be in the NFL right now."

"So," Deke asked, as he started to grasp Nicky's point, "your genes give you the muscle and the talent and all that, but you got to decide how to use it for yourself?"

"Word. Like LeBron," Nicky said. "Now he been great at hoops all his life and he's one of the richest stars the NBA ever seen. But he could've turned out a lot different if he'd gone another way. Like he's as big and as talented as he is by his natural gene pool. But his decision to be a world superstar? That's all him. All that practice and shit, that all worked for him, but his talent was there from the start."

Nicky, caught up in his own explanation, was excited about sharing it. "And the thing is, you can't change what your genes say you're going to be. You can only change what you do with what you got. Sometimes you can't even change that. Say like someone been born a man, but his genes are messed up and he feel like being a bitch. Sooner or later, that fool's going to put on a dress. He can't help it. That's what his genes say he is."

Deke turned his head away from Nicky and stared out the window for several minutes. Now he got it. Now he knew what Sharona faced. Nicky watched Deke absorb the information he had just presented.

Finally Deke rose and walked to the window. "So you saying ain't nothing can keep her from dying because her genes say she's gonna die That's it?"

"I ain't saying that's what I know is going to happen. In science they have what they call irreversible conclusions. You hear that when they say someone has cancer or what not, and they got only a short time to live. From what you told me, it sounds like Sharona has one of those irreversible conclusions. If that's the case, then nothing can be done. This gene is there and this is what it says, and that can't be changed. Otherwise, those folks at the labs would have already started reversing this business."

Deke had been calm until now. "Motherfucker! Sharona ain't never been nothing but a good woman. All her life she's been up against that rat-sucking mother of hers, who steals from her and gets down with every drive-by john that'd give her two dollars for a blow job. Living in this bullshit neighborhood and never having any money. Sharona was always studying her books and taking her Gran to church and being good to everybody she ever met. If that girl ever had anything she'd give it away to someone else before she kept it for her own self. She took me in when I got out. Gave me an address and introduced me to Tommy at the tire store so's I could get a job. Why she has to get this, Nick? Why?"

Deke was pleading now. "I ain't never loved no one, Nick. You know that. I never knew my father, and my mother made damn sure

I knew I was nothing but a welfare check for her. Nobody ever bothered with me about nothing till I met her. For sure she's the only person ever seen any good in me. And now she got to die? What kind of bullshit is that? I could kill someone right now, Nicky."

He started toward the door as Nicky quickly jumped in his way. "Easy, brother. Don't be going out there all mad and shit. You'll get your ass in trouble and then you'll be back in jail, and what good are you for her then? Think about it. Be smart, my man."

Deke turned and sank onto the couch.

"You love her?" Nicky asked.

"I don't know, what do I know about loving someone? She's the only person outside of you and maybe Tommy at the Firestone store I care about. I do know that."

"How you feel when you come home if she ain't there for some reason?" Nicky wanted Deke to really see himself.

"Don't like it. Feel empty."

"How about when you watch her walk across the room?"

"Like I could fuck her, sure enough. Even if we just got out the bed. I can't never get enough of that. No woman ever make me feel the way she do. It's way beyond all the trash I ever been with. Making love with her makes me feel like I left this earth, Nicky. Like my whole body been lifted up to someplace besides where I am. I swear I see stars with her."

Quietly, Nicky asked, "How did you feel when she told you about this bullshit going on with her?"

Just as quietly, Deke replied, "First I felt sick inside. Then I felt like I was going to cry. Kind of like the first night I spent in jail and that big ass guard took me out of my cell and beat me into the hospital ward. Felt like I was all alone in an ugly place and no one was ever coming to help me."

"And after that?"

"I know this sounds crazy, but I wanted to swallow her up so I could protect her from this thing that's coming to get her. I want to be afraid for her, Nick. Like I could use my body to take the bullet or whatever is coming for her. I wished it was me dying because that woman is too good to die. I ain't never been nothing. And never did nothing for nobody. She's worth dying for, Nick."

"Sounds to me like you met your true love, fool," Nicky smiled. "Listen. Sharona is all those things you said about her. Everybody been knowing that. Most of the people we run with all our lives ain't worth shit. Some people are just born different. Something about them says 'don't even think about disrespecting this one.' Sharona always been like that. That trash mama of hers was always trash and everyone knew it. I wish it was me that Sharona had an eye for. You a lucky man, fool. That woman sees something in you that ain't nobody else ever seen. She sees your soul. And what she sees tells her that you're worthwhile. You may not ever meet another person on earth that looks at you like that. I know I ain't ever found no one like that. But I'll keep looking till I do. And I swear to Jesus that if I do, I'll never ever leave her. Whatever she wants from me she can have."

Deke was surprised at the depth of feeling behind his friend's words and even more surprised that he knew Nicky was right.

But Nicky's lesson wasn't finished yet. "Now what you got to do is go home to her and quit this bullshit. Just do what she needs. She'll let you know what that is. Remember this, don't listen to what the woman say, listen to what she mean. If you know what she mean, then you'll be cool. Sharona is worth living for, fool. And probably worth dying for, like you say. How many women you think you ever gonna find you can say that about?"

Deke stood up again and walked to the door. He didn't say anything. He stopped and turned and Nicky tossed him the keys to his car without being asked.

"I'll have someone run me by later and pick the car up," he said. "Be good to her, Deke. You'll be the man you always thought you could be if you stand by her. I know that. You know it, too. Now go at it, fool."

Deke gently shut the door behind him and pulled out his cell phone. He entered a text message as he headed to Nicky's shiny Mercedes Benz, wet from a winter's drizzle on a miserable late January night.

A minute later Sharona's cell vibrated and she picked it up off the floor next to their bed. The screen read, *b home soon baby sorry but I needed to get it real its all good now luv u D.* She held the phone a moment and then speed-dialed her grandmother. It was time now to get it real, as Deke had said

Sharona had called Gran and they agreed to meet the next morning. That night Deke came back home and they sat up until late trying to make sense of it all. Deke told her how he felt about her and more than that; he knew she was his last great hope to find strength to try and put a life together for himself.

Sharona understood too well what and where he came from, and most of everything about why he had spent so much time in jail. But she also knew that she'd kept an eye on him ever since they were children in the same grade school. She told him now that she'd always avoided him and all his friends, "especially that Nicky Storms, because those boys always seemed to be in some kind of trouble."

"You was right about that. Now you know why I don't think I'll ever amount to anything if you go away. You're my reason to want to be something in this nasty world, Watts. You're all that, girl.

Then he said something she wasn't ready for. "We should be married, Sharona." He looked straight into her eyes.

"You just saying that because I'm dying or you really mean that?" she said, only half-kidding. "I ain't got no big insurance policy, damn sure."

"That's cold, Watts."

"I know, Deke. I'm sorry, I was just fooling with you. I just wasn't expecting to talk about getting married and I'm just surprised, that's all. Can I sleep on that idea? I need to give it some time. Right now I'm still trying to think about what I want the rest of my time to be. Or even if I want any time at all."

Tears began welling up in her eyes. "I don't think I can stand walking around knowing that each and every day is one less.. I'm scared, Deke. I'm really scared. I don't want to go into the ground."

Deke put his arms around her and pulled her closer. "I know, baby, I know. This is all such bullshit. We got to find a way to get you out of this. I know those doctors got all their tests and shit, but there has to be some way that this could be wrong. It just ain't right. Not to you." He held her while she sobbed into his rock-like chest.

After a few minutes, she heard his breathing hesitate and felt his chest begin to stutter and heave. She bent her head back, looked up and saw Deke's eyes aimed at the ceiling and tears rolling down his cheeks..

Before she could say anything, he spoke haltingly. "Lord, take me instead. I deserve to die for all I done. This woman ain't never done nothing but good. Leave her here and take me. Please leave her and take me."

He broke down entirely. They held each other long into the night and eventually fell in to a deep but troubled sleep.

At dawn Sharona woke up and threw a cover over Deke. He stirred and stretched out on the dilapidated couch. Before she climbed into the bed, she gazed at him and saw in his face a kindness and gentle spirit. She knew that last night was perhaps the only prayer he had ever uttered in his life. She knew that she had found her soulmate. Perhaps she had always known that even back in their school days.

His tears were real, as real as anything she had ever known. Somehow she felt that there was a strength in this man that would help protect her against any troubles she faced. What she didn't know was how she would be able to leave him so soon, after waiting so long, to be so deeply loved.

<hr />

"Gran, I can't even think about dying without getting all knotted up in my stomach. I'm afraid to go in to the ground. You know how I am about bugs. I can't even think about them without feeling sick."

Gran listened. They were sitting at her kitchen table, two cups of tea before them and some honey biscuits on a small cracked plate at the center.

For the past half hour, Gran had allowed Sharona to vent. First her granddaughter attacked the Cold Spring Harbor Lab, and in particular Dr. Russo. She said they were guilty of interfering with God's laws on life and death and would be punished for it. Then she lit off on the unfairness of life for a poor black girl from the projects in "the rich man's world." How it was altogether a different world for people like "us"'cause "We don't get the same schools or the same anything as the white folks get." Then she targeted the black male, complaining "they about the shiftiest species God ever made. Ain't none of them that I ever known could be trusted for a second," she said, adding that once they got their "booty call done," they usually headed for the door. Finally, she turned to her own family. She saved a special level of repugnance for her own mother, turning to her Gran and asking, "How did that woman ever come from you?"

Sharona rose from the table and walked to the kitchen sink, where she stopped. She wrapped her arms across her body, grasping her hands behind her shoulders, and began to sob. Gran was about to go to her but stopped as Sharona's words revealed what was in her soul. "I always thought that I was going to be something in this world. You always told me that I could be anything I wanted to be. I believed you. And I planned on that happening. Only thing is, I could never decide what it was that I wanted to be."

She turned and ran her hands through her hair, pushing it back from her face. "So I stayed between the lines, did what I was supposed to do, and hoped that one day something would come to me and that I would know what it was I was meant to do. But nothing ever came and here I am, working at the Target store and still living in the projects. "You know why I don't want to die, Gran?" Sharona took a deep breath and continued. "I'm mad, Gran. I'm mad at God for taking my soul back to him before I had a chance to do something great on this earth."

Gran let out a sigh and signaled for Sharona to sit by waving her hand toward her seat. Sharona stomped back to her place and folded her arms silently across her chest, staring at the floor the whole time.

"Shoney, honey, you right about one thing and I can't find any

argument against what you said, no matter what I think about."
Gran paused for a second, gathering her thoughts. "Black men are
the shiftiest species on the earth and what you said about 'booty call
running' has certainly been true far as I can recollect. 'Course, my
memory is a bit faded being how time has taken its toll, if you know
what I mean. But I will keep it in mind if ever I get another chance
at some rock and roll."

The two of them burst into laughter and Sharona slapped the
table in glee. "I hear you, Gran. I only wished I'd known that. Except
every black woman alive thinks her man the one's gonna be different."

"Now, let's get down to business here, Sharona honey. You got
some serious thoughts on your mind and I got some things to say
that you need to hear." The older woman lifted her teacup, took a
sip. "Listen to me, child. When you was born, I looked at you in your
little bassinet right back in that bedroom down the hall and I knew
there was greatness in you. I don't rightly know why. Lord knows
your mama had showed me enough to know she wasn't made from
anything special. When I see the Lord, come the day, I'll ask him
why he sent me such a foul-hearted person. Because I know I did
everything I could ever do to try and make that girl go right. But she
was a bent coin from the day she was born."

Gran slid her teacup back onto the table. "But you were different.
There was a look on your face; it was like the face of one of God's
own angels. Your smile was like a lightbulb. And you were so cute
when you were little. Everywhere you went, people would always
be stopping and looking at you. Black and white folks all. Seemed
sometimes like more white folks would pay attention to you then
even your own kind. Lord, you were something to see."

Sharona couldn't help but beam with pleasure at Gran's description, and didn't interrupt the older woman. "See child, some people
are just born with natural airs about them that send out signals to
others that say they special. You were such a child. I'd go to your
school and there'd be two hundred children all running about the
yard, and I could pick you out in a second, because you had something about you that just made you stand out. I don't know why,

except I recall one time asking my reverend about it and he said, 'That's just the Lord's grace showing through.'

Sharona stood and took the two teacups to the sink. Gran followed,,held her granddaughter's hands and stood face-to-face. "So while you was saying your prayers, asking the Lord to help you find your greatness, I was saying the same prayers for you, child. And I do believe that those prayers can be answered. You see, child, the world thinks that greatness is about money, fame, power. Some would say it's about how many folks know your name. Well, that ain't what the Lord thinks. Jesus didn't say we should measure ourselves that way. He never taught us greatness was about any of the things that most people think is great. This is what Jesus taught us."

And then, from memory, Gran recited a verse from the Bible: "And they brought young children to him, that he should touch them: and his disciples rebuked those that brought them. But when Jesus saw it, he was much displeased, and said unto them, suffer the little children to come unto me, and forbid them not: for of such is the kingdom of God."

Before Gran could utter another word, Sharona knew where her thoughts were going. She began to feel a sudden lifting of her fears and tensions as she listened. She was calm from that moment.

The old woman smiled at her beloved granddaughter. "Child, Jesus tells us that children are the kingdom of God. Life is your greatness, baby girl. God made us to create his likeness. If you really want to do something great before you leave this earth, whenever that may be, give God what he asks of you. Give him life like he has given it to you. Have a child, Sharona. There isn't anything on this earth as great as a child."

Gran took Sharona's chin in her hand and lifted it slightly. "If you can bring another person into the world, then you'll be doing the greatest thing that any person ever gets the chance to do. There isn't anything that can match the creation of a child. Make a child and you are building the kingdom of God, Sharona. Baby, you was born to be special and by creating life, you'll be fulfilling your destiny. And the child you leave behind will be a living monument to the life you have lived."

Tears of joy were welling in Gran's eyes now. "I believe that God sent Deke into your life at just the right time.and I believe Jesus has touched Deke's heart with your soul so that he ain't gonna be no booty-call nigger running out the door on you. You already seen that. He could have been gone already. What did he do instead? He came back and cried for your soul. He asked you to marry him. Sharona, that man ain't known anything in his whole life but trouble. Now he's at peace with the world 'cause he's entered inside that grace of God the reverend says you have."

Gran reached across the table and took Sharona's hand. She hoped to get the last words out before her emotions choked her. "Lord knows my heart is broken beyond any repair I been praying to Jesus to take me instead. But child, while you still have time, don't look back. Look ahead. The promise of your life is still out there, Sharona. The dignity of being a good mother will live long after you and me and all of us are gone."

Sharona locked her eyes to Gran's gaze. Tears ran down her face, but for the first time since the nightmare had begun she felt at peace. Gran simply sat silent. She had emptied her soul.

"Gran, the grace that I may have around me doesn't come from God. It comes from you"

———————«(●)»———————

Deke left for Citi Field and Sharona lay on the couch, where she fell into a dreamy sleep.

When she opened her eyes, she glanced at the clock and saw that the Mets game had probably begun. She powered on the TV and just as she found the ballgame, her cell phone rang. Glancing at the caller ID, she saw that it was a New York City number. "Hello?" As she punched the mute button on the TV remote, she realized she was feeling better.

"Sharona?" A woman's voice, feminine but strong, was on the

line. "This is Doctor Guitton from Cold Spring Harbor Lab. We met again last week when you were here for your checkup. Do you recall?"

"Yes I remember you, Doctor. Is something wrong?" Despite Gran's encouragement and Deke's support, which was helping to lift her spirits, Sharona still walked on eggshells, as if more misfortune might befall her at any time.

"Not at all, Miss Watts. I'm calling to let you know some wonderful news. You're going to be a mother. Your tests are positive for pregnancy. Congratulations!"

"Oh my God!' Sharona shouted. "You sure, Doctor? How? When my baby gone be here?"

Ellen laughed at Sharona's reaction. "I have a number for an ob-gyn near where you live. You should call for an appointment. She'll be able to get an accurate estimate and we'll work so your delivery is timed well before any possible condition that might complicate it. But, Miss Watts, you are going to…"

Sharona finished Ellen's sentence. "Do something great before I die," she whispered.

"Yes, you will. You're a lucky woman," said Dr. Guitton.

Chapter Twenty Six

April 4, 2013, 3:45 p.m.
Cold Spring Harbor Laboratory, Office of the President
Cold Spring Harbor, New York

Tod rose from his desk and walked to the seating area of his spacious office. Ritu and Ellen were already chatting with Zach, who was joining them by speakerphone for their biweekly meeting on the p63A gene project.

Russo flopped into one of the chairs facing the picture window and the Queen Anne sofa, where the women sat, and listened as Weitzman, from his office at Memorial Sloan Kettering Cancer Center in Manhattan, briefed them on the condition of Father Ted Hayslip, now a full-blown cancer patient. "He's coming in here on Tuesday and we'll complete the workup, but I've seen the initial biopsy reports, and from the scans we've already done, the prognosis is very grim," Zach said. He sounded discouraged, unusual for an oncologist. This case was different for him. In fact, it was remarkably different. And personal. They all felt that, even though no one had talked about it yet.

"How long do you think he's got, Zach?" Russo asked.

"Can't be certain yet, but I'd guess anywhere from six to nine months. No more. Maybe a lot less if we can't control this with radiation." Zach replied.

"How is he doing? When he was in last week, he seemed so distant from the others," Dr. Mhatra asked.

The four test subjects, who had taken to calling themselves the lab mice, were now meeting every two weeks at Cold Spring Harbor and had begun to bond. The results of their biweekly workups were being compared to benchmarks established at the beginning of this study to identify any medical similarities among them. The research team was keeping an especially sharp eye on the group's oncology reports now; they dreaded the possibility that Father Ted's fatal diagnosis might also show up in the others, which would identify why these four souls would all be coming to their ends possibly on Christmas Day. Now that one of them was marked, and not much could be done to change his fate, it was possible the same malady could afflict the others. But so far that had not occurred.

The lab worked with each of the four separately to trace their genealogy. That part of the task was overwhelmingly difficult, as they had little available detailed information or records for any of their ancestors going back more than two generations. The assignment to find their family histories had gone to Ritu and she had attacked the problem with her typical round-the-clock diligence and fervor. But so far, she had come to a dead end beyond the grandparents of each subject, except for Janet Bates, who had produced her great-great-grandmother's diary, which dated from the Civil War. The researchers were beginning to be encouraged as they delved into her lineage. But the other family histories remained blank.

"I spoke with him this morning and he didn't sound like the happiest man I'd ever heard," Zach said. "But that's to be expected. I'm not sure he was the most outgoing person even before all of this. Anyway, if he has any success at all with the protocol, assuming he accepts it, he'll likely succumb on or about the date his DNA results have indicated."

"On a more positive note - at least I think so - Ms. Watts is definitely pregnant," Ellen announced to Zach and Ritu. Russo had seen the report earlier. "She'll be due anywhere from late December to early January."

"Wow, that's cutting it close," Dr. Mhatra said, concern in her voice.

"Yeah, close is right. I have an old friend who has an ob-gyn practice out in her area and I'm taking steps to put them together. We'll need to take my friend - she specializes in high-risk births - into our confidence and get a clear idea of the delivery date once she's had a chance to examine Sharona, but I'm thinking we can go with a C-section if the baby is nearly full-term. God, this is awful," Ellen added.

"Is this what she wanted? I mean, she actually tried for this? Seems odd to me," Ritu was having a hard time understanding Sharona's decision. She could never be anything but pragmatic.

"It's actually one of the more noble things I've ever heard," said Ellen. "She confided in me that her grandmother gave her the idea. She wanted to do something great before she died and her Gran told her the greatest thing she could do was to leave a life behind. So she and her boyfriend decided they would have a baby while there was still time."

"Wow, that takes a lot of courage for both of them," Zach said. " He has to commit to being a single parent as well as deal with losing her. Not exactly your everyday pregnancy, is it? It's kind of amazing to me as we've seen this unfold," he added. "These four individuals seem to be acting the opposite to what I would've expected. I mean, I kind of thought that if a person were told they had a year to live, they'd go around the world, or quit their jobs and stay at the beach, spend time drinking, gambling, partying ... I don't know what. But that's not what we've seen so far. Each of them has kind of just taken it slow. They are depressed, we can see that, but there haven't been any excesses in any of their behaviors. At least not as far as I can see."

Ellen thought she had an explanation for this and responded quickly. "That's true, but to be fair, they were all pretty well-grounded people from the start, so what kind of out-of-the-ordinary or excessive behavior would follow? Each of them is going through a very tough self-mourning period. Mrs. Bates is angry and has shut out everyone around her except her son in the military overseas, who doesn't know her fate. Father Ted admits to being semi-comatose, and Brannigan seems as nervous as a cat on a hot tin roof. Of the four, Miss Watts seems to be the most even-tempered. Who knows, though? She may be keeping her troubles to herself."

Ellen turned to Russo. "What were you thinking you'd see, Tod?"

"I don't know. Certainly sleep disorders. Massive anxiety. Alcohol abuse. Drug use. Compulsive spending. Any of the outward negative characteristics that accompany threatened physical trauma or pronounced fear, I suppose."

Ellen Guitton was sitting with her hand under her chin. "It's true they were grounded in their own ways, but each of them also has a lot they're going to have to step away from. They've had time to assess the damage to themselves personally and know what they must leave behind . I expect this'll get harder for them to deal with. The clock will keep ticking away and each day brings them closer to the end. Not an easy thing to accept."

She had zeroed in on the same conclusion each of them had reached. It was still very early in the process and the four subjects might still fall victim to emotional trauma or massive anxieties as their fates loomed. As soon as Father Ted's diagnosis became known, it would be certain to hit home.

Russo spoke for them all. "Definitely not easy to accept. We need to be very attentive to their behaviors and see if we can catch any changes, especially for the worse. I think it's great they've begun to bond, and there seems to be some group strength emerging from their sessions. But I'm still very troubled by the search for the common thread. Ritu, I know you're doing your best, but I tell you, there's a link here and we need to press every possible resource to find it. I pray it won't be terminal cancer."

"I hear you, Doctor," Ritu replied. "I may have found something interesting in the diary of Janet Bates' great-great-grandmother but I need further confirmation of some of the data. If it's a good lead, that will give us at least a starting point. The problem is, even if we find something for one of them, matching it to the other three is almost a mathematical impossibility. The odds are not even calculable to tie together all four. But if it can be done. I'll do it," she added emphatically.

Russo knew even before Ritu said this that tracing family histories linking all four was improbable, but that didn't curb his need to see if there was something inside this mysterious happenstance that would possibly intercept the fate that was coming to them. "Let me ask you all something, and I don't want this to get out of this room," Tod spoke bluntly. "I'm having a very difficult time feeling detached from this professionally. Like all of you, I've dedicated my life to research, which has kept me from having to deal with the human element of this work. But this couldn't feel more personal. I feel as if I'm a personal tour guide to their graves, and keeping myself from coming emotionally involved is a challenge. Do you guys feel the same?"

"Yes," Zach snapped back.

"Yes, absolutely," Ellen said, almost simultaneously with Zach.

"Not so much," Ritu said. "I've been able to compartmentalize so far. But I'm buried in charts and history, and not as much on the front line as you guys."

"I'm not sleeping well," Ellen said, shaking her head.

"OK," Tod said. "I'm glad it's not just me. I mean, I'm sorry about this for each of us.. Not that we're not professional, but … Well, you know what I mean. I'm shocked that I'm being drawn into their lives and frankly, don't know what any of this will do to me longer term. I honestly wasn't prepared for such a late-in-life discovery of emotion."

Ellen looked into Russo's eyes. For the first time since she had worked with him, she saw compassion there. Her immediate reaction was warmth and admiration. But she put that aside as Russo continued. "OK. Enough about me; let's talk about me," he chuckled. "Thanks to the persistence of our PR people and the well-known and socially connected Doctor Guitton, I will be on *Face the Nation* this Sunday."

"Really! Well, congratulations," Ritu said.

"I'll finally see you without your Mets hat?" Zach, a Yankees fan, kidded him.

"One of the obligatory stops on the way to the Nobel Prize, learned Doctor?" Ellen joked from across the table

"Or not.. After millions of people get a chance to hear me, I'll probably fall all over myself and our license to operate will be pulled," he said dismissively. He was embarrassed by the team's reaction. But he had even more stunning news. "And, if I hadn't told you earlier, I am scheduled later this month to have lunch at the White House with the President and his science adviser as well as the Secretary of Health." Several other public appearances were on Russo's calendar, too. None of which he was anxious to be a part of, but all of which he knew he was obligated to do. After all these months, their discovery needed to be put into perspective, and, like it or not, he was the voice and the face of whatever that perspective was to become. Tod Russo was becoming world famous.

"Oh my God! That's wonderful, Ted. When?" the three team members asked in near-unison.

"The twenty-fourth or twenty-fifth. I'm not sure," Tod mumbled back.

"How are you doing with all this new found fame?" Zach asked, concerned. He knew Russo was a private, humble man.

"Wanna know the truth?"

"Sure. Why ask otherwise?"

"I'm ashamed of it. I'm embarrassed by it all." Russo set his gaze on the speakerphone in the center of the coffee table, unable to look Ritu and Ellen in the face.

"Why? This should be the crowning jewel of a lifetime of achievement. You should be proud of what you've brought to humanity." Ritu argued, trying to mask her own indignation at his suggestion there was anything about their discovery that needed an apology.

"Tod, why?" Ellen asked as well. She was stunned that Tod would suggest that their research, on which they worked so hard, was a burden.

Tod became uneasy, knowing he had hurt their feelings. They had their lives and reputations tied up in their work. His confession was unexpected and unwelcome. Once he realized this, he spoke quickly to soothe them. "I am proud of our work, doctors. Please don't be insulted. But I'm uncomfortable with being cast into the limelight when good people - really good people - are walking to their deaths as an outcome of our discovery. I'll be seen in the bright lights or in the press by millions around the world, and Janet Bates will be crying alone on her pillow tonight. Father Hayslip will be taking his chemo and enduring a three day stay at the hospital because he can't go twenty seconds without wrenching his guts out. Or Sharona feels her baby move inside of her and knows that child is going to grow up motherless. And Brannigan - he plays with his grandchildren, knowing in less than a year he won't be there to see them."

His eyes rose up to meet Ellen's now and he spoke a little louder so Ritu and Zach wouldn't miss his point. "So I'm proud of what we've done. And I know it's a turning point in the science of genetics. But as I said, I'm deeper into the weeds on this than anything I've ever done before. I'm not a man who has been intimately involved with his emotions. Just ask my former wives. This is different. Really ... different."

His gaze settled on Dr. Mhatra. "Ritu. Find it. I don't care what you have to do or how much it costs. Just find the link. We can't let them go to their end not knowing why."

Chapter Twenty Seven

April 7, 2013, 8:45 a.m.
CBS News, Studio 16, Stage 2
120 West 53rd Street
New York, New York

"What a dump," Tod thought. Everywhere he looked, equipment was scattered. Furniture was piled up, along with an array of lighting fixtures, scaffolding and screens. It looked like a warehouse to him. A warehouse for half-empty coffee cups,: every horizontal surface held one.

He was seated at a table as the technicians were testing the lighting. Under his chin, a bib prevented the makeup now slathered on his face from dripping onto the shirt and tie he'd been fitted with when he arrived at eight-thirty. His own camel hair jacket, white shirt, and red tie, had met with disapproval from the assistant producer, a scraggly woman of about twenty with a head of unkempt, shoulder-length curls.

She took a look at him from above her glasses and made a notation on her clipboard. "No one told you? Dark jacket, blue shirt. We'll have to dress you. The tie will be fine. Please come this way ... Mister Russo? Did I get that right?"

"It's Doctor Russo, but yes, you have it right. Dress me?"

"Whatever!" She had already walked off into the cavernous studio, leaving him standing with Dr. Ellen Guitton. Ellen had come along to offer support for his first televised interview..

"Monika, I need you on two; we have a dressing change and makeup is ready for Russo," the curly-haired producer shouted. "Please find me! Hurry!" She was yelling into the headset,which appeared to be required equipment for the workers on set

At one end of the room, he could see a team of assistants carrying boards that he guessed were about to come together to form the familiar backdrop of the Sunday morning news show, Face the Nation. But so far, there was nothing resembling a set.

"Yes." Curlytop now peered at Russo from above the rims of her glasses. "We need you in a high-contrast color for the cameras, so we require a dark jacket. Your publicist or whoever managed your appearance was informed, I'm sure. We also require a light-blue shirt, which will appear white on screen. Monika I need you now!" she shouted into the headset.

Ellen glanced at Russo with an incredulous expression. Tod smiled back, but he was nervous. He had resisted making this appearance until he'd been dragged into it by the lab's public relations director, who - he now realized - wasn't here yet, as promised.

"Just a second." Curlytop was speaking into her microphone. She had not yet told them her name or asked who Ellen was. "Are you expecting a … what's his name?" she said in to the headset, then looked at Russo, "someone named Neiporte?"

She had butchered the name, pronouncing it "Nee-port" when it was "Nee-a-port-ee," but she wasn't the first person to mispronounce Tom's last name. "Yes, Russo's with us." She continued into the microphone. "He's … OK, send him back." She had interrupted Russo's reply and was moving her microphone back up to the middle of her forehead. Now she noticed Ellen, standing a step or two behind Tod. "And you are? Wife? Friend? What?"

Ellen instinctively knew exactly how to cut this self-absorbed whirlwind down to size. She paused for a good ten seconds, while making eye contact. "I am, I believe, a guest at this studio, as is Doctor Russo. We're here because Mister Moonves and I share a floor in our apartment building and we're close friends, and he assured us we would be accorded exceptional courtesy as guests of the show and the CBS team."

Ellen paused again to allow her words to sink in before she continued. "Doctor Russo and I, so far, have not learned your name, nor has Doctor Russo been treated with any of the CBS courtesy that Mr. Moonves promised."

Satisfied that Curlytop had stopped in her tracks, her mouth agape, Ellen continued. "Now, you seem like a very wise young person, and you apparently have considerable talent and responsibility here. We can plainly see the lack of support you have from your colleagues. However, we would like to know your name. Then, we'd like you to explain the procedures that Doctor Russo will need to follow so he can contribute to this program."

Then Ellen delivered her knockout punch. "We are meeting Mister Moonves here at this studio, because he is joining us for brunch after the broadcast. That information, my dear, is a favor I extend to you. I am sure you wouldn't enjoy the surprise of having the President and Chief Executive Officer of CBS Corporation walking in on your broadcast unexpectedly. My name is Doctor Ellen Guitton, Doctor Russo prefers Tod, and I hope it's very nice to meet you," she said as she stuck her hand out just as Tom Neiporte arrived.

"Thank you, Ellen," Curlytop said as she reached out to accept Ellen's firm, warm handshake. "I'm Peggy, Peggy Brunner, and I apologize. I am sooo strung out today. I've been a jerk. I'm sorry. The set was supposed to be constructed last night and when I got in at seven this morning, it wasn't. The stage crew doesn't arrive until eight and they are union and there aren't enough of them to set up, so we had to. ... Oh, and if that isn't enough, our host called in this morning and is delayed on Amtrak coming up from Washington - he was at a White House dinner last night - so he's going to be late, which means no run through, which means I'll have to walk through your appearance with you, and I hate doing that!"

Despite the pressure she was under to get the show on the road, Curlytop Peg knew she needed to apologize. "So please, this isn't me. I'm really not a witch. You must be Tom? I'm Peggy and I'll be working with you until Brian gets here. Nice to meet you and thanks for coming."

At that moment, an attractive Asian woman in her mid-thirties appeared. "Have no fear, Monika is here," she said. "Which one is Doctor Russo?"

Peggy pointed to Tod as she shook hands with Tom Neiporte, who by this time was looking at an outline from the show's producers of what might be discussed today. "Hi, Peggy, Yes, I'm Tom. I assume you have these already?" They stood shoulder-to-shoulder as they turned away to discuss Russo's appearance.

"OK, Doc, you're mine for the next twenty minutes or so," Monika said. "Let's go back to wardrobe and get you fixed up. Mrs. Russo, you can come with us if you like, or we can meet you back here. I think we can find you a safe place to sit while they finish setting up."

The set now appeared complete; workers were placing microphones and lighting and cameras aimed at different angles were testing their shots. Suddenly, everyone seemed to be moving in a preordered direction; they all appeared to know exactly what their assignments were.

Ellen blushed at being called Mrs. Russo, which surprised Tod. She was usually a cooler customer than that. "I'm Doctor Ellen Guitton, Doctor Russo's colleague. And I'll go with you both."

"Oh, sorry," said Monika. "I just assumed." Tod sensed he was also blushing, which surprised him even more. Looking ahead to avoid eye contact with Ellen, he muttered clumsily, "Well, I guess we qualify as a couple," and they followed Monika across the warehouse.

"Lenny, I need this place cleaned up NOW!" they heard Peggy bellow. "It's a shithouse. It's your ass if these coffee cups are still here when we go to broadcast."

Chapter Twenty Eight

April 7, 2013, 12:38 p.m.
International Passenger Arrivals Terminal
John F. Kennedy International Airport
Jamaica, New York

Michaela saw him coming long before he reached the glass security doors which opened into the massive arrivals hall from International Customs. She ran to the entryway, but a burly security guard stopped her, telling her she had to wait behind the yellow line, which she'd already crossed. She'd known that, but was hoping for a sympathy pass. "But that's my baby brother coming home from Afghanistan!"

"I understand, miss, but you'll have to wait behind the line. He'll be here before you know it." The guard gently steered her back by her arm.

The guard was right. As she glanced back over her shoulder, she could see Michael ten steps away, smiling from ear to ear as he jogged toward her. She turned and threw her arms around his neck as he dropped his bag to the floor.

"Oh, Michael, I missed you so much!" She buried her head into his shoulder and immediately began to sob. He was in uniform. This scene had been replayed daily for the staff at the terminal for a long time. The homecomings of military personnel were always highly emotional.

"I missed you too, Mick. I missed you too," he said as he tightened his grip and tried to keep his own feelings under control. After a few minutes, Michael slowly began to release his grip and Michaela was able to catch her breath. "Nice luggage, you dork," she said as she kicked his duffel bag. "Doesn't look big enough to be carrying all the presents you should be bringing for me." She wiped her hands across her face, and ran her sleeve under her nose. She knew she looked like a train wreck, but she didn't care. Michael was standing in front of her.

"I went shopping for something for you before I left, but they didn't have anything in fat ass sizes," he said, laughing so hard he could hardly get the words out.

With that, he picked up the bag, threw his arm around her shoulders and they headed to the parking lot.

———————

It was Palm Sunday; typically cool for an early April day, but sunny and cloudless as they rolled down the street where several residents were out, raking the remains of the gray winter from their yards. If you looked closely, you could see bulbs beginning to emerge from the still-cold earth.

As Michael and Michaela turned into the driveway of their home, they could see their father in the garage under the house, where his pet project, a 1965 Mustang convertible, sat under a tarp awaiting a long-promised renovation. Rod's attention was focused on the rake in his hand. He needed to re-tape the handle to the teeth for the third or fourth year in a row in time for the annual spring cleanup.

Michaela shut off the engine and saw that her dad had not looked out to see who had arrived. She was about to hit the horn but Michael swiftly unbuckled his seatbelt and rushed out, grinning his trademark ear-to-ear smile. "Hey, Pops, got a rake for me?"

Rod jerked his head around. Stunned, he couldn't believe what he saw. Not knowing what to say or how to act, he felt foolish after his first words of greeting: "My God, look at you! You must have grown a foot since you left!"

"Nah. I got lifts in these boots, Pops. I see the rake still isn't fixed!" He wrapped his arms around his father and the two embraced.

"Mike! It's so good to see you. What are you doing home? Why didn't you tell us you'd be coming? Mickey, did you know about this? How long can you stay? Was the flight OK? Are you OK?" Rod's questions tumbled out without giving his son a chance to answer.

"How 'bout if we find Mom, and I'll answer everything at the same time?" Michael said.

Rods face showed his surprise. "Oh, Christ. Of course. Your mother. She's up in the kitchen. Where else? Let's go!"

But Janet wasn't in the kitchen. She had left about ten minutes before Michaela's car approached. She'd been at the sink, peeling potatoes, when she had gotten the familiar signal from down deep in her abdomen. The telltale sense of rising anxiety when her children were near.

Laying the potato peeler aside, she walked to the window of the front room. She was about to turn back to her chores when she saw Michaela's car turn onto their street, a passenger sitting next to her. As the car approached, Janet could make out the familiar shape of her son. She nearly collapsed with joy. Grabbing the kitchen towel she'd slung over her shoulder, she pressed it her face and cried. Tonight he would sleep under her roof, just a few feet from her heart. She felt dizzy, so she sank into the sofa and tried to regain her composure. She didn't want Michael's homecoming to be ruined by her lack of control.

She listened to his footfalls as he clumped up the stairs, and when he entered the house, with Michaela and Rod following behind, she could barely see him through her tears. Choked with emotion, she couldn't utter a single word.

Michael sat at her side on the sofa and pulled her head to his shoulder. "Mom, Mom, it's OK. It's me, Mom. I'm fine. Don't cry.

Everything's going to be fine, Mom. Come on, Mom, how about a smile?"

But his encouragement didn't work. Not for Janet, and not for Michael, either. He stared up toward the ceiling and tried to hide his own emotions.

Michaela turned, crying, toward the kitchen and returned with a box of tissues, while Rod placed his hand on Janet's heaving back and tried his best to comfort her. "Some surprise, eh, Jan? He looks taller."

Michaela had suggested on the ride home from the airport and that their mother needed to do things in her own way. Michael wasn't altogether happy, but he'd agreed to go along. He had questioned Michaela very closely about what he called the "weirdness" of the whole thing.

Michael had told Michaela that his platoon leader had helped him get the time off to come home. Mickey had abeen surprised to find out she was a woman, Carly, and that she had also been good at internet research.

Carly had provided him with information on DNA and the Human Genome Project, as well as a thorough breakdown on Cold Spring Harbor Lab, including the first press release on the study. So, Michael was up to speed on the facts. What he couldn't understand was how his mother had become one of the poor unfortunates who had participated in the research.

Michaela wondered if all platoon leaders in the Army were as empathetic and caring with their troops as this Carly. She knew her brother was considered a "hottie" and could easily have made a living off his good looks and sculpted body. Although she had been a year ahead of him at school, she had heard that Michael, a two-letter athlete, had been dubbed one of the "hung guns" by admiring cheerleaders. She hoped this Carly, whoever she was, wasn't targeting her baby brother for her own reasons.

But her first concern right now was their mother. "It's not that the test is killing her, Mike," his sister explained. "All the test can tell us is that her genes indicate that she is supposed to die on Christmas Day, and if they're right, that would have happened regardless of whether we knew it was coming or not. The shit of this whole thing is they can't say how it will happen. And like Dad says, maybe it won't happen."

Now, as Michael answered his family's questions about his life in Afghanistan, he wondered how long it would be before his mother would disclose what he had come halfway around the world to hear. He wanted to tell his parents the news of his impending transfer home, but he wanted to wait until after his mother had shared her tragic news. At last, he felt sure that his surprise would be the medicine his mother needed.

"So, I have some good news, guys! My unit is being rotated home. I'll be stateside this September. Should be here by the ninth if all goes as scheduled. I'll be getting some leave before I have to report back to Fort Hood in Texas. So get ready, folks, I'll definitely be in effect back in the 'ville!"

"We'll be sure and let the eligible women know, you dork." Michaela said as she jumped across the couch and put her arms around his neck. "It might even be nice to have you home for a change."

"That calls for another round!" Rod exclaimed as he headed to the refrigerator to grab some fresh Coors Lights.

Janet had been churning inside throughout their discussion. She had been completely taken off guard when Michael burst in so suddenly. She hadn't thought about how she was going to tell him about her death sentence. Now she wondered if his announcement might offer her a chance to put that off until he returned in September. She needed to think about that. Why tell him anything that could interfere with his judgment while he was still over there?

The internal struggle was pulling her apart. She was preoccupied and it showed.

Michael masked his disappointment. He had expected Janet to do cartwheels. Instead, seemingly distracted, she got up and left the room. She needed to be away from them, to think for a few minutes.

"I'll be right back. I need to go potty."

Michael looked at his sister with a quizzical expression on his face. "What's that all about?"

"I have no idea." Michaela was confused as well.

"No idea about what?" Rod asked as he returned, holding three fresh long necks.

"Nothing, Pop," his children answered in unison.

Chapter Twenty Nine

April 9, 2013, 12:37 p.m.
St. David's Roman Catholic Church Rectory
Oceanside, New York

T ed's depression was beating him up. He wasn't sleeping; waking nearly every hour on the hour, his mind preoccupied by the devastation of that battlefield long ago and the prospect of the utter darkness of the coffin waiting for him.

Now indifferent to the parishioners, his homilies had gone from simply weak to positively banal. He had also cut out his sisters. After Patty's visit in January, they'd promised to keep in close touch. They hadn't.

For her part, Patty had tried. She called every other day and e-mailed anything new she had found about the "God gene," as the media had dubbed it. Colleen tried to speak to him at least once a week as well, but he avoided the calls and if he returned them, it was always from his car or someplace where he could claim to be in a rush. He wanted distance. He knew he was deep in the throes of self-pity, but right now he felt he had earned that.

The morning visit to Sloan-Kettering wasn't encouraging. The doctor's worst suspicions had been confirmed by the biopsy reports. He had a large mass centered in the cortex of his brain, which was deemed inoperable. The deadly cancer was flourishing. It had grown since the initial MRI had exposed it only a short while ago. Dr.

Weitzman had said that he suspected it could be a very aggressive "incident," and had recommended radiation and chemotherapy immediately.

"Doctor, we both know my fate is sealed and my due date is on the calendar. So here are my questions. What is the prognosis? What happens to my quality of life? What care will I need as the cancer proliferates? In short, Doctor, what would you do in my place?"

The two men had walked out onto a terrace that adjoined the physicians' lounge. It was a sunny spring day, so they sat on chaise longues sipping their Starbucks. Weitzman promised an, blunt discussion of Ted's condition, the impossibility of surgery, and the hopes for treatment, under the caveat of making his recommendations based solely on medical reality. Ted understood the facts, but he was also dealing with his personal reality, and to him, the stress of cancer treatment, especially since it would not prolong his life, seemed pointless.

"Father, I'll be as brutally honest as I can, if that's what you're after." Zach said.

"Proceed, Doctor. I need to hear the truth. My time is limited, so I have none to waste."

Zach looked directly at the priest. "Here's the deal, then. The protocol for this treatment is rough. Very rough. We'd need you here for several days at a time because the treatments will kick your ass. There will be a loss of strength, weight and energy. The degree of sickness from side effects will intensify as treatments go on, and your physical decline will be noticeable."

"I've witnessed chemo and radiation with my parents, Doctor, so I know what to expect. It's not pretty, but in all likelihood I am going to accept the protocol. There is always hope as long as there is life," Father Ted said.

Weitzman nodded. "The quality of life question is difficult to answer. You appear to be very robust and you should be able to go for a considerable length of time without any dependence on supporting care. How long is hard to say until we get into the actual treatment."

Zach put his unfinished coffee on the table. "The sessions would be anywhere from four to six days here at Sloan. Aside from that, and from what I've told you to expect in terms of physical decline, you should enjoy normal activity. How full that will be or how long is subject to your physical reaction to the protocol."

The priest nodded. "How much time do I really have, Doc?"

Zach felt his stomach tighten. He was never comfortable answering this question. He was a superb oncologist. But like all physicians, he relied upon the protocols administered to cancer patients and each of those had a field of expectations assigned to them. Most doctors avoided making predictions, as it was better to not set expectations that could vary widely during treatment. He liked Father Ted right from the beginning, respected his seemingly gentle nature, suspecting that beneath the quiet exterior lay a steely resolution that made him strong.

"My opinion is that you will probably see somewhere from six to nine months. Six months if we can't control the tumor, possibly less if it grows. But whatever the treatment, your cancer, unfortunately, is terminal."

Ted rose from the chaise longue to throw away his drained coffee cup. Then he turned back to Zach. "How long before I become bedridden? I have no family nearby and I am not sure what my status as an employed priest will be. So I need to consider my care requirements."

"What do you mean your status as an employed priest is in question?"

Hayslip wore a sardonic smile as he returned to his seat. "My diocese is quite upset with me for participating in this study and I could lose my privileges as a priest."

Zach looked shocked. Father Ted smiled ruefully at the doctor's reaction. "I know. Ever since the draft card burnings in the '60s, they've cracked down on clergy joining the picket lines or getting involved in anything that's embarrassing to the Church. It's mostly political self-preservation, but as they say, Doc, them's the rules."

Zach sipped his coffee and then spoke his mind. "Believe me,

Father, I understand. My parents are Hasidic Jews and have lived for years in the same house in Brooklyn originally occupied by my great-grandparents. They're planning to move to Florida if my name is publicized in connection with this so called 'God gene' scandal. They would be refused service at the local stores if their community found out. Incredible!"

Zach's dismay had turned to anger now. "What is it about religions that they have to be a hundred percent right about differences of opinion? Why the hell is everything with them either black or white? Most of the world is gray. Can't they see that? Hello? Wake up, people. This is 2013, not biblical times. Ugh! I'm so sorry, Father."

"I wish I understood why," Ted said. "In my case, it's this one Church lawyer who is the zealot chasing me. My name isn't even out there and you guys are keeping it that way, so why come after me?" Ted made no attempt to hide his annoyance. "But this lawyer is a monsignor and was part of the legal team that defended the Church back in the '90s when they had those sex scandals up in Boston. What they learned was that a cover-up can do more damage than the actual scandal, and now everyone walks on a tightrope over anything that could become public. Lucky me, eh?"

Zach shook his head. "Whether you'll be bedridden will depend on your level of health and strength from this point. But I'd say you'll probably be ambulatory through the summer and into the fall. As you get into the last few weeks, you'll need assistance. As for as nursing care, let me speak with Doctor Russo and see what the lab can provide. There may be some help we can offer. I'll let you know. You'll have no issues with obtaining all you'll need, Father."

The thought now in Zach's mind was that he would find a way to help this unfortunate priest even if he had to dig into his own pocket. But he doubted Russo would allow the situation to get to that point.

"Thanks, Doctor. I appreciate your honesty. Now what?"

"Let's get you scheduled for treatment next week. Please call me any time with questions."

Ted scanned the rooftops surrounding them on the terrace as

he let out an audible sigh. "One thing you didn't answer, Doc. What would you do in my place?" Ted continued to gaze skyward.

Zach stared at the priest he had known for just a short time. His intuition told him that this very kind man needed a friend. "If it was me, Father, I would move in two directions while I still had time. First, and as quickly as I could, I would lose my luggage. We all carry luggage around with us all day. Sometimes we don't even know how it got there. But these bags get tied to us and we end up carrying them forever. It makes no sense to keep dragging what weighs us down." Ted turned to Zach as the doctor continued. "Our faiths, both of our faiths, teach us that life ever after is our redemption. But what about our life on earth? Shouldn't we get to feel redeemed by that? How do we free the soul we live with each day? Shed the luggage. That's first on the list."

Now Zach walked over to deposit his still-full coffee cup into the trash. He turned and faced Ted as he spoke again. "Then I'd make sure that those I love most in this life know how much I love them. If it were me, I'd think the worst thing I could do would be to leave this earth without letting those I care about understand how much I love them. For that, they need to hear from me whatever my truth may be. Good relationships or bad. Those are the two things I'd do, Father." Zach sat back down.

Ted smiled. "Have you ever considered getting into my business, Doctor? You're good. Very good."

"Oy! God help us all if I did. But hey, every good Jew considers himself a rabbi first and something else second."

———— ⬥((◉))⬥ ————

When he walked through the front door of the rectory, Ted went directly to the table where the personal mail was left. There were several messages including a note asking him to call Father Schmidt's room when he got in. Leafing through the mail, he came upon a letter from the bishop's office. He quickly opened it and found the formal notice of the disciplinary board hearing. The letter stated that he was to be at the board hearing on June 30th at 10am, and to bring along any relevant documents or materials. The letter was copied to Father Schmidt, which told Ted what Schmidt's message was likely to be about.

Father Ted left the rest of the mail on the table and went to his room to call his pastor. As he did, he stuck the letter in his back pocket and muttered to himself,

"This is luggage that needs to be shed."

Chapter Thirty

April 9, 2013, 5:31 a.m.
35 Sunnyfield Lane
Hicksville, New York

The weekend had gone by in a flash. Rod, Janet and Michaela canceled their Monday plans so they could spend their last few precious hours together with Michael.

The night before, Michael had invited some of his friends round and they'd managed to clear out all of the beer in the house and a few extra six packs besides. Michael and Michaela were glad for the distraction of friends, as they had both been waiting anxiously for Janet to tell Michael what she was hiding from him. But she never had. The tension in their home was palpable.

Now, as Michaela and Janet were in the kitchen before dawn to put breakfast out for Michael before he left, they were circling the elephant in the room. Each of them could feel what hadn't been said, but none of them would take the first step. Only Janet had that right, and she wasn't talking.

Michael decided he had to share his secret with his family. He'd been bursting to tell them and had been patient long enough. "Mick, you know how you're always asking me if there are any female camels over there sniffing under my tent? Well, it turns out there is one."

Janet went on alert. Michaela, too, had a premonition about what

Michael was about to say. She had no idea that her mother had the same feeling.

"I have kind of hooked up with this girl over there who's in my outfit. She's from Virginia. Her name's Carly Hoffer. And, well, she's going to be joining the family soon. We're getting married when we ship back to the States."

Janet would look back on that moment as an out-of-body experience. She would see the crooked grin on Michael's face, hear his words as if they were on a record played at half speed, each and every syllable slowly dripping out as if muddy crude oil were draining from a can with a pinhole in it. She would remember the wide-eyed dismay on Michaela's face and the blank stare from Rod, as if he had lost his hearing and couldn't transmit the words that hung in the air to his brain. She would also recall with perfect clarity how quickly the discussion descended into a dark morass and then escalated to one of those moments in life that you can never truly explain. You just know life has changed forever.

Before either Janet or Rod could answer, Michaela recalled her suspicions as they drove home from the airport. "Excuse me. Is this the same Carly who also happens to be your platoon leader and is so helpful to you?"

"Yeah, sis. How'd you guess? She's great. Wait till you meet her. You guys are gonna get along great." Michael, overjoyed at sharing his news, didn't see the storm clouds gathering.

"How is it that you can be 'hooked up' with your platoon leader? Isn't she much older than you?" Janet was trying to keep herself in check.

"She's thirty-one Mom, but that's got nothing to do with it," Michael blithely replied.

Janet proceeded with steel in her voice. "Nothing to do with it? You're nineteen. It has a lot to do with it. How long has this been going on? Why would this person be interested in you in the first place? If she is your platoon leader, isn't that kind of like the rat watching the cheese? She's supposed to be looking out for you, not looking out for herself." Janet felt trapped and threatened. Someone seven thousand miles away held sway with her cub. Her neediest and youngest cub. She would claw back with every ounce of her being if need be. No quarter should be expected by this woman because none would be given.

"You have it all wrong, Mom. Carly's a great person. She's gotten her GED and two years of college while she's been in the Army and she's been promoted to staff. She's got fourteen years in and she's getting out in November. That's when we're planning the wedding. She's good people, Mom. You're gonna love her. I know I do."

"What would you know about love?" Janet erupted as she leaped from her chair. "You're barely out of high school. And why did this Carly need a GED in the first place? Fourteen years in the Army at her age? That means she was in the Army at what, seventeen? I don't like the sound of this at all."

Michael realized he had badly misjudged how his news would be received, but he still kept trying. "Hold on now. Don't be making any snap judgments here, folks. I'm not a kid anymore and you have no right to damn a person you don't even know."

His mother was spitting fire now. "No one is damning anyone. You have to finish your time in the Army and what about going to college and becoming a cop? That's a long road in front of you."

Michaela and Rod remained silent as Janet held the floor. Rod knew he wouldn't be able hold his wife back. Michaela agreed with her mother and thought her sibling was very much a wide-eyed school boy, vulnerable and emotional.

"Why not? Just because I'm married doesn't mean I can't go to school," Michael said as he looked at his father for support. But he saw there was none. Michael was on his own.

Janet knew she had to put her foot down, and immediately. "I'm sorry, Michael, but this whole thing sounds ridiculous and immature. You need to rethink this. I know you must be lonely over there and this woman has probably had her eye on you, but this has to stop right here."

Michael didn't back off. The discussion fell into one of those dark holes, where all sides remain resolutely convinced of their position.

At the moment when they were feeling more alienated than ever, Janet drew her sword. "Well, I have some news for you too, young man. I am dying. On Christmas Day I am going to pass over, they tell me. I've slaved every day of my life for you and I think that as your mother I had a right to hear that you were seeing someone before giving us this news. I think your father and I have at least earned the courtesy and that respect. We are owed something, Michael. Thank you very much for throwing our lives out of the window."

"Mom! I already know" Janet was speechless as Michael continued. "That's why I came home. I'm sorry you're upset but I thought this would make you feel better. That it would show I'm settling down and taking life seriously, that I'm planning my future."

"How did you know?" Janet's voice was so cold that Michael knew if he chose to, he could take his sister down with him right now. "That's not important."

"Well, regardless of what you think you know, here is something you don't know, obviously. You are not emotionally prepared nor are you mature enough to handle marriage. You are nineteen. Still a child. This woman is taking advantage of you. I doubt she will go through with it unless she's blind or stupid.. Now I want you to think this over carefully on the trip back. You'll see that what we're telling you is for your own good. Michael, don't do this. You'll be sorry. Do you hear me? Sorry!"

Michael glared at his mother. He could sense there was to be no compromise or negotiation.

No one spoke, but Janet's her heart and soul were raging. Caught completely off-guard, she felt like a defenseless animal about to be slaughtered. She wanted to grab her son and wrestle him to the floor, tie him up, keep him home. She felt as though she was fighting for his life. She had kept watch over him from the instant of his birth as a mother timber wolf guards her cubs in the wilderness. Janet could feel danger, but her confidence in her ability to protect him had been shattered by his revelation. There was something more, some other doom, she felt. This feeling of dread had started during her Christmas Day phone call with Michael. She had always known she was overprotective, but something else was pulling at her now.

What Michael saw was only coldness, darkness. He knew he had to leave. "Sorry? No, you're the ones who'll be sorry. I'm out of here. Dad will you drive me? I don't want to miss my plane. Bye, everyone. It's been real."

Chapter Thirty One

April 9, 2013, 10:25 p.m.
Reese Public Housing, Building Four, Unit 102
Middle Island, New York

"Twins? Did you say twins? Oh my God. Twins?" That was all Sharona could remember about the afternoon meeting when her obstetrician confirmed her pregnancy. It was still way too early to be able to know the sexes, but the doctor had given her the delivery date at around December 28th.

The doctor wanted to be able to adjust the date and, since she had also spoken with Dr. Guitton, she understood the need for accuracy. She assured Sharona they would be able to schedule her delivery by cesarean section before Christmas if necessary.

Sharona called Deke at work while she waited for a taxi to take her home. "Yeah, that's what I said, Deke. Twins. We will have two more mouths to feed, so you better be going for all the overtime you can get!" She had tried to sound giddy, but ambivalence was beginning to dampen her optimism.

"Takes a real man to make twins, girl. You sure got lucky with me," he teased.

Then she heard him shout to his boss, "Tommy, Sharona be packing two cakes in the oven! She's having twins. Yeah, I know about that." Deke chuckled as he spoke to her again. "Damn. Tommy said to tell you he knew you was good stock first time he laid eyes on you." She could hear several voices in the background, but it was hard to tell what anyone was saying with all the other noise accompanying a busy afternoon at the tire shop.

"That's great, Shoney. I knew you could do this, baby. I'm real happy. What Gran say? And how you like this doctor?"

"I haven't called Gran. She said she would stop by on the way home from work today. The doc's OK. She talked about delivering the babies before …" And the reality came back. She choked on her words and started crying softly.

Deke was alarmed. "What's wrong, baby? What happened? You OK?" And then it struck him, too. This was the first time she'd had to say aloud that the children growing inside of her were going to be orphaned soon after their birth.

"I got to go, Deke. My taxi's here. Be on time tonight," she said and rang off.

But he wasn't on time. He was hours late. When he hadn't shown up by nine, she covered the plate of food she had set out for him, put it in the microwave, and went to bed. She was exhausted. She had taken a sick day from the store, but she wondered how much longer she could keep working while carrying her babies.

Earlier that evening, Gran had stopped by. She looked drawn and fatigued. As she went to the kitchen to get herself some tea, she mentioned how sore her back felt, and said she didn't know how much longer she could keep changing hospital beds. But her spirit brightened immediately at Sharona's news. "Lord, Sharona, you don't do anything lightly! Twins. Well that's twice the blessing, isn't it? Ain't that a miracle? Two babies at the same time. I can't recollect anytime there ever been twins born in this family."

They talked about the delivery and the potential for a cesarean, but Gran saw that Sharona had become listless. She knew her granddaughter had reservations about parenting and, even more so, about security for her children.

Sharona recognized that Deke was still a work in progress. He was taking online courses at Empire State College, but because he worked full-time, he was at least four to five years away from a degree. Sharona believed his heart when he pledged his love and loyalty, but she didn't know if she trusted him enough to put one child in his care, much less twins.

"Child, I know what you thinking about now. How these babies going to be cared for with a con for a father and an old slappy mammy like me for the woman of the house."

"No, Gran, that's …" Sharona started to protest, but her grandmother cut her off.

"Girl, don't you lie to me. I know what you been sitting here thinking about all day. Tell you the truth, if you wasn't, I'd be surprised, so don't even bother saying you're not."

The old woman pointed her finger at Sharona. "Now you listen here, Shoney. The Lord ain't going to let you down. He done sent you the,things in your life that you always needed, didn't he? You got your health, you got your man, you got a roof over your head and you got food on your table. Now count your many blessings. You even got children coming to you. None of that is possible without the Lord's grace upon you. Don't you even think about feeling sorry for your situation."

"Gran, I'm going to die, maybe as soon as my babies get born. They'll be orphans from their birth. How you expect me to feel? I ain't got no money to leave them. It's for sure nobody's gonna give them any and how is Deke going to raise two babies? He don't know nothing about babies. Shoot. I don't know nothing to even teach him."

"I know whatever Deke needs to know about babies, Shoney," Gran shot back defiantly. "I sure took care of my share of them across the years. I'll be right here and your babies will be taken care of, Sharona. They'll never be dirty and they will never have a hungry moment long as I am on this earth."

There was a pregnant pause while the obvious question settled in on Sharona. Her face showed she was sulking, and Gran would have none of that. "I hear what you thinking, girl. How long this old coot be hanging around? Well, never you mind about that. I imagine

I'll be like a new person once I get them little angels in my arms. So you don't fret about that. I been thinking about ending my job at the hospital and taking my Social Security anyways. December be a good time to start."

Sharona threw her hands up. "And where will they be raised? Here in the projects like me? Gran, I want my babies to have their own house, not some public assistance hole in the wall with bars on the windows and junkies shooting up in the parking lots. I want them to be able to go to college and get somewhere. How's that going to happen?"

Gran answered first with a furrowed brow, followed by a forged-steel voice. "Sharona, don't you be making judgments about your children's character before they're even born. You thinking that if they don't have all the things that you never had that they'll have a bad life. That just ain't true. They'll have the same opportunity to get an education that anybody else has. And this country is opening up more and more to colored folks. It ain't like it was when you was coming up or, Lord knows, when I was coming up. Shoot, I had an aunt when I was a child was born in slavery and run away to freedom. That's in the past, honey."

Sharona couldn't help it. She burst into tears. "Gran, I'm so scared for these babies. How do I know how Deke will turn out? He should have walked in that door a half hour ago and he didn't. I know he's trying hard, but he's a man, Gran, and sometimes he's just a fool. How can I leave these two babies here not knowing how their father will take care of them?"

"Baby girl, I been telling you all my life you got to let go and let God. If you trust in the Lord, the Lord will never abandon you."

"I know you believe that, Gran. I'm trying. I'm trying."

Later, Sharona had fallen into a fitful and restless sleep. She heard the tumblers in the deadbolt on the front door and sat up in bed to watch the door as it opened. She glanced quickly at the digital clock; it was ten thirty-five. She could see beyond Deke as he opened the door; a car was pulling away after dropping him off.

"Where you been, Deke? Why didn't you call me? I been worried all night something happened to you."

"I'm sorry, baby. My phone's dead. I forgot to charge it. The boys at the shop took me out for a drink to celebrate the good news about the babies and then Nicky came by the bar, and we got to talking, and next thing I know it's almost ten. I'm sorry, Sharona. I should have come home right away. How you feeling, little mama?"

"Don't be thinking you'll be playing with me, Deke. And I might have guessed that Nicky was involved. His phone dead too?"

"Hey, Nicky didn't do nothing but sing your praises all night. Telling all the guys from the shop they should meet you and see how I 'outkicked my coverage,' he says."

"Is this how you'll be after the babies are born, Deke? Coming in here with wine breath?"

"Baby, I had one wine and then went to water. One. I swear. And that wine mostly sat on the bar till it was all warm and shit. Sharona, when will you believe me when I say I'm changing? I told you I'm sorry about tonight. I know I should have come home straight from work. I'm sorry, baby. Now tell me all about the doctor's meeting. They boys?"

"Don't be no fool. They too young to tell yet." He saw her smile. " Besides. I'm going back to sleep. If you'd been here when I fixed your dinner, I was ready to tell you all about the babies. Now you can wait 'til morning. Goodnight."

"Yeah, that's all right, Watts. I'll be here in the morning. Just like I'll be here every morning. Forever. Twins. Man, ain't that something," he shook his head, smiling broadly, as he quietly closed the bedroom door.

He stepped into the tiny living room and began to think about his conversation with Nicky earlier that night. He had already realized that his finances fell far short of the task of raising his new family with anything approaching comfort or style, let alone security. For an unskilled laborer, steady work was scarce and badly paid. He had hinted to Nicky that perhaps he could be of some use in his friend's nefarious endeavors

Nicky didn't warm to the idea. He told Deke to keep at the

computer courses, but added that he always could be counted on for help. Nicky made a habit of keeping his affairs to himself and Deke had no idea how Nicky was moving away from the darker side of earning his living. Nicky, like Deke, was leaving his former life behind. Deke wasn't sure exactly what Nicky meant, but he knew his old friend had means. He was also surprised that Nicky was pushing him toward the education that Deke was chasing. Maybe Nicky was getting soft.

Sharona was trying to go back to sleep, but her head was filled with the same worries. Gran hadn't convinced her that God would provide. She was asking herself a different kind of question now: Should she even go ahead with this pregnancy? It was still early and even though she wanted the children, she also believed they should come into a world where they stood a solid chance of succeeding. She wasn't going to be there to make that happen. Who would? An ex-con with a good heart? An aging grandmother with good intentions?

Was that the best she could offer her unborn children?

Who if not her? Who but her?

Chapter Thirty Two

April 12, 2013, 9:25 a.m.
35 Sunnyfield Lane
Hicksville, New York

It had been yet another restless night. Janet had felt Rod get up at about two. When he didn't return to bed, she went to find him on the sofa in the living room, sitting in the darkness. When she asked him if he needed something, he responded, "I need to have my son home."

"I know." She dropped into a chair and began weeping quietly. "I'm sorry, Rod. I'm so afraid for him that sometimes I feel like I can't breathe. He's just a little boy." She put her face in her hands and sobbed.

Rod remained quiet, lost in his own thoughts. What he was thinking wasn't going to help her. His fears went way beyond the news that Michael intended to marry.

Since Michael had stormed out, none of the family had been doing well. Michaela had followed Michael that morning out to the car and tried to get him to listen to her.

He refused. "Mick, just let me go. I'm sorry that none of you approve of my life, but that's how it's gonna be. See you in September." And he slammed the door of his father's car.

Janet had kissed him on the cheek as he left, but Michael offered no reaction. "Be careful," was all she could say.

"Yep, that's me, Mister Careful," he had muttered as he lifted his duffle bag and turned to leave. They were both still angry.

As Rod and Michael had driven away, Michaela was already in her room, her door locked. Janet sat at the dining room table and tried to make sense of what had just happened. At first, she thought Michael was being stubborn and selfish. But she knew that wasn't in his character. The truth was that he probably had some real feelings for this woman. What he was defending was very real to him. But Janet was paranoid about keeping her son safe. From everything. How on earth, she thought, do mothers ever let their children go?

The phone rang and the caller ID told her it was Rod's cell phone. Janet punched the talk button. "Hi Mom, I'm sorry. I shouldn't have dropped this news on you with no notice at all. I know this all seems sudden to you. But I thought maybe I could cheer you up if you knew I was coming home and getting married."

"Michael, I am thrilled that you'll be home soon and I want you to find a nice girl and get married. But you are still so young, and this has all happened so quickly, honey. I just want you to be happy and do the things in life that you've set out to do. We want you to find your future, Michael."

"I understand that, Mom. I do. I was going to introduce you to Carly on a Skype call, but when I found out about you and had to come home so quickly, we decided to wait. That was probably a mistake. So as soon as I get back, I'll set it up and you can get to at least see her and talk a bit. It's a start. OK? Mom, I need for you guys to be with me on this. If it has any chance at all, no matter if it's right or wrong, if we aren't all together on it, it can't work, Mom."

"I agree. Your suggestion's a good start. How about we at least see what she looks like before we start arguing over this whole thing. The Skype call is a good idea, honey. Deal?"

"Deal. And, Mom, I didn't mean any of the things I said to you guys this morning. Too much beer last night."

"Me neither, Michael. I just hate it that you had to leave. It got the better of me. I miss you so."

"I miss you, too. Tell Mickey I said I'm sorry, and I'm a dork, and that I love her and I'll call you when I get back to the base."

"Travel safe, Michael. Be careful," Janet said in a hush. And then she added, "Thanks for the call." But Michael had already hung up.

Afterward, Janet sat there, her anxiety building. She told herself it was because they'd argued, but deep inside she knew that somehow the connection she had with Michael was being disrupted. And she prayed it was only over a girl.

Tonight, nearly two days since Michael had left, Janet and Rod were fretting over why they hadn't heard from him, as he had promised. They were both starting to realize and to accept that Michael was growing beyond their boundaries. He had been a schoolboy only a year before, and his move outside their nest had happened so suddenly.

Janet felt nauseous. Her stomach was doing flips. She headed to the bathroom. Just as she closed the door behind her, the phone rang and she heard Rod call out that he'd get it.

"Excuse me? Yes, this is Mister Bates. Yes. Yes, I am at home. What is this about, may I ask? Excuse me? When? Are you certain? Is there any possibility there could be an error? Yes, we'd appreciate that. Yes we'll be here. Thank you."

Janet heard the conversation as she walked back down the hallway on her way to the living room. The tone of Rod's voice told her it was desperate news. Then she heard it. A guttural, tortured roar broke out of him.

In an instant, she was in the room. Rod was standing in front of the window, his right hand pulling at his hair, the phone still in his left. He turned to Janet as she entered, his face contorted in despair. Janet saw no life at all in his eyes.

She knew what he was going to tell her and in that instant she felt something she later realized was spiritual separation. It was a sensation of disconnection and going to some faraway place. The universe was claiming some piece of her and she would remain, for the rest of her life, less than she was before this moment.

"He's gone." Rod's voice was barely audible. "Our son is dead. He was killed yesterday by a roadside bomb on his way back to the base. He and two others. He's gone, Janet. The Army has a representative coming to see us now. They should be here within a half hour and asked if I wanted to alert our church. I didn't know what to say." Rod fell to his knees. Janet collapsed beside him on the floor, throwing her arms around him. The two of them clung to each other helplessly, lost in grief. Then Rod jumped up, ran to the sink and began retching.

Janet stayed on her knees. Alone. Between his sobs she heard him pour out his soul. For the first time ever, she knew she was seeing deeply inside him to the emotions of the man she loved.

"He didn't belong there, Jan. I did this. I should have kept him home like you wanted. What was I thinking? I wanted him to earn a living? Look what that got him! Jan, I'm so sorry. If you never forgive me, I wouldn't blame you. Oh my God! Our boy. Our precious little boy is gone. What will we do? Oh, Michael, I'm so sorry, son. I'm so sorry I let you go." He turned back to the sink, heaving.

Deep in her own grief, Janet couldn't help him. But then her thoughts moved to their other child. She had to reach Michaela as soon as possible. Mickey had stayed at her friend's house the night before and was going straight to her part-time job this morning.

Janet stood up and went to Rod and leaned across his back. "We need to pull it together now, honey. Michaela's going to need us to be her strength."

"I know. I know. Oh, God. What have I ever done to deserve this? Why Michael? Why you? Why?"

There was no answer, of course. Janet knew this.

Michael was gone. She knew it. She had been feeling it for months; she recognized that at this moment. Now she needed to protect her other child. And somehow, even in her overwhelming sadness, she clung to Rod and realized that perhaps she had never known his true depth.

As she saw Rod, and later Michaela, and Kathy, in the depths of their shared grief, she realized that she had been so focused on herself that she had failed to understand her family's love for one another and for her. What was happening to her was also happening to them. She wasn't dying alone. The sudden loss of a loved one reminds us that we do often take the blessings of our family's love for granted. We assume that other person will always be there. When we lose him, we come to know how ill-prepared we are for his loss and what that is going to do to our hearts and souls. Michael's death propelled Janet back into her life. The circle of her love had been interrupted, but tragically, it had been completed.

Chapter Thirty Three

June 28, 2012, 2:45 a.m.
Aboard Lady Katy,
41.2 degrees north latitude
71.2 degrees west longitude
Long Island Sound

There are days when the tropics visit the Northeast's summers. The temperature climbs above ninety and the humidity crowds the air's saturation point, forming a glare. The sodden daylight looks as though it could be sliced with a knife. The unforgiving sun beats into submission every form of life under its powerful gaze. Those who can, move into air-cooled structures. Others crowd the shores surrounding ocean waters, seeking relief.

Together with those languid days come the soft summer winds that follow the sunsets, when the ocean breeze, traveling above the great Atlantic Gulf Stream, makes a majestic arch east of Montauk Point, kissing the shores of America farewell before it heads to Europe. This provides some of the best nighttime sailing found anywhere in the hemisphere.

On such a night in late June, more than two months since he and Kate had spoken, Dan Brannigan watched the western sky surrender its palette of color to the distant horizon. Dan left Colcroft House as darkness settled, and drove to the nearby Seawanhaka Yacht Club, where his sloop, *Lady Katy*, had been brought by the dock crew from its moorings and made ready.

The moon had risen full that evening, after passing the summer solstice. That was significant, as he would be sailing a course to the spot he had selected just off the northern tip of Long Island at Orient Point. There, after setting his auto-pilot on a course north-northeast, he would drop overboard into the dark, cool waters of the Sound while the sloop continued its journey. After he tired of swimming, he'd be drawn under the soft, moonlit sea and taken peacefully to his death.

As he sat in the cockpit and gazed out at the reflected light shining upon the glittering sea, he went through the litany of the unforgivable pain he had inflicted on Kate. The sloop bloused her sails in full array, caught the prevailing winds from the south, and kept time with the roll of the sea while he made his last confession.

There wasn't any point waiting for the finale, Dan thought. He had gone ahead and signed his will and had left a note in the glove box of his car, now parked at the yacht club. Before he went overboard, he would text Kate a simple phrase, "glove box."

Earlier in the week, he'd had lunch with Russo. Tod had asked him for a get-together and Dan agreed to meet at Piping Rock Country Club, where they were members. Russo had been alarmed by the slide in Dan's spirits and wanted to help his friend. He was appalled when Dan confided that dying might turn out to be the most merciful thing that could happen to him, saying, "And the sooner the better."

"Dan, nothing could be that bad," Russo countered.

"Kate's left me, Doc. I can't go into the reasons why, but she had good cause. I earned her hatred and it's out of my hands. But I have to live the remainder of my life knowing that I broke her heart, and believe me, Tod, death seems better." As Dan finished, his voice choked and his eyes began to water.

Russo dropped his voice to a whisper so no one could overhear. He felt powerless to offer any consolation. He knew how devoted Dan was to Kate, and she to him. He couldn't imagine they would split up. "Dan, can't this be worked out?"

Dan glanced past his friend to the lush golf course, and reached for a water glass.

"I don't expect so, Tod. I really dug a knife into her heart. She gave me her love, and her trust, and all I did was abuse it. I'm in hell without her, Tod. You know, when you first told me what I was facing and I blew up, it was Kate who brought me back. She made me want to use my time left in the best way I could. It's like being at the theater, at intermission before the last act is about to start. If it's been a good show, you're glad to go to your seat but if it's been a stinker, you dread it. In my case, it had been a good show, but now if Kate's gone, it's a stinker."

Silently, Dan finished his thought to himself: and I can't wait for the final curtain.

⊷«(○)»⊶

The sea was at a two-foot swell and the sloop took each roll with confidence, moving silently to Dan's appointment with his fate. He had long ago passed the bright glare he recognized along the North Shore of Long Island, and he now saw the lights of Orient fading from view to his right. He had arrived at his watery grave.

Dan was content with what he was about to do. He and Kate had built a close family bond of parents, children and grandchildren. Their breakup would shatter that. If he was lost at sea, his legacy would remain. Kate would never reveal to the family what had brought him to that point.

He wanted them to have his wealth. But more important than that, he wanted them to stay together as the family he and Kate had created. Avoiding an ugly divorce was the only way. He owed that to Kate and he was about to surrender himself to what he considered a final act of love.

He reached into the knapsack to find his cellphone so he could send Kate his final message. He turned it on and waited for a signal.

In an instant, the cell phone began to buzz with the messages that had been waiting over the last few hours. As compulsive as ever, Dan waited for them to finish and he read with little interest. Among the list of names on his screen were two of his daughters. Allie's message began, "*You won't believe who we ...*" Diane, meanwhile, had sent some flight times for her summer visit. Dan's eyes filled. He gazed wistfully at the rolling sea and the moonlight glimmering on the water, which lit the course for his boat.

Then he felt a single buzz, which told him there was a newly sent text.

Dan's hand trembled. He sat looking at the screen and read the first few words for more than a minute until he was able to punch through to the full message: *be home in the morning keep house empty lot to talk bout need say many things first — still angry second — still a team third — am sorry more morrow luv k.*"

Through tears, Dan reversed his course. The moon, no longer behind him, illuminated the path ahead. It was as if he was cruising down a shimmering highway. The *Lady Katy* stretched her sails before him into the wind.

Chapter Thirty Four

June 29, 2013, 10:22 a.m.
US Airways terminal,
Pittsburgh International Airport
Pittsburgh, Pennsylvania

The wheels kissed the runway exactly as scheduled and the plane arrived at its gate three minutes before its arrival time. The flight from LaGuardia had been uneventful and Father Ted had actually dozed off after downing his complimentary coffee and plastic-tasting biscuit.

He moved quickly through the airport, boarded an Avis shuttle bus, and picked up his rented Ford Focus. His Google map showed the drive to his destination was thirty-eight miles.

In an hour, he would be keeping an appointment he'd made twenty two years ago in the desert of Kuwait with Lance Corporal Jason Bonnie, USMC.

He drove through the gates of Pinewood Cemetery and Memorial Park, slightly south of Zelienople, Pennsylvania, where the body of the only son of Durwood and Josephine Bonnie had been buried with full military honors. The casket had been sealed before it was shipped to Andrews Air Force Base in Maryland. The Bonnies could have had him interred in a grave provided by the military, but they wanted him at rest near their family home so they could visit often.

The parents never knew that their son's body was not whole. He had been decapitated by his murderers and his head had never been recovered. The military presumed it had been destroyed or buried in some long lost location by the bloody soldiers under Saddam Hussein's command.

Father Ted's memory of February 1991 was crystal clear. He had been sullen and disconsolate in Germany while the nurses and doctors tried to coax a positive outlook from him, trying to sell him on the miraculous prosthetic devices available. Everything they described about his recovery and treatment he was going to find miraculous.

It was bullshit, he thought.

He had been told the commanding officer of the hospital would be visiting at some point and would fill him in on the exact circumstances of his injury.

More bullshit.

He'd tried to make contact with his unit to see what their status was, but that, he was told, was now classified. Only the commanding officer could release information to him.

Bullshit again.

On his fourth day in Bullshit World, he saw a phalanx of Army brass coming down the hallway as he sat on his bed, which had been pushed outside of his room while the doctor was performing a procedure on the trooper in the next bed. As the brass hat got closer, Ted was surprised this crisp-looking commanding general was so young. Ted thought he might be under forty, although he probably wasn't. He had light gray eyes and a trim body, and he sported a buzzed haircut . He looked like a baseball rookie as he halted in front of Hayslip.

"I'm Glenn Barrett, Father, and I owe you an apology. I should have been here when you woke up, but I was on duty that night at my wife's bedside. We now have a son named Glenn, like his daddy." Taken aback by the general's casual familiarity, Hayslip said the first thing that came into his head. "Congratulations. Is this your first?" Then before Barrett could reply, he added, "I've been here four days."

He hadn't meant to sound like he was scolding.

"Actually, he's our fifth. We have three girls and now two boys. And please call me Glenn." He reached his hand back to one of the three other officers who stood behind him. A woman with captain's bars handed the general a chart. "Yes, this is your fourth day under our hospitality, Father. So even though Marines like you deserve better, nothing keeps the Army from practicing its favorite thing—bullshit."

Hayslip was starting to like this guy, despite the depths of his depression. "Now, Father, you and I are going to go down to the solarium at the end of the hallway and have a long discussion about your case, so if Captain Moranda here will lend me a hand turning you, I think I can remember how to push a hospital bed. May I call you Ted?"

"I actually prefer Father, if you don't mind."

The young general laughed out loud and looked at the other officers, who also were smiling. "I don't blame you, Father. A title worth earning is one worth keeping. I hate being called 'doctor.' It sounds old. My wife hates me being called 'general.' So I'm always trying to get everyone to use my first name. Makes me think I'm cool."

Once they had reached the solarium, the general tried to convince Ted that the worst of his troubles would be behind him when he got back to the States. He pledged that his therapy would render him fully mobile and even fit for running.

After some time, Barrett sensed that Ted was losing interest, so he asked if he had any questions.

Father Ted asked him what he knew of the combat that had left him with one leg.

General Barrett's entire demeanor changed. Ted sensed that the general was uncomfortable as he described the action, and grew impatient listening to what he already knew. "General, what aren't you telling me?" he interrupted "I can tell you're hiding something."

The general's reply was immediate and forthright. "It hasn't been confirmed fully, but we think this was friendly fire. But the truth may never be known."

Father Ted just shook his head in disbelief. "Would this have any bearing whatsoever on my case?" he finally said.

"Not really. There was one fatality among your group, and that could get dicey, but the 'casualty of war' evidence here would rule any final disbursements for support issues, monetary considerations, etc. Friendly fire is not supposed to happen, but it does, and since we haven't figured a way to avoid wars, what chance do you think we'll have to avoid friendly fire?"

In the short time that Father Ted had been with this extraordinary young general and surgeon, he had grown confident that the man was speaking to him as an equal, not as a subordinate. He decided to take advantage of that and use the commanding officer's power to wrap up unfinished business. "Glenn, I need your help on something," he said. "I want to know where the unit I was attached to is now and how they're doing. I was about to do some work with a Marine lance corporal, and if there is any way, I'd like to alert his senior officers to a possible problem he may be dealing with before it becomes an issue. Is there any way you can assist? It's important; his continued presence in his outfit could be a danger to others."

"Sure, Father. I'll tell you what. Tell me the name of the Marine and his outfit again, and I'll see what I can do to get patched through to the C.O. out there myself. My rank will give me a better chance of getting someone on the horn quickly. I have some time this afternoon and I may be able to get something set up for you. If I do, I'll get them to call you here. How's that?"

The phone on Ted's nightstand rang the next morning as he was working on his scrambled eggs and coffee. He had to admit the chow was pretty good for a hospital as he picked up the receiver. "This is Captain Hayslip, how may I help you?" He reverted back to his military bearing, which felt as natural as it ever had to him.

"Good morning, Father. General Barrett here. I have Major Cleary of the Third/Second on the line. I believe you two already know each other, so I'll get off and you can proceed with what we talked about yesterday. I'll be up to see you a little later."

Hayslip did know the major, although they had never been too familiar with each other. Cleary was a no-nonsense, by-the-book Marine, with a reputation for strictly enforcing discipline. "Captain Hayslip, we're glad to hear you'll be recovering. Sure glad it wasn't any worse. We'll miss your services here. Now, what can I do for you, Captain? I understand from the general that you had some contact on twenty five February with Lance Corporal Bonnie of Third Platoon, Delta Company? I see your contact was not reported, from looking at Bonnie's jacket."

Father Hayslip felt the wrist slap. Chaplains were required to update jackets after any contact made with enlisted men, regardless of timing or circumstances. He ignored the reprimand. Instead, he explained that Bonnie had approached him in the field and had indicated a potential combat disorder.

Major Cleary listened as Ted told him about his concerns regarding Bonnie. Then he spoke directly. "Well, Captain, what I am about to tell you is classified, which means your disclosure or acknowledgement of this discussion outside of this venue could earn you a court martial. Is that clear, Captain?"

"Yes sir, perfectly clear." Ted was annoyed at the tone the major used, but decided to overlook it.

"Chaplain, I won't bother to read you the actual field reports, but Corporal Bonnie was captured on twenty five February while at his post. His weapon had not been fired, and what's even more strange, it was recovered intact at the scene of his capture. You know these people steal anything they can get their hands on. Bonnie's body was found about three quarters of a mile from where he had been posted. He was decapitated, but his head was not recovered and remains missing."

The rest of what Cleary said to Hayslip came in a blur, delivered in typical military jargon. Ted wasn't really absorbing it. All he could see was the face of Jason Bonnie, the terror in his eyes. Ted now recalled that fear in Jason Bonnie's eyes that morning in Kuwait when he reached out to his chaplain.

And Jason's chaplain had failed him.

Cleary was still speaking. "There was no other evidence of any physical struggle to the body. There was, however, a handwritten note attached to the protective jacket Bonnie was wearing. We got it translated. The usual hate messages. 'All Americans will die. Send us more Marines who are cowards and who wet their pants. See you all in hell. Send this child back to his mama.' I can go on, Captain," Cleary said, his voice now less rigid. "But the essentials here appear to be that Bonnie was on a forward listening post and somehow these cocksuckers got the drop on him. His platoon leader had posted him atop a two story building which became occupied by the enemy while Bonnie was on the roof. We have no way of knowing how he engaged the enemy, but in light of what you just told me, I suspect he froze. He was just a kid in his first real combat. Hell, he never once used his radio to alert anyone he was in trouble or that the goat eaters were in his ass."

Cleary hesitated for a second, as if pondering Bonnie's fate. "Putting two and two together, I think he must have tried to hide on the roof and was found. What a mess. Anyway, we sent an old gunny who stayed with the remains, which were sealed in his casket until they went into the ground, so his family wouldn't have to know exactly what happened to him. If it's any comfort, we believe that we probably caught up with the animals responsible. There were no survivors of that engagement. It's a shame you didn't have the opportunity to do more, Captain, but that's sometimes what we have to deal with here in the field."

Ted took Cleary's last comment as an offer of absolution. It was an offer he knew he wouldn't accept.

"Is there anything further, Captain?"

"No, sir. Nothing further. Oh, wait, excuse me, sir, where was Bonnie from?"

"Let's see here ... ah Zelionople, Pennsylvania. I'll spell that for you, Captain. I have his home address if you were thinking of writing his parents."

The major gave Hayslip the information. "Now, I don't need to remind you, Captain, that this information is military classified."

"I understand, Major. I doubt I will ever speak of this again until the day I die."

"I hear you, Captain. I hear you. Semper Fi."

The line went dead. As it did, a light in Ted's soul went out, too.

Now, on a June day all these years later he sat on a small stone bench. He could see the headstone, "Bonnie" carved in granite underneath a cross. Then he read:

Jason

Beloved Son

Born May 12, 1972

Died February 25, 1991

The grave wasn't as well-kept as some of the others nearby. The dirt was not fully covered by grass; in fact, it was mostly weeds. There were no flowers or plants.

Father Ted silently went through the prayers for the deceased and administered the Catholic rites for the dead. When he'd finished, he walked the few steps to the grave and placed his hand on the stone. " Jason, I'm so sorry for what happened to you," he said. "If I could live my life over, I would have taken you that day directly to your C.O. and had you relieved of duty. But I didn't. You see, Jason, you weren't the only one that day who didn't know what he was doing. I've been thinking about you ever since I learned what happened. You came to me because the war was a surprise to you and you didn't know what to expect when you got there. When you found out what it really meant, it repulsed you, and you knew you didn't belong there. My mistake was much the same. I didn't really understand what fear was in another person. You let yourself be captured and killed rather than do the thing that you feared the most—kill another human."

Ted paused a moment as he pondered his role in the tragedy. "And you came to me thinking I would know what to do. I let you down, Jason. I know that now. But here's the thing, Jason. War is not for people like us. I shouldn't have been there any more then you. You didn't have the experience and the knowledge to know what an enemy's death meant. I didn't have the experience or the knowledge to know you needed to be protected. And so the war took your life, and my heart and soul died right along with you. Until today. You see, Jason, you didn't live long enough to understand that you were a victim of a senseless war, but I have. I've had more than twenty years to figure out that we both died out there that day."

Ted's thoughts turned to his fate now as he continued speaking to the lost Marine. "I only have a short time left now, Jason, and soon we'll meet again. I've thought for all these years about you. Every day I offered Mass for you. I wish I could have been a better chaplain for you when you needed me. But I just wasn't, and there isn't anything I could do that would change that. I pray that you'll continue to rest in God's care and share in His kingdom and that you've forgiven me. I believe God welcomed you as a true believer because rather than kill another, you allowed him to kill you. Like our Lord Jesus, you gave yourself rather than accept something you couldn't believe in. It takes a very brave man to do such things, Jason. Semper Fidelis, my young friend."

Ted returned to the rental car and sat staring at the grave of the boy he had met in Kuwait who had changed the course of his life. It had taken him twenty two years to understand that he simply hadn't been qualified to look deeply enough into the soul of Jason Bonnie and save the boy from his fear. He could admit that to himself now.

Facing his own end soon, he had prayed for a release that would allow him to understand that not all things in our lives are possible. Sometimes the path we must walk isn't clear to us.

He smiled as he recalled how it was that his prayers were answered. It happened one day about a month ago, as he strolled along the boardwalk at Long Beach. He was saying the Lord's Prayer slowly and fervently to himself, "Thy kingdom come, thy will be done." And it had hit him. The words of Christianity's most often-repeated prayer held the key to his freedom from himself. "Thy will," he suddenly understood. "Not my will."

He stopped and stood there, absorbing the simplicity. This keystone of his faith had escaped him all this time. He shed his guilt.

What happened in Kuwait to both of them was God's will and he had failed to listen to the prayer had had said thousands of times since then. He was so consumed with his guilt, so closed to the rest of the world, he had forgotten that his faith could help him find peace.

"Rest in peace, Jason. I'll see you soon," he whispered, as turned the ignition and began his journey home.

Tomorrow was the Disciplinary Review Board.

He was ready. He was home.

Chapter Thirty Five

As Kate Brannigan turned her Jaguar through the gate and drove the length of the stone driveway, she saw Dan's car and felt a flush of anger. She quickly took a deep breath to suppress her emotions. It wasn't what had happened in the past that mattered now. She had a mission.

On the drive back from the Westhampton Beach house, where she had spent the last month, she'd contemplated the parts of her marriage that were forever damaged by Dan's confession. At the same time, she'd realized the role she had played. And then, finally, she brought the two realities together with a plan to salvage the love and purpose in her life in a way that was fair to everyone, but especially to her.

Kate had played it by the book every day of her life. Obviously, Dan had not. But still, she needed him in every way, just as she believed he needed her. Being separated from him brought her, for the first time, to a full understanding of what their life together had produced. After she had arrived at that conclusion, she could see their union wasn't perfect but that it was, at least for her, the life she would choose to live again. That meant Dan must be in her life. God help her, it meant she must be with Dan.

She entered the house and went to the solarium next to the kitchen, where she would usually find Dan reading *The New York Times.*

Sure enough, he was there, quietly waiting for her. He looked at her contemplatively as she walked toward him. Kate hadn't thought how she would act when she saw him again, so she did what she usually did. She acted naturally. She walked over to his chair and as he began to rise, she leaned over, said "Hi," and kissed him on his forehead.

"Hi, you look great. The tan looks good." Dan was able to get the words out, but he was flustered. He felt a bit like a condemned prisoner waiting for the judge's sentence. The message the previous night had sounded hopeful and conciliatory. More than he deserved, he thought.

Kate put her bag down on a chair. "Thanks. The sea did me a lot of good. There's a leak over the fireplace, by the way. You may want to get a roofer to look at it. I checked outside and it looks like a few shingles are missing."

"I hope that's the least of my cares, Kate."

"I know." She needed to take control of this now. "Dan, let me get this out without you interrupting me."

Dan remained silent and she began. "I love you, Dan. And I have been a good wife, a good partner, and a good mother to our children. I know this." She paused and let that sink in. "You love me. You've been a good husband most of our marriage, and a good father to our children. I know that, too."

Dan sensed that a storm cloud could burst over his head at any second.

Kate's anger started rising as she spoke. "Why the hell did you have to spoil that? Who did you think you were? Do you think you're some god-like superpower who can walk through this world entirely without consequences? Yeah, you screwed up. You cheated, lied, deceived, broke your vows, and you stole . My question to you is this, Dan: Why did I have to hear about it?"

Dan was about to answer, but she held her hand up to stop him. "I didn't need this crap, but you've dumped it all over me, Dan. I could have gone to my hundredth birthday and never missed it. Why did you have to share this? So you could cleanse yourself? Thanks a lot. I'm so glad I could help you out."

Kate's sarcasm was growing as she glared at him. He was startled that her focus seemed not to be on what he had done, but rather that he had confessed it. He hadn't expected that.

"I know you felt the need to unburden your soul, Dan, but the things you had to get off your chest landed on mine like a ton of bricks and I'm really angry at you for doing that to me. It ranks as the most selfish and inconsiderate thing you've ever done, and I will always be mad at you for that."

And here she drew in a sharp breath. "But, it's over and done with," she said. "You'll have to answer to a much higher power than me for those things you've done. I 'm not your judge. Having said that, I owe you an apology and I hope you'll forgive me."

When Dan heard Kate's apology coming, his first thought was that she was going to admit to an affair, too. But he was wrong.

"I'm sorry, Dan, for sending you to another woman. I'll never forgive Loretta for what she did to both me and my brother, but I understand now why you did it. I always knew that you were immature and ego-driven. Especially back when the girls were little and you were coming up in the world. What I didn't realize then was that you were also insecure and needy. I always thought your head was too swollen, and I still do. But back then, I thought your ego needed to be deflated and I deliberately tried to counterbalance it. I really thought that it would keep you from being a big-mouthed braggart. I never imagined it would make you want to degrade yourself and our marriage by being with another woman. But I now see I was wrong and I'm sorry I wasn't smarter. That was a very demanding time in my life with the girls all so young and close in age. I know we didn't have as much sex then as you may have wanted. But I'll take my share of the blame for not seeing you as the emotional equivalent of a teenage boy."

Kate's anger was draining away as she continued to talk. "Brannigan, you have been a wonderful person to share a life with. We've seen so many dreams come true. And in just about every way I can think of, you've made our world better. And, more than anyone, I've seen how generous and kind-spirited you've been. But now it turns out that money wasn't yours. I could never stand being a rich woman and now I feel as though I'll never be able to scrub away the stain of knowing it all rests on what you stole. I don't want you to confess to the Attorney General and go to jail, but you need to make this right."

But Kate wasn't finished. "Now, regarding what you did to my brother. That also needs to be fixed, Dan. I don't care how you do it, but he needs to be compensated for what he should have had. He was your partner. He trusted you and you deceived him.. Now you need to make good on that. I expect you to put that high on your to-do list. She looked down at her wedding ring now. "Then, finally, there's us."

Apprehension clutched at Dan. After listening to Kate this morning, he was in awe of her nobility. He hoped that would allow him to remain her husband.

"We've been husband and wife, lovers, parents, confidants, and partners all these years. I still love you for being the man I always wanted to marry. The father you've been to our children. The friend you've been to so many. The generous person you've been to the poor. The life we've lived has been worth the lifetime it took to build it. Your confession to me shouldn't be allowed to destroy all that. It needs to become an opportunity to use the gifts granted to us to do more with what we have. They say you're going to die soon. If they're right, then nothing I say will change that. But what I say until then—that right, that decision—belongs to me."

Her eyes rose from her ring finger to catch his gaze again. "I haven't been selfish in our life together, Dan. But I'm going to be selfish now." Kate's eyes began to swell with tears. "I know I still need every minute of the life we share and until the day I can no longer feel your heart next to mine, I refuse to think that anything is over. Especially not us, Dan. But you better not have anything left you want to confess."

Dan tried to speak but he couldn't. He trembled and let the tears roll from his eyes. Everything she had said told him what his life amounted to. He'd taken a corrupt path, but their marriage stood above his character defects. He'd never really understood what the term soul mates meant. Now he did.

Kate had brought him back from the edge of a watery grave and given him a vision that would leave him with a task that would honor his life and their family.

Then he looked deeper and knew what he owed her. He prayed. Why was I so rewarded? God, how did you decide to give me this woman's heart? What was the great plan for all of this and what part was I supposed to play? Was it all intended to come down to this? Was I supposed to be a thief so that this woman could find a greater purpose and use for that tainted fortune? Ha! What irony there can be in sin and what joy there can be in truth.

"Kate," he finally said, "all of what I've told you, and anything that I stand guilty of, I have never, not for a single moment, stopped loving you. Everything you've described will happen."

"OK," Kate said. "Now I want to go shower. The shower at the beach is OK, but not like this one."

"Can you use some company? I need to do the same thing." Dan said half jokingly, assuming he would have to work his way back into their lovemaking together and that it might take some time.

"There's no lock on the door." And as she turned to head upstairs, she wiggled her butt playfully in his direction.

The first act had ended. The lights were flashing. The final act had begun and he was gratefully in a front-row seat.

He had never loved Kate more than at that moment.

Chapter Thirty Six

June 30, 2013, 10 a.m.
The Diocese of Rockville Centre Headquarters
Meeting Room 206
Rockville Centre, New York

Father Ted was running late. His car didn't start when he was leaving the rectory and he'd had to get a jump. He still had half a cup of coffee when he was called from the reception area.

The meeting room was unpretentious. Wide tinted windows were covered by gray blinds, a nondescript color painted on the walls. The table at the center of the room was cheap Formica the color of mahogany. Prints from WalMart hung; recessed fluorescent lights and steel chairs with black vinyl seats and backs completed the austere look.

Five people sat around the table, all clergy. Petraglia, his monsignor's purple sash around his ample waist, was at one end. Father Ted took the single open chair opposite him. The three other men and the woman at the table were then introduced. He wondered if they were here by choice or by command.

No one said anything to him as he sat, uttering a pleasant "good morning."

Petraglia wasted no time. "Now, Father Hayslip, I assume you are familiar with the document I hold in my hand bearing your signature. I refer to the Agreement of Subjugation. You have a copy that was sent when you were notified of this board hearing. I presume you've read it and understand your signed obligation?"

"Yes, Monsignor, I am familiar with that document and I have my original signed copy with me," Ted replied as he met Petraglia's eyes.

"Then, Father, may I ask if there are any provisos in the agreement that you could not comply with?"

"No, Monsignor, there are none." What else could he say, he thought. To argue against the terms of the agreement would make him a fool.

"So you agree that the spirit of the accord and the stipulations do, in fact, remain within your concurrence?" Petraglia's language was getting flowery.

"Yes, Monsignor, most emphatically I do." By confirming his willingness to remain obedient, Ted thought, would put him in a better light.

But Petraglia was a lawyer and he saw through Ted's response. That became clear as Ted felt the noose tighten around his neck. "That being said, Father, then perhaps you can enlighten us as to how you came to take part in this scientific project conducted over in Cold Spring Harbor? First, without permission from your immediate supervisor, Pastor Schmidt, and secondly, in direct conflict with your stated and signed agreement with which you now say, quite clearly, you have no issues. Please, Father, go ahead." Petraglia sounded pleased with himself.

Ted sipped his coffee and put the cup down. "Let me say I appreciate this opportunity to be heard and I hope you'll understand that I have in no way sought to disregard any of the rules of my ordination. My participation in the tests was anonymous. I'd seen an advertisement by Cold Spring Harbor Laboratory in the *Sunday Times* seeking DNA donations for a blind study. There was no information on what the DNA was to be used for. At no time did it occur to me that this would generate any findings that could be considered controversial to the Church. Had I suspected anything of that nature, of course I wouldn't have participated. I knew before I proceeded that Cold Spring Harbor Laboratory primarily works to find cures for diseases. I am as shocked as everyone in this room by the revelations. Obviously, had I known such information would be the final outcome of this study, I would not have participated."

Ted's reply was the answer of an honest man. But sometimes it can be dangerous to be honest.. It was this last point, which he had volunteered, that would be his undoing.

"Now, Father, what was your reaction to these scientists delivering such a morbid message, telling you that you only had, I believe, less than a year to live?" The monsignor tried to sound sympathetic.

"Well, it wasn't very good news, Monsignor. I found it difficult to accept."

"Father, did you offer any ecclesiastical rebuttal when told that you were to die in a year?" Petraglia, believing himself to be a fair man, thought he would give the priest one last chance to shine a favorable light on his actions.

"No sir. I was too shocked by the news."

"So you took them at their word? Their blasphemy didn't upset you?"

"The presentation to me of the science and the procedures used to quantify and qualify the results, after four years and four hundred subjects, was impressive, comprehensive, and clearly accurate. I, of course, know that God alone makes such decisions and not the Cold Spring Harbor Lab, but I felt under no obligation to debate theology with the good doctors."

"And let me ask you, Father, do you believe that the claim that they have found what has now become known as the 'God gene' is credible? Do you believe you'll die on Christmas Day?"

"Monsignor, I have an inoperable brain tumor. I hope to see our Savior's birthday this year and many more to come but the doctors would tell you not to count on it." Ted dodged the direct question as he refused to condemn the lab. Ted could sense the others' discomfort. But he was a dying man, so why persecute him?

A true inquisitor, Petraglia's glare never faltered, his features indicated pure disdain. Ted knew that the monsignor had a hard-nosed reputation, but the venom in his face was still shocking. "Do any of you have any questions?" Petraglia asked as he reclined slightly in his stiff-backed chair, unmoved by Ted's description of his terminal illness. The monsignor was ready to wrap up his game of cat and mouse.

"I have one for you, Father," said Father DeAngelis, who drew a sharp glance from Petraglia. "You said the presentation the lab made about this so-called 'God gene' was clear and comprehensive. Do you think what they have found will truly become a scientific fact? That each of us has a birth date and a death date assigned by our genes?"

"Father, I can't answer that. I have no idea where I would get the information that would allow me to speculate on that question. I was healthy when I took the test, and I was healthy when I received the results. Weeks later, I am a terminal cancer patient with a life expectancy close to the date the scientists have predicted. They say December twenty fifth will be the day that I die. I draw no conclusions."

Petraglia quickly took the meeting back. "If there are no other questions? Then, Father, you may go. This board will report its findings and recommendations to the bishop. You'll be notified by his office directly as to the outcome. Thank you for coming in today. We wish you well with your treatment." Petraglia icily dismissed him as if he was reading from a script.

As Father Ted crossed the room, Petraglia's oily voice posed one more question. As Ted heard it, he knew it was the order of execution. "Father, I understand that you are continuing to participate in this study, which, given that you have a signed document on your person that compels you to refrain from such activities, wouldn't you agree is somewhat … peculiar?"

"That's true, Monsignor," Ted admitted, "but the lab is trying to establish some connection between the death date common to me and three others. My cooperation could be key to unlocking a link among us that can shed light on the positive use of this of information. Possibly life-saving data may result."

"Yes, Father, that is, as you say, kind of you. Ah, are you also compensated for this … kindness and how much money is involved, if any at all?" Petraglia did not even try to dampen his sarcasm.

Ted had stepped into Petraglia's trap.

"I'm paid a thousand dollars for each day I participate at the lab," he admitted with a slight blush.

"Thank you, Father. I think we have all the information we need. You'll be hearing from the bishop."

Ted nodded his head and quietly left the room. That's that, he thought as he retraced the steps he had taken fourteen minutes ago on his way into the meeting room. That was all it took. Fourteen minutes and a life's work could be wiped out. It was now in their hands and he was sure that Petraglia would lead the board to recommendations that were not in his favor.

As he walked back to his car, he tried to suppress the anger building inside him. If they don't want me, that's their loss. I've been a good priest and I've done absolutely nothing to hurt the Church, he told himself. He turned the ignition, but his car remained still. He put his hands on the steering wheel, leaned his head down until it rested between his two hands, poised at ten and two.

What next? Why me?

Chapter Thirty Seven

July 3, 2013, 3:15 p.m.
Cold Spring Harbor Laboratory, Board Room
Cold Spring Harbor, New York

The researchers were now in the seventh month of their study and the four "lab mice"—as their subjects had taken to calling themselves—struggled with daily life as they tried to reconcile themselves to their fates. So much had changed for them in such a short time and their bonding as a group provided the support they could not find anywhere else.

Every two weeks, each of them was given a comprehensive medical exam. At first, each had wanted to remain separate; an attempt at self-protection. When they first met, they were reluctant to share feelings and fears. They felt no connection to each other; they were strangers just starting a journey together.

The first meeting had been conducted by Dr. Guitton. She noted that Janet Bates and Father Hayslip were detached and isolated, their comments more banal than insightful. Dan was upbeat and encouraging, but not emotionally engaged. . And Sharona Watts, who was younger, less privileged and less educated than the others, seemed wary and kept her distance from the others.

Their transformation to a cohesive group began to take root at their second meeting, when Sharona offhandedly referred to their group as lab mice. The others broke out laughing and the ice began to melt. As the weeks went by, the bonds strengthened through hope, fear, acceptance; eventually becoming loving and caring toward one another, dependant on each other's spiritual and moral support.

Now, when the meetings took place every two weeks, the researchers could see the obvious joy they found in one another. The level of trust within the group was profound. They suffered along with Father Ted when he told them about his brain tumor and masked their own fears of a possible similar fate. They rejoiced at Sharona's news that she was bearing not one child, but two. Janet, who had suffered the most difficult blow of all in losing a son, was supported with compassion and love. She had learned that there are greater things in life than one's own self and surrendering herself to that thought opened her to gratitude for her loved ones and her time remaining. Their emotions had traveled through peaks and valleys. The depression and fear were at times unbearable. Together, they got through it.

But Dan Brannigan had gone from being a cheerleader, into a deep, morbid abyss.

His spirits had declined It was Dan that had brought up the subject of suicide as a way to avoid the fate that had been predicted. He had told them he and Kate had split and all he would say was that it was his fault. He didn't seem ready to open up any further and the others gave him space, but maintained a supportive dialogue with him.

And so today, they were surprised when Brannigan entered the meeting whistling and buoyant. Dan didn't give them long to speculate about what had happened. "I have great news, everyone. My wife has come back. And she has brought me back to life. I can't express enough the gratitude for all the great things in my life and I want to share my happiness with all of you, my friends."

The group embraced him. They were glad he saw them as confidants and that his heart was healing. Then Dan asked them to all be seated; he had something more he wanted tell them. "I can't tell you how much I've learned from each of you . I see in you the bravery and dignity you live with day to day, and it makes me ashamed of myself for being the coward I am." Dan looked around the table at each of them. "In the last few weeks I had decided that I would kill myself if Kate and I couldn't work it out. I saw what you went through, Janet, and I couldn't find it in my heart to be as brave as you or as compassionate toward my family."

Dan eyes began to fill; he spoke haltingly. "I have children, grandchildren. But I was so fixated on myself. I was blinded by my own selfishness."

He turned to Ted. "Father, you've had more bad luck in one lifetime than anyone could ever imagine... I don't know how you do it. You have the strength of ten people. I'm ashamed of myself when I see your dignity day to day without complaint. Sharona, you amaze me. You choose to give new life before your time runs out. Honey, you may be the bravest of us all. With what you're facing, you're saying, 'Hold up. Not before I'm finished doing something great.' I have none of your character. I've chased money all my life. Turned out I was really good at it. I've tried to buy my way into respectability by being charitable. I never even got within driving distance of the kind of backbone you people have shown."

He looked up at the ceiling and continued. "Since Kate and I have reconciled, my thoughts have turned to dreams. I imagine that each of you has dreams you may never see realized because of what's coming.. I know I do. I always wanted to go to Tahiti with Kate. Whatever yours is makes it special, I think. Money can make some dreams come true. The thing is, some dreams can't come true without money, that's for sure. So I've said all of this because I want each of you to have your dreams come true while there is still time."

Janet, Ted and Sharona glanced at each other before looking back to Dan. "Each of these envelopes contains a bank check in your name for five million dollars. It's yours. Do whatever you need to do to make your dreams a reality. I know you'll make the right decisions because you're all really smart people."

And Dan placed a single white envelope, their names typed on the front, before each of them. "By the way, there will also be separate checks to follow that will offset any tax obligations. The idea is to make certain that the entire five million dollars is yours to do with as you see fit. My accounting guys have to figure that out, but there wasn't time, as this idea kind of came to me suddenly. I thought of it in the shower," he laughed.

The other three lab mice were speechless, and sat with their mouths open. Dr. Guitton quietly pulled a tissue from her sleeve and dried her eyes, moved by the magnitude of Dan's gift.

"Five million dollars?" Sharona finally uttered as she began to weep. "Five million dollars?"

Janet just sat, shaking her head from side to side and staring at the envelope, completely dumbfounded.

Ted reached out and took the envelope and opened it. "I have never seen what one of these looks like. Wow! I don't know what to say," he smiled. "What does one say to a gift like that? Thank you."

Janet spoke next. "Dan, this is beyond anything. Oh my God. Five million dollars? I won't know what to do. Five million dollars …"

Dan just sat and beamed. He was truly joyful about doing this.

"Mr. B," which was what Sharona called him, "you have no idea what you've just done for me and my children. I been staying up nights, wondering how my babies were going to get their education when I got nothing to leave them. Deke is trying to get a college degree now, but that's a long ways off and who knows if he'll make it?"

Her emotions overwhelmed her so she couldn't speak. She rose and walked over to Dan, who stood from his chair. She threw her arms around him and began sobbing. "Now my babies can go to college, just like you said. That was my dream and you've given it to me. Now I can have my babies and know they got a chance at life. Thank you so much, Mr. B. Thank you from the twins, too."

Dan reached down and put his hand on her belly, smiling. Tears in his eyes.

"You guys have a great mama.' He whispered.

Chapter Thirty Eight

September 4, 2013, 7:30 a.m.
Roman Catholic Diocese of Rockville Centre
Office of the Bishop
His Excellency Bishop Terence Thomas Molloy
Rockville Centre, New York

Ted had expected some kind of a formal letter. Instead, he had gotten a pink "While you were out" message in his box at the rectory the weekend before. Marge had gone home for the night, but Ted recognized her writing. Bishop Molloy had called.

Ted immediately dialed the number on the message slip. A message started "This is Bishop Molloy …." but suddenly the recording was interrupted and to Ted's surprise, a live voice sounded in his ear. "Father Ted, thanks for the quick callback." Molloy was sometimes referred to as "bishop sanctimonious" by parishioners at St. Agnes Cathedral, where the six foot plus, white haired, patrician presided and governed his diocese. He was considered a conservative. Molloy was also a three handicap, four times a week golfer at the nearby Garden City Golf Club. He was a *gratis* member, along with several other seniors of the diocese, including its counsel, Monsignor Petraglia.

Molloy had never met Father Ted despite his sixteen years in the parish, so Ted was startled by the familiar tone. He hoped the bishop wasn't just being charming.

"Yes, Bishop, I just received your message,"Ted said as his mouth began to dry up.

"Actually, you caught me between holes at the club, so I'll be brief. The review board has recommended to me that you be relieved of your parish duties forthwith and considered for a full suspension of your ecclesiastical privileges in accordance with your Agreement of Subjugation. I've read their full report, but before I pass along my decision on the recommendation, I'd like to speak with you. Can you be at my office Monday morning?"

"Yes, of course, your Excellency. What time, and will I need any of my documents?"

"Any time before noon Father. I usually start by seven. I'll be working at my desk, so just show up and ask for me. And no, you won't need anything. My secretary comes in later, so if you get there early, just knock. See you then."With that, he hung up.

Now, just after seven thirty, Ted stood before the bishop's door. He knocked softly just below the engraved brass plate bearing the bishop's full name and title. Hearing a muffled "come in,"Ted opened the door.

The room smelled of stale cigar smoke, and Ted was surprised to find the bishop crossing the office toward him in an orange golf shirt and khakis held up by a lime green web belt. He looked every bit the country club member. He was tall, tan, fit, clean-shaven and appeared to be in a hurry. He had a no-nonsense reputation; Ted knew he was not a man to be taken lightly. And he had no intention of doing so.

"Come in, Father, come in," Molloy motioned to Ted. "I'll be with you in a second. I just need to leave this on the secretary's desk."

He meant it when he had said he'd be only a second. Before Ted could drop into a chair opposite the modest desk, he heard the door close as the bishop re-entered and began speaking.

He wasn't saying what Ted had hoped, but he was direct and to the point. "Father, you've left yourself wide open to the board's recommendations, and I have a duty to uphold the Church's rules and regulations. I have no wish to pass judgment on you, or anyone for that matter, but you've left me no choice."

Ted began to speak, but the bishop continued as he walked to his chair behind the desk. "I've actually met Doctor Russo at a couple of charity golf outings. We were once in a foursome together. Lousy golfer. But he seemed like a decent sort. This 'God gene' crap is pure nonsense. For thousands of years, we've known that life is in the hands of the Almighty.. First it was the abortionists. Now it's the death squad. What's wrong with people? What is it about the teachings of faith and religious doctrine that lay people, especially scientists, just can't leave alone? And why did you leave your butt hanging out on this? What were you thinking?"

Then the conversation abruptly changed course. "You want some coffee?" the bishop asked. "It's right behind you. Help yourself."

"Thank you. I think I will," Ted said.

As Ted began to pour his coffee, the bishop busied with some papers on his desk. Ted intuitively felt he could reason with this blunt man. He couldn't imagine Molloy being sanctimonious.

Ted had been unable to sleep since the call. He'd been thinking how he would approach the bishop, how he would defend himself. He believed the only issue in the charges against him was that he had fogotten that he was prohibited from taking part in this type of study. He was not a spokesman for the lab—he was still an anonymous participant. Above all, the lab had done nothing to position the findings as a repudiation of anyone's religious beliefs.

As he turned to the bishop, Ted knew that his only possible avenue was to be truthful. He also knew the end was creeping closer as he was beginning to feel the effects of his cancer. He might as well shed the luggage, as Dr. Weitzman had suggested, even though he knew this could risk his priesthood.

Ted knew it was time to fight back. "Your Excellency, I've done nothing to contradict any doctrine or teaching of our church's faith," he said.

"How dare you say that, Father? The board considered your case very closely and unanimously recommended that you be farmed out of your parish and quietly defrocked. That board was composed of your peers, Father, not me."

"How dare I? How dare they? How dare you, your Excellency? For twenty seven years, I have faithfully executed my duties and followed every order I've ever been given. I've served every parish I was assigned to, and not once, not once, have I ever been accused of insubordinate actions, attitudes, or conduct."

He heard his voice rising and felt his neck turning red. But he was not going to stop now. "So I when I found myself struggling to find enough money for a new a car I took advantage of an advertisement that required an anonymous donation of my spit for a thousand bucks. Well, it turns it has gotten me a whole lot more than that. It's gotten me nothing but heartache. But am I being asked to defend myself against any real disgrace I've brought upon the church? No. No one outside of the lab and you, my superiors, even knows my name or my association with this mess."

Ted thought he should calm down now; he felt his temper might move the discussion off his aim —to state his truth. "And then there is this question, which I bring before you, your Excellency, because I consider you a fair man."

His temper wasn't entirely gone. "Why is this an issue at all? What has the lab done that has, in any way, repudiated the doctrine of our Church, or any other faith? What they've said is they've found a gene that can identify date of death. They've never claimed this proves science triumphs over God's will."

Ted took a deep breath before continuing. "Here's a question: How did the gene get so deeply implanted in us that it took so long to find it? Can anyone explain how the complexities of the human genome could be anything but divinely placed?"

The priest was getting flushed now. "Why not see that God is the only answer for what they've found? Who but God could have created such a sophisticated mystery within our bodies? And what exactly would the church refute? The Vatican jumped the gun, in my view. The only ones calling the discovery the 'God gene' are the media. They're looking to stir the pot so they have something to write about. They made it an issue. So why isn't Petraglia standing by me rather than trying to get me fired from a vocation that has been nothing but loyal service to God?"

Ted paused for a second, calmer now. "Look, I am a dead man walking. I'm about to enter stage four cancer. The sight is nearly gone from my left eye, my hair has fallen out, I grow weaker each day, and I can barely feel the tips of my toes and fingers. Now, would this have happened had I not participated in this study? Of course it would have. Am I going to get to the date predicted by my DNA? God only knows. Have I brought disgrace upon our church? Ridiculous. Absolutely ridiculous. Take my collar if you have to, Bishop. Maybe you'll replace me, but you'll never get anyone better than me."

The bishop sat with his arms folded during Father Hayslip's tirade, listening intently. When Father Ted took his seat, the bishop unfolded his arms and snatched up the priest's file. "Father, your record of transfers over the years indicates you demonstrate 'interpersonal apathy' and that you 'lack the dynamism for public speaking' that we like to offer our faithful. That has been a distinguishing characteristic of your reviews throughout the years. I see no evidence of that here today. Your voice on this matter is impressive in its logic and fairness. I congratulate you on your argument and tell you now that I will not be accepting the board's recommendation. I will convene the board so that I can personally explain to them my reasons for my decision. I know that those boards can be tilted by the monsignor's position and personal prejudices, but you didn't express yourself to them the way you did here. And in the end that doesn't matter. My decision is final."

Molloy smiled. "You're a very impressive priest, Ted, and from your record I see that you have sacrificed greatly for our church— and our nation. Congratulations, Father. I will always remember the meeting we had here today. I learned a good deal from you."

Ted blushed, then smiled in relief. He felt like he had just dropped a heavy piece of luggage. "I learned a lesson too, Your Excellency," he said.

Chapter Thirty Nine

August 11, 2013, 11:24 a.m.
Cold Spring Harbor Laboratory, Office of the President
Cold Spring Harbor, New York

The lab's team members had evolved into roles based on their experience and specialties. That is, except for Russo, who, to his chagrin, had had little choice but to spend a good part of his time over the last few months facing the worldwide media. He did so throughout the summer, and his life story was recounted in a feature in *The New York Times*.

He hated this new celebrity, which had destroyed his privacy. But media hype was something he was beginning to understand and he was working to make it bearable. Dealing with the four study volunteers was far more challenging.

He was brooding now that although his team had been testing molecular cell samples and blood work, and taken oral histories since January, they had yet to come across a single common element.

The genealogical search had become a shared chore for Doctors Weitzman and Mhatra, whom Russo was about to meet. He was desperate to ensure that the lab would provide the information that answered the question posed by the common death date. The p63a gene order of execution defined their date of death, but the mystery of their identical dates remained unresolved.

Only one - poor Father Ted - looked likely to meet his end as predicted by the study's results. The others all remained healthy and, in Sharona's case, robust and fruitful. Their contribution to the project, which put great demands on them personally, had yielded nothing. None of them had complained, but he wondered how long it would be before they threw in the towel.

Tod needed to cover today's session and move to his schedule for the afternoon. He was due at CNN for a live interview with Anderson Cooper, followed by dinner at Ellen's apartment. She was to meet him at CNN's studios.

He had found himself enjoying Ellen's company more and more and depended on her to help him navigate the endless receptions and speaking engagements that now took much of his time. She acted as his compass in all discussions, save those involving the DNA discovery; he was immersed in that. Ellen seemed to glide in and out of conversations without appearing presumptuous or intrusive. She had a unique skill that allowed her to present her thoughts in a way that sounded as if her words were coming from them both.

She also remained the medical and scientific analyst for the test group. She became their counselor, therapist and adviser. She presented the human face to the lab's extensive attention, the anchor of sanity in a fate that seemed unthinkable. Patiently and lovingly, she created a calm environment where the confidence derived from her guidance allowed each of the four subjects to temper the panic inherent in those assigned to certain death.

Remarkable woman, he thought.

"Doctor?" Ritu Mhatra's voice broke through Russo's reverie and brought him back to their meeting. Ritu had found his office door slightly ajar and was smiling at him.

"Yes, come in, Ritu. I was just daydreaming," he smiled as he came around his desk.

"I wasn't sure I should interrupt you. You looked so peaceful." She moved to the seating area.

"Where's Zach? He's joining us, isn't he?"

"Yes, he's had to take a call just now. He'll be along shortly. Sorry."

"OK, let's get started, and he'll just jump in when he gets here. I've got some concerns about the blanks we're drawing on all these tests and the lineage issue. Is there anything we can do to accelerate the process? I don't want these brave souls to depart without us finding the explanation for their connection. I still can't accept that there isn't something that ties them together."

"I agree, Doctor, but so far, it doesn't appear that there are any physical connections. There isn't anything that we've been able to match." Ritu opened her files as if she was looking through them for something.

All the scientists were equally frustrated by their inability to establish a connection, but neither Zach nor Ritu had taken it as personally as Russo had. "What about this DNA patterning we've ordered? I know we went to that later than we should have. Is it progressing satisfactorily? It's costing a fortune."

Dr. Weitzman entered the office. "Sorry I'm late. I heard your question as I was coming in. Can I jump in here, Ritu?"

"Sure, please do," she said.

"OK. The mapping is very time-consuming and complex, as well as expensive, as you know." Zach continued to define the core problem, which did not allow them to get accurate reads on the DNA-based cross-mapping of the four subjects. He pinpointed the trouble as protein mutations within the subjects' DNA that changed unpredictably depending upon when tissue samples were taken; the team hadn't been able get a handle on that and it was complicating their efforts to find a common denominator.

Dr. Mhatra added, "The general rule of thumb, as I realize you know, Tod, is that of the three billion units in the human genome, sixty per generation can change randomly. Protein works within the DNA and can alter what we see at the time we are trying to get a comparison. The devil in our case is in the mathematical calibrations. They are endless."

Weitzman jumped in to continue Ritu's point. "That appears to be caused by chemical changes in each of the four subjects. But those same changes may not necessarily become permanent as the protein values change. That can happen for any number of reasons, but it alters the patterning, and invalidates the comparisons when we view them, even if only on a temporary basis. In other words, what we are looking at from sample to sample can be changing even as we are examining it. That said, we're seeing patterns that regulate themselves and give us useable ranges that we can accept as permanent. But the glitch is timing. We need accelerated results and the proteins move about at their own discretion." Zach sounded defeated; he had his hands turned upward and his shoulders hunched in frustration.

"So will we be able to find what we are looking for - assuming there is anything to be found at all - before December twenty-fifth?" Tod sounded weary.

"I'm hopeful ... er ... we're hopeful," Zach said as he nodded toward Ritu, "but not optimistic. It takes a very long time to complete a single DNA string even under the best of circumstances, but if you multiply the equation by four and ask for a cross-map among them that might - and I stress might - offer us verifying evidences, it's like trying to find a single point of light in an entire universe."

"I knew you were going to say that." Tod pushed his chair back and tossed his pen down on the coffee table.

"I'm making small progress in tracing the family lines, finally," Ritu said, in an attempt to share something positive with Russo. "I've found recorded documents of the name Hayslip going back to the turn of the last century. I still don't have it locked down, but I'm hopeful that it will check out and at least I'll have a starting point. I have also identified a pretty clear path to Janet Bates' ancestors. Her maiden name was Bell, and there are a lot of those, but the family records she gave me indicate that her great-grandfather lived in Brooklyn and also served in the First World War. But again, there is a lot to uncover before we find the right Bell family. It's a start."

She opened the file marked Brannigan. "As for Mr. Brannigan, there isn't much. There aren't any immigration or military records, so we still have lots of work there. Miss Watts is going to be even tougher. Her grandmother has been really difficult to get information from and the family names are not unified across even the present generation. What's her problem Tod? Why won't the grandmother meet with us?"

"I suspect she is embarrassed by her family. Sometimes families have been through generations of turmoil, broken homes and absent parents. I understand Sharona's mother named her after a man she suspected was the girl's father. If you see this from Valerie Stalls' world, perhaps discussing genealogy is painful. Sharona's mother recently ran off to Texas with a convict she met while working at the county jail. So we have a mountain to climb to try and piece that together. Tough assignment, but not impossible."

Ritu shook her head. "That poor girl. What kind of a life would she have had if her grandmother hadn't been there for her? And still is, for that matter. Amazing."

"Not to sound pessimistic," Russo said, "but it appears you're still a million miles away from putting this puzzle together."

Zach exhaled deeply, and Ritu nodded, although she wasn't in total agreement. "It sounds worse than it is. What I've discovered is that you need one strong starting point for each family tree. If you can get the first fact established, you can build around it. I'm sorry, Tod. I wish I could be more positive. I'm ... we're on it, around the clock."

"I know, I went past your office this morning at about five and saw you in front of your computer. I thought it best to not interrupt you. You had to have been up since three-thirty to get here from New Jersey at that hour.. When do you sleep, or see George?" Tod blurted without considering that, as her boss, this was an inappropriate question.

Ritu just laughed. "George is worse than me, if you can imagine that. Usually when I get home, I need to peel him away from his computer. He has gotten into Pacific Rim investments lately, and all he can think about is Shanghai and Indonesia. He's going there for a month. As for sleep? Who cares about that?"

Tod stood, signaling the end of their meeting. "I used to care about sleeping, but since this project, I find I get less and less. I keep waking up, thinking about our four and what their nights must be like. Ellen tells me they're sharing more all the time in her meetings with them. One of the things they've been saying is how difficult night time is for them. They find themselves walking around in the dark, anxious. What a curse we've put on them. Sometimes I wish we had never begun this project."

"You shouldn't feel guilty about this, Tod," Zach said, trying to find something positive. "If nothing else, our discovery also allows them time to prepare."

"Prepare for what? Prepare for leaving their families?" Russo's voice took on an edge that matched his mood before he caught himself. "Thanks, Zach, I know you mean well and I realize that I'm taking a negative view here. But for the first time in my life, I'm seeing what 'scientific progress' can mean on a personal level. And honestly, I wasn't prepared. Not for this."

Russo looked into his colleagues' eyes. He sensed the disappointment over his increasing disenchantment with their research. He knew his leadership was hanging in the balance, but he didn't think it was all that important anymore.

What had touched him as he watched the months slip by was the unselfish spirit of the four volunteers. The lab mice showed him a side of life he had never known. He had never felt that depth of love for someone else. His world had shrunk to a single focus. He stood alone in his small universe, never having understood what these brave, ordinary people knew—that loving others above ourselves is what makes our life here worth its creation, its living, and, somehow, grants us a graceful exit. That our world is here for us to share with others and the sharing is what gives it meaning and substance.

His parents and relatives had died and it had all seemed to him to be part of the natural order of things. His only living relative, a cousin in Rome, was merely an annual Christmas card contact. He had had no interest in politics or social issues, or, for that matter, the environment, world history, entertainment, global warming. Nothing.

That had all changed when he sat in this room and watched as

Sharona Watts, who had just received the news that she had less than a year to live, said she was going to miss her grandmother. There was no "poor me." There was no anger. There was no blame directed at anyone or anything. No swearing at God about the unfairness. She simply didn't want to leave the woman next to her, who had given Sharona love all of her days.

And the others. Janet had lost a son in Afghanistan and yet she carried on taking care of her remaining family, who were about to lose her.

Father Ted was fighting against cancer without a word of self-pity while struggling to keep his priesthood active. He worked so that others might find comfort from him, rather than he from them.

Brannigan was distributing his wealth so he might see the benefits of his generosity before his death. And Kate worked hand in glove with him to make certain that happened.

"In some ways, I envy our four lab mice," he said. " They know what their lives have been worth and what matters. They're lucky. They have something they're going to miss—and people who will miss them."

He stared at Zach and Ritu. "Please keep me in the loop on what turns up. Thanks." He turned back to his desk as his colleagues glanced at each other and rose to leave.

Part III

Chapter Forty

Janet could see his name carved on the stark white limestone marker as she rounded the curve in the road. Now one of thousands of silent memorials that populated Pinelawn National Cemetery, Michael's grave was, by far, the newest in this section. The others around him had served in the Korean War. She had turned to her congressman to help pave the way for her son's remains to be interred close to home.

Pinelawn, the closest national cemetery, had been closed for years, but a few plots, inadvertently left empty, were still available. The other national cemetery on Long Island would have meant a hundred mile round trip for her each day. Pinelawn was a six mile ride.

Since Michael's burial, Janet had begun each day at a convenience store, where she bought a large coffee, trimmed it with lots of milk and three sugars, and got a copy of the daily newspaper. Then she went to share her morning coffee with her son. She would "communicate," as she called it. She'd fill him in on news and gossip, family happenings, and read to him from the paper. Her visits lasted roughly an hour.

In the beginning, she tried to get Rod or Michaela to come with her. They did, a couple of times, and then stopped. Kathy also accompanied her once. Janet knew they all thought she was crazy, but her morning ritual seemed perfectly normal. She remained convinced that Michael's spirit was there and that he enjoyed her company.

Today she was excited to tell him that she was actually going to meet Carly soon. After Michael had so suddenly been snatched from them, Janet decided to reach out to Carly Hoffer. They were in touch throughout Michael's funeral arrangements, and, to Janet's pleasant surprise, she found Carly intelligent, articulate, and devastated over Michael's loss.

Janet realized at once that Carly had been deeply in love with her son. There were no scars that needed to heal between them; Michael had not had a chance to tell Carly about his family's reaction to the news that they planned to marry.

"Hi Mike, how are you honey?" Janet said as she sat down on a small bench near her son's resting place. "Listen, before I read you the latest, I have some really exciting news.. Carly's going to be here in three or four days and she's going to register at Hofstra to start in the January semester. In the meantime, guess what? She's going to move in with us. We've been on Skype all weekend and it's all worked out. Oh God, Mike, she's wonderful. No wonder you loved her so much. We all love her. Aunt K thinks she's way too good to waste her time in the Army."

Janet shifted her weight on the hard bench. "Anyway, honey, I hope you don't mind, but we're going to give her your room when she comes. I'm not going to change anything and she said that would be fine. She said she'd love to see your things and stay in your bed so she could feel close to you. That's why she applied to Hofstra, so she could be on Long Island, where she'd be near you. Oh, what a treasure she is."

She was smiling, as if Michael was seated next to her. "Your unit gets to the States this week, and when she's released, she'll head right over here. She's still really pissed at the Army for not letting her come home for your funeral, and even though she was planning on getting out anyway, she says now she wouldn't stay for any price."

Janet rose from the bench and stooped to pull a few strands of crabgrass that had sprouted up. "So she got accepted at Hofstra and she's going to be your neighbor soon. We're all excited. She's going to be a finance major."

In that instant, Janet's mood went from bubbly to morbid. She had been thinking more and more about her own end, now a little over three months away. She constantly asked the doctors at the lab if they remained convinced of the results and each time they confirmed that their evidence continued to be validated: Several more volunteers had reached their predicted death dates since the initial announcement last Christmas Day.

Outwardly she remained calm, but inside, she felt a time bomb ticking. "I'm scared, Michael. I need your help, if you can give it to me, honey. I mean, this is getting harder every day. I feel great and it feels impossible that I'm going to die soon. I don't let anyone but you see me like this. You know, I was a raging bitch when I first found out, and I tore the hearts out of everyone around me."

She began to pace back and forth before his silent headstone. "But your passing opened my eyes. I realized that your father and Michaela were really going to take the brunt of this whole thing. Kathy, too. You know, first you, then me. I've realized that loving others more than we love ourselves is the best thing we have in our lives. But losing them is the price we pay for that. When you lose someone you love, a piece of you dies, too."

She shook her head from side to side as she continued pacing. "They've really been hit hard. I never, ever saw your father show as much emotion as when he learned that you were gone, Mike. He'll never be the same; I know he won't. I try to tell him every day that it wasn't his fault, but I know it isn't helping. And Michaela just can't get past it, either. She's really quiet now. I worry a lot about her 'cause she doesn't say much. So while I'm still here, I'm keeping up a good face and trying to keep things as upbeat as I can. I don't let them see …"

She was starting to cry now and picked up her coffee cup and clutched it with both hands. "I just don't know what's going happen to them when … I leave. Oh, Michael, I'm sorry … I shouldn't be making you sad. I'll stop now."

She tried to think what she could say to Michael that was more positive. "Did I tell you we're going to Italy next month? I probably already told you this." She had. Several times. "Yeah, we rented a villa for the month in Positano, and Kathy and Bill and their kids, and Michaela and Carly are coming, too. Yep. Imagine that? The Bates bunch in a villa with an ocean view on the Amalfi Coast for a month! And listen to this: Dan Brannigan has offered us his private jet to fly us there and back. Imagine us arriving in Italy in a private jet!"

She stopped her monologue while she extracted a tissue and blew her nose loudly. "Boy, was I wrong about Brannigan. He is the sweetest man. Of course, it's easy to say nice things about a man who hands you five million dollars. But he really is. He's always talking about his grandchildren and his kids, and he adores his wife. They must have gone through a rough patch, but, God, how he goes on about her. Michaela said she heard he is the biggest philanthropist on Long Island and that he's worth nearly a billion dollars. But you'd never know it if you met him. He's just like the rest of us."

She paused and sipped her coffee and gazed around the cemetery. The peace and quiet had finally eased the churning that Janet had been feeling inside. It was a sultry, hazy, late-summer morning and most of the grass had turned a straw-colored yellow from the summer's constant sun. Already, some of the trees had surrendered a few dark green leaves to the changing multitude of autumn colors. She watched a monach butterfly flit across the area where her son now lay. As it perched on one of the headstones, she wondered if butterflies are people who have come back. As a little girl, she'd once believed that.

Realizing her thoughts were wandering aimlessly, she focused on speaking with Michael again. "I still haven't decided what to do with all that money, honey. Ha! That's cute isn't it? Money honey!

I'm going to leave a chunk to Michaela and, of course - oh, what am I thinking! I do have some big news. Guess what? Your father quit his job - finally. His last day is next Friday." She'd forgotten that she had told Michael this already too. "I've been after him all summer since we got the money, but he just didn't want to let go. Finally, he came home last week and told me he'd handed in his papers. Said I was right that he'd been doing it long enough. But I know it was because of me."

Janet stood again, walking a few yards to a nearby trash receptacle to dump her unfinished coffee. "It's funny, but I have never felt as close to him as I do now. Isn't that odd, Mike? I mean, we went through a whole lifetime together and raised you two, and we did OK as married people, but it never really felt, you know, close, until all this other stuff started happening. I'm glad, though. He's a good guy, your father. I call him a late bloomer."

She sat again and paused, taking a deep breath. She was trying to think of what to say that could keep her physically near Michael. "I do have to do something about all that money, though. Kathy is trying to get me a financial adviser. Your father … well, he's your father, you know. 'Whatever you want is fine with me,' he says."

She wasn't aware of it, but her talks with Michael were becoming more and more disjointed with each visit. Often, she just rambled on about anything that popped in to her head, repeating herself from day to day. "Except for the cars and paying off the mortgage and the credit cards, it's just sitting in the checking account. I'm almost afraid to touch it for fear if I start spending, I'll never stop. So anyway, what's new in the world today? Let's take a look."

After she had read through the paper from cover to cover, she stood, then bent and kissed his headstone goodbye. As she had each time, she sobbed a little. She straightened up, said a silent "Our Father" and told Michael she'd see him tomorrow. Then she tiptoed back to her new Lexus as if afraid that she would wake the sleeping souls if she put her foot down fully.

She started the car, sobbed a little more, and slowly left the cemetery, thinking about a snapshot she had in her head of Michael, standing in the sunshine with a beach ball in his hand, looking back at the camera, the sun making him squint and wrinkle his nose. He was five years old when that picture was snapped at the beach.

To her, it was as if it were today.

Chapter Forty One

September 4, 2013, 5:15 p.m.
9 Bay Road
Brookhaven Hamlet, New York

When Sharona had brought home her five million dollar check from Brannigan, she went first to Gran's apartment and sat across from her at the kitchen table, where they usually held serious discussions.

"Gran, I been thinking about these babies, how they was ever going to break out of this life that we live. See, I always kept the dream like you told me, but I never did see anything great come along until I had these babies inside me. Now I got to leave these sweet children before they're even a month old. And I can't bear the thought of that, Gran. You know that. I especially have been thinking 'bout you and Deke taking over after I'm gone. You know he ain't the most educated, and even if he tries, who says he ever going to get his college diploma? Or what he going do with it? I ain't saying he'll quit on these babies, but truth is, nobody knows what Deke might do till he does it."

Gran sat in her chair staring at Sharona through her thick glasses, wondering what her grandchild was leading up to.

Sharona picked up a kitchen towel and began fiddling with it. "Now, before you go telling me how he's such a good man, let me tell you something. Nicky Storms told me Deke been sniffing around, hinting that if things don't go so well, he might want to work for him again. You see what I'm saying, Gran? Nicky told me about it, because he say I got to keep an eye on Deke. After I'm gone, you especially got to know the devil you dealing with."

She set the towel down and moved back to the table, where Gran remained seated. "Nicky always been smarter than Deke and he thinks he can keep Deke out of his business, but that might mean Deke would go somewhere else if he gets down on his luck. You know what I'm saying?"

"Why you telling me all this, Sharona?" Gran was still in her uniform from work and she was tired. She was anxious for Sharona to make her point.

Now seated opposite her, Sharona held her hand up. "I'm getting to that part, Gran. See, you getting along in years, and I was thinking about what would happen to the babies if you pass over. And that scares me almost as much as me having to die. Because left alone, ain't no way Deke could ever be to those babies what you were to me, what you would be to them."

Sharona nodded as if she had just concluded some great lesson. Gran, meanwhile, was ready to put her head on the table and begin snoring. "Anyway, I been just as afraid of all this as I could ever be of anything. So here's what I decided to do, Gran. First off, I'm going move us out of this project and find us a nice house with some property so the babies will have plenty of room to grow up and play, and even ride horses if they want. Then I'm going to buy you a car, and Deke a car, and maybe even one for myself. Something with a lot of room behind the wheel, because I'm so fat from these babies."

Sharona was smiling broadly now. Sharona stood and walked back to the sink. "Then you and me's going shopping, Gran. And we going to buy furniture for that house and stuff for the babies' nursery, and have it all decorated as beautiful as anything you ever seen. Then I'm going to make Deke quit his job and enroll full time in college, so he can get his studies finished and get a degree so he'll never be a dumb daddy that has to work forever changing tires in Riverhead."

Sharona spun around and folded her arms across her chest. She looked defiantly at her Gran, who could do nothing but stare at the girl she raised, horrified at the thought that she'd snapped under all the pressure. Sharona was ready to drop her news on Gran now. "Then I'm talking to Mister Brannigan and have him invest the rest of this five million dollars he gave me today so that our family is set for life and my two babies is as good as anyone in this whole world. So they grow up with all the opportunities that you and me ain't never even dreamed of seeing or having. So that someday their names will be recognized for being smart and classy and beautiful and rich."

Gran had struggled out of her chair and was moving with her arms outstretched to comfort her granddaughter. Sharona's last few words hadn't really registered. Instead of hearing Sharona's declaration that the family was leaving hard times behind, she thought a confused and delusional young woman was falling apart right in front of her.

"Child, what you talking about? You sound crazy. Now stop making no sense and tell me what's on your mind. I ain't be staying up all night worrying about you losing your mind, you hear?" Gran wrapped her arms around her beloved grandchild.

Sharona took her Gran's arms from around her neck and squeezed her hands.

"Here it is, Gran, right here for you to look at," Sharona said as she took the check out of its envelope and handed it to her grandmother. "Tomorrow I'm going to the bank where I got seven hundred and forty-three dollars and sixteen cents in my checking account and I'll deposit this check for five million dollars. Ain't that going to put a surprise on the face of that snotty teller down there, think she so high and mighty. They be calling me Miss Watts from now on, instead of asking me for my license every time I go there to cash my check."

Gran felt as though she had been hit by a stun gun. She stumbled backward as she stared, unbelieving, at what was in her hand. "Oh, Lord save us. This can't be real. I …"

Sharona now crouched so she could look directly into her Gran's face as she grasped the old woman's shoulders. "Oh, it's real, Gran. Mister Brannigan gave one of those to each of the lab mice that's set to die on Christmas along with him. You know how I been telling you the lab mice been coming together and how we all helping each other think out our troubles and fear of dying and whatever? Well, Mister Brannigan says that's meant a lot to him and that he realized how he had all his dreams come true while he's been on earth and how he wants the same to happen for us while there is still time. So, he handed us each a check for five million dollars—and then he said he hopes it enough," Sharona laughed uproariously now.

She released Gran's shoulders and took the older woman's hands in hers. "Gran, my babies are rich and they will go to college and they will live in a nice house and they'll never worry about food on the table. And you'll be treated like a rich woman everywhere you go from tomorrow to the day I see you in heaven. And Deke will have an education and he is going to be somebody."

Halfway through her outburst, Sharona began weeping. She wrapped her arms around her still-unbelieving Gran, the old woman's eyes glazed as though she left the earth on some mystical journey. "Gran, your prayers has been answered. The Lord has answered all our prayers," she said.

Sharona's words brought Gran back. "Oh my Lord. Oh my Lord Jesus. I can't believe this, Sharona." Now Gran was crying.

And so began their journey, later joined by Deke, to a destiny that both women had believed could happen only to the lucky few in life.

Now, it was happening for them.

———⊱✦⊰———

Today, with summer's heat behind them, was move-in day. They were leaving their past behind. The little family had looked at dozens of properties and homes, and had finally settled on a former farmhouse with a barn on an acre and a half of land in the rural hamlet of Brookhaven. The property and surrounding community was bursting with bucolic charm and the three of them were sold the minute they pulled up to the house, built in the style of a Nantucket cottage. Their new home had everything they would have sketched for themselves if they had drawn it with an architect.

Built in 1885, the elegant, welcoming home was near the center of town, but also a short drive from the beach. When the broker first brought them to see it, it was a working bed and breakfast. The owners had maintained the property perfectly: new roof, authentic silver cedar siding, and all new windows, some of which overlooked the wraparound porch and a small lily pond at the side of the house. The gracious original woodwork and classic Victorian details were complemented by the spacious new kitchen and renovated baths. The seven bedrooms and four full bathrooms included two master suites, so Gran could occupy the one on the main floor, while Sharona and Deke took the upstairs.

In the yard were huge old specimen trees, an in-ground pool, and a pool house that also doubled as a guest house. The restored barn could garage four cars. Now that they had quietly gotten married, Sharona insisted that Deke do the bargaining. Their broker had patiently brought them to multiple houses at various prices, high and low, while trying to figure out their financial status. She was stunned, as were the Bay Road home's owners, when Deke's offer exceeded the asking price by ten percent, but only if they met two stipulations. The first was that they had three hours to respond, or the offer was off the table. The second was that the closing would be in thirty days. Skeptical, the broker asked Deke if he was certain that he could acquire financing in just thirty days. He simply said "yes," smiled, and handed her a binder of twenty-five thousand dollars. "We got babies coming; can't wait any longer," he said. The house was theirs by the time they returned to the nearby realty office in the hamlet's small downtown area.

Later, when the three of them were alone, Deke told Gran and

Sharona that he had been prowling online real estate sites so that he knew the asking prices of similar homes. He had discovered prices in the area had climbed fivefold over the previous ten years; the recession that had afflicted the nation had barely been felt here. He also had learned that empty property within the hamlet was all but gone, which kept driving prices up, too. He then looked up sales over the previous six months; the average time on the market for houses in a similar price range was nineteen days. The area was hot. This house had been on the market for only eight days.

He figured the property's value would probably grow at least five percent over their first year. Rather than risk losing the house, he decided to overbid the asking price, taking the offering to just over a million dollars. There would still be enough money left to provide economic stability for Sharona's children after she left them. Deke knew that after a year he would still have made a profit, but what was more important was that they would quickly get the property they wanted. He wanted Sharona to be well settled in before the twins arrived.

Gran chuckled and looked at Sharona with an expression that said, "I told you so."

Sharona just laughed. "I'm going to start calling you sneaky Dekey," she said, as she kissed him gratefully. "Thanks, Deke, good job." Sharona was amazed at how quickly Deke was adapting himself to their new life. As she faced the cold sense of foreboding that had descended when the lab had delivered her sad verdict, Deke's calm and determination was a rock she found herself leaning on more and more.

Deke was the one who convinced her the fees she was being paid by the lab were comparable to her store salary and that she should quit and enjoy her pregnancy. So she had. It was Deke who wisely informed Sharona, who wanted him to leave his job and go to school full-time, that doing so would violate his probation. It was Deke's idea that if she got pregnant they should marry, so there would be no question of the children's parentage if and when Sharona died. And it was Deke, who enthusiastically agreed with Sharona about getting

Brannigan's help on protecting her new fortune. "Keeping money can be harder then getting it," he had said. Dan had come through with ways to keep their windfall safe that neither Deke nor Sharona could have ever imagined.

The courses Deke were taking showcased his aptitude for finance. He had quickly found that he was skilled at working with numbers. He had taken only three courses so far, but two of them were accounting classes, and he dove into learning, which excited him, and helped him to see that he had talents and skills beyond pure brute strength. His third course, the basic principles of trading equities, completely enthralled him; he pulled an A.

"I been telling you all along, Deke, you just needed to find yourself," Sharona constantly reminded him.

His reply was always, "Uh huh, Watts. I just needed to find you."

Moving day had been long and arduous. By sunset, Sharona was completely drained. There was still, it seemed, days, perhaps even weeks of work ahead of them before the house would really be theirs. For all of them, though, it was a day of triumph and rejoicing. Gran was nearly ready to burst with pride. Deke directed the movers throughout the house as they toted in not only the meager remnants of their former homes in the projects but also a stream of deliveries from stores including Pottery Barn, Buy Buy Baby, and Ethan Allen Galleries. Gran and Sharona had furiously shopped for the essentials to set up the home, especially the nursery furnishings. They were all eager to see the babies' room assembled before tackling anything else.

Deke was moving a dresser from one side of the master suite to the other as easily as if it were a matchstick when Sharona felt a stitch in her side. She walked downstairs and out onto the porch, sitting on the top step to listen to the quiet as twilight gathered. To the west, the fading sun had turned the skies a bright autumn rage of color; swirling clouds, all shapes and sizes, appeared as if painted against the sky. Sharona felt heartsick as she hugged her expanding belly and felt the twins move. Her doctor had confirmed the sexes, and she and Deke had decided on the names Tulip and Thomas. At this moment, Sharona was torn between their good luck and reality. She knew she was carrying two children who would never know their own mother. Her due date was December 28th, but the doctors planned to induce labor on December 23rd or 24th if she hadn't given birth yet.

When she had first heard that she had a date with death, all she could focus on was that she'd be leaving Gran. Now, she knew she had found a man who loved her deeply, and who was changing his life to become worthy of being the father of her children. Her pregnancy had been perfect. They had the home of her dreams, cars, security. Everything she could have ever wanted had become a reality. And soon, for her, it would be all gone. Gran kept telling her to ask the Lord for comfort. But she couldn't understand that. Comfort for her was where she was right now. She had prayed and it gave her some peace. But that peace was temporary. The demons taunting her always returned. They were here now, spoiling yet another dream come true.

She felt Deke softly walk across the boards of the porch and gently sit beside her. He reached out and took her hand. "Beautiful, isn't it?" he said with a hint of wonder in his voice.

Sharona sniffled and nodded her head silently as the tears began to fall.

"Come on, baby, don't be crying now. This is your moment, Shoney. You're here, alive, the babies are good, tonight this roof will be over our heads and your Gran will say her prayers for the first time in all her life in a house that has her name on it."

She looked away from him, back toward the sunset. "I know. But I have to die so we could get it, Deke. It don't seem fair. Everything I ever dreamed of is here, and all I can think about is having a life raising my children with you in this beautiful house. I don't want to go, Deke. I don't want to go. Please, please. I just want to have my babies and see them grow up." Her pain overcame her.

"I know, baby girl, I know. Come here." Deke took her in his powerful arms and stroked her head while she sobbed on his shoulder.

Behind them, Gran had come out to the porch; she silently sat down in a rocking chair. She listened as her beloved granddaughter suffered and once again she prayed for a miracle. There were a hundred and twelve days left before Christmas.

"Jesus? When will you answer my prayers?" she whispered.

Chapter Forty Two

September 4, 2013, 7:20 p.m.
Colcroft House
Cold Spring Harbor, New York

Neither Dan nor Kate could recall how long it had been since they'd had Joe and Loretta to the house. But as part of her reconciliation with Dan, Kate had insisted that he compensate her brother.

Dan had come up with an idea that he was going to put in Joe's pocket tonight. After their partnership had dissolved, Joe Kelly had remained at Morgan Stanley and become one of the firm's top people. He was a rich trader, and he and Loretta had lived a comfortable country club life. Or so it appeared. Unable to conceive, Joe and Loretta had adopted a son. They were planning to adopt again soon..

Their child, James, was born in Korea and arrived in their home at the age of three. He was sledding with his parents one winter evening at the Piping Rock Country Club golf course when their world turned upside down.

When it snowed, the club's members and their families used the gentle slopes for sledding when the course was closed. Joe, Loretta and James were on a three-person toboggan. They placed the boy between his dad's legs and Loretta sat behind Joe as they joyfully slid down the rolling hillocks of the golf course.

A group of teens were on the same slope, using plastic dish spinners that gave a faster ride but were harder to control. They crossed the path that Joe and Loretta and James were navigating. Joe steered their toboggan to the right to avoid the teens, but the maneuver tipped the toboggan over.

Usually a spill like that would mean nothing more than a few laughs as they brushed off the snow afterward. But as the toboggan began to tip, James tried to stand. The boy was tossed up in the air, and landed head first a short distance from either of his parents, who also tumbled off the sled. Loretta knew immediately that something was wrong. Normally, James would have been rolling around in the show and laughing after a spill like that.

Joe had landed farther downhill, but was within three feet of his son, who was lying still on the frozen surface. Loretta, who had never taken her eyes off the boy, reached out for him, shouting, "James! James! Are you all right?"

He never answered. When the child had landed, his head had hit the ground at an odd angle, snapping his neck.

Their lives were never the same. They remained childless. Loretta had more than doubled her weight and began to drink. Her happy hour at the club, which used to begin at five in the afternoon, now started at about the time she finished her first nine holes, around noon.

Many days, the club manager would call a car to take her home. She would be sound asleep in their comfortable Oyster Bay Cove house by the time Joe arrived home from work. Rarely was Loretta awake to see the clock strike nine at night. And even if she didn't make it to the club, she had stashed plenty of alcohol in the house. Her addiction was beyond Joe's ability to manage.

Joe remained the steady, silent, brooding man he had always been, uninterested in anything but his work. Joe and Dan had drifted apart. Loretta and Kate went their separate ways, too, as Loretta descended further into depression and an empty existence. Dan had considered the potential for Loretta to ruin his life, so the less time she and Kate spent together, the more secure he felt. And while

Dan felt guilty about the business relationship with Joe that he had severed, he justified the split to himself: He knew Joe wouldn't have gone along with his illegal scheme.

Tonight was to be a redemption for Dan. Joe was going to walk out of Colcroft House a very rich man.

Loretta was already toasted when the couple arrived for dinner; and by the time the four of them had finished, she was slurring her words and staggering as she and Kate walked to the veranda to watch the sunset. The men went to the library when Dan said he wanted to talk with Joe about an investment. That was partially true. The January deal with the global communications company and China World Airways had netted Dan just under two hundred million dollars. They first shared some Morgan Stanley gossip. Then Dan told his brother-in-law about his lucrative deal. Not that he needed to; Joe had heard through the grapevine that Dan had backed the communications-airlines deal.

Finally, Dan spoke up. "Joe, it has always bothered me that you were out of the mix in the stuff I did after we were separated. I've never been comfortable with the fact that I had all this good luck and you could have been, or should have been, part of it. We were partners. It wasn't fair that Morgan Stanley drove a wedge between us." Joe looked suspiciously at his brother-in-law. "Dan, I always thought that you wanted the split. I have no complaints about my career after that. I've had a pretty good time and Morgan has been good to me."

Dan was startled at the hint that Joe knew the truth about how their partnership ended—that Dan had engineered their breakup. But he wasn't going to get into that now.

"In my mind, it still doesn't seem right, so I've decided to try and catch us up. My take on the initial deals I did back in the early years was roughly a hundred and seventy million. My recollection of the way they were developed was that the seminal relationship began while the two of us were still partners, but the deal didn't actually come together until I was out on my own."

Dan paused to gather his thoughts before proceeding. "You

should have been a full partner in those years. I've created a numbered account in the Bahamas - here are the details - with you as sole owner. It contains eighty-five million. At five o'clock today, it became yours.." He smiled and extended his hand to Joe.

Joe didn't take Dan's hand. "Are you crazy, Dan? I can't accept this. I didn't do anything to earn this. The Lucent hookup was sealed between you and Barnes back at Villanova, way before we worked together. You would have pocketed that business no matter where I was. Why are you doing this now?"

Dan was stunned at Joe's understanding about what had gone down all those years ago. "Joe, it's eighty-five million dollars. What the fuck do you care why I'm doing this? Who's crazy here?"

Joe was not naive. "There's more to this, Dan. There has to be. You just don't drop eighty-five million dollars on someone because you used to work with him. Even if he is your brother-in-law. There's more to this, Dan. What is it?"

Dan just shrugged and leaned back. "There's nothing Joe. I'm just trying to balance the books. You're Kate's brother and we feel bad that we've acquired so much. Not that you and Loretta haven't done well, but we should have been partners all along, Joe. This is what your share should have been and now you have it. It's got nothing to do with anything else."

Dan knew he didn't sound convincing, but he was thrown by Joe's grasp of the truth. Joe sat still, running a mental chronology of events since they'd parted at Morgan Stanley.

When his memory put everything in place, he stood and handed Dan's file back to him. "I can't take this, Dan. It's not mine. Thank Kate for me. But you keep it. Give it to charity or build a library. I don't want it."

"Why?" Dan was shocked.

Joe hesitated for a minute before speaking. "I know you had a deal with Barnes before you ever left Morgan. He told me so because he thought I knew; he thought I would be coming along with you. You cut me out, Dan." Joe smirked across the table at Dan. "You're surprised? Why? Barnes knew at the time we were partners and brothers-in-law. One day he called looking for you. You weren't there and the discussion just went in that direction. By the time we hung up, I knew what you were doing."

Joe stared deeply into Dan's eyes now. He had hoped for years that someday he would be able to tell his former partner that his deception had always been obvious, and that he had always known what was going on. Joe held his hand up, silencing Dan, who he sensed wanted to speak; he wasn't ready to hear what his brother-in-law had to say. "That's OK, Dan. I wouldn't have taken that risk. You guys could have gone to jail for that one. There's no way I would have been a part of that."

Brannigan tried to interject, but Joe spoke first. "You knew me well enough to know I wouldn't have bought into a scheme like that, so you got me out of the way before the machinery started grinding. Makes sense, so I never brought it up and it's something I don't begrudge you for. In fact, I'm grateful you respected my honesty."

Joe paused for a moment, and then went on. "What I am bothered by is what happened between you and Loretta."

Dan's heart pounded. Joe leaned back in his chair and crossed his legs. After all these years, he was enjoying Dan's discomfort immensely. "Oh, yeah. I know about that. She's told me about it repeatedly through the years. She despises me, Danny. Blames me for James. And so every now and then, in one of her drunken stupors, she'll tell me how you were so good together and how Kate was the lucky Kelly, because she got you."

Joe's face hid his dark feelings toward his sister's husband. Dan had betrayed him in every way. Confronting Dan now was his own reward for years of silence. "Yeah, I've known now for a long time, Dan. At first I thought it was a fantasy she was making up, but I soon realized that it was real. Why Dan? Why her? Why me? And how could you have done that to Kate and the girls?"

Dan was unable to speak. He'd always been ashamed of himself for these betrayals, but at this moment, confronted with the undeniable truth that he had stolen both money and marriage from Joe Kelly, he was speechless and utterly defenseless.

Joe grunted, mocking Dan's weakness. "Well, whatever. Thanks for the offer, Dan, but I don't want your money," he said, spitting out the words. "I'd never feel comfortable with it. Money can't buy honesty - or dignity. I have a clear conscience, Dan, and I want to keep it that way. You did what you did and now you have to live with it. Some admire what you've pulled off. But I wouldn't want to be in your shoes. Does Kate know any of this? Is she the reason you're doing this now?"

Dan could only whisper, "It's not as simple as that. And as far as Loretta and me, it wasn't sport fucking, Joe ..."

"I've heard that, Dan,' Joe interrupted Dan,' you both used each other. The two of you were full of insecurities and found something with each other . I get it. Loretta has sober moments every once in a while and she told me everything."

Joe's expression darkened. He was controlling himself but he wasn't sure he could continue. "But you were wrong. Loretta was wrong. She still lives inside that fantasy. She still thinks of you as one of the big things that happened in her life. I never measured up. What a crock."

Joe stood and looked down at Dan, still seated on the sofa. "I don't care anymore. When we lost James, everything changed. She went to the bottle; I went to my desk. I can't do anything for her. Maybe I never could. I hope for my sister's sake that whatever came out of you screwing Loretta did you some good. My sister seems content with her life, at least as far as I can see."

Dan stared at Joe and ran his hands through his hair. He knew now that he could never redeem himself in Joe's eyes. He had sunk to a depth from which there was no redemption.

Sounding broken, he began to apologize. "I'm so sorry, Joe. Everything you say is true. Loretta and I—we both needed to grow up. I got lucky. My time with Loretta taught me a valuable lesson. I learned that I needed to be exalted by a woman. And Loretta made me realize that it wasn't flattery or great sex that did it. What she made me see was that it was the woman who was willing to walk the floors with your children at night so that you could sleep; the one

THIS'LL BE THE DAY THAT I DIE

who did the dishes, folded the laundry at midnight after a twenty-hour day; who washed the toilets; who had great sex with you even after all that even though she was exhausted. Loretta made me see the truth in my life was Kate."

Dan confessed, unable to mask his shame. "And I fell in love again with Kate, but this time with a love so deep it hurts my heart when I think of her. Your sister means everything to me. I would rather take my own life than do anything to hurt her. She's the best woman I could ever meet on earth or that I would expect to meet in heaven. And that was what came out of my affair with Loretta."

Dan rose from the couch and put his hands in his pockets. There wasn't much left to say. "I'm sorry, Joe. I thought when she and I parted that Loretta had realized something similar with you. I never understood how much you two had lost. I'm sorry."

The apology was humbling for Dan, Joe knew. But it was too little and too late. He simply nodded. "Oh, well, she probably did, for a time. We were very happy when James came along. But when he died, she first thought it was punishment for her adultery, her affair with you. Then some priest talked her out of that. Told her God didn't work that way and she believed him. Eventually she gave up and drowned her sorrows in booze. Her family has a long history of problems with alcohol. It was bound to happen." Joe took a few paces away from where they had been facing each other; his back was now turned toward Dan.

"Why didn't you ever confront me?" Dan was genuinely curious.

Joe looked Dan in the eye. "Simple. I wanted to protect my sister. This shit we're talking about is beneath her dignity. I wanted to stay at her level and not get soiled by all of this."

Dan nodded. "Amen, Joe. You've got that right. Are you sure you won't take the money? Find some use for it?" Dan really had no need for these millions, but he did need the forgiveness and absolution..

Joe waved his hand dismissively. "No. I'd never touch it, Dan, and I'd probably die with it in that bank forever. Take it and do something good with it. That's a better idea. Be a saint, Dan. You can afford it," he said, a mocking tone in his voice.

"Ha," Dan smiled ruefully. "Money can't buy you sainthood, Joe." Dan knew that if absolution for his sins were to come, it wouldn't be from the man he had betrayed in so many ways.

"But maybe it can help pay off your sins," Joe said, not very convincingly. It was Dan's problem and Joe wanted nothing to do with it.

"Not if you're the buyer. As this little chat of ours just proved," Dan said. "Well … better luck with God, then." His brother-in-law shrugged as he began to leave Dan alone with his thoughts.

Dan didn't bother to tell Joe how apt his words were. He just let Joe walk quietly from the room. No handshake. No forgiveness. Not another word spoken.

Dan's reckoning with God was coming fast.

Chapter Forty Three

September 4, 2013, 2:10 p.m.
Amtrak, Track Number Six
Penn Station
New York, New York

The numbness in his toes was now creeping through the rest of Ted's right foot and toward his ankle. Worse, he was feeling the same phantom sensation in his left leg, making it hard to use his prosthesis.

He could still maneuver well enough, but he sensed that if this continued, his mobility would be affected. That didn't mean he couldn't get around; there would still be wheelchairs or crutches. But they required strength, and that was something he was running out of.

Ashamed that he had delayed seeing his sisters for so long, Ted planned a visit to Baltimore, checking the Orioles schedule to see if they were playing at home. It was the last home stand in a dismal season. At least he'd know where to find Patty.

Father Schmidt dropped him off in Jamaica to catch the Long Island Rail Road train to Penn Station, where he'd pick up Amtrak to Baltimore. He'd be there before dinner and head straight to Colleen's; he expected she would cry for hours when he showed up unannounced.

By now, his appearance gave away his dire condition. His hair was a whisper of slight, dust-like strands that he usually covered with a Kangol cap, but his weight loss was even more obvious and his teeth were beginning to protrude because his jaw and face had changed so much. He knew Colleen would try to control her emotions when she saw him, but she would fail.

He was sad about this trip. He knew it was likely to be the last time he would visit his childhood haunts. He also realized he didn't have too much time left with his sisters. Slowly, the curtain was coming down. Time was the enemy now.

As the train left Penn Station, he plugged in his iPod, in the hope that some music would raise his spirits. After the train came out of the tunnel in New Jersey, Paul Simon's "Graceland" began playing. The genius of Simon's song about a trip to Elvis Presley's home in Tennessee seemed to move in time with the rumble of the train. As he listened to the words about being received in Graceland it filled him with tears. He was surprised by the emotion the lyrics drew from him. But these were happy tears, he thought.

He turned his head toward the window to hide his emotions from those around him and swallowed hard. He was coming to the end, and the idea of being received in Graceland struck a chord. He clicked to listen to the song again. Calmed by the melody, he then switched to a Dave Mathews tune.

In Baltimore, he grabbed a taxi to Colleen's house. As he handed the driver a tip, he was shocked to see a for sale sign hanging out front. This trip to see his sisters was about to turn into a revelation for him, he thought. He took two steps up to her door and heard Colleen's voice as she emerged from the adjoining house. "Teddy, is that you? What are you doing here?"

He could see Colleen's stunned look as she drank him in for the minute it took her to get down the steps and put her arms around him, as she stretched across the low boxwoods that ran between the two row houses.

"Hi, Col, it was a spur-of-the moment thing. I had some time off and decided to surprise you. Looks like I'm the one getting shocked.

You're selling?"

Instead of answering, she turned to the adjoining house, where her neighbor, an enormous woman who filled the doorway, stood. "Hilly, look here," Colleen said. "My brother Teddy is here. What a surprise! I'll see you later, hon. Let me get him settled."

Ted had met Hilly over the years. He waved unenthusiastically, "Hi, Hilly, how are you?"

"Good, how are you?" she said, just as weakly, smiling and displaying a set of the yellowest teeth Ted had ever seen.

"Here, let me have that," Colleen said as she took Ted's duffle bag. "Oh, it's so light. Not planning on staying long?"

"No, just a day or so, Col. I have Masses on Sunday I need to cover, so I'll be heading back Saturday afternoon." They entered the house and Colleen put his bag on the stairs facing the front door.

"Let me get you something. I have iced tea. Or would you like something stronger?"

"Any cold beer?" he asked.

"Let me see." As she bent down to look into her refrigerator, Ted crossed the tiny living room and sat on her sofa, placed in front of the windows.

"Here we go. Can't tell you how long it's been in there, but there's another if it's not any good." She handed it to him. "Glass?"

"No this will be fine," he said as he twisted the cap off the long-neck Bud. "So what's with the for sale sign, Colleen? Where you going?"

"What's that?" she said. When she wasn't prepared to answer a question, she always fell back on phrases like "excuse me?' or "come again?"

"The house, Colleen. How come you're selling?" She came out of the kitchen with a plate of stale crackers and a jar of Wispride cheese; Ted thought he should check the sell-by date on the cheese before even considering it.

And then she had started to cry. "Teddy, I didn't want to tell you, but I was let go by the school district in June. They were downsizing and they were going by seniority. Remember, I worked for the first nine years as a temporary? My job was eliminated." She slid into a chair. "Oh, Ted, I don't know what I'm going to do. I had no money saved and this month I missed my mortgage payment for the first time in sixteen years. There's just no jobs around and I get unemployment, but it isn't much. I thought it best to sell the house before I get too deep in the hole."

Ted was surprised but sympathetic. "Colleen, I'm no financial expert, but you must have some equity in this house. Couldn't you get refinancing until you get back on your feet?"

His sister picked up a tissue box from the end table. "The bank wouldn't let me do anything because I'm not working. They said they'd consider my application when I could show proof of six months' employment."

Ted pursed his lips. "Typical. Banks are always there when you're flush, but gone when you're broke. Can't Patty help you? What did she say?"

"Nothing, Ted. The usual. 'Oh, honey, I'm so sorry to hear that. Let me know if I can do anything for you.' Then I call her and she doesn't call back. She's never got any time for me, Ted. We're very different people. You know that."

He did know that. Patty had made the same kind of vows to him last winter, when she came to Long Island armed with every fact she could find about human genes. She'd kept up the weekly calls for a while. Then the calls dropped to every other week. Now, he hadn't heard from her in nearly two months.

Meanwhile, his life revolved around cancer and biweekly visits with the Cold Spring Harbor Laboratory researchers. Recently, he'd made an effort to polish his fading reputation at St. David's. He'd made significant progress there; his sermons were getting better as he shed his luggage, got more in touch with his feelings, and spoke from his heart.

"But enough about me, Teddy," Colleen said, blowing her nose loudly. "How are you doing? You look great."

"Yeah, feeling great," he lied, giving his sister the only answer she would hear no matter what he said. As he answered her questions about his treatment and how he was coping, he took his cell phone out and sent Patty a text: *"In B'more at Cols. You around?"*

Two minutes later, his phone vibrated. *"Holy S---. How long? At the store. Will call u"*

A minute after the text buzzed through, her call came.

"Hey," he said. "Surprise, surprise. Come and get us; we want to see some free baseball tonight."

"Sure. There's lots of available seats. Who's with you? Surely you don't mean Colleen is coming to the game. She hates baseball."

He smiled. "Yeah, but she loves hot dogs and so do I. You get a fifty percent discount, as I recall. What time will you pick us up?"

"Can I just send a car? My car won't hold the three of us. It's a two-seater, remember?"

He'd forgotten that. Or was she hinting that Colleen shouldn't come? "Hey, that's great. I love the executive treatment," he answered.

"You in uniform or a civilian tonight?" she asked.

"Civvies. Even polished my fake leg." He smiled as he spoke.

"Oh, God, Ted! That's awful, even for you. OK. You're at Colleen's now, right? Then you know what going on there, right?" It was more a statement than a question . Before he could respond, Patty continued. "OK, the guy who'll be driving the car is Eugene. I'll have him there in about a half hour to forty minutes. Game is at seven eleven and we'll have time for dinner."

"Dogs, Patty. Dogs with the works. I can't go back to New York without a Bird Dog." Ted squeezed a word in before his breathless sister ended their call.

"OK, OK. Dogs for you. But I'll have something fit for humans and Colleen will not like anything she gets anyway." He was disappointed by her snarky remark, but let it go, glad that Colleen couldn't hear her. Even if Patty was right. "See you later, Pats."

He hung up and gazed at Colleen. "Baseball, sis. The American pastime. It will do you good."

Colleen whined. "Teddy, I don't want to go and I don't really want to see Patty. I'll wait here for you."

But he was firm. "Colleen, please. I need both of you together. I have news. News you can use. OK?"

"Oh! What kind of news? I hope it's good news, Ted. told Hilly I'd help her tonight. She's trying to paper her kitchen." She looked at his face. "OK, Ted, I'll come. But I'll hate it."

He shrugged and smiled. "I knew that before I made the call."

"Oh, you're still such a scooch. I'll just go next door and let Hilly know. Have some cheese and crackers meanwhile." And she headed toward the front door.

"Thanks, but I'm saving myself for the Bird Dogs," he said just before he put the beer bottle to his mouth. I t was hard enough to hold onto his health, he thought. He didn't need to touch that cheese.

Patty had snagged a glass-enclosed luxury box for them; plenty of these suites were empty. For Orioles fans, the baseball season had ended sometime in June, when the team fell to bottom of the league and stayed there. There was a sparse crowd for the game tonight as the home team faced the Blue Jays, passing through town on their way to the playoffs.

Keeping her promise, Patty provided hot dogs for her brother while she and Colleen had corned beef sandwiches. Colleen only nibbled at hers, saying she didn't really eat processed meats as a general rule. Patty raised her eyebrows at Ted.

"Patty, I promised Hilly an Orioles cap," Colleen said during the third inning. "Is there a souvenir stand on this level?" They could see she was bored, since she had been working her way through any reading materials she could find.

Patty nodded. "One level down. It's about twenty yards down the corridor. You'll see it. You want me to come with you?"

Colleen rose from her seat. "No. I'll be fine. This is Suite 105, right? I'll find my way back."

Ted waited until the door closed before he glared at Patty. Ever since they'd arrived at the ballpark, he'd been waiting to lecture her on her responsibility to her siblings. "What's going on, Pats? Why are you and Colleen so distant? She lost her job and now she's losing her house. She reached out to you and she tells me you won't call her back."

Patty waved her hand back at her brother, a sad smile on her face. "Is that what she told you?"

"Yes. Is it true?"

Patty uncrossed her legs and spun her chair to face her brother. "Well, yes. But there's more to this, Ted. C olleen has no money because she loaned most of her savings to that beast next door. Hilly's on welfare and can't pay her back. Her husband walked out three years ago. Who could blame him? And she keeps crying poverty and Colleen keeps lending her money. She has our sister completely under her spell."

"What? Why haven't you said something to me sooner? Is Hilly … you know … straight?"

Patty just shrugged her shoulders. "I couldn't answer that. I don't think there's anything like that going on, but Hilly kind of bullies Colleen. When Col called and told me she got fired, she let it slip that she was almost broke. I worked at her till she told me she'd loaned all but a few thousand dollars of her savings to Hilly over the last several years. She told me Hilly kept saying that she was going to sell her house as soon as she got clear title to it, but who knows the truth?"

Patty took a bite from her sandwich and swallowed. "In the meantime, Colleen has been paying that moocher's bills. Now Col needs cash herself and it's all gone. Did she tell you I asked her to move in with me?"

Ted showed his surprise. "No, she didn't mention that. You did? Would you two get along?"

Patty took a swallow from a long-neck beer bottle. "It would be a disaster, Ted. It wouldn't work for a day. But what else could I do? She has to sell her place, and right now she has no job. And, truth to tell, I may not have a job after this weekend, either. This place is going through a major shakeup after the season ends Sunday and I could be gone. Eighteen years out of the playoffs. I'm sure management thinks it's time for some changes."

"But you're on the business side," Ted said.

"Yeah, but we sell the sponsorships, the signage, and the ads. Attendance and media impressions are at an all-time low. The place is hemorrhaging money and no one—no one—is safe. Ownership is sharpening the knives as we sit here."

"Wow. This family is walking under clouds these days, isn't it?"

"I'll be OK. I've had some pretty good years and I have a decent stash put away. But if I want to stay in baseball, I may have to move to another city. I've already talked to a few people and there are other opportunities. Of course, most of my contacts are here, but my track record is pretty good and I can probably land something. But I'm not sure I want that. I've been thinking about a change myself." Her voice trailed off.

"What kind of change?" he asked cautiously. He saw that she had started to cry. "Patty, what's wrong?"

"I'm what's wrong, Ted. I have nothing worthwhile in my life. Sure, I have a super apartment overlooking the Inner Harbor, and a hot car and a glam job, but there's nothing permanent in my life."

"By permanent, you mean male companionship?"

Patty nodded. "You know me, Ted. Just sailors home on leave. Never anyone who stays too long. Yes, a steady man would be nice. And couple of kids and a dog, too. Right now, I'm everybody's good time, and when they're done, so am I. I hate my life, Teddy. I'd give everything to have a normal life, with someone who makes my breakfast on Sunday mornings."

"So what do you want to do?" Ted asked. "You're still young. Move away and start new somewhere else. No baggage when you get there. You can be anything you like."

Patty shook her head. "I know. I'm kind of leaning that way. I'm tired of keeping up this image and playing the happy hooker. It never has a happy ending. No substance. Just laughs."

The click of the door told them that Colleen had returned. Patty jumped up and headed to the bathroom to wash her face while Ted turned off the closed-circuit TV. He was now itching to share the news that would change their lives with his sisters.

Ted and Colleen talked about the cost of souvenirs while they waited for Patty to rejoin them. When she did Ted went right to the point. "Listen, girls I have some business with you both. It's among the reasons I came down here this weekend."

"You're not going anywhere, are you Teddy?' Colleen asked.

"Colleen, for Christ's sake! What's that supposed to mean? What's wrong with you?" Patty lashed out.

"I'm just asking, Patty. He's been sick and all. I don't know. You don't need to jump down my throat for every little thing I say."

Ted held his arms up between his sisters. "Just a second, ladies. I'm not going anywhere, Colleen. At least not for a while. But the truth is, there isn't anything more the doctors can do for me. He paused to let that sink in before continuing. "But God has been very good to me and to this family, so we need not dwell on the negative. I have something to share with you that is all good."

Then Ted told them about Dan Brannigan's gift and his decision to divide the windfall. Two accounts for his sisters had been set up with Charles Schwab Financial Investments. The final third was to be split and donated to each of the parishes where he had served as a priest over the years.

His sisters' jaws dropped as he spoke. Colleen dissolved in tears, and even Patty began to cry. He kept talking without waiting for his sisters to regain control; he thought they might never allow him to finish. "So, it isn't a king's ransom, but it should be enough to provide each of you with a comfortable and secure lifestyle, provided you let it work for you. I have all the documents with me back at the house and you'll have the contact information for your account executive. He's a good guy, young, but smart. Use him."

Patty was speechless, a rarity for her. She realized that Ted's gift meant both she and Colleen could escape the unhappiness in their lives. But then dark reality crept in, as it dawned on her that this good luck was only possible because Ted was dying. Soon he would be gone. If he hadn't been involved in that experiment, he never would have met Brannigan, and there would have been no multi-million-dollar gift to solve all their problems. Patty sank deeper into tears, mumbling something they couldn't make out.

Ted reached over and rubbed her back.

"Can we go now?" Colleen asked. She seemed totally lost in her brother's news. Her silence betrayed the depth of her emotion, Ted knew that she understood that he was getting his affairs in order, but she couldn't talk about it.

"Sure." Ted replied. But as he stood, he suddenly grew dizzy and nauseous. He turned to grab the chair to get his balance and saw the room moving around him in slow motion. Colleen rushed to catch him.

He saw Patty watching him, fear replacing the sorrow on her face.

"Teddy! Are you all right?" Colleen shouted.

"Sit down! I'll get you some water," Patty called.

He felt his cap slide down across his cheek and chin as it fell off; his face seemed to rush toward the floor where the cap had just fallen.

Then nothing but blackness.

Chapter Forty Four

September 4, 2013, 7:20 p.m.
1048 Fifth Avenue
Floor Seven, Apartment One
New York, New York

The late afternoon interview with Anderson Cooper had been one of his better ones, Russo had thought. Ellen agreed. The CNN operation had been the most professional either of them had seen up to now. And Anderson was indeed a "very special guy," as Ellen had promised Tod he would be.

The interview stayed within the scientific boundaries that Russo preferred and Cooper had avoided the "God gene" angle.

When the show's director signaled that the interview was over, Cooper shook hands with Tod and said, "Thank you for your time today, Doctor, and congratulations on this wondrous discovery. Have you submitted your own sample to find out your date, Doctor?"

"No, thanks. I'm a coward," Tod responded. And as soon as he said that, it hit him like a punch from a heavyweight boxer. He did feel like a coward. He had asked four volunteers, to accept their death dates so that the lab could poke and prod and continue its research. But it hadn't occurred to him that neither he nor any of the team members were willing to take the same risk. That darkened his spirits.

The dinner Ellen prepared for them was, like her, simple and elegant. They enjoyed a glass of wine while she mixed a salad and steamed some vegetables to accompany the tasty veal Oscar she had cooked. They ate on the terrace of her apartment overlooking Central Park. The weather earlier that day had threatened rain but as the sun began to set, they realized it hadn't happened.

"Are you still struggling with all this?" Ellen asked after he had described the dismal meeting with Ritu and Zach at his office.

He decided to open his heart to Ellen. He trusted her instincts. "This case has turned into an obsession for me," he told her.

"Really?" she said, not sounding surprised . "I suppose that kind of fits your character, Tod.. This is your work, hence it is an obsession for you." Ellen hoped he wasn't as desperate as he sounded. She had noticed that he appeared increasingly troubled. She had felt much the same way herself.

He furrowed his brow. "It's complicated, Ellen. I'm proud of our work. This discovery is important. But I can't help feeling sorrow for the four people who had to know their death date so we could continue our research. And also. .."

He stood and walked the few steps to the balcony wall. He leaned on the railing, putting his elbows on the bricks. Ellen picked up her wine glass and moved to his side. "Want to talk about it?" she asked.

Tod nodded. "I can see from the four that having a life sur-rounded by people you love and who love you means everything. I have none of that. I've driven myself to be so goddamned buried in research that I've let all the wonder of love pass me by. I've blown two marriages. I have no children, no parents, no sisters, brothers. No one. The friends I can count on one hand are all through work, and I'm really not intimate with any of them."

He shrugged his shoulders. "This talk we're having right now is the most intimate discussion I've ever had with anyone, Ellen. Even my ex-wives."

He walked a few steps away from her and then spun round to face her. "So I've been asking myself why I go on like this. Haven't I done this long enough? What's in store for me before my gene kicks in? And what the hell have I been missing while I've had my eyes fixed on a microscope?" He shook his head remorsefully. "But I'm afraid, Ellen. I don't know how I would start over again. How would I do that?"

"Let's step inside and finish this conversation," Ellen said. "It's starting to get chilly out here and I want to give you something." They walked through the French doors into the apartment.

Russo felt better after unburdening himself. He took a chair near the fireplace as Ellen headed to the far side of the room and took an envelope from an enormous writing desk.

She handed it to Russo and sat in a chair across from him. "Open it."

He opened the envelope and removed the letter. It was her resignation, formal and concise. A deep sense of loss began to enshroud him as he finished reading her words. He refolded the letter, slipped it inside the envelope, gathered his rising emotions and looked into her eyes. "Why?" he said.

Ellen nodded. "Because I have been going down the same path as you, Tod. What we've been seeing has been an example of people at their best. I've always been amazed at how people can be so brave when faced with the worst. Remember how everyone just showed up and worked so feverishly and unselfishly when the World Trade Center Towers were attacked? How, whenever there are natural disasters, people come together and help?"

She shifted her gaze from Tod to the blaze dancing in the fireplace. "Those people, our lab mice, have kindled an epiphany in me. And for you too, I see. They've put aside their own tragedy and focused on the ones they love most. Oh, they have had their moments. That's only natural. But have you ever thought about what you'd do if you knew the exact day you were going to die? Just imagine if you had to walk around with that?'

Her gaze returned to Tod now. "Like you said to Anderson today, I'm a coward, too. I don't want to know. But I sure have respect for the people who do. I want to be like them. I want to care about someone else more than I care about myself. So I'm going to

England to be with my brother. He's all I have in this world now. We've lived apart for years and it's barely a Christmas card relationship now. Maybe not permanently, but for a start, so that we can fill in the years we've lost."

Tod, still seated and looking up at her, listened as she continued. "You never knew my husband, but John was a good man. Since he died, I've gone underground. I keep up with a few friends and acquaintances, but really, my world has narrowed down to my job, and there isn't a whole lot of passion. People passion is what I'm talking about; not career passion. The kind of passion that Dan and Kate Brannigan have for each other. The kind that exists between Sharona and her grandmother; what Janet has for her children. The kind that Father Ted has for that poor marine whose death he never got over."

Tod stood and was now about an arm's length from Ellen, facing her as she continued. "I had that for my John. I miss it now. And I'm going to try to rediscover that in me somehow. I'll start with rekindling the relationship I had with my brother."

Tod's mind had been churning while Ellen opened her heart to him. He felt himself clutching her words and feelings in a kind of syncopation - almost a dance - that felt completely right to him. In fact, the calm that came over him left him as comforted and as secure as he had ever have felt.

Tod had controlled his life and emotions for as long, and with as much diligence, as could be expected of any man. He had relied on his experiences to serve as his compass point. He operated with deliberate and careful calculation. That was especially true with his emotions, which he buried under reason and logic. He never expected to submit to impulse or sudden emotional commitment. Such changes could affect his reasons for living. But that was what happened to Tod the instant Ellen finished talking.

A few moments passed. Ellen returned to her chair. Tod stood still. Finally he spoke. "Then I will resign, too. I have a cousin in Rome and I'm going there to pick up our relationship again while there is still time."

He leaned his elbow on the mantle and recognized his own truth now, the truth that was greater than reason or logic. "Ellen, I don't know how you're going to take this, and please don't be offended. But I think I have fallen in love with you. I say that because I have never felt for anyone what I now feel for you. I have long admired your style and class and intelligence and your worldliness, but I always kept it disconnected from my feelings. . But working so closely these last few months … I don't know. My emotional life has opened and I felt a change. And just now, as I listened to you, it all came together for me. I feel like somehow we are growing closer. You finish sentences for me. And I love that about you. You can choose from the menu for me and I always enjoy what you pick. You can tell me the box score from the Mets game, and you can just as easily explain 'Madame Butterfly' and make me want to understand the power of Puccini."

Ellen sat stunned as he turned toward her. "I've never let anyone into my life like I've let you in. And now we feel exactly the same about our work and yet we haven't said a word about it until tonight. To me, that's more than just casual. I don't know or pretend to know what it means to have passion for someone. But I feel a growing desire to be with you, to be a part of you."

Her face betrayed nothing, but Tod was too far into it to stop. "I have no idea what to do about it and I don't know how you'll accept what I'm saying, but among the things I'm learning is that I need to say what I feel. I'm probably making an ass of myself, but there it is."

There was a pause as Ellen placed her glass on a nearby table and looked at Tod, now sitting and fidgeting, avoiding eye contact.

She took another few seconds to gather her thoughts as clearly as she could. "You're not the only one who has fallen in love, Tod. I would never have said it to you because I was afraid it could never be, but I've been feeling the same way."

Now it was Tod's turn to meet Ellen's gaze as she continued. "For me, it's different. I've had another man in my life. I loved him very much. Since he died, life for me has been about wondering what's next. I want to love you but I have to move cautiously, Tod. Last

Christmas Day, when we arrived for work, I got out of my car next to you,and saw you in that stupid Mets hat. And as I stood there freezing, something happened. I knew what it was because I'd felt it before. It's a feeling you get when you see someone - really see them - for the first time. Everything changes. And I've kept it to myself all these months because I didn't think you felt that way and I wouldn't want either of us to be embarrassed."

Ellen leaned forward in her chair, never losing eye contact with Russo. "Then, finally, I decided I wanted to bring love back into my life, and I needed to start with my brother. I still do. But that doesn't mean we can't try to find out if what we both think we feel is real."

Tod said, smiling broadly, relieved that this moment, which could have gone so badly was going so well. "You know, there is one other thing that I love about you," he said.

"What's that?

"You always surprise me."

"Well, long ago, a wise teacher I had in India told me that the way to keep a man in love with you is 'Every day he should be surprised by how you love him and he will never take his eyes off you for another woman,'"

"If you can love me, Ellen, that will be enough of a surprise for a lifetime."

Chapter Forty Five

October 13, 2013, 12:45 p.m.
Cold Spring Harbor Laboratory
Cold Spring Harbor, New York

The first words spoken that day by Dr. Ellen Guitton shocked the lab mice.

"I wanted to tell you all directly that I have resigned my position here at the laboratory and I'll be leaving when they can find my replacement. I've decided to take some personal time. My brother lives in England and I'm going there to be with him."

She had earned their trust as the lab's go-to person for guidance and decision making. Ellen had been an oasis for them. They had each turned to her for assurance.

"Is anything wrong?" Janet asked fearfully. "This seems so sudden. We'll miss you, Doctor. You've been our rock."

"Thank you, Janet. Nothing's wrong. I just thought it was time to close the gap that has built up over the years between my brother and me. He hasn't been here in several years and I haven't been there and … well, we used to be so close."

"Does he have a family?" Dan asked.

"Just me. He never married. Lots of women, but never a bride."

"But we'll still see you until you leave, right, Doctor Ellen? I couldn't have gotten through this without you," Sharona said. She had grown in many ways since they'd met, but in no way more obviously than the enormous belly now housing her twins. She waddled now, most of the time walking with both hands placed against her lower back for support.

"Oh, I'm not going right away. As I said, they have to find a replacement. I'll still be here when the babies come. I don't want to miss that."

The chatter among them continued as everyone asked how long Ellen had been at the lab, how she had come to this career, and was it true what they'd heard—that she lived in a fabulous apartment overlooking Central Park? And had she really been friends with Jackie Kennedy?

Ellen answered all their questions with humility and grace, and a dose of self-deprecation. Her travels and her privileged life sounded fabulous, but it was impossible not to see that it had been built on great personal loss. While she'd inherited a fortune, the lack of a loving family weighed on her despite her world travels and famous friends. It became evident, as the discussion went deeper, that sometimes the life we lead is shaped by forces outside our control. "It's amazing to me, Doctor, that you didn't lose your bearings with all you had to absorb at such a young age," Brannigan said. "You didn't take anything for granted and never abused the privileges given you. And you turned your life into something really productive. Good for you. Well done."

"Oh, I'm no saint, Dan, I've committed my share of sins."

"It's hard to imagine you a sinner, Doctor." Janet chimed in.

"It's hard to imagine anyone who isn't both," Dan said. Looking at Ted, he added, "Isn't that right, Father?"

Ted's fading condition was now more obvious than it had ever been. He had been having fainting spells and had some bruises on his face from the falls. After he had returned from Baltimore he had kept his schedule as much as he could, but his strength was waning and he knew he didn't have much longer to stay connected at these group meetings.

"A saint and a sinner? Absolutely. We're born with free will. That allows us to choose between good and evil," Ted replied.

"I'm troubled by having been both, especially now," Dan said. "I'm afraid of answering the roll call and wonder if my list of sins will be outweighed by the plus column on the books."

"Well, you're my favorite saint, Mr. B," Sharona said, drawing a hearty laugh from the group. Dan got the joke and enjoyed it. But then an awkward quiet descended as they considered the stark truth in Brannigan's comment. Each of them came from a religious background that had taught them to believe in life after death as an everlasting reward. Did breaking God's laws earn you eternal damnation?

"I was reminded recently that you can't buy your way out of your sins," Dan said. "I tried it, but my offer was rejected." Everyone laughed, but then Dan's voice was grave. "I'm serious. It was a lesson I'll never forget. I don't know if all sins can be forgiven in God's court of justice."

Ted found his voice, the priest, that he had wanted to be. The word of God was something that Ted Hayslip knew, and he shared his thoughts with his friends. "The Gospels are filled with Jesus's love for the sinner . Our Lord doesn't cast us out into the fires of Hell because we sinned. He made us in His own image as flesh and blood, man and woman. And He gave us our free will to choose between right and wrong. None of us can be perfect and none of us ever will. The difference between a saint and a sinner is in our desire to do God's will. It's all in the Lord's Prayer. On one hand, we ask God to 'forgive us our trespasses'; in return, God asks us to 'forgive those that trespass against us.' And He tells us we can turn to Him to 'lead us not into temptation, but deliver us from evil.' This is God's message to us. The Lord's Prayer. Jesus came into this world to deliver His father's prayer to us and it is amazing in its simplicity. But sometimes we forget to remember. I know I've been guilty of that."

He paused as he realized how quiet the room had gotten. "I'm sorry. I sound like a sermon and I don't mean to, but..." The exhausted priest suspected he had held the floor for too long but he was determined to deliver one final point. "In the end, God gives us all we need to be either a saint or a sinner. Most of us will be both at different times and for different reasons during our life. And that is exactly how it is supposed to be. Who are we to judge God's creation? We are what God intended us to be. Sometimes a saint, sometimes a sinner." He shrugged, indicating he was finished.

"Thank you, Father. I very much needed to hear that." Brannigan quietly said as the others lost themselves in their own thoughts, pondering Ted's words.

Time was getting shorter now.

Perhaps God's judgment was not something to be feared.

Chapter Forty Six

November 1, 2013, 8:15 a.m.
St. David's Roman Catholic Church Rectory
Oceanside, New York

Things had moved much quicker than Ted had imagined. As he looked out at the chill rain splattering against the windowpane of his room at the rectory, his sadness grew.

He'd spent a couple of days in Baltimore, then Patty told him she would accompany him back to New York. Colleen had stayed behind. After receiving Ted's gift, she had announced she'd decided to move to a warmer climate and was looking for a place in Florida. She was determined to write children's books, a dream she'd always had.

Eight weeks later, her house was sold and she had called Patty, who was still in New York, to say that she'd be coming up so they could spend Thanksgiving together. She was excited about a family album she had found in the basement of the house. She said it had pictures and documents in it that went all the way back to the Civil War. Patty suggested she pass it along to the lab since so little had been traced on their family.

Ted was in hospice care now and Father Schmidt had insisted he stay at the rectory instead of a nearby facility. The diocese had stepped up and offered financial support. "Father, this is your home.

You stay here," Schmidt had insisted, as he arranged for Patty to stay in a furnished apartment just a two-block walk from her brother's bedside.

Although Ted was shocked about his rapidly deteriorating physical state, the sadness he felt was more that he had seen his ability to be intimate with others, so long lost to him, had blossomed over the past year. Now it would all simply slip away. The empathy for others which had been dormant in him for so long, had now returned and flourished in his life. His uncanny judgment about people and his ability to help them search for peace or comfort was renewed and his ability to assist the spiritually afflicted was once again second nature. Everything he had lost was reborn.

He recalled his last meeting with the lab mice two weeks before; the thought of it warmed him. His balance had begun to deteriorate rapidly and the pain he was suffering required an increase in medication; he now needed an intravenous device that constantly administered morphine.

Strange, he thought as the rain pounded harder against the window. All I have left is time, and what I don't have enough of is time.

Chapter Forty Seven

November 17, 2013, 3:18 p.m.
Aboard Gulfstream R4TW8
Over the northeast United States

"We're just passing over Hartford out to the left, Mister Brannigan. We should be on the ground in another thirty five minutes. I'll let you know when we start our descent."

Dan listened with one ear as he talked on the phone with his assistant. They were going over the final paperwork. Kate was gazing out the window at the changing colors of the New England landscape in the golden autumn afternoon. They were coming back from Tahiti, and had stopped for a single refueling in Seattle. After twenty hours in the air, they were both anxious to set foot on the ground.

Dan was particularly exhausted, bothered by an annoying swelling in his leg. He had mentioned it to Kate and she had spoken with Tim, their pilot, who had been with them for years. Tim told her that such swelling was common in long air trips.

"Look, I want all of this complete by the end of this week so I can sign off on it," Dan said into the phone. "I'm shutting it down this Friday before Thanksgiving at my daughter's in Washington next week, and then I'm spending the next month Christmas shopping and decorating the house. What part of that can't these fucking lawyers get?"

Kate looked at him sharply, knowing that he was speaking with his assistant, Laureen, who didn't usually stand for that kind of language. Kate wasn't surprised when she heard Dan apologize. "I know it's not your fault. I'm sorry. But this was all supposed to be finalized before we went to Tahiti and it's still not done. Yes. Yes. OK. We'll be on the ground in about a half hour and we should be at the house by five. OK, leave the papers and I'll drop them off in the morning. Then sit on these knuckleheads to get the rest of this done before Friday or their lives are going to become very miserable. Yeah, I know. No one is better at misery than me. Bye."

Dan punched the off button for the air-to-ground phone. "I hate lawyers."

"What now?" Kate quietly asked, hoping her calmness would settle him down.

"I don't know," he said. "Everything's ready. The girls' trusts and the grandkids' college savings are all done, so we can sign those tonight. But the papers putting everything else into trust and identifying you as sole proprietor are being held up.. She's going to put the heat on them. I told her I'm done by Friday."

Dan had been on edge over the last few days of their trip and had been restless for most of the flight home. Kate hoped that anxiety was just the result of making a long trip halfway around the world.

"Are you sure you want to do this, Dan?" Kate asked again. Before they had left Dan had set the wheels in motion; not only had he planned his funeral, he had also set up the distribution of his vast estate. Nearly everything was to be held in trust, giving Kate, as sole proprietor, full control. She had warned him that if she was put in charge of the estate, she would put it to work for others. Kate made no secret of her disdain for the corrupt foundation of Dan's wealth, and she intended to see that it benefited the needy and afflicted.

"No regrets," he answered. He gazed out of the window for a few minutes and then turned to her and reached across the aisle and took her hand. "This was a great time, babe. You're still the hottest bod on the beach."

"Yeah, right. Your eyes are going, old man." She waved off his flattery.

Dan turned serious. "Listen. It's a lot of cash, but you'll find the right places for it, so enjoy the process. I would never be the right person to do that."

"Stop, Dan," she said as her eyes filled. "You sound like you're saying goodbye. I told you no talk of that. I look into your eyes and all I see is life. And based on what we just experienced over these last ten days, I know you haven't lost any of your … skills,"

She knew from Dan's lascivious grin that he also was recalling the frequent, exuberant sex they had shared under the Southern Cross. This vacation had definitely done wonders for their libidos. "I'm talking about your scuba diving skills," she teased.

Dan felt a rush thinking back to Tahiti. The vacation had turned out to be one of the most romantic times in their marriage. They chartered a small sailboat and went out sailing for several nights, exploring Bora Bora and several uncharted islands. They'd slept on deck under the stars and swam naked in a lovely, isolated lagoon. Their lovemaking had never been as exciting or fulfilling; it left them exhausted and gratified. If Dan's life was ending, they still knew that the love they'd shared had survived even the rockiest of times and would go on, and that the spirit that bound them together made each of them so much more than either would have been alone. On the second night of their sail, under a starlit sky, they tried to recall their wedding vows and laughed until they cried when neither one could get the words right.

"What do you mean? I was talking about my scuba diving as well. You need to clean up your mind, Kelly," Dan chuckled.

"We're beginning our descent, Mr. Brannigan. I'll need you and Mrs. Brannigan to fasten your seatbelts. We'll be on the ground shortly," the pilot announced.

Chapter Forty Eight

November 17, 2013, 11:22 a.m.
St David's Roman Catholic Church Rectory
Oceanside, New York

Father Ted answered the phone. It was Bishop Molloy; Ted quickly asked if he was standing under a tree somewhere around the third hole.

Molloy let out a loud roar of laughter. "I'm glad to hear you still have your sense of humor, Father. Actually I just wanted to see how you were coming along. And I also wanted to let you know I finally met with the board and rejected their recommendation. The meeting was fascinating." The bishop sounded almost like Ted's conspirator. "All but one person agreed with my decision. I'll bet you can guess who that was. In fact, he went a bit off the rails as he debated my decision. It became apparent, as you suggested, that he has an agenda. Actually, that's why I took so long to schedule the meeting. I needed time to do some research."

Ted was amazed at how candid the bishop was being, but he said nothing and kept listening.

"What I found encouraged me to ask Monsignor Petraglia to step down from his position with the diocese. It doesn't matter what his issue is, so I won't bore you with it. He harbors a certain bitterness that affects his judgment, and he'll be considering other options going forward. I just thought you'd like to know my decision is now formal, and that the board members pass along their best wishes, as I do, for a wonderful Thanksgiving next week."

"Thank you, Bishop. I appreciate this call very much. It means a lot to know I have your support."

"Well, thank you, Father. It means a lot to our church that we've had your career."

Ted knew what the bishop meant. He was saying goodbye. "God's been good to me, Bishop."

"He is good to us all, Father." Then the line went silent.

Ted looked across the room at his sisters, huddled around a laptop on the coffee table. They were scanning real estate listings for Naples, Florida. They'd decided they were both going to start a new life there. Together.

He thought to himself that as strange and fearful as the last year had been, in some ways it had also been the best time of his life. He'd always believed that God worked miracles in strange ways and Ted felt that now he saw His plan. He was grateful at how so many of the things outside of his control had come to be purposeful. He understood now that his quest as a priest and humanitarian was as it was meant to be. His sisters would be able to find the lives they'd always hoped for, and they had turned to each other and regained a relationship they'd lost. He had come to terms with the tragedy that had been so deeply buried inside of him for so many years, going all the way back to that single encounter with a young marine a world away. And he had found the voice he'd lost and the confidence to use it in a way that brought comfort and peace to others. As one of the lab mice, he had gone from being passive and indifferent to positive and encouraging, almost as if it was his mission to be so. Within his church, he had regained his stature and enlightened those who would listen to reason.

As he watched his sisters, it occurred to Ted that perhaps his life was never meant to be about a large congregation. Maybe it was as simple as making a difference in a single life. Perhaps that life was Patty's or Colleen's, or maybe even his bishop's. Maybe it was the other lab mice. Maybe what he had shared with this handful of people would help someone else in need.

As a younger man, he'd fallen in love with the Broadway musical *Les Miserables*. He always cried at the end when the protagonist, Jean Val Jean, utters the last line before he dies. Now, here with his sisters at St. David's, Ted felt grateful he'd somehow finished the job he was born to do. He whispered Jean Val Jean's words to himself and was softly comforted by their grace and wisdom.

"To love another person is to see the face of God."

Chapter Forty Nine

November 25, 2013, 4:38
9 Bay Road
Brookhaven Hamlet, New York

It had been a Thanksgiving celebration they had only dreamed about. Sharona invited Nicky Storms to join them and to their surprise, he enthusiastically accepted, offering to bring desserts and wine. Gran and Sharona were up early that morning to begin the preparations.

While the sounds of the Thanksgiving Day Parade blared from the huge flat screen TV, Deke kindled his first fire, which would turn out to make the house stiflingly hot on an Indian summer afternoon when the temperatures hovered near seventy at midday.

The turkey went into one of the double ovens; pies in the other. By the time Nicky arrived, the house was filled with the smells of the pastries cooling. The turkey, with all the trimmings, was nearly ready to be served.

The picture-perfect image of a family holiday dinner had come together. And although Sharona knew they weren't the typical American family on a magazine cover, at the moment, setting the table with the elegant new china and the table linens she and Gran had bought, it certainly felt that way.

Deke confessed he'd never carved a turkey, so when it came to the table accompanied by Gran's beaming smile, Nicky offered to take on the assignment.

"Gran, you say the grace," Sharona piped up while Deke brought the side dishes to the table and Nicky did a credible job of carving up the poultry.

"Sharona, as this is your house, and you the one holding those babies, I think you need to say the grace," her grandmother said. "You the one has so much to be thankful for."

"Gran, I can't say no prayers. You know that. Come on."

"Nah nah nah, Shoney. Saying prayers is nothing but speaking to the Lord. Now go on. You got some things you got to say, I know."

Sharona sat smiling at her grandmother while she gathered her thoughts. Deke put his water glass down, and Nicky sat still, as did Gran. The only sound was the crackle from the fireplace as Sharona blessed their Thanksgiving. "Lord. We thank you for all the many blessings you have sent us. We thank you for this food and for this table where we gather. We thank you for these babies that you have sent us and we pray they always please you as we know they will please us. We thank you for this home. We thank you for our Gran, who is the strength and the love that helps keep our family together. And we thank you that she can cook. 'Cause I sure can't!"

Everyone burst out laughing, except Gran, who whispered something about being blasphemous. Sharona caught her breath and looked toward Nicky. "We thank you for our friend, our brother, Nicky, who always guards us and helps us to see the light, even when there may be darkness. He's a good man, Lord. Please keep him safe and near us. And we thank you for the many friends that have helped me down this road where I walk with you by my side. Especially all my friends at the lab that have shown me that white people can be my friends. Thank you for the lessons that I learned from them, and for teaching me to open my heart to others different from me. We ask you for mercy on their souls, and peace and comfort for their loved ones."

She began to choke up and turned so she could face Deke, who was seated to her left. Tears began to swell in Deke's eyes too as he gazed back at her, but she hurried her prayer so she could get the words out. "And above all, dear Jesus, we thank you for my husband, Deke. I ask you to watch over him and our babies when you take me to your heavenly kingdom. Keep him always safe and let my spirit always be in his heart, and the hearts of our children. Amen."

Sharona bowed her head. All four of them each touched their new linen napkins to their eyes.

Gran had been right. Sharona did have some things to say.

Chapter Fifty

December 9, 2013, 5:05 p.m.
American Airlines Terminal
John F. Kennedy International Airport
Jamaica, New York

Ellen had chosen a window seat in business class on her Heathrow-bound flight, which was scheduled to board in an hour and fifteen minutes. They stopped at a coffee bar and Russo ordered two cappuccinos, although neither of them really wanted one. The tasteless, overheated drinks had lightened his wallet by eight dollars and reminded him why he had long ago ceased to purchase anything to eat or drink at an airport.

Ellen had decided to go to England before the holiday travel rush to spend a few days with her brother. The lab had not yet found her replacement. Tod was disappointed that she had chosen to go, but he also knew this wasn't about the two of them. After they had revealed their feelings to each other, they had begun exploring the depths of their newly discovered connection. Their relationship as a couple was warm and growing closer day by day. Tod was absorbing the tranquility that came from sharing his life and heart with another person. Ellen felt much like a girl in love for the first time, and looked for chances to share her thoughts and experiences with her newfound companion.

Today she was flying to London, and Tod was putting the finishing touches on his resignation letter to the lab, which Ellen had read while they drove to Kennedy from her apartment. His plan was to hand in the letter before Christmas break and, like Ellen, leave the final date open-ended until the board named his successor. His letter recommended Dr. Ritu Mhatra as his replacement, a move Ellen had endorsed.

"Are you going to be all right?" she asked Tod calmly.

"You mean with our lab mice? Not really," he said, but he quickly admitted, "the truth is, I can't say that I'm looking forward to this." He wanted to stay off of that subject. "I'll miss you, Ellen. It sounds so strange for me to be saying that. I don't think I've ever said it to anyone before."

"I'll miss you too, Tod. And I know what I'm talking about. I have said it before."

"Is this working out for you like it's working out for me?" he hated to sound needy, but he had to know.

"Better than I'd even hoped, Tod. You have so much to offer. I'm discovering that more and more."

"Really? I find that fascinating. Tell me what you mean. I didn't know there was anything there," he joked.

"I will. But not now. There's too much to say and it's a long way to go to the gate. Let's both go to England for New Year's and I'll keep you enthralled with my psychobabble." She pushed away the nearly full cup of cappuccino and reached for her carry-on bag. "I'd better get going. The line at security is getting longer."

"Yeah, you're right. OK. Maybe I will join you for a New Year's trip. We'll see how things go here." He reached for her bag as they headed to the security area. They looked like any other couple saying farewell at the airport as he handed over her carry-on, softly kissed her cheek, and asked her to text him when she landed. She promised she would, and then softly cupped his face in her hand. She said she'd be back before Christmas.

"Yes, please do," he said. "I'm sure I'll need a friend that day."

As Ellen walked to the security line, Russo's cell vibrated and the

LED told him it was Ritu.

"Please tell me something good," he said as he answered the call.

"OK, I will! Father Ted's family dropped off a family album today that is chock-a-block filled with records like birth certificates, Army discharge papers, and all sorts of goodies. And from the looks of it, the thing goes way back."

Tod could hear the excitement in Ritu's voice. "That's great," he said. "Anything jump out at you yet?"

"Too soon to know. I only just got it. I'm beginning to scan it through my trace against the Bell family. Sharona's family is really hard to track, but Zach says he finally has an agreement from her Gran to sit down with him at the end of next week."

"And how are you doing with the Brannigans? We need a break there too."

"Still stuck,' she sighed. "I have clear records back to Dan's great-grandfather, but I've hit a wall beyond that. Dan himself hasn't been much help and apparently the family didn't keep any history once they got to America."

Tod hit the lock on his keys as he approached his car. "OK, well, you're starting to break up now, but keep at it. Maybe this Hayslip album will take you somewhere. Let's hope." But Ritu didn't answer and he knew he had lost signal.

As he climbed behind the wheel of his car he felt a flash of anger and wondered why the Hayslips were only now producing this possibly useful information. Why had Gran been so stubborn, and why had Dan been so unconcerned.

"Hello!" he muttered to himself. "Does anyone know the clock is ticking?"

Everyone knew the clock was ticking.

Christmas 2013

Chapter Fifty One

December 24, 2013, 11:04 p.m.
Brookhaven Memorial Hospital Medical Center, Room 203
Patchogue, New York

Gran proudly strolled from the nurse's station with yet another floral arrangement. This one had two balloons tied to it, one saying 'It's a Boy," and the other "It's a Girl." The flowers inside the blue and pink teddy bear vase were blue and pink carnations. A nurse, seeing the familiar face of her co-worker, immediately began to squeal about Gran's new twin grandbabies. After a few minutes chatting, Gran used her shoulder to open the door for Room 203. Sharona was tending to the infants in their bassinets. The twins peered out from underneath tiny knitted stocking caps, one pink and one blue.

Tulip had come in to the world first, at 3:57 p.m. on December 23; Thomas had followed eight minutes later. They had been weighed, cleaned, tested, and pronounced perfect.

Sharona had cried throughout the delivery, from the first drip of the drugs that delivered the local anesthesia to the moment of overwhelming joy at seeing her children. The Caesarian section had gone smoothly, but the procedure called for her to spend several days at the hospital. They were all scheduled to go home on the morning of December 26th. But Sharona did not expect to be leaving with her babies. She was certain that tomorrow, December 25th, her part in this story would end.

She tried not to think about it, and avoided discussing it. As did Gran and Deke. Everyone proceeded as though the plan was for Sharona to take the children home to their freshly painted, scrubbed, and decorated nursery the day after tomorrow. "More flowers! Oh my, where we gonna put them? Who they from, Gran?"

"The nurses on the surgical wing, baby. I worked there for a long time."

The hospital had been Gran's employer right up until Saturday, when she had officially retired after twenty-four years as a nurse's aide. Sharona and Deke had encouraged her to do this sooner, but she had resisted, claiming the longer she worked, the more Social Security would give her. When they pointed out that she wouldn't need Social Security now, she snapped at them. "How would you know that? You never know what life brings. Besides, I worked all my life for my Social Security, and I want to get every penny I earned."

"Old school," Deke said.

"Been knowing that," agreed Sharona.

Sharona saw Deke glance at the clock and his eyes met hers as he registered the time. The same thought had occurred to both of them. In less than an hour it would be December 25th.

Her day to die.

Earlier, as they gazed into the faces of their sleeping children, Sharona had talked about trying to stay awake as long as possible. "I'll have no sleep from now until tomorrow night at midnight," Sharona had told Deke. I ain't missing any of my time with these babies. I figure I'll be asleep long enough after." She didn't need to say after what.

Deke agreed; that this was his plan, too. "I'll be right here with you every minute, baby girl. Right here."

The babies had just been fed and were due to nurse again at half past midnight, so Gran, who was staying at the hospital along with Deke, told them she would be back. The nurses' break room had a reclining chair where she could nap. She'd return for the midnight feeding.

As Gran left the room, Sharona watched her wistfully peek at the sleeping babies and saw a tear drop from her eye. Then Gran turned and walked straight out the door without looking at her granddaughter. Sharona knew what Gran was thinking. These two little babies were about to become motherless. How could this be happening?

Deke went to the bassinets and gazed at their tiny miracles. Sharona silently said a prayer as she watched Deke absorbing the wonder of the newborns. If you have to take me, please make it sudden so I don't know it's coming and please not where anyone else will see me. If I can, let me go in my sleep, dear Jesus. Let me go while the others are sleeping, too. When she'd finished the prayer, she felt nauseous and began to tremble. She'd never imagined fear like this.

Chapter Fifty Two

December 24, 2013, 11:20 p.m.
Colcroft House
Cold Spring Harbor, New York

Dan yawned as he spoke. "My leg is killing me, Kate. The swelling is not going down."

Kate closed the refrigerator door, and asked, "Have you exercised at all since Tod spoke to you?"

"Who needed exercise? Getting Christmas to happen was exercise enough."

"Well, you should have gone in to see him and gotten it looked at. It's been over a month since we came back," Kate scolded.

Since they had returned from Tahiti, Dan had ignored follow-ups exams that had been recommended after the biweekly sessions at the labs. He complained about the pain in his leg to the doctors, but refused to take the time for any further examination or diagnosis. He would continue to submit his DNA samples and participate with the other lab mice, but he skipped everything else despite entreaties from Russo and Ellen.

'Yeah, yeah," he said as he went to the utility room at the side of the house with a bag full of Christmas wrappings. With their eye on the calendar and the clock, Dan and Kate had sold the family on gathering together for Christmas Eve rather than Christmas Day.

They told their kids that the rush of getting out the door for Mass in the morning was exhausting for Kate, who put so much effort into their holiday traditions.

"But, Mom. First the kids will be up late, and second the 'midnight' Mass at St. Pat's is at nine p.m.," Allie had objected.

"That's exactly right," Kate had said. "We can have a nice dinner and then open gifts and go to the nine o'clock. And when we come home, the kids can play with their toys while we have dessert. Then, after the kids go to bed, you guys can have your gifts. It'll be nice. We won't have to rush the next morning, and when the kids get up, they can play with their toys. Let's try it just this once," she'd begged them.

The Brannigan daughters suspected something was up. They knew this had been an unusual holiday season; they speculated that the changes they'd seen had something to do with their mother spending the month of June at the beach house alone. She had told them then to stay away, that she had some thinking to do. Back then, Diane had called her father secretly and asked if Mom was sick. She told him that she and her sisters thought Kate was acting strangely. Dan assured her that wasn't the case. The girls never knew the truth.

The night had gone well to this point, and Kate and Dan had suppressed their anxieties enough to enjoy being with their family. Dan was playing his role to the fullest and did a better job than Kate, who at times grew distant. Over the past month, Dan had turned every minute of his time toward holiday planning with Kate. He shopped until he couldn't walk another mall concourse, wrapped gifts, wrote Christmas cards, and even offered to help the decorating company that each year trimmed the house and grounds.

They'd gotten to St. Patrick's a few minutes after nine and found seats in various parts of the church. No one got sick this year, so they were still seated when the choir performed the "Hallelujah Chorus" from Handel's "Messiah."

After the Mass they returned home and the Brannigan youngsters and their parents were all their beds for the night. Kate and Dan were still up.

"Where are you going?" Kate asked as she saw Dan grab a ski jacket from the utility room.

"I want to get some air before bed," he said. "Maybe walk this swelling down. I'll just be a few minutes."

"Want me to come?" she asked, even though she dreaded going back out in the cold.

Knowing her aversion to winter weather, Dan smiled at her. "No. Go ahead up to bed. I'll only be a few minutes."

"OK. But don't be long. It's almost midnight," she said, just a slight hint of apprehension in her voice.

Dan knew what she meant. "I'll be back soon," he whispered.

He left by the side door and headed toward the bluffs that descended sharply down to Cold Spring Harbor. The cloudless night made the air seem especially clean as he inhaled deeply. Stars twinkled above the water's silence. A brilliant crescent moon hung low in the east of the starry night and cast shadows from the trees now emptied of their foliage. The silhouettes of the silent trees reached upward, as if surrendering to the darkness along the harbor's shoreline. Only a few clam boats floated quietly at their moorings.

Dan stood looking out across the expanse and told himself for the last time that fear of death was worse than death itself, and that living a life pursuing one's dreams, was a life well spent. He knew he had neglected the swelling in his leg, believing it was probably something he should be concerned about, but he also believed that his hand had already been dealt, so why bother?

What Dan had feared more was the possibility that if his leg had required treatment, it would take away what little time he had left.. After they'd returned from Tahiti, as far as he was concerned, every second of every day belonged to him and Kate and the family. Dan had lived life on his own terms; he wasn't about to change that..

Turning back toward the house Dan thought about the family that he and Kate had made. His children and grandchildren sleeping under his roof this night. Warm, safe, secure. Their lives in front of them: their dreams yet to be.

As he looked at the tall chimney spires of the mansion against the clear, star-speckled sky, he saw the glow of the lamp in their bedroom. In his mind he could see Kate leaning back on soft, downy pillows in her special Christmas pajamas, reading the holiday cards they'd received. She did that every Christmas Eve.

What a joy his life with her had been. What wonder this person had brought to him. He remembered a quotation he'd seen some-where, "If I get to heaven and my wife is not there, it shall be no heaven for me." Well, he thought. Maybe tonight I'll find out about that and see if it's right. He took a deep, long breath and said aloud to the night, "OK, I'm ready."

He walked slowly back to the house and labored up the stairs, his leg still throbbing. In their bedroom, he saw that Kate had dozed off with the cards on her lap. He turned off her lamp, gently took her reading glasses off her nose, slipped into his own Christmas pajamas in the dark and kissed Kate softly on the top of her head. He sat by the window, looking out over the harbor and glanced over at the digital clock on his night stand. It read 12:06. The day was here. And so was he. He was sleepy now and soon he nodded off.

Kate woke with a start. Her neck was stiff, as her head had drift-ed off the pillows. She glanced at the clock to see the time - it was twenty after three - and then realized that Dan was not in bed with her. Across the room she saw the shadow of his head resting against the chair facing the window.

She walked over to him and looked to see if his eyes were closed. In the dark they appeared to be, but she sensed something was not right. His jaw was hanging as if he was in deep sleep, but she couldn't hear his breathing. She leaned in closer and suddenly her blood ran cold. Dan's eyes were open. And she was right, he wasn't breathing.

She dropped to her knees in front of him and leaned into his chest, listening for a heartbeat. Nothing. She took his wrist and felt for a pulse. His skin was cold. Kate moaned softly as the reality struck her.

Kate dropped to her knees beside his chair and put her head on his shoulder. "Oh, Dan. I'm so sorry I wasn't awake when you came back up. I wanted to tell you that I love you. I always have, Dan. Ever since I first laid eyes on you, I knew we'd be together. I wanted to tell you how happy you've made me all these years, and how grateful I am for the girls and our life together. And I wanted to tell you what a good man you are. You are, Dan. You're a good man. I hope you're happy, Dan. You've worked hard to make life better for so many. I'm sure God knows that and you'll be rewarded."

She could barely whisper to him now, her words coming in spasms. "Sleep in peace, Dan. I'll miss you every day until I see you again."

She clung closer to Dan to muffle the sound of her sobs. At long last, the tears began to ebb.

She reached up and closed Dan's eyes and tilted his head forward so that his jaw would close. Then she kissed his head and went to her closet, drew her robe around her and went down the hall to Diane's room.

⇒»((●))«⇐

Because Dan had died at home, an autopsy was performed. The medical examiner would determine that the long flights to and from Tahiti had probably brought on the embolism that had had continued to grow and expand, eventually dislodging and settling in his brain. Had Dan been examined after they returned from vacation, this may have been found and treated. But would that have meant that he could have cheated his date with death? There was no way of knowing, the researchers acknowledged. He had fallen asleep in the chair and never felt it when the blood clot in his brain stopped telling his heart to pump. The swelling in his leg had ceased. Dan was gone.

Chapter Fifty Three

December 25, 2013, 8:28 a.m.
St. David's Roman Catholic Church Rectory
Oceanside, New York

Sister Cathleen O'Rourke had been assigned to hospice care for some eighteen years now and was very gifted in her ministry. Not only was she an outstanding nurse, she also had the capacity to offer compassion to families as life drained from the dying souls she assisted through their final days. And, when the last hour was at hand, she helped those families with their grief in ways that made each of them feel as though she had been acquainted with the deceased for years. The survivors would recall her contribution for the remainder of their lives. It was her gift.

The Hayslip sisters were going to need her. Watching the monitors on Father Ted through the night, Sister Cathleen saw his heart rate fluttering; the blood gases were nearing a critical point. There wasn't much time left as the sun came up Christmas morning. She'd sent word to Father Schmidt, who had quietly come to Ted's room. Colleen and Patty were at Father Ted's bedside, as they had been throughout the night, while the priest administered the sacrament of the Anointing of the Sick. It was a quiet ceremony of prayer and absolution, which took only a few minutes as Ted's breathing labored under his oxygen mask. The irregular beeping of the monitor was evidence of how threadbare were his chances of survival.

He'd been in a drug-induced coma for ten days, when his pain had become too much to bear. Each day since then, there had been no change in his condition, although his "numbers", as Sister Cathleen and the doctor referred to them, steadily declined.

In the last hour, his pulse rate had accelerated alarmingly, signaling that the last battle for his life had begun. Soon, the inevitable would come, and he would pass over.

Colleen had spent the last eight or nine hours in constant tears; Patty had been solemn and quiet. They exchanged few words, but stayed vigilant at their brother's side. Before Ted had lost consciousness, they had each taken a private moment with him to say goodbye. Sister Cathleen offered them the opportunity to have a final word before she administered the sedative that would alleviate his pain; the point of hospice care was to prevent the patient's suffering. She had explained that once the dosage began, Ted would have no awareness and would feel no pain. But even though he was unconscious, Sister Cathleen told them that Ted could still hear their voices.

Each sister took a turn at his side.

"Teddy, it's Colleen, honey. Don't be afraid, Teddy. Mom and Dad will be waiting for you when you get there. Say hi for me. We'll miss you, Teddy. I love you. Goodbye." She lost herself in her tears. She never noticed the slight flicker at the left side of Ted's mouth as it turned up in a smile. She ran from the room and collapsed just outside the door into Patty's arms, sobbing, until she felt entirely drained and exhausted.

Patty helped her to a chair, found her a glass of water and some tissues, and asked her if she was going to be OK. Her sister nodded. Then Patty turned quickly and entered Ted's room. She walked to his bed, took his hand in hers and leaned down to his ear. "You probably never knew this, Ted, but I always thought of you as my best friend. I did what I wanted to do all my life, and I know it wasn't always what I should have been doing. But you never once questioned me or passed judgment. You were always there, and you loved me, no strings attached. You were the only one who ever gave me that. I'm your sister and you're my brother. We didn't have any choice about that. But I had a choice about who I pick as my friends." She paused now as her words were sticking in her throat. "And you're my best friend, Teddy. My best friend. And I will be your friend forever."

She looked up, her eyes brimming. "God, be good to him. He's the best man we will ever know." She paused again, the tears streaming down her face, and finally said, "I love you, Teddy."

She heard a sound from him, almost a grunt, as if he had received her message, but then nothing except his breathing. She kissed his hand, stroked his head, and lingered, looking at him. Then she turned and tiptoed out of the room.

As the lights on the Christmas tree in the corner of the room twinkled, Sister Cathleen kept watch, applying the stethoscope every few minutes and checking the monitors.

At twenty eight minutes after eight on Christmas morning, Ted's breathing was interrupted by a great, deep sigh. Then nothing. Sister Cathleen applied her stethoscope and felt for a pulse. She turned to Colleen and Patty. Exhausted, they hadn't noticed that he had stopped breathing. The nurse looked at them and shook her head. She turned off the oxygen and the IV fluids, and extracted the feeder line from his arm. She removed the oxygen mask and gently stroked back the wisps of hair on his head. She made a sign of the cross and looked back at Ted's sisters. "I'm sorry. I'll wait outside. Please take as much time as you want."

The sisters sat on the love seat, holding each other's hands, and stared at their brother's lifeless figure. He looked peaceful, like he was only asleep. From next door, the bells of the church steeple calling the parish to Christmas Mass rang out.

Patty smiled as she envisioned her brother's spirit, walking in his vestments to begin the Mass.

Chapter Fifty Four

December 25, 2013, 10:44 a.m.
135 Sunnyfield Lane
Hicksville, New York

J anet had worked feverishly, preparing her home for their first Christmas since Michael had died, knowing it might be her last Christmas with her family. She'd steadfastly presented an external appearance of calm, but inwardly was filled with fear and dread.

Carly Hoffer, now discharged from the Army, had joined the family until she could find her own place.

Michaela was still beyond being comforted. She had remained distant even during their vacation in Italy, which had ended early because Janet decided she couldn't stay for the full month. She needed to get back home to Michael. Her visits to the cemetery resumed the morning after their plane touched down.

Rod had no idea how to help his daughter. Kathy was equally at a loss.

Alone with Michaela one afternoon, as they addressed the family Christmas cards, Janet finally started the long overdue discussion they both needed. Her dying wish, she said, was that Michaela complete the life that she could not complete for herself. Janet told her she had learned that our time on earth is our best chance at heaven, and that this earth offers us all the goodness and happiness that we could ever imagine heaven would be, if we could just recognize it.

Janet told Michaela that the great lesson of Michael's death, to her, was the revelation that he was a part of everyone who loved him. She said Michael's spirit had helped her through this sad time, and gave her the strength to go on. "Michael will always be there for us, Mickey. And soon, so will I."

She then asked Michaela to marry and have children, and if she had a boy, to name him for her brother. "Teach your children who he was and who I was, and why you loved us. Stay close to Aunt Kathy and your dad. The ones we have loved since our birth are the ones we want to keep with us until our deaths."

There had been a wall between mother and daughter ever since Janet had blown up on that night after learning her death date. This conversation broke that wall down and Michaela seemed to open up again. Michaela wasn't quite the same person, but maybe, Janet thought, she never will be. She and her children were soul mates, she knew. And perhaps there is pain in our human lives that just can't be soothed.

Janet had told Rod of her conversation with Michaela and her hope that it might have done some good. He looked at her, sighed and said, "Have any magic words for me?"

His question struck her deeply. They really hadn't dealt with Rod's grief. She knew he was in turmoil, but she hadn't yet turned her thoughts to him.

That changed the next day, when she woke up in the middle of the night and saw Rod was not in bed with her. She found him in the living room, in the dark, staring out of the window. He told her he was angry at God. Losing his son, and soon, perhaps, his wife, was more than he could bear.

Janet sat next to him, put her head on his shoulder and began speaking from a depth of her soul that she had never known she could reach. "I always believed that God gave life. And God gave us the gifts of family. But it's not a lifelong contract, Rod. It's love that is eternal. It doesn't leave our hearts when we die. Michael is still your son, and your love for him is still with you. And it was our love that gave us Michael. And Mickey. So you aren't really losing anyone as long as you keep that love in your heart. And I'm not leaving you, Rod. I will always love you, no matter where I am. Michael is here with you and me right now. You have to believe that if you believe that you loved him."

They talked through the night; by dawn, they'd awakened both Carly and Michaela with their laughter. The two young women found Rod and Janet looking through their wedding album, laughing at the hairstyles and recalling who were the bad dancers.

On Christmas morning, Janet was up before dawn and had all the gifts and the decorations ready when Rod, Michaela and Carly awoke. She was jubilant, and wore a Santa hat and a new floor-length red robe. Christmas carols played loudly.

The Bates and Jonas families attended an early church service, and afterward, when the others agreed to go back to the house and start making breakfast, Janet and Kathy climbed into Janet's van, planning to stop on the way home at 7-Eleven for orange juice.

Despite an underlying feeling of dread about reaching this fateful date on the calendar, Janet and Kathy were in high spirits as they pulled into the bustling parking lot of the convenience store. It was busy and they found themselves waiting for an available parking spot.

Janet seemed at ease, her Santa hat discarded for church, now perched back on her head. Janet stepped out of the van. It was a tight spot, and she was very close to a snow bank that had hadn't been fully cleared away.

Janet was laughing and wasn't paying attention to her exit from her vehicle, causing her to lose her footing as he stepped onto an ice-covered curb. As she started to stumble, she struck out her right arm, to grab something to prevent the fall. That instinctive, simple maneuver drew her arm back, the result being that she was unable to break her fall or cradle her head, which struck the concrete curb.

Kathy, meanwhile had turned to apologize for bumping the door of the car next to them in the parking lot. She didn't see Janet fall.

At first Janet saw stars flashing, then blackness. A small light grew more intense as it advanced toward her. She felt no fear, nor pain from the blow to her head. She could hear Kathy's voice, as if at a distance, shouting for an ambulance and asking, "Janet, can you hear me?"

But Janet couldn't answer. She heard voices saying they'd seen her fall suddenly; one man said she'd cracked her skull. The light got brighter; Kathy's voice grew more faint. Now, somehow from above, Janet could see herself lying between the van and the curb, her purse next to her, her Santa hat in the snow. She saw strangers standing round her and Kathy on her knees, leaning over. The store manager was running inside.

Suddenly, the light began to spin and shift as if tossed by a breeze. She felt as if she was being carried towards the great light. And then, as if in a dream, Janet was moving through a cloudlike tunnel, completely silent and calm. The air was cool, clean-smelling.

Janet felt the familiar sensation telling that her children were nearby. But the intensity was much greater than it had ever been before.

Then she heard Michael's voice. "Hey, Mom, I've been waiting for you."

And Janet knew her soul and her heart would be at rest, in peace and happiness forever.

Chapter Fifty Five

December 25, 2013, 3:44 p.m.
Cold Spring Harbor Laboratory,
Office of the President
Cold Spring Harbor, New York

Ritu's cell phone was vibrating across her desk as she gazed at the computer. She glanced down at the caller ID and knew who it was. She didn't want to answer it. She knew it was bad news.

"Hi, Tod. Where are you?"

Russo was on his way to Oceanside to offer his condolences to Father Ted Hayslip's sisters. Patty had just called to tell him that Ted had passed away. That made three out of the four lab mice who had died on the day their DNA had predicted.

"I'm on my way to see Father Hayslip's family. We're just waiting to hear from the hospital on Miss Watts."

The board had taken Russo's suggestion that she succeed him and Ritu was now acting president of Cold Spring Harbor Laboratory. Tod was to stay on until December 31 and then remain as a consultant for another year.

"I'm sorry to hear about the priest," Ritu said. "He suffered so much. Zach told me when he was first diagnosed the doctors didn't think he'd make it to his death date."

"Yeah, he fought quite a battle. But he'd been in a coma for the last ten days. It was awful for his sisters. They weren't doing very well when they called me."

"Well, at least Janet Bates died quickly. She probably never knew what happened to her. And Dan went in his sleep. That was kind for him."

"I suppose," Tod said.

"How are you doing with all this?" Ritu asked.

He thought for a second before answering. "I feel like I've been hit in the head with a bat. I have a pounding headache, and I feel almost semiconscious, like I'm walking in a fog or something. That's why I called you. I needed to hear a voice so I'd know I wasn't asleep."

"Maybe you shouldn't be driving, Tod."

"I'm OK. Listen, anything further on the mapping results of the DNA now that you've gotten some of the family histories?"

"Not yet. I've gotten confirmations on a lot of good data and the families have provided some really useful information in terms of diaries and clarifying dates and such, but it still isn't all hanging together. Zach sent me a file this morning that was locked, but he didn't give me the password. His note said I'd find it interesting. I sent him a text hours ago asking for the password, but he hasn't gotten back to me yet."

"What's the file title?"

"It's labeled 'grandmother.' That ring any bells?"

"Nope. I know he spoke with Sharona's Gran this week. Maybe there's something there. Anyway. I'm almost here, so I'll ring off. Wish me luck."

"Good luck. Sorry again."

"Yeah," he sighed. "Bye."

A text came through just as Ritu hung up with Russo. It was from Zach, and just a single typed word: "*BINGO.*" She entered the letters b-i-n-g-o in the password field and the file opened immediately.

She read the notations that Zach had made under the heading "*Notes from interview with Valerie Stalls, grandmother of Sharona.*" The first two pages were standard questions and answers, most of which they already knew, about Gran's missing husband and

Sharona's mother who couldn't identify Sharona's father. But then halfway through the fourth page of the report, Ritu reread an entry twice, then ran out of her office and to the lab, where she could view the DNA samples drawn from the test subjects under the powerful microscopes.

If what she had read in Dr. Weitzman's report was true, then a critical piece to the puzzle had been sitting in front of them all along.

There was a change that could have occurred after they had studied two samples; when they had originally checked them, the specimens hadn't released the clue to the mystery. The effects of proteins on certain SNPs in the sample DNA were subject to alteration. In simple terms, this meant was that it was possible that samples previously considered as unmatched could now be matched.

Ritu quickly found the two sample slides she needed and put them simultaneously under the scopes. There it was! What they had previously considered as unmatched samples were indeed matched. There was the connection.

"Bingo, indeed," she whispered, as she returned the slides and ran back to her office.

The circle of understanding was beginning to close.

Chapter Fifty Six

December 25, 2013, 10:15 p.m.
Brookhaven Memorial Hospital Medical Center, Room 203
Patchogue, New York

None of them could bear the strain. The day felt endless. Gran and Deke had remained in Sharona's room since midnight. That meant they'd been watching the clock tick away each minute for twenty hours. Neither Sharona nor Deke wanted to fall asleep, and Gran was doing her best, but she was exhausted by the vigil.

The babies had kept to their feeding schedule throughout the day. Nicky Storms had visited, which had been fun as he rolled two tricycles, one pink, one blue, into the room, saying that their Uncle Nicky wanted to give them their first bikes and the new parents had decided to ask Nicky to be the babies' godfather.

The most recent feeding and diaper changing had gone as all the others had, without problems. Sharona had decided not to start the babies out with breast milk for obvious reasons, but the twins had taken to the formula. In every way so far, things were just as they should have been.

Nicky had left and Gran said she was going to just sit outside the door of Sharona's room for a while, which Deke and Sharona knew meant she was going down to the nurses' break room for another power nap.

Deke opened his laptop and started working, while Sharona stared at her two little treasures until her eyes began fluttering closed. She caught herself and glanced at Deke, whose head had dropped; he was leaning to one side and breathing deeply, gently snoring.

Sharona gave into the idea of taking a page from Gran's book. She'd get in a quick power nap. She let her eyes close. Just for a minute, she told herself.

Deke heard the babies crying as if they were off in the distance. He began to waken, but he couldn't get his eyes to open. He could feel his body start to move, but opening his eyes was still a struggle. Finally, as he moved his laptop, he realized where he was and his eyes snapped open. Both infants were crying in harmony, but his first reaction was to peer at the clock. The small hand was at twelve and the long hand somewhere between the three and four. It was past feeding time. How long had he been asleep? He hadn't realized he had dozed off. He felt completely disoriented.

Then he remembered. Sharona.

He looked at her on the bed. She was still. Her hands were folded in front of her, her head rolled to one side. The cries of her babies went unheard.

His spirit collapsed. The inevitable had happened. He began sobbing as he turned away from where she was and reached into the nearest bassinet and took Tulip up in his arms; then he reached a hand under Thomas and lifted his son. He held his children close, tears falling on their swaddling blankets. He felt a sadness come over him at the thought of these two perfectly born children never having a single moment with the wonderful woman who had given them their lives.

Then, as if it were an illusion, Deke heard something move from the other side of the room. He turned slowly and saw Sharona push herself up from the bed and rub her hands across her eyes.

"I'll take one of them," she said. "You get the bottles ready. Leave Thomas here with me. Where's Gran?"

Deke was thunderstruck, eyes widening and now gushing tears.

Sharona looked at him, puzzled, not yet fully awake. "Well, what are you waiting for?" she asked him.

Deke realized she didn't know what time it was. She hadn't yet realized that it was after midnight. The date had moved ahead to December twenty sixth and she was still alive. She had escaped the death sentence her genes had predicted.

"Sharona, look at the clock!" He exclaimed. His hands still filled with howling babies, he pointed toward it with his head.

She focused on the digital readout. As the reality sunk in, her expression turned to shock. Her day to die had passed. And here she was, alive. She turned to Deke, watched him embracing the children in his arms.

He couldn't contain his laughter or his tears. "Look at that time, baby!" he shouted. "We got peoples waiting for us."

He felt his legs trembling underneath him as he walked to Sharona's bed. She took her children from him, one on each side, as she sat quietly, sobbing. She couldn't speak, choked with emotion now. Grateful to be in this moment, beginning a new life she sensed was meant to go on for a long time to come.

Deke put his hands over his face. The door to the room slowly opened, and Gran entered with her arms wrapped around herself, wearing the soft, confident smile of one who was seeing the miracle she'd prayed for. Sharona was still with her.

Life - and hope - would go on.

Epilogue

February 10, 2014, 2:47 pm
Whiteshire Mews
Bournemouth, England

Ritu ended her call to Russo, as contrite as she could ever recall feeling at any time in her life. Tod, of course, told her she had nothing to be sorry for, but he suspected she heard the hesitation in his voice. The doubt clouding the closing chapter of his illustrious career was something he would now live with.

Tod gazed out of a small window near the fireplace where he was seated in the cozy country kitchen of an ancient English farmhouse. He and Ellen had been together since they had returned from the States on New Year's Eve. They were alone while her brother was working in London and had cemented a firm foundation under the new relationship both had embraced. Their romance was still in its discovery stage, but passion had germinated and they were slowly finding out how to be a couple.

The winter had been typical for the southern part of England: wet, hostile, unforgiving. Outside, beyond the reach of the crackling fire, the rain moved nearly horizontally across the sodden field, stretching up to the road, where he now saw Ellen coming. She was returning from the village in a classic Aston Martin, one of several cars her brother kept in this seaside retreat on the southernmost English coast.

Ellen would be inside in a moment, and Russo welcomed that. Ellen would bring him perspective. As he heard her enter through the back of the house, the kettle he'd put on to boil for the tea began whistling. He knew she'd need hot tea to banish the harsh English cold.

"Oh my God, it is so raw out there," Ellen said as she came in, rubbing her hands together and trying to infuse some warmth back into her body. She headed directly for the blazing fire.

Tod smiled and began steeping the tea. A couple of sliced lemons were on the work counter between them. The dim daylight from the small windows and the glow of the fireplace, beneath the timber beamed low ceilings, lent a warmth to the room, a four-hundred-year-old kitchen in an English farmhouse.

As Tod poured the tea into two mugs, Ellen turned from the fireplace and asked if the file he had been expecting from Ritu had arrived. He said it had, but he hadn't opened it yet because Ritu called just as he'd received it.

"That's no surprise," Ellen said. "It's probably chock full of data and information that she wanted to boil down for you to save you time. She doesn't skimp on details."

Tod handed her the mug and sat by the fire. "She wanted to apologize. It turns out that what they found, in the end, was probably there right from the beginning. And now the whole project is in question."

"Why? What have they uncovered?" Ellen asked as she took a seat opposite Tod.

"It turns out that the four subjects we've had under our microscopes for a year shared a previous date in their family histories back in 1864."

Ellen sipped her tea as Tod continued. "They each had a relative present on Christmas morning in 1864 at a plantation in Cottageville, South Carolina. And at least three of those relatives were murdered that morning by Confederate troops searching the grounds of a plantation that belonged to the great-great-uncle of Dan Brannigan."

"Oh my God!" Ellen's hand flew up to her face. "How firm is the information?"

"It's all backed by public records and archived stories uncovered by the genealogical search we've been doing for the last thirteen months. The documents that prove it are all part of the file Ritu sent."

"Wait, you said three of them had a relative who was murdered. Which ones and what about the fourth?"

"The three were Brannigan, Janet, and Father Hayslip. Brannigan's great-great-uncle owned the plantation and the slaves, but he was a Union sympathizer, apparently, and hid slaves in his barn. It was a stop on the Underground Railway. But that sympathy evidently didn't prevent him from taking advantage of his position by fathering children with some of the slaves who worked for him and his family in the main house. He'd get them pregnant and sell them for more than he had paid for them, since the buyers would see them as a two-for-one deal. Horrible! He employed a straw boss who had a married daughter with two young children. That woman's son was the great-great-grandfather of Ted Hayslip."

Before Ellen could ask a question, Ted raised his hand to stop her. "For reasons never uncovered, there was a schoolteacher at the house that day who has turned out to be the great-great-aunt of Janet Bates," he said.

"How did Ritu get all this?" Ellen asked with a trace of professional admiration in her voice.

Tod nodded knowingly in agreement. "Now, for the horror of their story." Tod continued.

"Wait," Ellen interrupted. "Does Sharona's family have anything to do with any of this? I mean, she is our mystery woman. She survived her DNA death date."

"Central role to play," Tod's eyes narrowed. "Her part is the punch line to all of this. But let me tell you first what happened in 1864, which became known in that area as the Christmas Day Massacre."

"Oh my God! Don't say it."

"Oh, yes. It was uniquely American for its times. The Confederate troops found the hidden slaves that Brannigan was transporting North. They put every living soul they could find on the property, regardless of age, race or gender, in the barn, locked it, and set it on fire. The Brannigan family, the Bell family and what later became the Hayslip family had blood relatives who were murdered that Christmas Day."

"How did Ritu track all this down?" Ellen asked,

Tod leaned forward in his chair, speaking quickly, eager to lay the entire story out for Ellen. "She broke the search open with two pieces of evidence that came at separate times. Last spring, she received a family album and a partial diary from Janet, which had records of her relatives, including her great-great-grandmother, back to 1864. So Ritu began with the Bell family name and put the lineage pieces together. Much later, in early November, one of Ted's sisters was clearing out a closet in preparation for a move and found a family album. In that book were details of the family's ties to Cottageville, South Carolina. The hunt was on after the coincidence. Ritu contacted local newspapers and area libraries to see if there was any information that would put the names together and—bingo! Up turns the name Brannigan. The pieces all fell into place, from that night in 1864 to the present day. All the way across these hundred and forty-odd years there are records linking these families."

"But for the Brannigan, Bell, and Hayslip names to have come out of that night, some obviously survived the fire. How?" Ellen asked.

"Ah yes. How indeed? More tea?" Tod offered.

"No, thanks. In fact, I need to take this sweater off. This story has my adrenaline rushing."

"OK," Tod said. "Here we go. Turns out that the married daughter of the straw boss was the great-great-grandmother of Ted Hayslip. When she saw the soldiers, she hid her two children in a root cellar under the main house. The children saw their parents and grandparents dragged to the barn, but they stayed hidden while the massacre took place. The next day, slaves from nearby farms came looking for survivors. They rescued the children and sent them North through the Underground Railway. The boy was adopted in Baltimore by a family named Bishlip. When he was old enough to understand, his adopted family told him the story. His real family's name had been Hayes. He decided later to change his last name legally to a combination of the two and created the last name of Hayslip for himself."

"Wow!" Ellen face showed both her respect for the work Ritu hand completed and wonder at the intricacy of the puzzle she had unraveled.

Tod took a swig of tea before continuing. "The mother of the schoolteacher, who was probably just an innocent visitor to the plantation that morning, eventually left South Carolina. Her husband, who served with the Confederacy, never returned home and was presumed dead. She went to New York and was raped by her boss at a shirt factory. This was all found in her diary. The child she gave birth to as a result of the rape was born in a convent and she gave him up for adoption. But he never left the orphanage. That child kept his family name, Bell, and was the great-grandfather of Janet Bell, who married Rod Bates."

"And Brannigan? What happened to their clan?" Ellen asked.

"It turns out that Ronan, the owner of the plantation, had a twin brother who immigrated to America long after the Civil War ended. His name was Seamus, and he is confirmed through the records as the great-great-grandfather of Dan Brannigan. This is where the story takes its final twist and why Ritu feels she failed in her research," Tod said.

"OK," Ellen said. "But I just want to make sure I have this all straight. All three family names trace back to that single event on Christmas Day 1864, and the genealogy leads directly to the three subjects we lost on Christmas Day 2013?"

"Exactly. All three of the people we lost on Christmas Day had relatives killed by Confederate soldiers as Christmas Day dawned in 1864."

"This is blowing my windows in. I need a drink, and something stronger than this tea."

"Wait. After I tell you the rest, you may want more than one."

"Ready when you are."

"OK. Hidden in that same root cellar with Father Hayslip's ancestor was a young black girl, placed there by her mother, Tanya. The child's name was Tulip. When the two white children were found the next morning, Tulip was with them. She was also sent via the Underground Railroad north to Baltimore, where she lived to be well over a hundred years old. Her mother had stashed her in the cellar that Christmas Eve and told the child she was going to hide in the woods nearby. She said she'd come back when the soldiers left. She never returned, but Tulip insisted all of her life that her mother ran in the opposite direction from where the troops were taking prisoners, and she believed that her mother never was locked in the barn. Tulip had no idea what happened to her mother and she never saw her again."

As Ellen sat in suspense, Tod drank some more tea. "Now we come to the final twist. Grandmother Stalls—Sharona's Gran—as you'll recall, resisted working on the genealogy research until just a few days before Sharona's twins were born. When she finally did sit down with Zach, she told him of a great-aunt she recalled from her childhood, who shared a story about bearing a white child. The child didn't survive past its first birthday, but it was quite a scandal. Her aunt was a devoted Christian, as was her husband, and she never would have cheated on him. It was assumed that at some point in either her or her husband's family trees some white blood had been introduced, and that's why she had a white child. But along with that story, Gran also told Zach the great-aunt's history. Great-Aunt Tulip had escaped from the plantation where she was born because the Confederates came and killed everyone. She said it happened on a Christmas morning, and that she survived because her mother, Tanya, hid her under the main house with two white children. She always said that her mother disappeared in the woods. Tulip believed until her dying day that her mother escaped the murderous Confederate soldiers."

Ellen shook her head, amazed at how the threads of the story were weaving together. She kept still as Tod continued. "Ritu only got that information on Christmas Day, but she immediately thought it was possible that Aunt Tulip was a surviving child of Ronan Brannigan and quickly went back to her slides to once again match Dan Brannigan's DNA against that of Sharona Watts. The previous crossmatches carried out during their months with us had never kicked up any unexpected similarities. Sharona's test results, because of her pregnancy, showed a major portion of her SNPs moving all over the place."

"That would make sense, actually," Ellen added, "since her hormones and proteins would be in constant shift as her condition progressed. But it still could have been possible that certain of the slides we had for her, at least the more recent ones, had conformed back to their original formations. Ritu can't take the blame for not nailing down moving targets." Ellen was on the edge of her seat as she waited for Tod's conclusion. "And?"

"Dan and Sharona are cousins. There was a verified match."

"But, Sharona did not die like her cousin Dan and the rest of them on Christmas Day," Ellen pointed out.

"Let's think about this," Tod responded. "Sharona's DNA SNPs were constantly active during her pregnancy. Her proteins were playing a chess game. At some point in her final test, just before the delivery, they apparently returned to their original structures and settled there. Those samples had not been run for exact matches before Christmas Day, as it was presumed—and this is the cause of Ritu's discomfort—that there would be no change."

Ellen saw where he was going now. "But she was wrong. When Ritu learned of Zach's findings from Gran's story, she put the pieces together and found that Dan and Sharona were genetically linked. And though no one can prove it, based on the story of Aunt Tulip, they were probably linked historically as well."

Ellen sat silently while Russo stared at her. He knew that she was running what he'd just told her through her mind and that she was trying, as he had, to line up the possible conclusions they could make from these new-found facts. All four of their lab mice could be historically traced to a slaughter over a hundred and forty years ago. In the twenty-first century, multiple generations later, the descendants of the victims are identified by their DNA as being marked for their own certain deaths. Their mutual death date turns out to be the same date that their ancestors were murdered nearly a century and a half before. Three of the four meet their fate on the anniversary of the death of their ancestors. One survives.

Before Ellen could speak, Tod did. "One of Sharona's ancestors, her great-great-grandmother Tanya, perhaps didn't die on Christmas Day 1864. Tanya could have lived after she stowed the child and disappeared into history. Perhaps by the time she returned for Tulip, the girl had already been shipped north. But Sharona did lose a relative in the fire, so her DNA dictated she was going to die along with the others on December twenty-fifth," Tod said, the question obvious in his voice. "Why? We know she is part Brannigan. We now have her DNA matched to Dan's and we've recertified, over and again, the original finding—that Sharona's death date was indeed December twenty-fifth."

Ellen felt weak from the conclusions playing out in her head. "Then all this adds up to no conclusion at all. If our original finding was correct, and we know it was, then does this evidence suggest the farfetched possibility that our four subjects were living reincarnated lives? Come on, Tod!" Ellen continued thinking out loud. "Somehow Sharona escaped the prediction of her genetic determination, just as one of her ancestors escaped the murder sentence of the Confederate soldiers on that plantation. In the end, as these subjects have shown, could we be looking at reincarnation! Tod, do you think it's really possible? Two sets of 'executions' within the families carried out over a century apart?"

Tod answered immediately. "I don't, and in my discussion with Ritu I went through the same conclusions you just did. Ritu reminded me that in her native India, there is a profound belief among Hindus as well as Buddhists in reincarnation. In fact at one time, there was a fairly solid belief in reincarnation among early Christians as well. Eastern religions often explain our human differences as a result of previous lives, good or bad, which bear their fruit in the present life through karma.

Reincarnation repudiates the Christian teaching of a final judgment by a just God, with the possibility of being eternally condemned to Hell. Reincarnation seems to be a perfect way to punish or reward one's deeds without the need to accept God as the final judge. Ritu isn't supporting reincarnation. She does respect it however, if only for its widespread acceptance." Ellen's face told him she would need to take a step back from what lay before them now. Tod thought like a scientist, as she did. They believed in facts that were proven by data and which supported conclusions without equivocation. Their entire careers had been disciplined by that intellectual rigor. If a hypothesis bore even a millimeter of doubt, the conclusion could not possibly be extracted. Any work under study would be repeated over and over again until the last facts were discovered and an irrefutable resolution achieved. And even then there can always be new information that will unseat formerly accepted scientific facts. The truth of science, particularly human science, is that it is never static. Their lab work irrefutably concluded that Dan Brannigan, Ted Hayslip, Janet Bates and Sharona Watts were going to pass from this life on December 25, 2013.

The conclusion was flawless, Tod had no doubt of that. That the four souls had been linked since December 25, 1864, was documented and proven. The conjunction of the two dates in history— astounding and mysterious— was central to the puzzle. As was the fact that they now knew Sharona and Brannigan to be cousins, based on DNA evidence. Finally, they knew that somehow Sharona had not died on the twenty-fifth, their collective death date.

"Tod," Ellen said, "right from the beginning we said all we'd uncovered in our research was that we could predict accurately what a person's death date would be. Today we know that, in at least one case, that didn't happen. But that could have happened in any one of the cases we tested across the four years of the study. We came across Sharona's case when we found the coincidence of the four all having the same date. In trying to link the four together, we finally found a historical point in time where their paths crossed. So what are we to believe this proves?"

Ellen shrugged her shoulders. "Is it possible that her grand-mother prayed to God fervently enough that Sharona was spared by divine intervention? Maybe it's because she chose life and gave birth to twins? That would suggest some form of divine intervention, I guess. It could also be that our research needs a lot more refining. We looked at Sharona's genetics from a single point of time and analysis, and drew our conclusions. Those conclusions, in her case, didn't bear out our findings ..."

Tod finished the sentence for her: "... suggesting that perhaps we are looking at years of further tests before we can safely predict what we thought we could when all this began. We have yet to es-tablish the actual mechanism that links the date of the deaths with the cause. We have an embolism that could have been diagnosed and prevented, a fatal cancer in a man who had two parents who both died of cancer, an accidental blow to the head ... and a complete miss on the date of the last subject. The science here doesn't go far enough. It may be that it never can. If we're up against reincarnation or divine intervention, we're over our heads."

Ellen looked deeply into Tod's eyes. She was trying to find a hint of where his thoughts might be taking him. Did he feel he'd failed? Was he about to re-enter the quest to find the answers they now knew remained unresolved?

He knew she was waiting to hear this. "Ritu and I already went over this. She now sees that the study of DNA is work that will likely go on beyond our natural lifetimes. I think she's right. And I believe the science is there which will eventually lead us to provable summaries and facts."

Tod dropped his mantle of scientific authority and reached for the emotions that had been awakened in him. "What we have proven here is more about our humanity than our science. I think we opened the question of mortality to four people and they very clearly answered it. 'What would you do if you knew when you were going to die?' They embraced not material values. They moved toward their loves and passions. They clung to what their hearts had led them to during their lives. They sought redemption in their loved ones. Ellen, for me, the lesson of this whole thing is what those four people showed us. That peace can be found through love and happiness. That it exists in each of us, and it's here for us if we share our love and our soul with others. In doing that, we have the courage and the strength to transcend even our deaths, because our lives will have had meaning."

Ellen placed her empty mug on the counter as Tod turned and shrugged his shoulders. "The science we have dedicated our lives to will continue. The complexity of the human body and mind has been a puzzle challenging man's understanding for eons. With all of our accumulated research and intelligence, we still can't explain how Sharona stayed alive."

Tod walked over to the fireplace and stared out at the cold, damp gray winter. "Maybe we aren't meant to know, Ellen. Maybe there is such a thing as divine intervention, maybe there is such a thing as reincarnation. Maybe our science missed something. We both know there is much more to be learned. And we lost three good people on Christmas Day, which our work predicted."

Tod paused and he gazed at the fire. "I wished Ritu luck, Ellen, and told her if anyone could get to the bottom of this it would be her. I'm not going back to it, Ellen. Just as Sharona brought new life to the world, I've found a new life. I've found you."

He returned to his chair and lowered himself into it. Ellen crossed over to Tod, and knelt before him as she clutched his hands. She had no need to say anything. For several minutes, they both stared at the flickering flames.

Then Tod began laughing quietly. "I'm thinking of Ritu's final words just before we hung up. I asked her if she thought it even remotely possible that we had somehow found credible evidence of reincarnation. That what we were really seeing in p63A was simply a notation etched in each of us that closes our current story until we are called upon to play it over again."

"And what did she say?" Ellen asked.

Tod smiled before responding:

" 'God only knows.'"

Dedication

This book is dedicated to my eighth grade Nun at Saint Michael's, Sister Germana Maria, SJS.

The life of a nascent adolescent needs many guiding influences. She saw something in me that made me want to find my imagination and put it to the page. Her belief, guidance and sheer will to drive me to the winners circle lodged in me something that I've kept all of my adult life. My life would have been so different if she had not brought me to believe in my mind. The seed she planted fifty years ago never left my soul. This work exists, indeed, the encore of my life is possible, because she insisted I not miss out on what only she uncovered in me. She will never read this work here on earth. For that, and for all the years I never told her how important she was, I will always be remorseful. Rest in Peace Sister.

Finally to my bride and soul mate Patty. You gave me my life, to live in love. Then you gave me the wonder of our children. Even better you gave me you to share it with. No man has ever been blessed more than I.
JMG/2014

Acknowledgments:

To the very best of my limited knowledge on the subject there is no work being done along the lines described in the body of this work by the Cold Spring Harbor Laboratory of which I am aware. The imagination of the writer is solely responsible for the fiction behind this story although the plausibility of someday finding just such a discovery as that described ,while given a chance by medical professionals with whom the author spoke, remains, for the moment ,pure fictional speculation.

There is no such place anywhere on Long Island's glittering 'Gold Coast" known as Colcroft Hall described as the former Taiwanese Embassy. Although Madame Kai Shek did in fact populate the general area for a long time as she succeeded her late husband. The location of her former home shall remain as it was, anonymous.

There is no place in Kuwait known as B'har Albein that I am aware of. And according to the map there is indeed a place known as Cottageville South Carolina however the story of the events that purportedly took place there as told in this work are entirely products of the authors imagination.

The descriptive of the demise of Lucent Technologies and all of the surrounding information and characters depicted within that particular portion of this novel are strictly the author's imagination. Lucent Technologies in fact was purchased in 2009 by another networking equipment company and is, to the best of my knowledge, still viable as a supplier to the telecommunications industry.

"This will be the day that I die" was a dream of mine for over twenty five years but a dedicated effort for only the last two and a half. Without the support and guidance of so many this dream could never have been in any readers hands. For that I must now express my forever gratitude.

To my four adoring children, Erin, Shannon, Kevin and John; thank you for believing in Dad. I believe in you too. You know that. Thank you.

To Beverly Swerling who took the endless illiteracy of the first manuscript and found a potential novel then patiently nurtured the work to a birth. Without you Beverly this work would have remained a dream. Thank you.

To Judy Bernstein, for always fixing my clumsy wording and so gracefully bringing each page to sensibility. Your codes and standards dignify everything you touch. Thank you.

To James Van Pragh, thank you for the early encouragement. Your support as I was heading down the runway with this idea gave lift to my wings. Your generosity will always be recalled. Thank you.

To Sister Ann Fitzgerald. Your truth told me how right, and how wrong, I could be. The lesson kept me going.

To Greg Walsh, there is enormous comfort in knowing that you approve. Your gift of grammar and respect for the language was always a beacon. Thanks Coach.

To Larry Leible, you are my best friend and my brother in life. Your unwavering enthusiasm helped more than you can ever know. And your analysis and perspective on story lines and characters was critical in assuring me I was going in the right direction. Never leave my back dear friend. Semper Fi.

To all the friends, colleagues and relations that suffered the early awful manuscripts in kindness; and graced me with their support and enthusiasm so lovingly. Thank you.

To all the friends who took me in at the Palatine group when I hit bottom nearly forty years ago. Thank you. I never forgot your love.

CPSIA information can be obtained at www.ICGtesting.com
Printed in the USA
BVOW04*2125020414

349502BV00002B/131/P